# EARTH
## is the
# LORD'S

**THE SUNFALL TRILOGY**
**Book One**

# The
# EARTH
## is the
# LORD'S

*William James*

ORBIT

An *Orbit* Book

First published in Great Britain in 1992 by Orbit Books

Copyright © William James 1992

The moral right of the author has been asserted.

A CIP catalogue record for this book
is available from the British Library.

ISBN 1 85723 084 1

Typeset by Leaper & Gard Ltd, Bristol, England
Printed in England by Clays Ltd, St Ives plc

Orbit
A Division of
Little, Brown and Company (UK) Limited
165 Great Dover Street
London SE1 4YA

# CONTENTS

# Tarvaras

*The principal land masses and seaways*

ICE CAP

NORTHERN PASSAGE

SURASAI

SURISTAN

SEA OF TEARS

N'PAN

CH'KASIA

CH'NOZIA

C'ZAKJA

KHITAI

KERAISTAN

INNER SEA

N'TALAN

EASTERN SEA

GREAT NORTHERN SEA

Y'FRIKE

N'ZUAN

GULF OF MISTS

Y'RABE GULF

DR'GASIA

MARAKAN

Y'VROPE

TIDAL SEA

K'CHIN

SOUTHERN SEA

HEÜRISTAN

GULF OF STORMS

# Tarvaras

*The extent of the known world during the Khanate of Arjun*

GREAT NORTHERN SEA

SEA OF TEARS

SURISTAN

N'tan

CH'NOZIA

Turtai

Pantai

CH'KASIA

Khitai

Ch'npai

INNER SEA

Jaroselsk

Zereislav

T'iver

J'slav Plain

Shermetyevo

M'skva

N'TALAN

Perceislav

Vaslav

Y'RABE GULF

Ruysdal

Miroselsk

Losan

KHITAI

SIT R.

Pesth

C'ZAKIA

Kinsai

Khirgiz Steppe

D'NIEPER R.

N'PAN

T'sosci

EASTERN SEA

KERAISTAN

X'nadu

Khara Caves

GREAT ESCARPMENT

Serai Gorge

Camp

Y'NTZE R.

City of the Dead

G'bai Desert

Susley

MOST R.

M'roke

Y'RABE

Y'FRIKE

# The Khanate of the Golden Clan of the Altun

*Chart showing principal bloodlines and family relationships.*

The names of characters appearing in the books of the SUNFALL trilogy are indicated by capital letters.

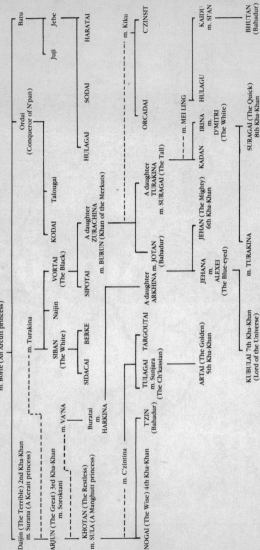

Note: Broken lines indicate second marriages and subsequent step-relationships.

# Kuriltai

Burun sat cross-legged on a large flat rock and narrowed his eyes to stare out over the dead land of the G'bai. It seemed to stretch endlessly south from the foot of the escarpment upon which the army was encamped. Already the baked plains shimmered with the early heat. The mountain peaks on the distant horizon were an indistinct haze; a band of wavering whiteness which vanished upwards into the awful blue of the sky above. Burun grunted, as if he had become aware only at that moment of the impact of the angry red glare of the sun, and from his belt pouch he drew a stoppered horn container. With care he applied a little of the charcoal-based mixture to his eyelids, darkening the permanent blue stain which was the mark of the Merkut clan. It seemed unbelievable that the solar intensity could increase still further, yet he knew that it was so. The escarpment was close to the equator, and by midday only the men of the Yek clans, who were unaffected by extremes of heat or cold, would be moving around the camp. Everyone else would be sheltering in the yurts.

Experimentally, Burun touched the sun-blasted surface of the rock upon which he sat. The slick of moisture at his fingertips sizzled briefly, and he grimaced.

Burun's yurt was being erected on a flat piece of ground at his back. He caught the undercurrent of fear in the murmuring voices of the two Y'rabe slaves who were hurrying to complete the task and, for perhaps the tenth time since he had placed them there, he glanced at the pair of baked white clay discs which lay

3

at the forward edge of the rock. Still they were free from discoloration.

Burun muttered an invocation, and spat left and right. Even though the Sechem had explained to him the manner in which the constituents of the discs detected the presence of lethal radiation, the reputation of the G'bai produced a hollow feeling of disquiet in the pit of his stomach.

He studied the pattern of the arid landscape again, as if repeated examination would reveal some previously hidden secret about its nature. The sound of a voice impatiently raised intruded upon his thoughts, and Burun turned his head.

Osep, his C'zak orderly, was attempting to speed up the operation of yurt erection. The burly body servant was issuing orders in badly accented Yek, and Burun grinned to hear the villainous use of his native tongue. The language of the conquerors was universal, but it still amused him to hear a foreigner from the east coast of one continent employing it to a couple of slaves from the north coast of another.

'This pole here.' The C'zak was gesturing. 'Now the other. No! Name of Names! Not like that!'

Burun wondered what it must be like to be a slave, subject always to the will of others, required to be obedient even to fools. For himself, he knew that he would hate it. A slave was a beaten man; one who had chosen perpetual servitude as an alternative to death. And defeat was not a concept he knew much about.

Slavery was not natural to a proper man.

But then again, according to the Yasa, they were all slaves of the Kha-Khan.

Reflexively Burun tensed his right hand and the silver-tipped talons glittered momentarily as they emerged from their protective sheaths, then were retracted again. The C'zaki, like the Y'rabes and most

4

of the other subject races, possessed no talons. Their
fingers were tipped with nails which, although they
grew, were hard and immobile like plates of horn. And
yet the C'zaki seemed no less human than the Yek.

For the most part the Y'rabes seemed to ignore
Osep's criticism and interference. Their smooth
brown faces remained blank in that manner which
said far more than any facial expression. A corner of
Burun's mouth twisted in wry amusement as he
watched the C'zak show the younger slave how to
draw the coated felt tight before lacing it to the poles.
Probably it was something the Y'rabe had learned
before he was waist high to his elders, but he stepped
back silently until Osep had finished fussing. Then he
continued work as if he had suffered no interruption.

Burun snorted and shook his head. The C'zaki made
excellent conscript cavalry. They lacked the imagination to be afraid and would charge anything they
were pointed at. In riding ability they were second
only to the Yek; however, they possessed neither the
temperament nor the application for domestic service.
Even as a military orderly, a C'zak was the next thing
to useless.

Burun reflected on Osep's bovine stupidity, then on
the fact that, in spite of it, he kept the fellow in his
service. It would have been too much trouble, he
rationalised, to train another.

He turned away again, shutting out not only Osep's
voice but also every other noise from the camp, and
thought about what he was going to say at the kuriltai.

A cheer from troops somewhere over on the other
side of the camp heralded Siban's arrival. About half of
the army consisted of conscript C'zaki or N'pani, and
Burun wondered if Siban was amused to be cheered
by the men he had beaten so soundly in battle.

He rose and turned in one elastic movement. Gesturing to a slave, he indicated the discs on the rock, then stalked over to his now completed yurt. Osep hastened to lift the door flap.

'Get me something to drink.'

'Yes, Khan.' The C'zak hesitated. 'Do you want tr'van or k'miss?'

'K'miss!'

Tr'van was a form of rice wine - a drink suitable for the effeminates who populated the court of the Kha-Khan. Burun glared at Osep for suggesting it.

'The Khan wishes.'

The orderly bowed and scuttled away. Burun started to spit, then stopped, remembering that he was technically inside. He hawked and swallowed.

Hooves rattled outside. After a moment the door flap was flung aside, and T'zin and Nogai stormed into the yurt antechamber. They halted in their tracks.

'Burun.' Nogai's face betrayed surprise. 'I thought this was Sidacai's yurt.'

There was a Merkut guidon on a lance outside the door, but Burun let the lie pass.

'Not hardly.'

'So you're here too. We heard you were in the west.'

Burun snorted. 'It's a kuriltai, isn't it? Of course I'm here.'

'You must have travelled fast.'

'I got in this morning. Eight days riding.'

Let Nogai work out for himself that Burun must have been at the Merkut summer pasture and not in Ch'nozia.

The Kha-Khan's grandsons were twins, alike as two peas. They wore the fancy gold coats of the Yek Altun, and they both had the odd red-gold hair of descendants of the Ancestor.

'So tell us.' Nogai started to loosen the wire fasten-

6

ings of his coat. 'Why are we here? All we had was Siban's summons.'

'You did not arrive with him?'

'At the same time, but separately.'

Burun spread his hands. 'I know no more than you.'

'Oh, I think you do.' Nogai's tone was disbelieving. 'There is going to be a new campaign, of course, or else you would not be here. You would still be hunting down Ch'noze rebels. Who else does Siban send for when he wants reconnaissance? So tell us.'

Burun thought about the Kha-Khan's order which reposed in one of his saddlebags, and particularly about the references in it to Nogai. He stifled a grin.

'No.'

Nogai reddened.

'I am the son of Khotan, the son of Arjun, and when my grandfather dies –'

'To speak of the death of the Kha-Khan is a thing you could die for.' Burun kept his face impassive. All Nogai was waiting for was a sign of weakness.

T'zin muttered something, and from the response Burun guessed that it had been offensive. Nogai slashed out angrily, his unsheathed talons gleaming gold. T'zin jumped back and he readied, his left hand moving towards the hilt of the d'jaga at his belt.

'Stop it, you two!' Burun stepped swiftly between them. 'You know the Yasa. All personal differences, all blood feuds, are suspended for the duration of the kuriltai.'

Nogai ignored the interruption. He launched himself forward and Burun moved a quick pace, setting himself so that his shoulder met the noyon's headlong charge. Nogai bounced back as if he had run into a wall. He landed among the cushions which were scattered on the floor, and rolled, spluttering.

'You – you weren't supposed to do that!'

7

Burun looked down at him. 'What did you expect, boy? That I would go witness for you? Get out of here, both of you.'

T'zin straightened out of his fighting crouch. His face was suffused with mirth, and Burun realised suddenly that he was drunk.

'Oh, Burun Khan,' T'zin reached out to pull Nogai to his feet, 'we are most heartily sorry for having offended you.'

Nogai swatted the proffered hand aside. T'zin only laughed, and Burun relaxed. He stepped back and waited for them to decide to leave.

T'zin was still laughing as he crossed the antechamber and pushed aside the door flap. He turned. 'Come on, brother mine. You'll have to kill me another day.' Ponderously, drunkenly, he bowed to Burun. 'Burun Khan, you always make me laugh.'

'I am sick over it.' Burun mustered his dignity.

T'zin laughed again. He went out, leaving the door hangings swaying.

Nogai picked himself up. Burun suspected that he had stayed on the floor deliberately, so that the engagement with T'zin could not be recommenced, and wondered why. It was not like Nogai to avoid a fight.

'I apologise.' Nogai spoke.

Burun tensed. Nogai was at his most dangerous when he pretended humility.

The noyon brushed invisible specks of dust from his coat. He inspected his long, slim hands, and the gold talons flashed again for a moment. Then he looked sideways.

'I apologise.' He repeated the words.

Nogai's voice sounded sincere enough, but Burun moved a pace, so that he was out of arm's reach. He was not afraid, but it would be unwise to be careless.

8

'Your apology is accepted, Noyon.'

He waited. Nogai wanted something, and Burun meant to find out what it was.

'They are all against me, you know. My brothers. Everyone.'

Nogai had lowered his head again, so that Burun could not tell if the tone of subdued self-pity was real or fake. He decided that probably it was pretended. Nogai was so proud that he would die rather than beg for sympathy. Burun wondered if the fight with T'zin had been staged, another pretence designed so that they would be left alone together. But surely even Nogai was not that devious.

'What would you have of me, Noyon?'

Nogai raised his head.

'You know it is my ulus. I should be Kha-Khan when my grandfather dies. Not Kodai, or Talougai. My grandfather -'

'Your grandfather sent you to the army.' Burun interrupted. 'As I remember, he said that you would learn how to serve, or how to die, one or the other. And since it seems that you have done neither, perhaps he underestimated you. Perhaps we all did.'

'Then help me. Support me. The rest will fall over themselves to follow if you declare for me.'

Burun shook his head. 'I am Khan of the Merkuts - not a noyon of the Altun Uruk.'

'You undervalue yourself.'

'I think not. Besides, the Ancestor fenced the Khanate about so that no one like you would ever come to it. Be satisfied with what you have, and with what will come to you in the course of time.'

'God, but you're blunt.'

'Your great-grandfather used to say that he kept me alive because when everyone else was telling him what they thought he wanted to hear, I told him the truth -

9

even when it was unpleasant. It's a habit I've grown accustomed to.'

Nogai appeared to ignore the uncomfortable reference to Daijin, whom men had called The Terrible. He picked up a scrap of silk from the table, and used it to wipe away the charcoal shading from his eyelids. When he had finished, the gold clan stain of the Altun was clearly visible. Burun was glad when Osep came out of the back of the yurt with the k'miss. He watched the orderly fill a cup, but when it was offered, he gestured it away.

'Serve the grandson of the Kha-Khan before you serve me.' He growled C'zak at Osep.

Nogai accepted the cup.

'What did you say to him?'

Burun translated. Nogai sipped, then made a face.

'Ugh. K'miss.'

Burun smiled. 'I'm an old Merkut. I like k'miss.'

For an unguarded moment, Nogai's face said what he truly thought of the remark. Then he caught Burun's eye.

'I am the Kha-Khan's grandson. I should be the next Kha-Khan.'

'Aaagh!'

Burun was not entirely pretending to be angered by Nogai's return to the subject. He uttered a wordless bellow, and Nogai jumped. One pace forward and Nogai was backing quickly towards the door, still holding the cup. Burun followed swiftly.

'You're like dogs after a rat, you and your brothers. You won't let it alone, will you? Go on, get out! I'm sick of the whole pack of you - forever picking the Khanate over, when none of you may ever have a chance at it.'

Burun raised a hand, talons exposed, and Nogai thrust the cup at Osep. Then he backed through the door hangings, colliding with someone who was coming the other way.

'Siban.'

Burun stepped back and grinned.

Siban's appointment as marshal of the army had nothing to do with the fact that he was the Kha-Khan's half-brother. He resembled Arjun in nothing. He was a different kind of man entirely.

'And what did Nogai want?' Siban let the door flap fall. He raised an eyebrow as he turned to look at Burun.

'Oh. To be the next Kha-Khan. What else?'

'God. Is he at that again?'

'Has he ever given up? They're all the same, except T'zin.'

Siban made a face.

'T'zin. Huh. Was he here as well? More to the point, was he sober? No, you don't have to answer that. He's a damn drunk, T'zin.'

Burun shrugged. 'He's your blood, not mine.'

'I know. But Name of Names, I can't be forever holding the reins on my blood-kin's offspring.'

They were both big men, Siban only a year older than Burun. But where Burun was broad, Siban looked as if the years of campaigning in the southlands had burned all the excess flesh from his body. He waved a hand to dismiss the subject and flung himself down on a mound of cushions.

'God, what a ride! I think my back's broken.'

He pulled off one riding boot and upended it. A stream of sand cascaded out. Burun snatched the boot away and tossed it to Osep.

'Don't mind my yurt floor, will you?' He yanked off Siban's other boot in one movement. 'Anyway, if you were riding so hard, how did you collect so much of the G'bai in your boots?'

11

'Oh. We stopped for a time at the Khara Caves. You know - where the post road used to run in Daijin's time. The Sechem insisted on trying his discs in a place where he was certain there used to be radiation.'

'A touching faith in his own invention.'

'Oh, I don't think the discs were discovered by the Sechem. Old Science, probably. But yes, I agree with you. I told him that if any of them discoloured, I would feed the whole sack to him, a piece at a time.'

'I gather from your presence here that they remained pristine.'

'Of course. And yours?'

'The same, obviously. They're on a rock overlooking the plain, with a slave watching them for any change.'

'How trusting we both are.' Siban stood up and stretched. 'That's better. I'm getting too old for campaigning. If I have to ride for more than a few days, I feel like an old cripple.'

Burun grinned. Siban reminded him of his father. Until the day he died, Sebu had complained of arthritis. It was an ill which disappeared magically whenever he had to fight.

'So the G'bai is passable at last.' Siban set his cup aside.

Burun nodded. 'I spoke to the hundred commander at Pantai. They rode until they could see the foot of the Moistr' Gorge. Their discs shadowed a little at one place, but they detoured with no ill effects. All the men live and are healthy. I excused them and sent them north.'

'So.' Siban sounded satisfied. He sat back, and Burun met his eyes.

'What do you wish of me? As if I did not already know.'

Siban chuckled. 'Reconnaissance, of course. I want to know the lie of the land, the mountains, the passes -'

'Yes, yes.' Burun gestured. 'You want to know it stone by stone as if you had set foot there yourself. Very well. I'll go.'

'It isn't a command –'

'I know that. That's why I'll go. Though you might have left me one summer with my clan.'

Siban shrugged. 'You know the Yasa as well as I. If your clan needed you, you would not have come.'

'And that's another thing. Why hold the kuriltai here, in God's name? I'll have to ride back to the 'Sit, collect men and remounts, then return here. We could have met at Pesth, or even in Losan.'

Siban made a face.

'It was the Kha-Khan's order. I think he wanted everyone to see the prospect clearly when the matter was discussed. And who are we to argue?'

'Khans ourselves.'

Siban smiled. 'You tried that argument with the present Kha-Khan's father. And with no more success as I remember. Anyway the ride will be good for my blood-kin. I had a look at the camp as I rode in. They've gone soft.'

Burun shrugged. 'A year of peace. Most of them haven't fought anything more than a few bandits.'

'Oh, well. No doubt you will find the time to bring them to a proper state of readiness.'

'Will I indeed?'

'Why not? I had a copy of the Kha-Khan's order to you. By arrow messenger, six days ago.'

'I see.' Burun searched Siban's face for some clue to his thoughts, but if Siban meant more than the simple statement of fact, he did not betray it. 'I'd like to know why I was chosen.'

Siban seemed to consider.

'Oh, I think simply because it was convenient. Yours is the hardest task the army will face until the full campaign next year. And idleness hasn't been good for them. The Kha-Khan had to get them away from Kinsai. Otherwise they would have torn the place apart with their feuding.'

'Hunh.' Burun grunted understanding. He picked up a cup, and used it to weight one side of a map of the G'bai.

Siban moved a plate so that it held down the other. 'Tell me how you want to do this thing,' he said.

Burun looked up, surprised. 'I await the decision of the kuriltai, surely.'

Siban snorted derision.

'If you and I cannot decide on a plan without the dubious assistance of the Altun, we should be back with our clans, old men telling tales by a dying fire. We will decide, and they will agree.'

'Oh.' Burun smiled softly. 'I see.'

The slaves had rolled up the sides of the kuriltai tent, so as to allow what little air there was to circulate more freely. Burun was inclined to think that the disadvantages outweighed the benefits.

'Look at T'zin.'

Sidacai, Siban's eldest son, nudged Burun and spoke in an undertone.

Burun looked across the tent at the group of seated Altun. It was clear that Nogai's twin had been drinking steadily since the incident in Burun's yurt. Now he was supported on either side by his half-brothers, Tulagai and Targoutai, and Burun guessed that if they moved away, the Kha-Khan's grandson would fall flat on his face.

'When Siban sees that, T'zin will spend the rest of the war commanding some Ch'kassy hilltop.'

Sidacai seemed to be enjoying the prospect, and Burun looked at him sharply. It was Sidacai who had

14

ordered the slaves to roll up the tent walls. Now the watching troops could see everything, even if they were too far away to hear. It seemed likely that they would find the spectacle of T'zin's imminent collapse quite edifying. Siban would be forced to take some kind of disciplinary action, whether he wished to or not.

So far as Burun was aware, there existed no personal animosity between Sidacai and T'zin. He had not heard that they were feuding, and certainly there was no political advantage to be gained from T'zin's public disgrace. It seemed therefore that Sidacai was prepared to promote trouble purely for the sake of the embarrassment it was likely to cause Siban. Father and son were too much alike in the strength of their character and it was well known that they did not get on.

'Kuchuk!'

'Yes, Khan.'

Burun's standard-bearer came out of a small knot of standing aides and orderlies near the tent entrance.

'Present my compliments to Tulagai Noyon and say that I suggest that T'zin Bahadur should be put to rest in his yurt. It is clear that he is sick, and so he may be excused. Say that I think that this should be done now, at once, before Siban Khan arrives to start the kuriltai.'

'Yes, Khan.'

Burun watched Kuchuk circle the crowd in the centre of the tent. When the standard-bearer bent to speak to Tulagai, Targoutai, who was on T'zin's far side, leaned forward to hear. He said something briefly to Kuchuk, then looked up to catch Burun's eye. His nod was an acceptance. Tulagai was signalling to two junior officers, and in a tight group they supported T'zin discreetly away.

'Damn you.'

Sidacai swore pleasantly, and Burun turned to face him, his expression carefully innocent.

'Your pardon, Noyon. I sought merely to save your blood-kin from disgrace.'

'I know very well what you sought. And I tell you that you will interfere with my entertainment once too often.' Burun met Sidacai's fierce stare steadily. After a long moment Siban's son shook his head. 'You shame me, Merkut.' He laughed in self-mockery. 'I think you really were concerned about Altun honour.' He turned away again, and Burun slowly let out the breath which he had been holding.

Like his father, Sidacai was a bad man to cross.

'Be quiet, all of you.'

Siban glared around the tent, but the noise lessened only slightly.

Haratai's sons were squabbling in the far-away corner. They had all been drinking, and Burun reflected that the Ancestor's harsh rule against spirits made sense. He watched as the youths pushed and jostled one another, encouraged by shouts and jeers from nearby uncles and cousins.

As a group the Altun all tended to drink to excess when they were not otherwise occupied. Some of them even used hashish, a thing which, because the Ancestor had never considered it, was not forbidden by the Yasa. Burun's eyes moved from face to face. In their present state most of them were probably incapable of commanding more than a shaman's cart in battle, although no doubt any one of them would be able to lead a raid. Briefly, he wondered if it was going to be worth the trouble and inconvenience to bring them to the required state of campaign readiness.

Siban seemed to realise that he was going to have to do something drastic to gain attention. He picked up a pear from a bowl on the table, and threw it accurately so that it hit Sodai full in the mouth. Haratai's brother started to his feet, spitting. Someone tripped him as he lurched forward, and he sprawled full length.

'Silence!' Siban thundered. 'This is a war kuriltai, not a Kinsai revel! Remember that you came into this tent between two fires. You offend not only me but also the Kha-Khan by your behaviour.'

The older men, Burun among them, growled in agreement. Sodai crawled back to his place, and gradually the noise died away.

'It was the Kha-Khan who summoned you here, not I.' Siban hooked his thumbs into his belt and scowled at the grouped Altun. 'So far as I am concerned, you can all go back to Kinsai. Saving the Kha-Khan's order, it would be easier to conduct this war without you.' He looked at their faces to see if the threat had taken effect. 'Very well then. We are here to discuss a campaign against the Alan. The G'bai is passable, and next year we will move an army across the desert, through the mountains, and we will invade.'

Siban's mention of the radiation-tainted G'bai produced a murmur of unrest and, in spite of himself, Burun shivered. The Sechem said that once the G'bai must have been full of life – that it was a desert made not by nature, but by men, in the course of a great war. Burun wondered how such a thing could be so. No dog fouled its own kennel; no man poisoned the land upon which he dwelled.

If radiation was indeed a curse made by men, then they were dead and gone long since, and a good thing too.

'Last year we sent an embassy to the Alan.' Siban stilled the mutter. 'The ambassadors travelled by the Inner Sea and made landfall at a port which the Alan call Suslev. After several months they returned, having

17

been permitted to proceed no further.'

News of the insult produced a growl of anger, and Siban raised both hands for silence. 'We obey the Will of Heaven.' He seemed to pause for effect. 'One Lord upon the earth, as there is one God above. An end to the chaos which was in the beginning. Universal order under the rule of the Kha-Khan!'

The Altun led everyone else in shouting agreement, and Burun smiled sourly.

'The Alan defy us!' Siban gestured. 'What must be our reply?'

'War!'

The response was a single unanimous cry which was taken up by the troops massed outside the tent. It spread around the camp.

Siban looked back over his shoulder and caught Burun's eye. Burun tried to read his expression, but failed. He wondered if Siban enjoyed speech-making, and supposed not. Then he wondered if anyone else had noticed that Siban had not actually asked the kuriltai to approve the war.

Siban waved his arms for silence.

'Very well. This winter Burun Khan will carry out a reconnaissance across the G'bai. We need to know much more than the old maps tell us. This camp will be expanded to form a base both for that operation and for the campaign.' Siban bowed in Burun's direction. Burun scowled. 'Burun Khan,' Siban spoke as if he was asking the question for the first time, 'how many men will you use?'

Burun pretended briefly that he was considering his reply. Already he had argued the matter with Siban, and had won.

'The first tenth of my own tuman and the tenth of T'zin Bahadur's that was with me on the Y'frike campaign.'

'Two thousand men. Yes. I can see that we are going to do this thing properly.'

Burun allowed the mild sarcasm to pass unremarked. He spread his hands for a moment, then looked up and spoke again. 'Also I will take those of the Altun, along with their personal guard, who may be available.'

Only Siban knew that this last was the Kha-Khan's order. His face remained impassive. Across the tent Nogai lifted his eyes from a seeming contemplation of his talons. He smiled unpleasantly.

'We are honoured, of course, Khan. But we decline, with thanks.'

Burun smiled back, and showed his teeth.

'You misunderstand me, Noyon. When I issue that kind of invitation, I expect more by way of reply than a bow and a wave of the hand.'

'Oh?' Nogai seemed amused. 'Explain it to me, please. Explain to all of us why we should pay any attention at all to the words of a snivelling Merkut - even one who is related to the Altun by marriage.' He looked around for support, and a group of Altun cousins sniggered agreement. Targoutai placed a warning hand on his half-brother's shoulder, but Nogai shook it off.

Burun sat back. It had been Nogai's choice to employ personal insults. Burun had not been looking forward to the exchange which he had known would take place, but now he decided that he was going to enjoy it to the full.

'My meaning was clear enough. You are coming across the G'bai with me, Noyon. You, and your brothers. Even your idle cousins, and that ragged, ill-trained assembly your family calls a guard. You are coming even if I have to start you on your way with the toe of my boot.'

Nogai flushed crimson. He started to his feet, intention clear, but he was both waved down by Siban and restrained on either side by Tulagai and Targoutai. He struggled for a moment against the arms which held him, then subsided swearing.

'It is not as if I particularly desire your company.' Burun managed to continue as if he had suffered no interruption. 'God knows I will likely spend half of my time keeping you from cutting one another's throats, and I have little taste for that. But you see, Noyon, I have no choice in the matter. I have the Kha-Khan's order, under his seal, that you are to go.' He ignored the whoops of laughter which erupted at Nogai's discomfiture, and met the outraged stare of the Kha-Khan's grandson squarely. 'Perhaps your grandfather hopes that I will manage to lose you, all of you, somewhere in the desert.'

It was the kind of situation which appealed to Sidacai's instinct for causing trouble, and he was laughing unrestrainedly, jeering at Nogai. Without seeming to glance in his direction, Burun swept one arm back like a scythe. Sidacai tumbled back off the cushions, but he was still whooping as he crawled back to his place. Burun looked up at Siban for assistance.

'I am glad that you are amused, child.' Siban's tone was mild. 'Because you are going as well.'

Sidacai stopped laughing. His face changed, and then he laughed once, unpleasantly. 'Beloved sire,' he bowed, 'I honour your command, of course.'

Siban ignored the insolent tone. 'Then it is settled. When Burun Khan has provided us with intelligence, we will decide how a full campaign is to proceed. Does anyone else wish to say anything? No? Then I declare this kuriltai ended.'

The announcement caught almost everyone by

surprise. Then a pear thrown from the shadows on one side of the tent caught Siban in the mouth as he turned away. He spluttered.

'You young dogs!'

His answer was a mocking cheer from the Altun. Several of them reached for the fruit bowls, and Siban stalked out of the tent in pretended anger.

Burun remained in his place. He waited to see if Nogai would ask to read the Kha-Khan's order. But the noyon left without a backward glance, shouldering his way out through a crowd of amused Altun.

Burun experienced a feeling of irritation.

It seemed wrong somehow that the grandson of the Kha-Khan should be mocked by lesser men.

'It went well, I think.'

Siban fell into step beside him, and Burun shrugged non-committally. 'Well enough, I suppose.'

'Have you decided when you want to start?' Siban gestured at the plain.

Burun calculated silently.

'The gold month. My own tuman is ready and I have no problem with remounts, but I will have to inspect T'zin's and the Altun guard, and make up any deficiencies.'

'You'll find T'zin's tuman well enough arranged, I expect.' Siban nodded in the direction of a group of officers. 'The commander of his second tenth runs things when T'zin is drunk - which has been most of the time lately.'

Burun deemed it politic to ignore the implied criticism. T'zin was no kin of his, after all. He nodded.

'Yoruba. Yes, I know of him.'

For a foreign conscript to rise above the rank of hundred commander was unusual enough of itself. Burun had already heard the man mentioned by

21

others. Now he followed Siban's eyes, and studied the tall dark-skinned Y'frike who was standing in the centre of the group.

'A clever man.' Siban's voice was not quite expressionless and, as if he had overheard the comment, the Y'frike looked up. He met Burun's stare and after a moment nodded politely. The other officers turned to see who was being greeted, and, when they noticed Siban, they fell silent.

Burun walked on. For no reason that he could comprehend, the incident bothered him. 'A man who will bear watching,' he observed at last.

'Yes. I thought to have him detached to your command.'

'Oh?' Burun reacted sharply. 'Why?' He wondered if Siban suspected the Y'frike of involvement in some kind of plot.

Siban seemed to search for an answer. 'Well, you may need him if T'zin goes on drinking.'

'He won't, if I have anything to do with it. Is there another reason that I should know about?'

'Probably not.' Siban hesitated. 'Although I would value your opinion of the man. They are not like us, the Y'frike.'

Burun grunted as if he understood. The absence of talons and the differences in skin colour of the subject races were things which troubled many. Some even said that those who were different were not of the true race of men.

'But we were discussing your departure.' Siban abandoned the subject as if nothing of importance had been said. 'The gold month?'

'Yes.'

'But surely you will not need a full three months to journey to Pesth and back?'

'No. But I have the clan to settle.'

22

'Of course. You will be taking all your sons?'

'All save C'zinsit. He can play at being Khan while I am away. God knows he's been doing it since he was old enough to walk round a yurt. His father and brothers are always away on the Kha-Khan's business.'

Siban ignored the implied complaint.

'C'zinsit. That would be - ah, yes - your son by your inestimable second wife.'

'The younger son. His elder brother, Orcadai, is in the Kha-Khan's guard. But I have leave to take him, saving only your agreement.'

Siban spread his hands. 'By all means. He can support his half-brother against Nogai. They are still feuding, I suppose?'

Burun gestured. 'I imagine so. Jotan is like me in one respect at least. Once he gets his teeth into a fight, it's hard to make him let go again.'

Siban nodded. 'Yet you managed to keep them from killing one another when they served under you in the last campaign.'

Burun laughed. 'I, a Khan of a lowly sub-clan, stand between the grandson of the Kha-Khan and the husband of his grand-daughter in pursuit of a lawful feud?' He enjoyed the memory. 'No. I simply kept them fighting the enemy until they were too tired to fight one another. And when they weren't fighting, I had them riding in opposite directions - one west, the other east.'

'Let us hope that you are as successful again,' Siban commented. He stopped. 'There's bad blood there somewhere.'

At first Burun thought that it was Jotan who was the subject. Then he realised that Siban was looking across the dusty assembly ground. Nogai was deep in conversation with Tulagai and Targoutai at the door of his yurt. As Burun watched, Nogai put an arm around

23

both their shoulders. Clearly they had come to some kind of an agreement, and he wondered what was involved. He shrugged.

'On that, I would not care to venture an opinion. Perhaps it is we who are to blame. We raise our children to fight. The feud and the quarrel are as natural to them as breathing. How can we complain when they use their surplus energies to fight each other?'

'Or to fight us?' Siban glanced sideways. 'It seems to me that there are times when Jotan would as lief fight you as Nogai.'

'Look to your own offspring,' Burun retorted, and watched as Siban's face grew thoughtful.

'You might have sent me warning.'

They were at meat. Burun had been waiting for Nogai to raise the subject, but now he sighed.

'You gave me little chance, Noyon. I would have spoken of it. But if you recollect, your intent was upon other matters.'

Nogai concentrated for a while on the platter on the table before him. He chewed, then spat out a pad of gristle. One of the dogs lunged for it. Finally he looked up and met Burun's eyes.

'It is true, you know - what I said. They are all against me.'

'Your cousins, half-brothers?' Burun remembered the scene by the yurt door - Nogai with his arms round Tulagai's and Targoutai's shoulders.

Nogai waved dismissal. 'Nithing men. They would as soon shout for another.'

Privately Burun agreed with the assessment, but he said nothing.

'Truly, it is as I said,' Nogai continued. 'If you declared for me, the rest would fall over themselves to follow suit.'

Burun met the green eyes steadily. Then he shook his head. 'No, Noyon. Apart from anything else, your grandfather is still alive. And the habit of obedience to him is strong in me. So I beg you - trouble me no further with this thing of yours.'

Nogai looked away, then back. At the far end of the table, Tulagai and Targoutai were trying to poke T'zin out of a drunken sleep. T'zin was lashing out like a bear coming out of hibernation and the attention of nearly everyone was on them.

'It is my ulus! I should be the Kha-Khan!'

Nogai spoke with such desperate force that Burun sighed again.

'How can you even consider it?' he asked, his tone reasonable. 'Think now. For more than ten years your mother plotted and schemed. And for what? To get for you that which was already yours!'

Nogai's expression was anguished. He nodded.

'I know. I know.'

'Very well.' Burun gestured dismissively. 'Maybe at first they were only women's intrigues. Little affairs. But consider. You were your grandfather's heir. In time the Khanate would have been yours, both by vote and by right. Which one of us would have opposed his will in council?'

'Dead man's shoes,' Nogai said.

Burun smiled grimly. 'All men die, boy. It is a disease which comes upon us as a result of living, a habit we have that we cannot break. You live still, and are fortunate. Your grandfather was merciful.'

'Merciful!' Nogai sneered bitterly.

Two slaves ran past carrying platters of meat to another table and Burun recollected that he was in a public place. He lowered his voice.

'Merciful indeed. Your mother sought to break the Will of Heaven, to interrupt the reign of the True

Khan. The moment you heard of the plan, you should have been on your face before your grandfather's throne protesting your loyalty.'

'Like my father.'

Nogai's tone was raw.

Burun compressed his lips, then shook his head at the stupidity of the remark. 'Your father lives. Where are your mother's brothers - her cousins, uncles, nephews now?'

'Name of Names, you call him merciful! He slaughtered an entire clan!'

Burun nodded.

'Yes. I helped him and your father with me. And in a thousand years, who will remember the Manghutt name? But you he suffered to live, because you were his favourite and there was no proof against you. Even your mother reprieved, though he made your father put her away.'

Nogai opened his mouth as if to protest, but Burun held up his hand. 'No. Don't speak to me of it again.'

Slaves brought bowls of fruit and cups of chilled wine to the table. Burun sipped the wine experimentally and thought that he still preferred k'miss. He selected an apple and started to peel it with his d'jaga. All the time he was watching Nogai out of the corner of his eye.

'You are right, of course,' Nogai said at last. 'I have deserved everything.'

'Eh?'

Burun was astounded. Then he guessed that the subdued tone of voice was artificial. He showed his teeth.

'Don't grovel, Noyon. It doesn't suit you.'

Nogai slashed out, talons extended, but Burun was waiting for the move. He caught Nogai's wrist and drew him in close. Then he moved slightly so that no one else could see what was happening. Sweat was starting out on Nogai's forehead, and Burun tightened his grip until he heard the grate of bones.

'You don't learn, do you, boy? You think you can win my support by appeal, or persuasion, or even by guile? I'd rather take a serpent inside my guard, and I have little fondness for snakes!'

'My wrist!' Nogai tried to wrench his arm free. Burun squeezed deliberately.

'Heed me, you perverted pig's dropping! Every hour of every day you are at my heels or someone else's, whining that you should be Kha-Khan – that it is your fate, your ulus. You think that yours is fit conduct for a Khan?'

Beyond the pain, there was a kind of torment on Nogai's face which was not caused by the force of the hand which grasped his wrist. Burun relaxed his grip by a fraction.

'Your grandfather was right, Noyon.' He leaned forward so that his face was inches from Nogai's. 'Before a man can be a Khan, he has to learn how to serve. Sometimes he dies in the attempt. Try that path, why don't you, and maybe some day a few of us will offer you our respect.'

Burun released Nogai and rose all in one swift movement. He was striding away from the dining area long before Nogai could react, and he was halfway to his yurt before he began to shake. He thought about how the Ancestor would have reacted to see the way his great-great-grandson had been used by a Merkut. The wrath of Heaven was supposed to be terrible. Then Burun reflected that if the Ancestor really could see how he had treated Nogai, probably he was laughing.

'You'll send me word by courier.'

'By arrow messenger, as soon as I have settled the

clan.' Burun looked down from his saddle. 'I've arranged to review all the troops - T'zin's and my own - at Pesth.'

'You're starting from there?' Siban looked surprised.

Burun gestured at the great ball of the setting sun. 'Yes. This time I'd like to give them a chance to acclimatise before I expose them to that and the G'bai both. Remember that my men have spent the last four months in the Ch'noze snows. Besides, Pesth is closer to the remount herds.'

'And the others - Nogai, T'zin and the rest - shall I keep them here, or send them to Pesth?'

'Oh, to Pesth, naturally. They may as well accustom themselves to my ways.'

Siban suppressed a smile. 'Of course.'

'You remain here?'

'At least until the relay and supply depots have been set up.' Siban nodded. 'After that I will hand over command to Vortai. I have to be at Kinsai by the end of the bronze month.'

At the mention of his father-in-law's name, Burun made a face.

'Vortai. Hunh. You think he'll be satisfied with command of the base camp?'

Siban shrugged. 'Probably not. But there's nothing for him to raid within a thousand verst. He's all right, Vortai. It's just that he has no patience.'

Burun managed a doubtful smile. 'If you say it, of course it must be so. He's your brother, after all.'

'How delicately you phrased that.'

'Well. You know how I feel about my in-laws.' Burun gestured.

'I believe you've made it abundantly clear these many times past. Personally, I wouldn't concern myself about Vortai. It's Sipotai you need to watch.'

Burun growled in his throat. 'Hunh. True enough.

28

We've a fight still unfinished, Sipotai and I.'

'I heard about that. Something to do with your second wife?'

Burun spat to one side. 'The way he looked at her, she could have borne twins, and he the father.'

'Oh well, I'm passing fond of looking at your wife myself.' Siban spoke mildly. 'Although I haven't had your brother-in-law's opportunities. It's your own fault for marrying a concubine. It upsets the natural order of things.'

Burun scowled. Then before he could compose a proper reply, he heard the rattle of hooves at his back, and turned.

Nogai was riding out of the camp gate. He was flanked on one side by T'zin, and by his half-brothers on the other. His st'lyan was a bay with brilliant black points and he was managing the reins economically with his left hand. His right was tucked inside the front of his robe.

Burun waited until the foursome had ranged up level. Then he raised an eyebrow in enquiry.

'We travel with you to Pesth,' Nogai said. His statement was not quite a challenge.

'Oh? And pray tell me, how did you come by the news that the assembly point was Pesth?'

'Tulagai heard your aide instructing the quartermaster.'

'I see.' Burun considered. Then he nodded. 'Very well. Since you are ready to ride, you may as well come along. But you'll find it no pleasure.' He pointed a finger at Tulagai. 'You, Noyon. Five hundred men and ride vanguard. Stretch it out to half a day if you wish, but stay in contact by messenger. I want to know if a gnat pisses in our path.'

Tulagai looked sideways at Nogai, who nodded. Before Burun could make something of it, Tulagai had gigged his st'lyan round. He galloped over to the waiting troops, shouting the names of section leaders. Burun watched the hundred commanders break away from the mass. He was surprised that Tulagai knew ordinary soldiers well enough to be able to pick out individuals. He started to point at Targoutai, then changed his mind and indicated Nogai.

'You, Noyon. Another five hundred, and ride rearguard. I want you an hour or so behind the main body, ready to move up in support if needed. Targoutai, you will be responsible for the right flank. T'zin -' he looked to see if T'zin was sober enough to understand, and decided that he was, '- the same on the left.'

Targoutai was looking towards Nogai for confirmation, and Burun jerked his reins so that his mount reared. The st'lyan's flailing hooves just missed Targoutai's head and he reeled in the saddle, cursing.

'I said take the right, Targoutai!' Burun showed his teeth. He sidestepped his st'lyan and Targoutai backed hastily out of range.

'Take the right, brother.' Nogai's tone was amused. He nodded politely to Burun, then trotted sedately past, still using his left hand. Targoutai's face was flushed. He stared at Burun for a moment, then hauled his st'lyan's head round and rode off towards the commander of the right flank guard.

Siban laid a hand on Burun's bridle. 'You're going to have trouble with Nogai. Are you sure you want him under your command? I can always have him sent back to Kinsai.'

Burun laughed unpleasantly. 'It is nothing I cannot handle.'

Siban stepped back. He looked unconvinced.

'Well. It's your decision, of course. But I can't help feeling that you will have to break his other wrist as well, before he learns to behave.'

Off the escarpment, the land was flat and featureless. Burun let the scouts decide the pace. He settled himself in the saddle, and tried to sleep. He was riding a gray, the oldest and steadiest of his string, and her economical trot ate up the ground in an unbroken rhythm.

'Green light about four verst ahead, Khan.'

Burun snapped awake. He looked to where the aide was pointing. There was no moon and an unshuttered lantern ahead was like a small beacon. The green light flashed twice, then quickly twice more.

'Four flashes. Is Tulagai practising lantern drill? Kuchuk!' Burun swung round in the saddle and tried to find his standard-bearer among the dim shapes to the right.

'Yes, Khan.' Kuchuk pulled up beside Burun. He was swaying a white lantern to the top of his signal pole.

'Signal that oaf for a repeat.'

The standard-bearer tugged his lantern cord once, paused, then flashed twice more. Burun waited for the reply. The green light ahead flashed once long, then twice short.

'A long green, Khan, followed by two short.'

'Hunh. I can see.' Burun nodded.

Kuchuk jerked his lantern cord once in acknowledgement. Then he lowered his signal pole so that he could attach a green lantern to repeat the signal to the rear.

Burun stood in the saddle, but the blackness revealed nothing. 'I wonder why Tulagai's swinging right?' He nudged his st'lyan so that she followed the rest of the line as everyone changed direction. He was sure that he had seen four flashes the first time.

'Khan?'

Burun located the speaker. 'Yes. What is it?' Only Hodai, his aide, possessed such a girlish treble.

'Courier from Nogai Noyon, Khan.' Hodai sounded nervous.

Burun looked past him at the messenger. 'Well?'

'Lord, my prince says that he will not ride this pace.' The orderly's tone was deliberately insolent.

'What?' Burun was unable to suppress the gasp of amusement. He heard chuckles as the gist of the message was passed down the line of the command post. 'Is Nogai suffering from saddle sores already?'

Kuchuk unshuttered a signal lantern and in the light Burun examined the courier's face. The man was a stranger, one of the family retainers, he suspected. His countenance was stiff with outrage.

'Oh, well.' Burun considered one reply, discarded it as too formal and decided to say what he was thinking. 'Tell the noyon that if he thinks that this pace is fast, he knows nothing about how an army travels. However, if he does not wish to keep up, I will permit him to return to the escarpment camp. On foot, of course. I can use the remounts and maybe Nogai will find it easier travelling to Pesth by cart.'

'Name of God, Khan!' Hodai's protest was muffled and Burun ignored it. He looked directly at the courier.

'Well?' he demanded. 'Can you remember all that, or do you want me to say it again?'

The messenger's mouth clamped shut, as if he was biting off some retort. He shook his head, then hauled his st'lyan's head round. He spurred away towards the rear of the column and Burun cocked an eyebrow at Hodai.

'Yes?'

Hodai gestured helplessly. Clearly he was torn

between his automatic respect for the rank of the Altun and his loyalty towards Burun.

'Well, Khan, I - oh -'

Hodai threw up his arms in exasperation. Burun grinned.

'I know. I should not treat the grandson of the Kha-Khan like an unruly child. Perhaps I would not, if that was not the way he behaved.'


Burun ordered everyone into camp just as dawn was breaking. One moment the files of riding men were vague shadows. The next, each trooper was an image thrown into sharp relief by the abrupt sunrise.

'Khan?'

Burun gestured to Osep to wait. He let his riding cloak fall back over the st'lyan's hind quarters and watched as Hodai set up the outposts. The ground was dry; a haze rose quickly and hung in the air above the camp as it was set up. Burun stepped off his st'lyan's back onto a rock. He threw his reins to Osep. The orderly had already unsaddled his own mount and now he ran towards the lines leading both Burun's grey and his own piebald. Burun stretched, squatted to take the stiffness out of his legs, then straightened again. When he looked round, everyone else seemed to be doing exactly the same thing.

'K'miss, Khan?'

Burun accepted the jug which Kuchuk was holding out.

'Aaah.' He rinsed out his mouth, spat, then drank. 'That's better.' He tossed the jug back and Kuchuk grinned.

'A good night's ride, Khan.'

Burun nodded. 'Good enough.'

They had travelled about two hundred verst from

the escarpment. At that rate it would take six days to reach Pesth. Except that once they reached the plain, it would be much cooler and they would be able to ride longer. Say five days. He walked over to the place which Hodai had selected for the command tent. Hodai's orderly was trying to lay out his master's bedroll. Every time he had it arranged just so, one of the troopers who was erecting the tent would charge through, and he would be forced to start again.

'Eh, Mago.' Kuchuk was laughing. 'Best leave that until the tent is up.'

The orderly snatched Hodai's p'yass out of the way of someone's feet and stood to one side. He held the thin, fibre-filled mat against his chest and cursed the busy troopers in guttural T'tar.

'Donkeys! Keep your dung-sodden feet off my master's bedroll!'

The troopers grinned good-naturedly, ignoring the tirade. They strained on the bindings attached to the strips of coated material and in a moment more Burun was standing in cool dimness. The tent's treated exterior reflected away most of the sun's glare, making it possible for men to eat and rest.

'Do you want to sleep first, Khan?'

'Oh, yes. No, bring me something to eat.'

'The Khan wishes.'

Osep left the tent and Burun tried to remember what he had been thinking about in that moment when he first felt the coolness of the tent's shadow. Perhaps he had been reminded of the first time he ever stood inside a solar tent, a boy of twelve offering homage to the Kha-Khan. The memory of the occasion still made him tremble and left his mouth dry.

His father had been killed in a battle the day before and Burun had been left with a clear choice; to go on his knees to the Kha-Khan, or to take what was left of

34

his clan to join Targatun, the supreme Khan of the Merkuts. He had chosen Daijin, the present Kha-Khan's father, because he had reasoned that submission to the Yek represented the best chance of staying alive.

For an hour he had stood shaking in his boots, while the Kha-Khan recounted in a gentle voice the list of penalties applicable to one who had been taken in revolt against his rightful overlord. When he had finally been allowed to leave the cool shade of the solar pavilion, he had been thankful to feel the beat of the sun upon his shoulders. The following day Targatun's head had been decorating a Yek standard and, in the absence of any other candidate who was both eligible and alive, Burun had been elected Khan of the Merkuts.

'Khan?'

Burun started, then realised that he was in a different tent, three thousand verst and forty years distant. He took the bowl which Osep handed to him and sipped greedily at the hot gruel. There were chunks of meat in it and he spooned them into his mouth with his fingers.

'More, Khan?'

Burun wiped his hands on a cloth and shook his head. 'No. I'll sleep now.'

'Yes, Khan.'

Osep indicated the corner of the tent and Burun saw that his bedroll had been laid there.

'Good, Osep.'

He could not be bothered to undress. He kicked off his boots and lay down. Osep draped the riding cloak up over his shoulders.

'Wake me at the noon hour.'

'The Khan wishes.'

But Burun only grunted his acknowledgement at

35

the formula. Already he had turned over and was composing himself for sleep.

The tent, indeed the whole camp, was silent when he awoke. He stretched for a pleasant moment, then rolled off the p'yass on to his knees. Osep had placed his boots beside the tent wall and Burun hopped first on one foot, then on the other, as he pulled them on.

He pushed the tent flap aside and stood in the opening, listening. Somewhere off a st'lyan snorted, and in one of the tents someone was humming a snatch of a tune, a soldier's song about a N'pan girl. Burun thought about Kiku, his second wife, and warmed at the memory of her.

'- Oh coil me in her long dark hair,
And there forever let me lie -'

The words brought to Burun a shudder of recollection, but it was as if the haze over the camp was like a blanket, preventing sound as well as movement from disturbing the air.

Burun was not sure how he knew, but it was near noon. It felt like noon. He turned and looked back into the tent.

Hodai was snoring, wrapped in his bedroll, and Osep and Mago were stretched motionless on the ground. Osep's mouth was open and some kind of insect was crawling across his face towards its open chasm. Burun had a sudden thought that this was how the orderly would look when he was dead.

'Lord?'

Burun had not noticed the sentry before, but now the trooper rose from the shadow at the side of the door flap where he had been squatting.

'Peace, Obulai. I woke early.'

'Oh yes, Lord. Do you want a drink?'

The proffered jug held k'vass and Burun sipped just enough to wet his lips.

'Thank you.'

He pulled up the loose cowl of his robe and stepped out into the full blast of the sun. It was not as hot as it had been at the edge of the G'bai, but it was bad enough to turn breathing into an uncomfortable experience. Great heat was really no more trouble-some to the Yek than extreme cold, but Burun wondered if men would ever evolve so that they would be able to move with complete freedom in either climatic condition.

He went first to the lines. The st'lyan of his string were all tethered together, and he fed each of them a double handful of grain. Their heads dipped and he had to step back to avoid the sweep of the great single horn which projected from the forehead of each as they butted at him, seeking more. With care he examined the hocks and hooves of every mare, starting with the grey he used for riding and finishing with the chestnut which was bred for battle. She turned to nip at him as he lifted her left hind and he swatted her lightly across the nose with his free hand.

'Ah, would you, you ungrateful wench? Take that!'

The st'lyan snorted and remained still while he completed the inspection. But as soon as he lowered her hoof, she sidestepped and tried to crush him against the black which was Hodai's riding mount. Burun fisted her hard in the side and she backed up again, screaming.

The disturbance brought a sentry tumbling out of the shadows at the far end of the lines.

'Who goes? Stand still, there, and identify yourself!'

'Burun Khan. Let me pass.'

Burun thought about criticising the slowness of the challenge, but there was time enough yet to tighten discipline.

'Oh. I'm sorry, Khan.' The sentry lowered his bow. 'I didn't see you.'

Burun grunted. He walked past the guard post towards the most distant line of tents and tried to identify the pennants. Most of the guidons hung limply in the still air, but finally he made out the colours of T'zin's command and pulled aside the door flap above which the banner had been mounted.

T'zin was awake, playing chess with one of his lieutenants. He raised a hand in greeting, then returned to his intent study of the board. Burun was surprised to note that he appeared to be sober.

'Khan?'

Burun accepted a cup of k'miss which an orderly held out to him. He drank a little, waiting.

'Check.'

T'zin moved his elephant down the board. The lieutenant crowed and brought his warrior out from behind the fortress.

'Mate, Lord. That's another ten koban you owe me!'

T'zin had been turning to address Burun. Now he looked back at the board. There was an impenetrable fence around his overlord.

'Aaagh!' T'zin sorted through a heap of coins, then tossed one across the board. 'Curse you, Wotai! I'll take a game off you yet!'

The lieutenant folded the gold coin into his wallet. He laughed. 'Not until you concentrate more, Lord. The game requires a commitment. You must bleed a little to win.'

T'zin rose and stretched. He faced Burun.

'Well, Khan.'

'Well, Noyon.'

'Are you surprised to find me sober?'

'I'm quite astonished.' Burun handed his cup to the orderly. 'Is this to be a permanent state of affairs, or only temporary?'

'Oh, I only get drunk when I'm not on campaign.' T'zin made a dismissive gesture with one hand. 'What else is there to do, after all, for the son of the son of the Kha-Khan, except get drunk or play chess?'

'Well. There are other pastimes, I believe.'

'Hunting? I have killed enough. So have we all. And as for women –' T'zin grimaced, '– you forget perhaps that I am my brother's twin. I have had enough of women's conspiracies to last a lifetime.'

Burun nodded, deciding to choose his words with care.

'Your brother, on the other hand, has somewhat wider interests.'

T'zin went to the door flap and pushed it aside. Then he turned and looked back at Burun. 'My brother's choice,' he said.

'But not yours?'

T'zin stared out at the silent camp for a moment. Then he spoke again.

'I would rather be a dog, than Kha-Khan.' His voice was intense and Burun shivered. 'I would rather be a slave.'

Burun was in the middle of the evening briefing when a sound from the lines made him look up. It was near sunset, and the deep redness which was reflected across the sky made it difficult to see anything clearly more than a few hundred paces away. A st'lyan screamed shrilly and Hodai too looked up.

'Khan?'

'I know. Where's the sentry who should be at the far end of the lines? Can you see him?' Even as he spoke,

39

Burun caught a movement among the st'lyan. 'There. We're being raided. Osep, bring my bow. Come on, the rest of you.'

He ran towards the lines with Hodai half a pace behind, shouting instructions.

'No. Forget your saddles. Follow your Khan.'

Osep raced up and Burun snatched the bow and a fistful of arrows. Off to the right, Nogai was running, followed by Targoutai and T'zin. Everyone else had been caught off guard.

At the beginning of the lines, Burun stopped. He waved an arm at the others, and then looked along the backs of the milling st'lyan and tried to spot a movement which was out of place. In the camp, the alarm was finally being raised and, as the gong sounded, he saw a sudden brief flurry among the mares tethered furthest from the tented area. Hodai trotted up, breathing easily.

'I've sent men to circle round, Khan.'

'Good.' Burun nocked an arrow. 'Let's give them time to get into position. In the meantime I would like to know how any raider got this far.'

'I don't know, Khan. I found one of our sentries over there, in among the rocks. But the others are not where they ought to be.'

'You mean the outposts?'

'Yes, Khan. There are no men along the outpost lines, nor any sign of their bodies.'

'So who was responsible for this sector?'

'Nogai Noyon, Khan. I spoke to him myself when he brought in the rearguard.'

'I see.'

Burun glanced right and left. All along the perimeter of the lines there were kneeling troopers. He could tell which were the old soldiers because they were bootless and half-clothed, just as they had risen from rest. All of them were armed and ready.

Nogai was kneeling twenty paces or so away. He was flanked by his brothers and Burun summoned him with a wave.

'We'll have to flush them out. Nogai, you take the point. You personally.'

Nogai looked startled. He opened his mouth as if he was going to protest, but he was forestalled by Targoutai.

'God curse you, Merkut! Are you trying to get him killed?'

Burun ignored the query. He stared steadily at Nogai. 'Outposts, Nogai.' He saw the noyon flinch. 'Take the point.'

Nogai flushed. Then he rose and stepped over the picket line and into the tethered rows of st'lyan. Burun waited until he had penetrated about twenty paces. Then he waved again and everyone else moved forward. The mares began to shift nervously.

Burun still had an arrow nocked. He half drew his bow and tried to spot the raiders again.

'They haven't tried to break out yet, Khan.' Hodai's voice was quiet.

Burun did not bother to turn as he replied. 'No. Either they're very sure of themselves, or else they're waiting for us to make a mistake. Get some men mounted. Hurry. I think if I was their leader, I would try to stampede part of the lines.'

Hodai turned aside and Burun heard him calling orders. A row or two ahead, a st'lyan screamed shrilly.

Burun started to trot forward. He made for the nearest part of the perimeter. A loose mare reared up in front of him and he seized a handful of her mane and scrambled onto her back.

The whole of the picket line in the area which was furthest from the tents had been cut. Loose st'lyan were spilling on to the plain and, as Burun watched, troopers on foot raced forward, shouting and waving their arms to turn the leaders. Burun readied his bow, and looked for mounts with riders on their backs.

'Yip! Yip! Yip!'

There was a flurry of movement from the direction of the cry and Burun saw that some of the st'lyan were being ridden by what looked like children. He aimed without hesitation at the nearest and loosed an arrow. The raider threw up his arms and tumbled backwards without a sound. Burun selected another target and fired again. This time there was a sharp cry of pain as the shaft found its mark, and at once the other raiders slid sideways off the backs of the st'lyan. Small figures ran in among the milling mares, then out on to the plain. Everyone was shooting now, and they were picked off one by one.

Burun bent forward to catch up the st'lyan's head rope. He guided her out of the lines. Mounted troopers were starting to herd loose mares back inside the perimeter.

'Khan! Will you come see?'

Hodai was standing over one of the fallen and, when Burun dismounted beside him, he rolled the body on to its back with his foot. The raider was a dwarf, twisted and misshapen. There was only one eye and one hand was like a claw.

'Name of God!'

Burun spat. He had seen mutants before, but never in groups of more than two or three. Within the Kha-Khan's domains, any who survived past puberty were suffered to remain alive. But the Yasa forbade them to breed, on pain of death.

'They're all the same, Khan. A family, do you suppose?'

'God knows.' Burun turned away. 'Burn the bodies

42

anyway. Then let's get away from this place.'

Osep ran up with a cloak and Burun wrapped himself in it. He looked for Nogai among the men who were walking back from the lines and, when he saw him, placed himself deliberately in his path.

Nogai stopped.

'I know what you are going to say. I should have placed outposts all along the far side of the perimeter and, because I did not, the sentry is dead. Hodai mentioned it to me, but I thought he was being unnecessarily cautious. I'm sorry.'

Burun kicked at a loose clod of earth while he considered his answer.

'Very well. But when my aide gives you an instruction, treat it as an order from me, will you? You owe the family of the dead sentry a fine. Don't make the same mistake again, or I'll have you replaced and sent back to Kinsai.'

'I won't. Thank you.'

It was clear that Nogai was shaken. Burun grinned.

'Oh, don't thank me. Now everyone will wonder why I was easy with you. Your enemies will say that you have no head for command and it will be rumoured that you escaped court-martial only because your grandfather is the Kha-Khan.'

'Is that why you are letting me off?'

'No, Noyon. You are not responsible for your blood. Anyway, I think that in some ways it is bad training for someone like you to be Altun, not an ordinary man. You are expected to be the best at everything you do, but no one wants to apply the discipline which you must learn before you can excel.'

Nogai's mouth twisted into the semblance of a smile.

'Perhaps nursemaid to the Altun Uruk could be made a hereditary title of the Merkuts,' he said.

Burun gave him a long slow look, then shook his head.

'Unlikely.'

Nogai walked on and Burun looked after him thoughtfully. Had he been sure that Nogai's disobedience was deliberate, he would have court-martialled him on the spot. But on the whole Burun thought that it was worth the near loss of a few head of st'lyan to place Nogai at such a moral disadvantage.

'We've rounded up all the loose animals, Khan.' Hodai came up and saluted.

Burun turned. 'Good. In that case you can tell them all to get mounted. Come on. We're losing riding time.'

Burun had determined to drive all of the Altun hard during the days which followed. He did not want Nogai to have time to reflect on how easily he had been treated, then perhaps to wonder if there might, after all, be a chance of obtaining Burun's favour. But in the event it became clear that such a plan was unnecessary. Nogai was apparently feuding with T'zin and the attention of everyone was on the progress of the quarrel.

On the third day Nogai managed to knock T'zin off his st'lyan, and tried to trample him. T'zin ducked in under the flailing hooves, smashed Nogai's mare hard across the nose, then danced away again as she crashed backwards, screaming. Nogai went sprawling. He vaulted back into the saddle at once, caught up with T'zin who had remounted and turned away, and they galloped the length of the line, lashing each other with their riding whips.

Burun watched expressionlessly. At the end of the column, T'zin sat his mare down hard on her haunches and yelled abuse at Nogai as he rode on.

'The whole army will criticise their lack of discipline.' Hodai's comment was sour.

'Nonsense.' Burun turned away. 'They will say that the Altun fight like leopards.'

Nogai had managed to haul his mount round and now he rode full tilt into T'zin. Both mares fell and a group of officers rode forward to pick up and separate the combatants.

'True,' Hodai observed mildly, 'but don't you think it's a little hard on the st'lyan?'


'Khan.'

Burun opened his eyes. They were two days out of Pesth, skirting the big bend of the 'Sit River. Burun had ordered the main body of men into camp early because the grazing was good. Here in the foothills it was cooler; and they were able to ride through the night and well into the morning.

He sat up. Osep was kneeling at his side and Kuchuk was waiting a pace or two away.

'Yes. What is it?'

'Khan, a message from Tulagai Noyon. A large body of riders, three or four hundred, has crossed his trail, and he suspects an ambush. He awaits your command.'

Burun rolled on to his knees, and stood up. 'Name of God, I hope not. If he has any sense he is continuing to advance, but slowly. Has he left this range of foothills yet?'

'Not quite, Khan.'

'And he is what, three or four hours ahead at normal riding pace?'

Kuchuk nodded. 'Yes, Khan.'

'So if there is an ambush ahead of him, it will be in the gorges at the base of the next range. Excellent. Well, what are we waiting for? Hodai!'

Kuchuk laughed and turned away shouting. A

45

command courier at one of the fires jumped up and ran to meet him. Kuchuk issued instructions and the courier saluted, leapt into the saddle, and galloped away.

Burun's aide was in conference with a pair of young officers. He looked up as Burun approached.

'Yes, Khan?'

'Get everyone saddled up again. And send to Nogai Noyon. He is to bring up the rearguard at once.'

'Yes, Khan.' Hodai saluted.

'Quick about it then. Come on - move - the lot of you! Or else by the time we catch up with Tulagai, it will be too dark to see what we're fighting!'

The camp exploded into activity.

Burun picked up his riding cloak and fastened it around his shoulders. He wondered if Tulagai had enough sense, as well as courage, to stay in contact with an enemy if he was attacked and forced to fall back. He considered sending more precise instructions. But if Tulagai hadn't learned more elementary tactics than that, he wouldn't have survived his first battle.

'Osep!'

'Yes, Khan.'

Before Burun could give the order, his orderly was running towards the lines. He returned riding his own mount bareback. He had Burun's chestnut on a leading rein.

'Be careful, please Khan. She's very nervous.'

Burun snorted. He threw his saddle across the st'lyan's back. Osep raced round to secure the girth and the mare bucked, screaming. Burun grabbed at the bridle.

'Easy, sweeting. Easy.'

The st'lyan screamed again and sat down on her hindquarters. Osep waved his arms in exasperation.

'Khan?'

'I know. Come up, you perverted spittle of a cross-grained she-dragon!' Burun hauled on the bridle and, reaching up, seized the great single horn and pulled down hard. The chestnut's head came forward and she kicked out sideways. Osep yelled as he was knocked into a clump of thorn bushes.

'Do you need help, Khan?' Hodai hovered anxiously.

'Help Osep.' Burun spat. He hung onto the st'lyan's horn.

Her next head toss lifted him off his feet and when the st'lyan reared again he jumped clear, then danced in again under the slashing hooves. A hundred commander caught at the mare's tail, but her next kick threw him off and he landed, rolling.

'Easy, you she-devil.'

Burun swatted the st'lyan lightly across the nose, and at once she came up standing. She trembled and snorted as two junior officers grasped belatedly at her mane.

'That's better.' Burun scratched the mare's forehead below her horn and allowed her to nudge at his shoulder. The mare whickered and nuzzled at him, and he chuckled.

Hodai rushed forward to secure the flapping girth. Another aide was pulling Osep out of the bushes.

'Name of God, Khan.' Hodai shook his head. 'You can't ride an animal like that into battle.'

'Why not? She's skittish, that's all.'

'Skittish!' Hodai elbowed the mare hard in the side, then pulled the girth tight. 'She's only half broken.'

Burun grinned and then swung himself up into the saddle.

'I like her that way. It's useful occasionally to be mounted on a wild animal, especially in the middle of a fight.' He fought the st'lyan's head round. 'Anyway, it's not my fault if it takes half a dozen Yek to control one miserable Merkut st'lyan. Come on. Get everyone mounted. Hurry up, or we'll miss all the good fighting.'

'Messenger coming up, Khan.'

Burun grunted. He had halted the command post momentarily on a small rise. When he stood in the stirrups and looked back he could see the dust cloud which was Nogai hastening up with the rearguard. Burun grinned. Ever since the incident of the outposts, Nogai had been working hard to make amends.

The courier spurred his st'lyan up the slope and reined in hard.

'From Tulagai Noyon, Khan. He is in the valley of the hills beyond this range, engaging an enemy force equal in size to his own. He asks if you are coming to his assistance.'

Burun looked at the sun and calculated.

'Yes. Say to him that I will be up with him in less than an hour.'

The courier threw up his hand in salute. Then he charged off down the slope again.

'Kuchuk!'

'Yes, Khan.'

The standard-bearer was sitting with one foot out of the stirrup, his free leg hooked across the pommel of his saddle. His pennant satchels were open.

'Signal the column, black at the dip!'

Kuchuk attached a long black streamer to his signal pole, hoisted it, and then brought it angling forward. Immediately the moving formation began to change. Hundred commanders shouted orders, and the lines of riders spread out, moving forward at a faster pace.

Burun urged his chestnut down-slope and let her stretch out until she was level with the front rank. He eyed the sun. If the light failed before he reached Tulagai, some of the bandits would get away.

'Hodai!'

'Yes, Khan?'

'Detach two hundred men to the command of T'zin Bahadur on the left. Send to him that he is to get between the fighting and any escape route into the hills.'

'Yes, Khan.'

Hodai spurred away, and after a few minutes the furthermost part of the left flank divided and files of riders galloped away.

Burun relaxed his grip on the reins and let his mind wander. He had been told once that it was a special gift - the ability to be able to detach himself before a battle from what was to come. So far as he was concerned, it was simply that he could see no point in worrying once every possible preparation had been made.

Bandits. Probably they were Ch'noze, although it was unusual to find them raiding this far south and east. No doubt they felt safe in such a large concentration. Burun had spent most of the previous winter and spring sieging a series of Ch'noze strongholds in the far north-west. The experience had taught him respect for the Ch'noze tribesman's courage and stubbornness, if not for his political wisdom. In appearance a Ch'noze was similar to a Yek or a Merkut. They possessed talons. But there the resemblance ended. The Ch'noze seemed to have no proper clan or family structure - no sense of order. They were barbarians. Individual tribes were only loosely associated with one another. Each was controlled by its own warlord, who held power for just so long as he could fight off the rising contenders. Ch'noze tribes had to be subjugated separately and when the people of one area had been

49

beaten into submission, a permanent garrison had to be installed. Otherwise they rose again in revolt the moment they sensed any relaxation of occupying control.

A strange people.

There was a screen of trees immediately ahead and Burun sat up in the saddle. There was a river or a stream somewhere in front. He could hear the sound of running water.

'Kuchuk!'

'Yes, Khan.'

The standard-bearer had anticipated Burun's reaction. He started to wave the red streamer which he had attached to his signal pole. The front rank began to slow, but already the riding men were breaking through the trees onto the steep incline down to a river bank.

Burun cursed quietly. He let his st'lyan have her head. Halfway down the slope, she began to slide. He grasped her mane with both hands, hanging on as she screamed shrilly and then splashed awkwardly into the water.

Hodai surged up alongside.

'It's not deep, Khan.'

Burun eyed the river water which was rushing past. The surface was only a few digits below the level of his stirrup irons.

'It had better not be. If I have to swim this animal, I'll have your ears.'

Hodai flushed red; when Burun kicked the mare into motion, he dropped back. All along the river, lines of riders were forging steadily across. The bank on the far side was less steep and Burun let the chestnut shake herself before he urged her on. Hodai ranged up beside him again.

'I'm sorry, Khan. One of the scouts reported to me

about the river. But all I asked about was the depth. I didn't think about the steepness of the banks.'

Burun grunted acknowledgement.

'Well, at least everyone seems to have crossed safely. But make sure the hundred commanders dress their lines once we are on level ground again.'

'Yes, Khan.'

Burun uncased his bow and levered off the top of his quiver. He could hear the vague murmur of noise ahead and he kicked the st'lyan into a canter. The plain here was only about half a verst wide and, in the failing light, he could make out a gap which must be the valley where Tulagai was fighting. Burun thought about the lie of the land as it had been described by one of the scouts.

'Kuchuk!'

'Yes, Khan?'

'Signal the right - double black at the zenith!'

A strong breeze had sprung up. It was coming off the hills, and the pair of black streamers topped by the right flank's blue pennant were whipped back from the end of the pole. Men cheered, and the whole right side of the formation diverged away. Burun moved the chestnut up into a gallop and headed for a low hill on the left.

The sound of battle was quite distinct now. Burun judged that it was coming from the mouth of the valley itself. He checked the st'lyan on the crest of the hill and surveyed the scene.

There was a flat plain at the entrance to the valley. A shallow stream meandered across it and Tulagai's vanguard was strung out across its width, fighting a holding action. The Yek were being forced to retire, but they were doing so slowly. Every time the enemy charged, the troopers trotted away. They turned in the

51

saddle and volleyed arrows back into the ranks of their pursuers so that each advance petered out in chaos.

There seemed to be very little return fire and, although he could not make out the detail of their standards, Burun decided that the enemy were definitely Ch'noze. The hillmen were not good archers and he could see no sign of proper organisation in the attacks.

With the whole of the left at his back, he waited until the action had progressed a little further out on to the plain. Now he was above the enemy and slightly to the rear of their right flank. He nocked an arrow and shot.

Everyone seemed to loose at the same moment. The sky was black with arrows. They slid down into the enemy ranks and saddles emptied everywhere.

'Eeiyah!'

With a roar, the detached right flank raced round the shoulder of the hill, up through Tulagai's open columns, and crashed into the Ch'noze front. Burun backed his st'lyan up a pace or two and then released her. She charged forward down the slope as if she had been released from a catapult.

'Yaaiyah!'

Howling troopers overtook Burun on both sides. The whole force cascaded down into the enemy, turning what was left of the Ch'noze right flank back upon itself, and the battle dissolved into momentary confusion.

Burun kept the command post moving forward with the rest. He rammed the chestnut into a smaller skewbald which was being ridden by a Ch'noze who bore the facial tattoos of a warleader. The bandit screamed as the st'lyan's horn caught him in the side, then he fell under the hooves of Kuchuk's black.

Burun charged on.

The press was too tight for organised fighting, but Burun knew that his men were winning. Yek warcries sounded triumphantly around him.

A Ch'noze on foot ran blindly past and Burun stabbed at him with the sharpened tips of his bow. Suddenly he was out in the open again. He hauled the chestnut's head round, ready to organise another charge, but there was no need. The ground over which the action had passed was littered with bodies. Within the screen of Yek troopers the only movement was from a score of riderless animals which ran loose out on to the plain.

The battle was over so suddenly that Burun was caught unprepared.

'Kuchuk?'

'Here, Khan.'

The standard-bearer had reined in only a length away. Again he had one leg up across the saddle and was folding his banners and signal streamers so that they could be stowed in their satchels. He looked up expectantly, but Burun only waved.

'Hodai?'

'Here, Khan. I don't think we lost a man.'

Burun digested the statement. It was always the same after a fight. First one felt surprise at being still alive. Then one looked around to see who else had survived.

Tulagai rode up. He was grinning broadly.

'My compliments, Khan.' He saluted Burun. 'I don't think they knew what hit them.'

Burun shrugged. He did not think that there had been great skill involved in organising the attack.

'Oh well, you did a fair job of holding them.'

Tulagai nodded, pleased. 'Yes, I did, didn't I.'

'Did you lose many?'

53

'A handful, no more. Their archery wasn't very good.'

Burun sniffed. 'Then you were lucky.'

Tulagai laughed. 'Oh yes, I know. My father says I lose too many men in battle. But it's the way I fight best.' He stood in the stirrups. 'I don't see my brothers. Did you leave them behind?'

'Not quite. I sent T'zin round behind you, in case we had to stop them from running away. I expect he'll be up shortly. Targoutai was leading the attack which came through your lines, so he's around somewhere. Nogai was still about half an hour behind me when we came off the plain.'

Tulagai made a face. 'That won't please Nogai - he missed all the fighting.'

'Yes. I'm aware that he wants to return to Kinsai with a bloody lance and if possible some minor scar which will not mar his looks. But someone has to command the rearguard.'

'Of course. Although if you keep him out of the fighting too often, he is going to think that you are trying to prevent him from making his reputation.'

Burun shrugged. 'I'm not responsible for what Nogai thinks, nor do I care. The war isn't being organised so that he can gain glory, or improve the minimal chance he has of becoming Kha-Khan.'

'No, but -'

'But nothing. Your grandfather ordered me to take you and your brothers on campaign and to re-introduce all of you to some kind of soldierly behaviour. So if anyone else tries to tell me when Nogai may be suffering from hurt pride, I think I may throw up.'

Tulagai's expression was startled. Burun ignored him and gigged the st'lyan's head round. He kicked the mare into a trot and headed for the mouth of the valley.

'Black banner, Khan?' Hodai ranged up alongside.

Burun reined in. He stood in the stirrups and surveyed the plain.

'Yes. Let's make a few verst before we camp. And I want a full complement of outriders.'

'Yes, Khan. What about –' Hodai gestured at the litter of Ch'noze bodies.

'Bring our own dead in for burning, if there are any. Leave the rest to feed the soil. Were there prisoners?'

'No, Khan.'

'Hunh.'

Burun suddenly felt cold and he reached behind his saddle for his riding cloak. The sun had set and the sky was dark except for a few pinpoints of light. There was what appeared to be a new star overhead. Burun wondered if it was an omen and if it was good or bad.

'All right.' He pulled the fur collar of the cloak up round his ears. 'Get everyone moving.'

PART ONE

Suragai

At first only the *Simonova*'s lights betrayed her presence amid the blackness of space. But when the barge was closer, the survey ship's resemblance to a floating junkheap became more apparent.

Although he had been forewarned, Rostov eyed the vessel with disfavour. That, he reflected, was what happened when the Navy was persuaded to hand over operational as well as administrative control of a ship to a pack of civilians. The scientists and technicians who were responsible for running the vessel were all ranking members of the Imperial Survey Service; but that did not mean that they had the slightest notion about running either a tight or a tidy ship. As the barge swept silently towards the docking bay, Rostov noted the clusters of scanners and other unidentifiable telemetry which appeared to have been attached at random to the hull. It was not unusual for the configuration of a deep space vessel to be unbalanced. The Infinity Drive exerted exactly equal stress – which was to say almost none – on all parts of the contained structure, and a ship like the *Simonova* was never likely to be required to approach even the outer atmosphere of a planet, far less to land. As he examined the clutter, however, Rostov was inclined to wonder if it was entirely the result of essential additions to survey gear. More probably it was the product of the average scientist's well-known unwillingness to get rid of anything if he thought that it might come in useful at some time in the future.

Rostov keyed his writer, about to make a note to ascertain the exact function of each of the assorted external mountings. Then he stopped, remembering that his status aboard the *Simonova* carried with it only a limited amount of authority.

The other occupants of the barge's acceleration couches were reacting in a predictably more vocal manner.

'- a collection of scrap metal -'

'- typical of civilian operation -'

The two technical lieutenants who had been attached to Rostov's staff were providing a running commentary for those who were not placed adjacent to a viewport. But it was Zukov, the Master-at-Arms, who summarised the survey vessel's appearance with typical force and economy.

'By the Sack!' He examined the *Simonova*'s outline critically. 'She's a repair-dog's bad dream come true!'

The panel in front of the barge pilot flashed red as the survey ship's watch-keepers belatedly demanded recognition codes. Rostov experienced a moment of irritation. They were already well within the shield zone and, had the barge been hostile, it could have inflicted untold damage. Rostov forced himself to remember that the planet on his viewport's horizon was Knossos, capital of the Imperium, and not some rebel outworld. Perhaps the Secretary of the Navy Board was right - he had spent too long on active service.

'Reception party, Admiral. Starboard side of the docking bay.'

The Navy pilot indicated with a nod of his head. His hands were busy shutting down controls.

Rostov nodded acknowledgement, but when the barge settled he remained seated. Cabin pressure equalised with a hiss of air. Rostov reached for the flat permahide envelope which contained his orders and for a moment he brushed absently at the crisp new admiral's stripe on his sleeve.

'Captain? Sir?'

It was the familiar title, rather than Zukov's voice, which recalled Rostov to the present. Half a universe away there had been another tunic cuff, the gold braid scorched and burned so that its imprint was fused on to the skin of his arm. He pushed aside the recollection and stepped out on to the dock.

If the pilot's warning had not prepared him to recognise them, Rostov would have been unable to distinguish the *Simonova*'s reception party from the deckhands working around them. Like others in the area, the three ship's officers were dressed in drab coveralls. Only one wore discreet jewellery. Rostov waited patiently while they arranged themselves in order of precedence and then touched hands with each.

'Rostov.' He introduced himself economically. 'Sergei Alexeivitch.'

He could not help it if his use of the colonial patronymic sounded like a challenge. Let them know from the start that they were dealing with a kulak, not a noble.

If there was a reaction in the eyes of the trio's leader, Rostov was unable to discern it.

'Admiral. Allow me to welcome you. I am Surveyor Scientist Bock, administrator of the *Simonova*. I present to you my deputy, Surveyor Scientist Markov; and this is Surveyor Scientist Grigoriev. The noble Grigoriev is the Imperial Adjudicator.'

Rostov bowed. As he had expected, Grigoriev's skin was tinted faintly golden, the result of prolonged use of Longivex. Rostov saw the Adjudicator's eyes widen in surprise as he recognised the same colouring in the skin around the admiral's high cheekbones.

Let him wonder. It was true that the longevity drug was available as a rule only to nobles. The substance upon which Longivex was based was scarce - located so far on only two worlds of the surveyed systems - and it had proved impossible to manufacture a synthetic substitute which did not possess deadly side effects. Rostov was one of a very few special exceptions to the Imperial edict which excluded commoners from access to the bi-annual treatment which was necessary for administration of the drug, but he saw no reason to apprise the Adjudicator of the fact.

Almost as a reflex, he smiled grimly to himself. Kulaks who joined the Imperial Navy, even in the commissioned ranks, did not normally expect to enjoy a long life.

'Gentlemen.' Rostov employed the outmoded form of address without thinking. 'These are the officers of my staff.'

He indicated the group which had now assembled beside the barge and made brief introductions, so as to permit the officers to pay formal respects.

'Yuan, pilot commander, senior aide -'

The Manchu's half bow and the response of the surveyors to it were equally cold. Of all the human races which inhabited the Imperium, Yuan's had been isolated perhaps the longest before re-integration. Probably for that reason as much as any other, the Manchu appearance seemed impossibly alien to the eye. Rostov was accustomed to his aide's height - no Manchu was taller than one hundred and fifty centimetres - his colour, a unique golden yellow which was almost metallic in skin tone, and his oddly lengthened features. Everyone pretended to ignore the reaction of the surveyors to the fact that the senior administrative member of Rostov's staff was a member of a race which could be expected to have little respect for the Imperial establishment.

'Antonov, pilot major, sailing master –'

'Sandor and Kubitsky, technical lieutenants on temporary attachment –'

All three officers executed the approved additional formal full bow in Grigoriev's direction. The noble seemed to relax visibly, and Rostov concealed sour amusement.

'Zukov, Master-at-Arms; Mubarak, Marine Gunnery Sergeant; and Vorontseff, Corporal, my personal servant –'

From a practical point of view it was probably unnecessary to name the non-commissioned officers. They stood to attention, but it was clear that both the administrator and his deputy were unsure of the proper response. Rostov used the moment to search for a formula which would ease his passage through the final introduction. Finally he settled upon a blunt statement of fact.

'Rostov, Alexei Sergeivitch, lieutenant, flag officer. The lieutenant is my son.'

It was clear that the ship's officers spotted simultaneously the gold caste mark which was imprinted on the lieutenant's cheek. Their nods of acknowledgement became full bows which were held uncertainly while they attempted to adjust to the fact that they were, unexpectedly, in the presence of a member of the Royal Family. Rostov saw that the Adjudicator was covertly comparing the obvious physical differences between father and son. He cleared his throat.

'Hrrrm. Thank you, gentlemen. But for the duration of his stay aboard this vessel, you will pay only the respects due to the lieutenant's Navy rank.'

He did not look at the still bowing surveyors as he spoke, but at Alexei. The eyes which met his were a stranger's and Rostov was unable to interpret the expression which he found there.

*

The addition of Navy personnel to the *Simonova*'s regular complement had clearly brought about a certain amount of re-allocation of accommodation. Rostov was not sure what purpose his stateroom had served previously but it was obvious that it had been occupied by at least four persons, all of whom had been possessed of diverse tastes with regard to the minimal decoration which was permissible aboard a ship designed for deep space exploration. Rostov decided that it was easier to go in search of what would pass in the *Simonova* for a command bridge than it was to remain in his quarters, while Vorontseff attempted to eradicate within the space of an hour the accumulated disarray of several years of civilian occupation.

He was carefully tactful about his appearance in the ship's operational areas. For the moment, at least, they were the exclusive preserve of the survey vessel's planetside watch-keepers.

The reaction of the midshipman who first observed his approach was predictable.

'Attention on deck!'

'As you were.' Rostov acknowledged the salutes, and the officer of the watch and his two assistants relaxed into their couches once again.

'Surveyor pilot Zarubin, Admiral.' The ship's officer bowed from his place in front of the command console. 'These are Cadets Ostrakov and Poliakov.'

'Ah.'

Rostov examined the two juniors. They were both small in stature and their complexions were dark and swarthy.

'*Sp'kochnoi Kulaki?*' Rostov addressed them in colonial argot and they grinned in response.

'*Da, polkovnik Admiral!*'

Rostov nodded approval. Few citizens entered the survey service, and for a kulak to obtain the equivalent of Navy commissioned rank required exceptional ability. He sat down in a vacant chair and at once the younger cadet hurried to serve him with tea from a spotless samovar.

'*Sp'seba.*'

The bridge of the *Simonova* was far larger than the Navy pattern to which he had become accustomed. Even so it was crowded, and there was little excess space. It was apparent that the compartment had a survey as well as a command function. Most of the control surfaces were inlaid with sets of viewscreens which were linked, when they were in use, to cloaked survey drones.

The unfamiliarity of his surroundings reminded Rostov of the ambiguity of his status. Although his orders placed him in theoretical command of the *Simonova*'s mission, in practical terms he was a guest of the civil servants who operated the vessel. Survey ships were carried on the Navy List, but Navy personnel remained aboard on sufferance only. The conditions attached to Navy participation in survey visits to quarantine planets were always the same. Not for the first time, Rostov reflected that the situation was the typical result of the Imperial bureaucracy's solution to any conflict of interest between the Civil Service and the Navy Board. The orbiting platforms which maintained the isolation of a quarantine world were a Navy responsibility. Their sophisticated plasma weapons required regular technical inspection. However, the location of planets not yet released from survey classification was information restricted to members of the Survey Service. Thus the *Simonova*, which was technically a Navy vessel, was crewed by civilians and carried its Navy complement as passengers. A Navy sailing master was permitted to take over command only for the duration of the brief period when it was necessary for the *Simonova* to be manoeuvred to allow technical officers to service the weapons and telemetry mounted on the platforms. Rostov's authority was limited at all times by the secrecy requirements which surrounded every incomplete survey, and he had already concluded that his presence on the mission was actually of questionable value.

His blind musing was interrupted by the sound of footsteps on the companionway. Rostov turned.

'Attention on deck!'

'*P'jalst.*'

Alexei was wearing undress blues. His gesture acknowledged the salute which was probably a compliment to his Imperial rather than his Navy rank.

Rostov raised an eyebrow. He had not expected colonial argot from such a source.

'*Svedanya.*' He spoke the word softly.

Alexei flushed and bowed.

'Sir. Admiral. Your servant said I would find you here. Surveyor Scientist Bock sends his compliments. He - er - requests the pleasure of your company at a reception in the crew lounge. Fourteen hundred, ship's time. Sir.'

Rostov nodded. He supposed that a certain amount of *p'vestrannyoi* - fooling around - was unavoidable under the circumstances. Briefly he wondered if it would do any good to tell the ship's administrator that the presence of the newly appointed Admiral of the White on an ordinary survey mission was not an occurrence of special significance. In fact it was the Secretary of the Navy Board's answer to the new admiral's heated demand for an end to sick leave. Rostov grinned at the memory of a recent face-to-face encounter. Orders assigning him to the *Simonova*'s mission were make-work, a temporary solution at best. They had removed him from the stifling atmosphere of the Court, but already he was finding that Civil Service protocol could be just as oppressive.

'Sir?'

Rostov was troubled by the knowledge that he had been wool-gathering again.

'Ah. Yes. Thank the administrator, with my compliments. I will be pleased to attend.'

'Yes, Admiral.' Alexei saluted and turned away.

Rostov pursed his lips. They were strangers, it was true. He had not seen any of his children for ten years; but he guessed that Alexei knew that he hated to be treated with formal courtesy.

The crew lounge of the *Simonova* apparently doubled as a recreation hall. It was too large and too brightly lit, and Rostov decided that the colours hurt his eyes.

'Admiral. Welcome.'

The administrator's greeting made everyone else in the room turn round to look. They bowed and a group came forward to be introduced. Rostov thought that it was undoubtedly Alexei who was the attraction, especially for the women. One of them dropped into a formal curtsey, revealing both her cleavage and her undergarment, and he smiled grimly. A crewman served him with a cup of mediocre wine, and he sipped at it cautiously. Bock was trying to introduce the senior members of his staff, but he was hampered by the constant movement of people. They all wanted to touch hands with Alexei.

After a while Rostov allowed the press to carry him into a corner. Grigoriev was already standing there.

'Your son is popular, Admiral.'

The noble raised his wine cup and Rostov could see

only his eyes. He guessed that a reaction was expected and shrugged.

'He has the social graces, as befits his rank. I, on the other hand -' Rostov lifted his free hand in a dismissive gesture, and then let it fall again. He waited to see what Grigoriev would say next.

The Adjudicator nodded. He was thin, and there appeared to be dark patches growing in through the grey of his beard. Rostov wondered if he had been isolated from the longevity treatment at some time in his life.

'Indeed, yes. A most personable young man, if I may be permitted to observe.' The noble was not trying to be condescending. 'I myself am of only minor nobility, you understand. But your son's true excellence of breeding is recognisable at once.'

Rostov hid a smile. It was not the first time he had been the recipient of an undiplomatic reference to the absence of colonial genes in Alexei's physique, manner and appearance.

'Your son's relationship to the Exalted -' Grigoriev paused delicately, '- is it close?'

Rostov shook his head. 'Not especially.'

It was clear that the Adjudicator had hoped for a more detailed explanation.

'Ah. Yes, I see. Your pardon, Admiral, if I have given offence.'

Rostov's mouth twitched, then he showed his teeth. 'Not at all.' He concentrated on producing a matter-of-fact tone. 'My wife is the Emperor's niece. My son was brought up at Court, where she remained while I was on active service.'

'The Federated Systems Wars.'

'That is correct. My son joined my staff only two days ago. He has just completed a year with the Praetorian Guard.'

It was an unemotional summary; Rostov thought

that it hid well the bitterness which he felt towards Irina's kin for their concerted opposition to her marriage, for the years of separation which had been achieved by her father's influence with the Navy Board and, not least, for the extent to which Alexei's upbringing had been influenced by the rigid infra-structure of the Court. With only half an ear for Grigoriev's response, Rostov stared across the room. Alexei was the centre of a circle of fawning civil servants. He looked up, and their eyes met. After a moment it became clear that Alexei was excusing himself. Rostov watched as he made his way through the crowd.

'Who are all these people?' Alexei's tone was light, amused. 'They're all mad.'

Grigoriev was watching avidly, and Rostov pretended not to have understood the remark. 'I believe you have been introduced to the Imperial Adjudicator.' He indicated the man.

A light seemed to die from Alexei's eyes.

'Oh. Goodness, yes. How are you, sir?'

The enquiry was accompanied by a courteous smile. The expression of good-humoured contempt had vanished as quickly as it had appeared, and suddenly Rostov realised that he had missed an opportunity to relax the tension which existed between them.

'Noble Born. An honour.'

Alexei waited until Grigoriev was bowing, then smiled sardonically. Rostov watched expressionlessly.

'We were remarking on your sudden popularity,' he said.

Alexei's face shuttered warily. He said nothing.

'Yes indeed.' The Adjudicator's agreement was swift. 'Although of course the majority of these people are provincials, unused to the presence of a member of the Court. It is something of a treat for them, you understand.'

The observation was made dismissively. Rostov realised that the noble was unaware of the cross-current which had passed over his head.

'But not for you, sir.' If Alexei understood and absorbed the derogatory allusion to Imperial subjects from the colonial outworlds, he ignored it. He touched hands briefly with Grigoriev.

The man flushed with pleasure.

'Of course, I am used -'

But Alexei had captured his hand and was examining a signet ring on one finger. He looked up.

'Your family and title, sir?'

'House of Andreeyev, Noble Born. A cadet branch only, and so -' Grigoriev shrugged, '- I am untitled.'

'Andreeyev. Andreeyev. Ah, yes.' Alexei's eyes seemed to stare for a moment into the middle distance. Now he focused once again. 'Your family was associated with the development of the Manchu worlds, is that not so?'

Grigoriev flushed.

'I - that is, yes, Noble Born.'

'Yes.' Alexei appeared to be unaware that he was causing embarrassment. 'The problems connected with the keeping of slaves are of interest to me. Discuss them please.'

The tone was peremptory and the voice suddenly louder. Rostov saw the heads of people in a nearby group swivel, and he smiled grimly.

'Oh, well. You must understand, Noble Born, that I was not -' The Adjudicator's smile was sick.

'Your pardon. You kept no slaves?' Alexei raised an eyebrow.

'Only Manchus, Noble Born. Only Manchus!'

All other conversation had ceased, and the protest seemed to echo across the room. Rostov looked at the faces of the people who were now staring at Grigoriev.

70

Only two were Manchus, but the rest provided an excellent sample of the width of the spectrum of variations of species homo which inhabited the worlds of the Imperium.

'It was not thought -' Grigoriev's voice faded with the realisation, '- that they were human.'

'An opinion not supported by the Court of Adjudication,' Rostov observed smoothly.

'No, Admiral.' The noble's agreement was subdued.

Rostov was well aware of the scandal. The House of Andreeyev had purchased the right to exploit the commercial potential of the Manchu system. Taking advantage of its remoteness from the administrative centre of the Imperium they had enslaved the native inhabitants. A survey record had been falsified to show that the Manchus were not entitled to the protection of citizenship - that in fact they were aliens possessed of only minimal intelligence. Only when a Navy vessel had force-landed on one of the Manchu worlds had the deception been uncovered. The Manchus had been full citizens with diplomatic privileges for more than thirty years now, but there still existed between them and other humans a coldness which could not be explained simply by xenophobia.

'You were connected with the original survey?' Rostov spoke curiously.

The Adjudicator was pale, and it took him a moment to formulate a reply. Quite clearly he was torn between his desire to excuse himself from further cross-examination and his obedience to the protocol which kept him in the presence of a member of the Royal Family until he was dismissed.

'I was a junior member of the earliest survey party. I was exonerated by the Adjudicator's Court.'

'Naturally.' Alexei's tone was frosty. 'Otherwise you would not be here.'

He turned his back. Grigoriev bowed and hastened out of the room. Suddenly everyone began talking again.

Rostov found it hard to feel sympathy for Grigoriev's predicament. He watched the man leave. Then he turned back to look at his son.

'An interesting exercise. How did you make the connection?'

'I'm not sure.' Alexei considered. 'The crest on the ring was familiar. Then there was the fellow's appearance. It was obvious that he had been under house arrest at some point in his life.'

Rostov nodded. Accused persons were automatically excluded from longevity treatment, and, since the Imperial law courts often took years over a complex case, the effects of the irreversible ageing process were usually apparent. He remembered the dark patches in Grigoriev's beard, and thought that he should have realised their meaning.

'You embarrassed him.'

Alexei shrugged. 'He annoyed me. You may not react to a casual slight about colonial manners, but I do. The more so since I possess your well-known restraint only in small measure.'

Rostov showed his teeth.

'I see. Well, I suspect that you have made an enemy, though I doubt if he will ever be in a position to offer repayment for your treatment of him. Tell me, child -' he concluded mildly, '- is there a chance that we might find some alternative mode of address towards one another, or does your capability for restraint exclude all the intimate forms usual between parent and child?'

Alexei seemed to consider once more.

'I had it impressed upon me that my posting to your staff was a matter of strict duty. However, I believe that I could manage to call you father if it is appropriate to the circumstances.'

Rostov hid his irritation. He understood now the reason for Alexei's remoteness. Irina's brother was a member of the Navy Board, and he must have taken pleasure in sowing any seed which was likely to grow into a further barrier between father and son.

'Very well.' Rostov drank the last of his wine and held out the cup. 'Then while you are considering what those circumstances may be, you may allow your regard for your duty to sustain you while you fetch me another of these.'

It was clear that Alexei was startled. He accepted the cup. Rostov looked at him levelly for a moment, then he turned away.

Rostov knew that the *Simonova* was underway only because he had been advised of the fact by the voder of the ship's information system. He would have been surprised if it had been otherwise. The effect of the Infinity Drive was to accelerate every particle within its field so that the transition from rest to motion was not discernible. Although the survey vessel was now travelling at a speed faster than light, its occupants experienced no sense of progress other than that which was fed to them through the navigational telemetry.

The *Simonova*'s sensors were geared to respond to the presence in her path of any mass approaching planetary proportions. The occurrence of such an event would have the effect of reducing her motion relative to contiguous space to zero. It was not that collision with anything of that kind of size was capable of damaging the field: indeed it had been established that it would require the power of several suns to put even a dent in the electric blue haze which now surrounded and protected the vessel and its contents. But it had been proved to the satisfaction of all but a few sceptics that such an event would result in an effect similar to the collapse of a dwarf star. The *Simonova* would hurtle unchecked into a black hole of its own making, emerging perhaps eventually in another universe, or even another space-time continuum.

Viewed from space, the normal progress of the survey ship was like the passage of a comet. What was visible to the eye or to the sensor, however, was a path which had come into existence long after the *Simonova* had vanished along its trajectory. The constant impact against the field's rim, of everything from showers of meteors down to stray molecules of gas, resulted in a cosmic fireworks display of spectacular proportions: a long tail of deteriorating matter stretched out along the path which the ship had taken. As the external surface of the field collided with the elements of space, an explosive force was generated which was the equivalent of that produced by an ion bomb. Inside the protective envelope, however, there was no hint of this maelstrom. The survey vessel's crew and passengers were able to follow their daily routine undisturbed.

'Guard!'

Rostov kicked off from the wall, twisted awkwardly in mid-air, and parried Mubarak's assault. They were wielding modified Shen-sei swords with hologram blades, and he grunted with satisfaction as his reverse registered on the Gunnery Sergeant's body shield with a yellow flash of discharge. Somersaulting before he reached the opposite side of the recreation room, Rostov flexed his legs and allowed himself to come gently to rest. The whole area was under zero gravity.

He hung in the air for a moment, then kicked again, tuck-rolled, and came out level with the combat-master's waist.

Mubarak's sword swept down, and Rostov parried two-handed, catching the blow on his cross-guard.

'Ho!'

With an explosion of breath Rostov straightened his forearms, attempting to gain the momentary advantage which would permit him to disengage and then to cut at his opponent's unguarded left. The force of their exertion against one another pushed them apart. Rostov's feet touched the floor and he kicked hard.

'Touch!'

As he rose he somersaulted, circled his sword down, and slashed at Mubarak's neck. The sensors in the Gunnery Sergeant's shield flashed and his head was encased in a yellow glow. Unshielded, and with real blades, the stroke would have decapitated him.

Hanging in mid-air, Mubarak reversed his sword and bowed. Rostov grinned, brought his sword back in a fancy two-handed reverse, bowed, then somersaulted exuberantly.

Yuan was anchored beside the control panel at the entrance. He adjusted the gravity delicately and Rostov dropped lightly to the floor. He sheathed the holo-gram blade, then, with a hand pressed against the bunched shoulder muscles, swung his left arm in a wide overhead circle. The laser injury which had damaged the tendons was months old, but it still ached after violent exertion.

Mubarak unclipped his shield belt and held it out.

'Who wants this?' he demanded. 'He's unbeatable today.'

Rostov cocked an eye at Yuan, but the aide shook his head. The expression in his yellow eyes was unreadable and, since his oddly lengthened features were incapable of displaying an emotion which would be understandable to other humans, it was impossible to know what he was thinking. It was unlikely that he thought that he would be beaten. Shen-sei was a Manchu cult, preserved during the centuries of their isolation from the Empire. Around it they had developed a rigid code of honour - Shen-sei-go - which contained the principles according to which every Manchu male was expected to live and die.

'*So desu, Sei-sen.*'

Rostov spoke briefly in Manchu and bowed ironically.

'*So desu*' was a courtesy phrase. It could mean 'oh well', 'really' or 'so what'. It was neither a question nor a comment. Yuan's eyes flickered at the vocative title '*sei-sen*' - 'sword bearer'.

'*So desu, Sama,*' he responded flatly.

Rostov grinned. His aide had employed the only Manchu equivalent for a recognition of higher rank - '*sama*' - the word which meant 'lord'. He unclipped his shield belt and slung it over his shoulder.

'Oh, well.' He stretched lazily. 'If no one else wants to fight me -'

Mubarak offered his shield belt to Alexei. 'How about you, lieutenant? Maybe you'll get lucky today.' There was a suggestion of insolence in the observation.

Alexei flushed. After a moment he took the belt. His eyes were on Rostov's face as he strapped it on.

Rostov showed his teeth. He backed off into the centre of the room. When Alexei had taken Mubarak's sword, he nodded to Yuan. The gravity started to alter as he was clipping on his shield. He kicked gently and rose at an angle towards the ceiling.

'Well?'

Alexei's face was set. He flexed at the knees and

rose slowly. Then he executed a half-somersault and twisted so that when he had stabilised he was level with Rostov, but inverted.

It was a permissible commencing position. They unsheathed together and brought their swords forward two-handed into guard. Alexei revolved his blade once and then attacked.

'Ha!'

Rostov's breath exploded in a shout as he parried. Alexei was cutting consistently towards the left quarter, striking three or four blows on each assault before reaction force repelled him backwards. As soon as his feet touched part of the wall or ceiling, he launched forward again. Rostov's left arm ached and he realised that Alexei was trying to exploit the weakness of his healed injury to make an early touch. He allowed himself to be driven towards one wall by a new series of attacks, then kicked, rolled, and dived forward under Alexei's guard.

'Touch!'

He completed a circular slash as he descended and Alexei's shield was bathed in yellow below the waist. In real combat he would have lost at least one leg at the knee. Rostov rolled again as he reached the floor. Then he kicked and came to rest against the far wall.

Alexei dived towards him and their shields flashed angrily as they collided, sword arms locked.

'Give up.' Rostov strained to gain the advantage. He was amazed that Alexei was so strong.

'Never!'

Alexei was attempting to put two-handed pressure on his sword to break Rostov's grip. He kicked out wildly. Still locked together they tumbled across the room.

Rostov brought his knees up. He kicked hard

against Alexei's abdomen. The force of the blow pushed them apart, and they arrived at opposite walls simultaneously, kicked again, and met once more in the centre. Alexei's sword blade swept round in a great circle and Rostov turned it off with one of the best parries of his life. Jabbing with the point he kept off Alexei's attack until the reaction of their mid-air collision made them drift apart again. Rostov knew that he was going to be able to kick again long before Alexei was in contact with a surface. He looked up.

Behind the slight distortion of the shield, Alexei's face was like a stranger's. His sword was extended in two-handed guard and suddenly Rostov knew that he would never admit that he had been beaten. He signalled to Yuan, and with the change in gravity he was at the entrance with his belt slung over one shoulder before Alexei started to cross the floor.

'Why did you stop?'

Alexei's voice cracked with the discharge of emotion. Rostov turned to face him.

'You were beaten.'

'Beaten? By one touch?'

Rostov ignored the implied denial. He tossed his sword belt to Yuan and walked out into the companionway. Alexei was shouting something, and he quickened his pace so that if it was abuse or a challenge, he would be able to pretend that he had not heard it.

He wondered if Alexei was angry because he had been beaten again, or if maybe he was beginning to realise that there was no way, short of an accident, that he was ever going to be allowed to win. Rostov kneaded the muscles of his left shoulder in an effort to relieve the soreness. He reflected that he would be glad when the *Simonova* reached her destination. The daily combat practice sessions were starting to have an interesting effect on Alexei's ability to control his temper, but since it was essential to beat him every time, they were also very hard work.

'It's called Tarvaras.'

The projection was a holographic recording and Rostov watched as the planet's revolving image expanded to fill the centre of the viewing well.

'How large is it?'

The room was like a small amphitheatre. A voder commentary accompanied the recording, but Rostov had switched off the auditory input to his chair so that he could converse with the Manchu technician who was running the session.

'About one third the size of Knossos, Admiral. The diameter is just over twelve and a half thousand kilometres.'

The Manchu obligingly keyed a console display and Rostov grunted acknowledgement. Privately he thought that the precautions which were being taken to protect the identity and location of the survey ship's destination were unnecessary.

The secrecy which surrounded the location of a world under survey evaluation was essential in most instances. Freelance trading cartels competed constantly to obtain advance knowledge of the assignment of new commercial concessions by the Court of Adjudication, and this alone was sufficient to justify the elaborate security measures which the Survey Service employed. Tarvaras, however, would never be opened up to trade. It was in strict quarantine, and the Navy weapons systems stationed around it in space ensured that no one would ever achieve a landing there. Even the duly authorised activities of the *Simonova* were going to be undertaken at a respectable distance.

'Two moons, I see.'

'Yes, Admiral.'

The technician tapped a series of keys. The image of the planet receded and Tarvaras was suddenly a component of a larger system.

'There are seven planets altogether.' The Manchu's tone was prosaic. 'Several of them have more than one moon. The sun around which they orbit is thought to be quite old. It appears to be in the early stages of transition into a red giant and normally we would not have expected to find intelligent life anywhere within its field of influence.'

'And yet Tarvaras is inhabited.'

'Quite so. In fact it is probable that it has been repopulated several times. There is evidence to support the theory that the whole system was disrupted at some point, either by the passage of a comet or else by an encounter with an interstellar storm. One of the moons is in fact the remains of another planet, and it is one of the conclusions of our survey that this is a world which was resettled during the Second Empire.'

'The present phase of degeneration is fairly recent then?'

The question was Yuan's, and the technician bowed from his chair.

'So it is thought, *Sei-sen*. Our records of the Second Empire are far from complete, of course, but it is certain that Tarvaras has been isolated for thousands of years. There is some residual radiation, indicating that atomic weapons were in use approximately five thousand years ago. No civilisation under Imperial influence would have developed in such a direction; it must be concluded therefore that they discovered the technology for themselves.'

Rostov watched as the image of the planet was expanded again. This time a tiny replica of the survey

80

vessel was circling the equator inside the orbit of both moons. A number of other small objects suddenly popped into view. They were following a similar orbital path, but they were at a slightly lower altitude.

'Your platforms.' The technician pressed a key to bring the view into focus. 'There are sixteen altogether, all in synchronous orbit.'

'That's a lot for a world of this size.' Rostov was surprised.

'Yes. But we take the threat potential of this world fairly seriously. There is no doubt that the inhabitants once possessed space travel. One of the moons has been mined extensively. Their present stage of development is primitive, it is true; but they appear to evolve quickly. There is always the chance that they could –' The Manchu expanded his hands outward as if to indicate the idea that the population of Tarvaras might explode out into the galaxy.

On the basis of the information which had been contained in the briefing, Rostov was unimpressed. He looked at Yuan and raised an eyebrow.

'Of course.' Yuan's natural impassiveness made his response appear innocuous. 'But you spoke of a threat –' He prompted the other gently.

'Oh. Yes, *Sei-sen*.' The technician's reply came after a brief moment of hesitation. 'It was my understanding that you knew. You see, they are mutants.'

'Aaah.'

Yuan nodded. Looking at Rostov he made a slow, palm-up gesture. Rostov recognised the Manchu method of indicating intense sadness. He nodded agreement.

Ten thousand years earlier the Second Empire had fought itself to collapse against a race of genetically altered super-beings. The possibility of an encounter with their descendants, and the inevitability of the conflict which would follow, was the recurring nightmare which disturbed sleep at the highest levels of the Imperium. It was the reason for the formation of the Survey Service and was at the root of its policy.

Rostov understood why the precautions which had been taken to quarantine Tarvaras were so strict. But, like a minority of Imperial subjects, he was not sure that fear was sufficient justification for the isolation of whole worlds from the rest of the universe.

Alexei was barring his progress along the passageway and Rostov sighed inwardly. He guessed at once that his son had been talking to Yuan, and even though the casual disclosure of information had been pre-arranged, he regretted the unavoidability of the confrontation which was about to occur.

'Is it true?' Alexei's voice rang with angry intensity.

'Is what true?'

'That I was posted to your staff because you asked for me. Is it true?'

Rostov considered his reply only briefly. His eyes were on a level with Alexei's and he smiled unpleasantly.

'You have learned some strange manners at Court, child. Do you always speak to your betters in such a fashion? Or is this another example of what is appropriate to circumstances? Get out of my way.'

He started to push past, but Alexei caught at his arm, swinging him round.

'Answer me, father!'

The last word was stressed insolently. Rostov looked down at the hand which was holding his arm. He grabbed Alexei's wrist, then used his other hand to unclamp the fingers.

'Make me,' he invited.

Alexei's right hand clenched into a fist and Rostov

82

tensed to receive the attack which he was sure he had provoked. But after a long moment Alexei stepped back, his hands loose at his sides. He laughed bitterly.

'No need,' he said. 'I have my answer.'

Rostov was disappointed. He had expected to fight. Alexei seemed to search for words and Rostov waited to see what he would say next. The noise of a lock operating somewhere made them both look along the companionway. Rostov cursed the interruption silently. He turned as if to walk away, but Alexei spoke at last.

'What was in your mind? Did you imagine that I would be grateful for the attention? Did you expect me to fall on your neck in some touching display of filial affection?'

Rostov pretended to consider the question seriously.

'Oh, hardly that, I think. It's been ten years, after all.'

'Your awareness of the length of the interval amazes me.' Alexei made the observation tartly.

Rostov grinned. He found it hard to take the superiority in Alexei's tone seriously.

'You thought perhaps that I had forgotten about your existence?' He shook his head. 'No. Blame your grandfather and your uncle for the extent of my absence.'

Alexei gave a snort of disbelief. Rostov met the accusing eyes squarely, then he shrugged. 'Believe what you like then.'

'Thank you. I intend to.'

Rostov was determined not to be the first to turn away. He stared hard. Finally it was Alexei who made a noise, which might have indicated either disgust or anger, then brushed past. He strode off along the companionway and Rostov turned to watch him.

After Alexei had walked about fifty paces, he

stopped and turned. When he saw that Rostov was looking, he raised one arm in some kind of gesture. Rostov guessed that the sign was rude, but he was too perturbed to pretend anger. Everything had gone wrong. When Alexei was out of sight round the curve of the companionway, he turned and walked on.

In the first place it was clear that it had been a mistake to let Alexei know that his transfer away from the Praetorian Guard had been requested - because if the boy was looking for an excuse for his antagonism, then the one with which he had just been presented was perfect. Rostov thought about Alexei's behaviour and wondered if it was human nature for sons to hate their fathers, even when they did not know them very well. If that was the boy's only motivation, then he could deal with it. But the possibility of another reason troubled him.

Rostov thought about the warning which he had received before leaving Knossos - an anonymous permafax which indicated that one of the members of his staff had been commissioned as an assassin. It was impossible, surely, for Alexei to be the one. He considered that assumption, and then frowned. Even though it was unsupported by evidence, the conclusion would have been allowable were it not for the second piece of information contained in the warning message. The text had been unequivocal; it specified the involvement of a member of the Imperial Court.

Rostov sighed. There had been a strong element of pretence contained in his behaviour towards Alexei thus far and, for the moment at least, the subterfuge was going to have to be continued.

Yuan was a lotus, suspended impossibly motionless in the null gravity under which he tended to maintain his quarters when he was alone. Rostov thought about adjusting the controls, but he hesitated to disturb the state of *kerei* - contemplation - in case the period was one of the five which were the daily requirement of the Manchu code of belief. There was a foot clamp beside the door panel, and he engaged it.

The Manchu opened one eye, then closed it again. His position altered subtly and Rostov knew that he was listening. Before he had entered Yuan's quarters, he had known exactly what he was going to say. Now he hesitated. He wanted Yuan to ask what had happened, so that he could relieve his feelings. But even if the Manchu was curious, his adherence to the code of *satori* - a system of behaviour which defined what was right and proper for every situation - would prevent him from giving the feeling expression. Rostov took a breath, and decided to wait until good manners forced his aide to behave in an approachable fashion. He would count slowly to a hundred. After that, slowly again, a hundred more. And if that wasn't enough ...

Yuan opened his eyes, emerged from the lotus, and then seemed to stretch effortlessly until he was in contact with the nearest bulkhead.

'*So desu, Sama.*' He greeted Rostov. '*Konnichi wa.*'

'*Konnichi wa, Sei-sen.*' Rostov responded automatically.

'*Ikaga masu ka?*' - Is everything well? -

The Manchu's hand gesture reduced the words to the level of polite enquiry. Rostov shrugged.

'*Domo. Wa genki desu.*' - Thank you. Well enough. -

'*Oh ko.*' - Oh dear. -

This time the hand movement expressed the Manchu equivalent of sympathy and Rostov grinned in spite of himself. Manchu features were incapable of displaying emotions which were understandable to other humans, which was why they accompanied normal conversation with a series of gestures similar

85

to mime in ballet. But their ability to detect the feelings of others was close to infallible. Rostov shook his head.

'*Shigata ga nai. Karma, neh?*' - It can't be helped. That's how it goes. -

Yuan nodded gravely. '*Hai*,' he agreed. '*Karma*.'

Rostov knew that he did not believe that his failure to resolve matters with Alexei was due to karma, or fate, any more than Yuan did. He had misjudged the situation, and if he had added to his problems, it was his own fault.

Yuan rolled economically, kicked the bulkhead with one foot, and glided down to Rostov's level.

'What will you do now?' He reached past Rostov for the gravity control panel.

'I don't know.' Rostov bent to release the foot clamp. When he straightened again, Yuan was watching him. 'I don't know,' he said again.

They were speaking in Anglic now. Rostov guessed that Yuan had decided that the emotional shield which was provided by conversational Manchu was no longer necessary.

'For a son to be involved in a plot against his father -' Yuan paused delicately, '- is surely unthinkable.'

'For a Manchu son,' Rostov observed, 'but mine was brought up at Court.'

He thought about the decadence which existed at the centre of the Empire. A few hundred years of Imperial rule and already a coterie surrounded the throne which, by its very nature, endangered the survival of the Imperium. Suddenly, Rostov was troubled by a recollection. If the historians were to be believed, there had been another Empire once, on long-vanished Terra. And the generals who had grown too popular had been commanded to perform one last service by falling upon their swords.

There was no similarity of course; Rostov's service in a dozen frontier system wars posed no threat to the succession - rather the reverse in fact - but for a moment he found himself wondering if the convoluted nature of the Court infrastructure made the most devious method inevitable.

He put the thought aside and met Yuan's eyes steadily.

'As to my son, I cannot be sure. And so for the moment I must be watchful, and patient.'

'*Yoku.*'

Yuan spoke the word softly and Rostov nodded. There was a subtle difference which Anglic could never have expressed. Manchu patience was inexhaustible.

'*Hai. Taihenyoku.*' - Yes. Very patient. -

Rostov thought of asking if his aide had a better idea, but Yuan only nodded again and stepped aside.

'Coming up on orbital track, Admiral.'

The Survey Service watch-keeper indicated the data which was flowing across the screen at his side and Rostov nodded. He raised an eyebrow at Sandor and the technical officer plugged a Navy pattern Personal Data Unit into the main transmission bank.

'Ready to transmit recognition codes.' Sandor's tone was prosaic.

'Very well.' Rostov turned in his chair. 'Mr Antonov?'

The sailing master was corpulent and red-faced, a civilian professional who held honorary Navy rank while he was employed on contract with the Fleet. Normally he was a member of the Special Piloting Crew which was stationed at Knossos refit yards. Not for the first time Rostov wondered why he had been selected for this particular mission.

Antonov's uniform was old and ill-fitting. He rose and addressed the *Simonova*'s officer-of-the-watch, his salute a travesty.

'Sir, I relieve you.'

The Survey Service pilot rose also. He stepped away from the command console and bowed.

'Sir, I stand relieved.'

The statement and the response were simply a formula, but Rostov still experienced a feeling of satisfaction. For the next four standard days at least, the Navy was running the ship.

'Entering orbit, Admiral.'

'Very well. Terminate drive - five, four, three, two, one, mark! Auxiliary thrusters to standby.'

Rostov watched his own screen as it duplicated the information which was being relayed to the sailing master. He addressed Sandor.

'Lieutenant, you may commence transmission.'

'Aye, sir.'

Sandor keyed the PDU and at once Rostov sensed the relaxation of tension which went round the bridge. He grinned. The manual operation of broadcasting a recognition signal to the platforms in orbit around Tarvaras had been duplicated simultaneously by four automatic sending stations which were situated at various points along the *Simonova*'s mainframe. Under the circumstances, however, there was not a man who cared to place absolute faith in mere machinery. The survey vessel's signal not only identified her, it also disarmed the platform-mounted weapons which otherwise would have reduced her to vapour.

The technical officer was verifying that all platforms within firing range were accepting the signal. Then he rose to his feet.

'Admiral?'

'Carry on, Mr Sandor.'

The lieutenant left in a hurry. Inspection and servicing of each of the platforms was to be carried out in the survey ship's main docking bay. Rostov was well able to appreciate Sandor's desire to be on hand when the first of the series was tractored in. At the forefront of his mind, no doubt, was an awareness of the relative inexperience of the civilian docking crew, coupled with a knowledge that accidental triggering of plasma weapons while they were inside the shield was guaranteed to be instantly fatal.

'Coming up on the first platform, Admiral. Serial number seven.'

'Engage tractor beam.'

'Aye, sir.'

Rostov located the controls which linked his viewscreens to the ship's external sensors and switched the selector to the vision receptors which were concentrated below and ahead of the *Simonova*'s path. He knew that the platform was there, but in the nightside blackness he could see nothing at first. Then it was drawn into the light cast by a battery of exterior spot lamps.

The platform was dead black - an ovoid perhaps a hundred metres long by fifty in circumference. It was perfectly featureless and reflected none of the light which was being directed on to its surface.

'*Bojemoi!*'

Rostov expelled breath in an involuntary hiss of awe. The survey briefing had included only a verbal specification. There had been no videofax, and as a result he was unprepared for the sensory impact of the image on his viewscreen. The ovoid seemed to project a kind of deadly aura and, as Rostov compared the black egg shape with his memory of the framework structures which he had encountered previously, he wondered if the designers had been striving consciously for the visual effect which they had achieved. The power of the platform's weapons and the threat they posed was enough to give anyone pause for thought, but now they appeared somehow more lethal because they were unseen - concealed behind gunports which had been engineered to such fine tolerances that Rostov could detect no hint of them anywhere on the curved metal skin.

Ten hours and two platforms later it seemed that at least a few members of the *Simonova*'s crew were still suffering from the emotional impact of the brooding menace which was represented by the presence of each platform in the docking bay.

The *Simonova* was in almost perfect space equilibrium - like the platforms it was following a geostationary path almost thirty-six thousand kilometres above the equator of Tarvaras. And since that state of stability had been calculated so that it would not commence deterioration until the next inspection had been completed, Rostov had delegated command of the bridge to Yuan, and had elected to watch the performance of his technical officers at close quarters.

Everyone else who was not engaged in either survey data collection or ship handling seemed to be doing the same. The upper catwalks above the bay were crowded, and even the lower levels were occupied by small groups of senior survey staff who could have no excuse for their presence other than curiosity.

'Admiral.'

The *Simonova*'s administrator and the Adjudicator were performing stiff little bows in his direction, but Rostov only nodded. Alexei was standing immediately behind the men. When Rostov had noticed them first, they had been deep in animated conversation - a conspiratorial group of people who were the least likely, considering all the circumstances, to be found in close and apparently friendly contact with one another.

Alexei alone returned the nod. His face was closed and empty of expression. He bowed briefly to the two surveyors, and then walked away. The embarrassed silence which followed was broken only when everyone turned to watch as the *Simonova*'s bay tractor beams started to draw the most recently captured platform through the force field.

At this level of the bay there were small promontories every hundred metres or so along the main catwalk and Rostov walked out onto one of them. When a ship of any size was docked, they were capable of being extended until they formed bridges across which stores or personnel could be transferred. Now they were simply handy vantage points.

The passage of the black ovoid through the ion screen which permitted the docking crew to work in breathable atmosphere, even though the main bay doors were open to vacuum, caused an electrical imbalance which crackled across the curved surface. As it was passing Rostov's position, a jagged blue flash bridged the gap to the platform, and he controlled the impulse to jump back.

'Earthing crew!'

Kubitsky was below on the main bay deck. He shouted angrily, and a three-man team hastened to attach the sets of magnoclamps which were designed to drain the static charge. The men were clumsy in heavy insulation suits and the technical officer waited impatiently until the operation had been completed. Then he looked up at Rostov and saluted.

'Your pardon, Admiral. I will instruct the docking supervisor to discipline those fools.'

'Thank you, lieutenant. That is not necessary.'

Rostov shook his head, concealing the knowledge that he had been briefly in danger of his life. Kubitsky's face was pale and clearly he was shaken. The technical officer could not fail to be conscious of the lethal potential of an electrical discharge from the platform. As Rostov watched, he seemed to make a deliberate effort to compose himself. Then he saluted Rostov again and turned away.

Rostov frowned.

The outer skin of any craft which passed through the air barrier of a force field stored static electricity like a giant capacitor. Ship interiors were specially insulated to combat the problem and an operation similar to degaussing was carried out prior to docking with other vessels. It was true that the *Simonova*'s earthing crew had been slow to react - the more so since they must have been required to perform a similar task on both of the platforms which had been docked and inspected previously. But in fact it was the docking crew as a whole who were at fault, because the platform's progress towards the support cradle should have been halted as soon as it passed completely through the field, so that earthing and other safety procedures could be instigated. It was possible that, like many of the casual spectators, the key members of the crew had all been frozen into temporary immobility by the looming presence of the ovoid, but Rostov was inclined to suspect the convenience of such a coincidence. As accidents went, it had been too well arranged.

Acting on a sudden impulse, he turned.

Bock and Grigoriev were behind him on the main section of the catwalk. They were only a matter of metres away but, due to the insulation which separated every portion of dock superstructure - a provision designed as a safeguard against just the kind of occurrence which had threatened Rostov - both had been safe from danger.

Neither man had time to conceal or alter his facial expression, and Rostov was struck by the disparity. Bock looked frightened, but Grigoriev's face was predatory and full of avid intent. Rostov scanned the platform above for Alexei and saw him finally on the topmost section of the catwalk. He was laughing with a group of female technicians and did not seem to be aware that anything unusual had happened.

Even though the *Simonova* was now technically under Navy direction, Rostov's administrative duties remained light and consisted principally of approving the expenditure of insignificant items of equipment during platform servicing. He glanced down the codings listed on the last of the semi-opaque sheets and imprinted his authorisation.

Alexei added the permafax to the others already contained in the folder in his hand. He turned as if to leave, then paused. Rostov waited impassively.

'There is something going on.' Alexei did not turn, but spoke as if to an empty room. 'Something I do not understand.'

Rostov made no reply. Conversation with Alexei had been limited for the past day to standard matters of duty, and since he had not been able to think of anything which he could say to change his son's attitude, he had allowed himself to accept that the state of affairs which existed between them was likely to be permanent. He looked at the back of Alexei's head and willed him to turn round.

Alexei seemed to look down at the folder in his hand. Then his head came up again.

'I wanted you to know,' he said, 'because whatever

it is, I am not a part of it.'

He reached for the door control and the lock hissed with the release of compressed air.

'Wait.'

Rostov forced out the word. He was not sure that he cared about the plot, if one existed. But if Alexei said that he was not involved, then probably he was telling the truth, otherwise there would be no reason for him to say anything at all.

After a moment Alexei touched the control again. The door hissed shut. He turned.

Rostov gestured. 'I'm sorry. I don't know what to say to you.'

He had never felt comfortable at a personal level. Irina knew and understood. But even if he had not been separated from Alexei by duty, and leaving aside the connivance of Irina's family, a gap would have existed between them.

'I just wanted you to know.'

Uncertainty made Alexei's face appear even more youthful.

'Yes. Thank you.'

Rostov hesitated. If he said that he had never entertained a suspicion, it would be a lie.

'You don't seem very surprised.'

'That there is some kind of conspiracy?' Rostov shook his head. 'No. I had warning. And anyway, there are always little plots. You know what Imperial service is like.'

He waited for a contradiction, but Alexei only nodded. He was clearly unsure of himself and, in spite of the seriousness of his expression, Rostov was amused.

'Sit down, will you?' He spoke more abruptly than he intended, but Alexei sat at once. Rostov tried to smile. It was obvious that Alexei would find it hard to talk. It was hard for both of them. But now that the opportunity had arisen, it was necessary for them to try.

Rostov awoke in suffocating blackness. He struggled for a moment, but he was enclosed so tightly that he could not even work an arm free from his side. He forced himself to relax and tried to register his surroundings.

In spite of his initial impression, he was breathing without difficulty. The material which encased him was permeable foam and there was an air supply somewhere. Rostov tried to move again, but it was hopeless.

A coffin? Certainly a container of some kind.

External sound was deadened by the density of the foam, but Rostov heard clearly the clunk of metal surfaces coming together. The shock of an impact struck him squarely between the shoulder blades, and suddenly he knew exactly where he was.

An escape pod!

He experienced a sensation of horror and his stomach churned.

Like every other large vessel, the *Simonova* was equipped with batteries of escape pods in addition to her full complement of lifeboats. Emergency locks were situated in most of the main companionways and, in the event that they were forced to abandon ship, members of the crew who were unable to reach a docking bay in time were assured of a moderate chance of survival.

An escape pod battery was similar to a quick-firing cannon, and operation of the inner lock was sufficient to commence the loading sequence. The pods themselves were quite complex, but essentially they were multi-skinned torpedoes equipped with minimal propulsion and life-support systems. Once it had been ejected into space, a pod assessed its surroundings. Then it headed straight for the nearest suitable planet and effected a landing. In the event that it could not locate a world in reasonable proximity which possessed both a breathable atmosphere and acceptable conditions of gravity and temperature, a pod was capable of maintaining its passenger in a state of suspended animation for an almost indefinite period. Under such circumstances it was programmed to select an orbit around the largest near planetary mass, emitting a distress signal until it was recovered.

There was no discernible motion, but Rostov guessed that the pod was already heading for the surface of Tarvaras. It was a pity that it would be blown to atoms long before it got there.

More as a means of occupying his mind than out of a desire to establish the facts, Rostov began to calculate the data which governed the interlocking arcs of fire of the Tarvaras platforms. Even if one of the ovoids was in the *Simonova*'s docking bay - a recovery sequence had been initiated shortly before Rostov had retired to his quarters - those which were adjacent in orbit would open fire as soon as the pod was more than ten kilometres from the survey vessel's shield zone.

Tarvaras was just over twelve and a half thousand kilometres in diameter and the *Simonova* was orbiting approximately thirty-six thousand kilometres above the surface. That meant an orbital path with a circumference of about two hundred and sixty-five thousand kilometres with - Rostov divided swiftly by sixteen - one platform roughly every sixteen-and-a-half thousand kilometres. Platform weapons were set to allow nothing to rise more than a thousand kilometres from the surface of the world below - or in other words they had a killing range of about thirty-five thousand kilometres. More than twice the distance between one platform and the next. Say twenty seconds to exit the *Simonova*'s shield zone, at which point the pod would be a target for both of the adjacent platforms ...

Rostov stopped, aware that he had been indulging his capacity for mental arithmetic for easily twice that period of time.

He supposed that he had been rendered unconscious when he had entered his quarters. Thinking back Rostov realised that he could remember nothing after the moment when he had operated the lock control and the door had hissed aside. The nearest pod battery had been only thirty metres from the entrance to his stateroom, and no doubt that fact had influenced the would-be assassin. It was an arguably effective method of achieving both killing and disposal of the body - probably ensuring that the perpetrator remained undetected - to load the victim into an escape pod which was destined to be destroyed as soon as it was tracked by any of the platforms in orbit.

Except that there appeared to have been a miscalculation - one which Rostov himself did not yet understand - so that the pod was now heading unscathed for the outer atmosphere of Tarvaras.

As if in confirmation of that fact, the pressure of the foam encasing his head eased slightly and a display readout began to project data onto a hitherto invisible screen in front of his eyes. It occurred to Rostov that there would be more point to the information if he also had some control over the pod's guidance system, but at least he now knew where he was going.

It was still hard to believe that the pod was not going to be destroyed before it reached the ground. The recognition codes which the *Simonova* was broadcasting should not in theory render any platform completely inoperative. Nor should the temporary protection which the survey vessel was acquiring by the signalling process extend to any other object in contiguous space. The pod began to shudder and Rostov quickly checked the visual display. It would be a neat trick of fate if he survived the plasma energy weapons of the platforms only to be burned to a crisp because the pod entered the upper atmosphere of Tarvaras at the incorrect angle.

There was a sharp crack as the first of several skins of heat-resistant material which coated the exterior of the pod shattered and then separated. The instrument readings remained unchanged, and Rostov was reassured. Thus far the internal structure of the pod had protected him from extreme variations in gravitational pull, but now he felt his weight increase as the slim capsule reached terminal velocity for the thin, wind-torn upper atmosphere. The pod was no longer strictly under guidance. Instead it was falling. Following the data which was being projected on to the tiny screen, it was clear that the telemetry and guidance modules had performed according to specification.

The second skin of heat-resistant material seemed to burn off unevenly - at least that was Rostov's impression - for the vibration increased and the pod appeared to tumble and then check as the first ribbon chute opened. The chute itself only lasted seconds. It provided one good hard jerk at nearly five gee, and then the tattered remnants were detached automatically. The second chute lasted all of half a minute, and when the third opened, Rostov began to think about landing.

There was no point in worrying about what was happening aboard the *Simonova*. Either they would send a rescue party, or they would adhere to quarantine regulations and he would be marooned on Tarvaras. In any case he had more pressing matters to worry about.

It was growing uncomfortably warm inside the pod, but with the third skin gone there was a transparent patch in the casing shell level with his face. Rostov's body was still firmly encased in the pod's foam safety envelope, but now the system obligingly extended a bar switch until it was at mouth level. He bit down on it, and the display began to supply proximity and ground contour information.

At least the ground fifteen kilometres below was fairly flat. Rostov peered past the screen at the porthole, but he could see nothing of the surface of the planet. The pod temperature rose a few degrees more, and then levelled out. The main chute cluster banged open and a second bar switch was extended. This time the display flashed a red warning signal:

**Danger – Pod Hatch Release –
Do Not Operate Until Pod Has Grounded**

Rostov grinned relief. He was pleased to discover that the *Simonova* was equipped with the type of pod which permitted the moment of release to be selected independently. Clusters of explosive bolts secured the hatch, and early models of the pod had been programmed to blow these automatically on grounding. There had been a series of rumours about accidents: pods which malfunctioned on impact, leaving their passengers trapped and helpless; pods which misinterpreted conditions of temperature and air pressure, releasing their human cargo while they were still several kilometres above ground. Rostov checked the visual display again. According to the proximity readout, the capsule was only a kilometre or so from contact with the surface of Tarvaras. He gazed out through the transparency and cursed. The pod appeared to be descending directly towards a winding ribbon of water.

The river - it stretched away as far as he could see in either direction, and could not therefore be a lake - was very wide. Rostov estimated that the distance from one bank to the other was over a kilometre. There was no way of guessing at the depth, and as the pod continued to fall it became increasingly obvious that his initial impression had been correct. He was going to land almost exactly in the middle of the widest part of the stream.

Rostov considered the alternatives briefly.

Either he could wait until the pod splashed down - at which point it would start to sink, and if the water was deep enough and he had difficulty in escaping from the safety envelope, or became entangled with the chute, he might drown before he was able to struggle to the surface - or else he could blow the hatch prior to landing, risking being either injured or knocked unconscious during an unprotected impact.

On the whole Rostov thought that he was more confident about his chances in the second case. He would try to detonate the hatch bolts when he was about a hundred metres above the river. After that he would fight clear of the envelope and hope to dive away from the pod. It was fortunate that he was able to swim, although he wondered for a moment about the presence of large predators in the water. He had paid very little attention to the section of the survey briefing which dealt with native flora and fauna. At the time the information had seemed to be of no consequence. Now he wished that he had listened more closely.

He looked through the transparency again, and was alarmed to discover that the pod appeared to have increased its rate of descent. Perhaps one of the chutes of the cluster had collapsed, but whatever the reason time had suddenly run out. Hastily he bit down on the bar switch.

The hatch bolts exploded in rapid-fire sequence, and at once Rostov forced both arms up to chest level and punched them forward, tearing the extruded foam casing. Now it was as if he was teetering on the brink of a lidless coffin. The water seemed to rush to meet him. He threw himself forward and dived clear.

The water was very cold. Rostov kicked hard, aware that somewhere above him was the pod. When he surfaced he saw it about ten metres away. The chutes had collapsed across the casing, and already it was starting to sink. Rostov spat out a mouthful of river water, and struck out for what looked like the nearest bank.

It was hard to tell what time of day it was. The ground was too warm, Rostov was sure, for it to be morning. But since he had only a vague idea about the length of the Tarvaras day, he could only guess from the position of the sun and the length of the shadows that it was mid to late afternoon.

The sun was huge: a glaring red ball which was almost touching the tops of the distant range of mountains. There were a few white clouds and, although towards the sun the sky was tinged crimson, elsewhere the shade was a deep oppressive blue. Rostov thought that the colour of the sky probably had something to do with the state of the sun, and he wondered briefly about the effects of prolonged exposure to solar radiation. For a long time it had been accepted that humans could not survive on worlds which were

101

in orbit around any sun which was capable of being classed as a red giant. But the Imperial survey had located colonies on Cerberus and on the Manchu worlds, all of whose systems were identifiably red-shifted.

There were only a few trees along the river bank. They were tall and straight, their branches covered with clusters of fine blue-green leaves shaped like needles. Rostov saw that none of the leaves which had fallen were withered or had changed colour, and the ground below every tree was covered by a soft carpet which was perhaps a metre thick. Away from the river in every direction the ground was practically level, a plain covered by broad-bladed grass which grew in some places to waist height. There were a few small brown birds in the trees, but no other sign of life. Mountains were visible in the distance both towards the sun and on the far side of the river. The range in the latter direction seemed to be closer, and some of the highest peaks were capped with what looked like snow.

Rostov thought about following the course of the river in one direction or the other. If people and habitation were to be found, it was likely that they would be located somewhere along the bank. He looked at the expanse of the river. The pod and chutes had disappeared as if they had never existed. As soon as it had been fired from the *Simonova* the pod would have started to broadcast a signal and, since the crew of the survey ship could not fail to be aware that a pod had been discharged, and that it was occupied, he supposed that his descent had been tracked and that someone at least knew where he was to be found. Perhaps under the circumstances it made sense to remain in the one place.

His coverall was already dry, and the sun was so

warm that Rostov was glad of the minimal shade provided by the trees. The shadows had lengthened, he thought, so that probably he had been right and it was towards evening.

There was a broken branch half-buried in the bed of leaves around the base of the tree under which he stood. He pulled it free. It was about a metre long and as thick as his wrist. When he struck it hard against the trunk of the tree it seemed solid and did not break or splinter. Thoughtfully, Rostov laid it to one side. He was not sure that he would need a weapon, but there was no harm in being prepared. If a large animal appeared, he thought that he could probably climb the tree. But predators came in various shapes and sizes, and he was troubled by the knowledge that any rescue party from the *Simonova* could also include the person who was responsible for dumping him in the escape pod. He guessed that somewhere aboard the survey vessel a meeting was in progress to determine whether or not the quarantine regulations were to be obeyed, and whether that adherence meant that he ought to be abandoned. It was a neat dilemma. From one point of view it could be argued that he should be rescued from Tarvaras before he had an opportunity to come into contact with any of the inhabitants. In theory, at least, his knowledge of technology, and in particular his military ability, could affect the whole course of the planet's history. But in fact, it was just as likely that he would be killed by the first group of native Tarvarians he encountered. If the quarantine regulations had already been broken by the landing of the escape pod, so the opposing argument would run, then surely it would be a second and far more serious breach to despatch a lifeboat on a rescue mission, especially since the size of such a vehicle increased the risk of inhabitant contact a thousandfold.

Rostov doubted if either his rank or his arguable status as both husband and father of members of the Royal Family would affect the outcome of such a discussion. It was possible that recovery might be organised, and for that reason he would remain where he was at least until morning.

There was nothing to be gained by worrying further, so he settled himself as comfortably as possible against the trunk of the tree. The sun was warm and he was tired. His eyes closed and he slept.

It was still light when the thunderclap of the passage of one of the *Simonova*'s lifeboats over his head woke him. The vessel dipped above the surface of the river and Rostov judged that it was hovering roughly over the spot where the escape pod had disappeared. Then the boat lifted away and settled on the far side of the river.

Instinctive caution made Rostov remain in the cover of the trees. He could see figures emerging from the lifeboat hatch, but he was too far away to be able to identify faces. Soon he realised that the coveralls which were visible on the far bank were Navy dark blue and not Survey Service drab grey. He stepped out of the shadows, shouted, and waved his arms to attract attention.

An answering shout came at once. A delay followed while those who had left the vessel, presumably to search, re-entered it. The craft lifted smoothly across the river and, as it grounded nearby, Rostov was treated to a view of the blistering which marked the heat shield around the blunt nose. Clearly the pilot had not wasted time calculating an entry angle, but had bored down through the upper atmosphere as directly as he was able.

The hatch opened. Rostov started to walk towards

the boat, then stopped. Slowly he raised his hands until they were above waist level, and turned the palms outward to show that he was unarmed. Disappointment made him feel suddenly weary.

Kubitsky was holding the weapon, but it was Sandor who was smiling as he watched the others - Yuan, Zukov, Mubarak, even Vorontseff - as they climbed unarmed from the hatch. Alexei appeared last. He jumped down and seemed to stumble. Then he straightened and dusted invisible grains of dirt from the knees of his coveralls.

Sandor laughed unpleasantly and shook his head.

'Admiral.' It was as if he was pleased by the outcome. 'I began to think that you had more lives than a cat.'

'And the luck of the angels.' Kubitsky's expression was sour.

Sandor disappeared inside the boat for a moment. When he re-emerged he was cradling an explosive projectile rifle similar to the one which was being trained on them by Kubitsky.

'It is a pity it has to be done this way,' Sandor observed. 'My other ideas were so much neater.' He cocked the weapon.

Rostov looked at the others. He caught Sandor's eye. 'All of us?'

The lieutenant nodded. 'Admiral, I am afraid so. We would have preferred not to have included the Noble Born, your son -' he indicated Alexei with a wave of the muzzle, '- but our orders are quite explicit. No loose ends.'

'Six of us.' Rostov did his best to speak without a tremor. 'You really think you can get away with it?'

Kubitsky sniggered. Sandor nodded cheerfully. 'No question of it. Officially you are all going to be victims of a surprise attack on the rescue party by the native inhabitants. An unfortunate incident; but on a rescue mission which was undertaken against the advice of the Imperial Adjudicator, no one will be suspicious.'

'I see.' If he had been concerned to compile a mental list of likely candidates for involvement in conspiracy - any conspiracy - Rostov would have placed Grigoriev at or near its head, and so reference to the Adjudicator was not a surprise. All the same he raised his eyebrows and pretended to consider the possibility for the first time. A few paces to the right Yuan was flexing arm and shoulder muscles as if to ease some strain or tension, and Rostov wondered if the assassins knew how fast a Manchu could move when the need arose. Instinctively he did his best to prolong the conversation. 'So you take your orders from House Andreeyev?'

It was Alexei who cut in on Sandor's response, his tone frigid.

'The Noble Grigoriev insisted that only Navy personnel be employed for the rescue attempt.'

'And my unscheduled departure from the *Simonova*?' Rostov looked at Sandor and ignored Alexei. 'How is that to be explained?'

'Oh. An accident, of course.' The assassin's tone and bearing were completely confident. If he noticed that Zukov was now edging further to the side, widening the arc of fire, he did not appear to be troubled. 'The report will show that you were examining one of the pod batteries when it malfunctioned.'

'Reports have to be counter-signed.'

'True. But we have a small advantage in that respect. You see, the *Simonova*'s administrator owes a certain - ah - obligation to House Andreeyev.'

'Or in other words, he will do exactly as he is told,' Kubitsky said.

'Indeed.' Rostov tried to think of something else to

say, but suddenly it was as if his brain had dried up. He had no idea why House Andreeyev desired his death, and in any case it no longer seemed to matter. Kubitsky was flicking the safety lock of his weapon on and off. Clearly he was bored with the conversation. Sandor glanced sideways. Then he turned to look at Rostov again. He shrugged, and the decision in his eyes was final.

'And now, Admiral -'

The rising muzzle signalled his intention, but it was not in Rostov's nature to stand passively to be slaughtered. It made sense to assume that Yuan and Zukov would throw themselves to the right of the line of fire, but he did not wait for them to act. Instead he shoved Alexei hard at shoulder level, and dived left.

'What?'

Alexei was unprepared. He sprawled untidily, grabbed at Rostov's arm, and brought him down.

Rostov was deafened by the explosion of a single shot. On his knees in the grass, he was aware that he was not going to make it - that in all probability none of them were. Determined to face the bullet when it came, he looked up.

There was an arrow in Sandor's throat. As Rostov watched, the lieutenant dropped his weapon and pitched forward out of the hatch.

Rostov froze.

Kubitsky was bringing his rifle to bear on a target which lay somewhere in the direction of the grove of trees on the river bank to Rostov's rear, but before he could open fire three more arrows took him in the chest and he fell over backwards without a sound. Rostov felt as if there was a bare exposed place between his shoulder blades. Then an animal snorted quietly and broke the momentary stillness. Slowly he got to his feet, extended his hands at waist level to

107

show that they were empty, and turned.

There were a dozen riders. Most of them were carrying bows, but even those who had arrows nocked were not aiming at anything in particular. Rostov drew a long shuddering breath.

Everyone else appeared to be unhurt. Yuan had somehow managed to reach the cover of the side of the lifeboat, but now he rejoined the others. He moved slowly and cautiously, and kept his hands in clear view.

The Tarvarians rode forward. Rostov watched them, absorbing every detail.

The mounts were huge. They looked like equine stock, but they were half as big again as any horse that Rostov had ever encountered. A single immense horn projected from the forehead of each animal.

'I thought the unicorn was a mythical beast.' Alexei spoke with studied calm.

'Not on this world apparently.' As he responded, Rostov remembered the survey briefing and wondered if he was seeing the first evidence of genetic mutation. If that was the case, then it was a mutation which bred true. Apart from the difference in the colour of the coat - there were blacks, chestnuts, a grey and even a piebald - the beasts were exactly alike.

The riders themselves appeared to be human. At least, they looked like men. They had light skins which were tanned to various shades of golden brown, and most wore long down-turned moustaches or straggling beards. Only one - the leader by the richness of his robes and the gold chasing on his equipment - was unhelmeted. Rostov saw that his hair had been drawn back into a neat queue which had been tied with ribbon then folded decoratively forward across the top of his head. There was a weird kind of shading or tattooing around the lids of each man's eyes and Rostov thought that the eyes themselves were oddly shaped. They were slanted somehow, and he recollected pictures he had seen of the early ancestors of the Manchu. There was a vague similarity.

The bows were short, stubby affairs which looked as if they had been bonded from several different kinds of wood. The main part of the bowstave seemed to bend back upon itself.

'Compound bows. Powerful.'

It was Mubarak who made the observation, and Rostov nodded. In addition to a bow, each rider carried a curved sword and a shorter dagger, both in a belt around his waist. Several of the warriors also bore long lances which were tipped with iron or steel, and a few had shields slung either from the saddle or on a strap around the shoulders.

The Tarvarians halted in a semi-circle which enclosed Rostov and his companions against the side of the lifeboat. The leader seemed to eye them for a moment, then he spoke briefly. Clearly he was asking a question, but the gutturals of the language he used bore no relationship to any form of speech which was in use in the Empire.

Rostov realised that signs and shrugs were going to be inadequate. He struggled for a moment to remember the rules for first contact with alien cultures. Most of them were inapplicable, but there were procedures for language which might be appropriate. He stepped forward and addressed the riders solemnly in Anglic.

'Your father was a peasant, mine had an emporium. But there's nothing in that. Even if you offered me two hundred thousand, I would refuse. I'm a free man, and all that you hold dear, you rich men - and beggars too - none of it has any power over me.'

The lines came from a play dimly remembered. It

was a comedy which was said to have originated on Terra. Rostov had chosen the speech simply because it was the first thing which came to mind. He might as well have recited a passage from a Navy field manual. The purpose was to show that he too used spoken language and that it and Tarvarian were mutually incomprehensible.

The Tarvarian leader digested the announcement. Then he said something, his tone amused, and the other riders laughed.

Alexei came forward so that he was at Rostov's shoulder. 'Second stage?'

Rostov nodded. He touched himself on the chest. 'Me.' Then he touched Alexei. 'You.'

Alexei copied the movement. 'Me.' He tapped his own chest. 'You.' He addressed Zukov, touching the Master-at-Arms at the same moment.

The process continued down the line. When Yuan stepped forward to touch Rostov and complete the circle of address, there was a murmur of comment from the Tarvarians. Rostov pointed to himself again.

'Me - Sergei Rostov. Sergei Rostov - *name*.' He caught the eye of the Tarvarian leader and pointed. 'You - *name*?'

The man spat to one side. He muttered a few words and his companions chuckled. Then he addressed Rostov. He was speaking Anglic and, though his accent was strange, the words were perfectly understandable.

'Me -' The man tapped his chest, '- Arghatun, Leader of a Thousand. You -' He showed his teeth and gestured to include the whole group, '- prisoners.'

The Tarvarians were laughing openly and Rostov cursed under his breath.

To Rostov's surprise, the Tarvarian warriors showed no interest in the lifeboat or its contents. Either they operated some kind of taboo against such things, or else the technological relics of past civilisations were commonplace enough for them not to attach importance to a vessel which they must at least suspect to be in operable condition. Rostov had hoped to be permitted to seal the hatch, and thus to preserve the interior of the ship from incursion by animal and insect life - as well as from the potentially damaging effects of atmosphere and temperature - but Arghatun had rejected the request out of hand.

'No,' he said. 'First you will talk to my Khan. He will decide.'

Several of the Tarvarians were leading strings of three or four remounts, all of them unsaddled, and Rostov and the others were each assigned an animal. It did not appear to occur to Arghatun that they might not be able to ride. After Vorontseff had fallen off twice he was hoisted up by a grinning trooper and thrown face down in front of the saddle. The party set off downstream along the river bank and Rostov concentrated on making it look as if he had been riding bareback all his life. The pace was fast, but after a while Arghatun reined in until he was riding at Rostov's side.

'Back there,' Arghatun gestured to his rear, 'when I asked who you were. What was that nonsense you recited about rich man and beggars?'

'Oh.' Rostov hesitated. 'Just some words from a play. I was supposed to be trying to show you that we also had a language, but that it was different from yours.'

'Hunh. I see. That explains the game you played - naming one another. But most of the Yek can speak C'zak as well.'

'C'zak?' Rostov queried the word.

'The name of the language you speak. Although you don't look like C'zaki - especially that one.' Arghatun

111

indicated Yuan with a nod of his head. 'He doesn't look like a man at all.'

'Oh, well. In the first place we call the language Anglic and it is spoken by people on worlds all across the universe. And my friend is quite human, but he comes from a world very far away. You cannot even see it as a star in your sky. A long time ago - many thousands of years - something happened to the sun which shines on that world. All the people changed until they began to look as he does.'

It was a simplified explanation. Rostov expected the mention of other worlds to excite a reaction, but Arghatun only nodded understanding.

'Ah. I knew you could not be C'zaki,' he said.

'These C'zaki -' Rostov paused to disguise his interest, '- are they many?'

Arghatun shrugged.

'Who knows? We conquered them years ago in their land to the west of here. Most of them are soldiers now.'

'The women as well?'

The answer was a snort of derision. 'Only a fool uses women to fight. No, some follow their men. Others - well, I for one have a C'zak wife.'

The Tarvarian grinned and urged his mount forward again.

Suddenly the sky behind them flashed brilliant fire. Animals shied and the warriors shouted. Rostov turned to meet the eyes of the other members of the Navy party and in a moment of mutual intuition, they dismounted.

Rostov caught at Arghatun's bridle. 'Quickly, tell your men to dismount. If they can make their animals lie down, they should do so, and lie down with them. Very soon now there will be a wind, greater than any you have ever known. If they are caught in its blast,

112

they may be killed or injured.'

The Tarvarian was busy calming his mare. He stared at Rostov as if he was calculating the value of what he had said. Then he turned in the saddle and shouted briefly. The warriors hurled themselves at the heads or horns of their animals to make them lie down.

Rostov sat down quietly. The shock wave was delayed by only a few more seconds, and then it rolled over them like a small hurricane.

No loose ends.

The words had been Sandor's before he died and Rostov wondered if the assassin had ever suspected that he too was scheduled for termination once he completed his assigned task. Either the power plant of the lifeboat had been rigged to explode, or else the area of the landing site had been fired on from space.

In either event it would be assumed that everyone had perished. There would be no attempt at rescue, and it came home to Rostov with sudden force that he and the others were marooned on Tarvaras for ever.

Already the warriors were climbing back into the saddle. Rostov saw that Arghatun was watching him, and waited for the man to ask how he had known what was going to happen. But the Tarvarian only muttered something under his breath, and spat left and right. Then he turned away.

The party began to encounter scouts or sentries along the way, and Rostov guessed that they were approaching a camp or a settlement. Mounted men in ones and twos appeared suddenly from the cover of trees, or out of folds in the ground. They galloped up until they were within shouting distance, exchanged words with Arghatun, and then rode away again.

The size of the camp when they came in sight of it made Rostov's eyes widen with surprise. From the

113

river's edge it stretched back on to the plain for a distance of over a kilometre, and he thought that it must contain well over three thousand men. The tents were straw-coloured, ranked in orderly rows, and every so often they passed a larger pavilion which Rostov guessed belonged to some kind of nobleman or senior officer. The lines of tethered animals were guarded by patrolling sentries, and even those long stretches were under the shelter of strips of fabric.

Many of the men who sat outside the tents were stripped to the waist and some of them were barefoot. Most were working to clean weapons or saddlery, and only a few looked up and gazed incuriously as the party rode past.

There was a clearing among some trees close to the river and a number of two-wheeled carts had been parked there. On the tail of one of the carts a man was sitting. He was about Rostov's age and his clothes were very fine, although the colours were sombre. Four younger men were lined up in front of him and he was addressing them. All of them were richly dressed, but it was their hair which attracted Rostov's attention at once. It was an odd shade of reddish gold and, coupled with their tanned complexions and slanted eyes, made them look like young eagles.

When Arghatun saw the man on the cart tail, he tossed his reins to one of the troopers and dismounted. He crossed the clearing, bowed respect-fully, and started to speak.

At once one of the younger men interrupted. Argh-atun stopped speaking and bowed, but it was the older man who growled a reply and showed his teeth. The others laughed. The young man spoke again, and this time it was clear that he was angry. Then he spun on his heel and stalked off round the side of the cart. His three companions followed more slowly.

Rostov did not wait to be told that he could dismount. He was sore from the long ride and, as he tried to walk the stiffness out of his legs, pacing in limited circles under the eyes of his guards, he saw that the man on the cart tail was watching intently. Arghatun was speaking again, and he gestured once or twice in the direction of Rostov and the others so that it was clear that he was making a report.

After they realised that the warriors did not care if they stayed in the saddle or not, Yuan, Alexei and the others got down as well. They left their animals and gathered round Rostov in a group, but none of them said anything. Rostov asked one of the guards if the man sitting on the cart was the Khan, but the trooper only grinned insolently at him and replied in his own tongue. Rostov walked a little way off, squatted on his heels on the grass, and tried to pretend a calm he did not feel.

The process of report and interrogation took quite a time, and Rostov began to suspect that if he and the others were to be subjected to some form of tribunal before their fate was decided, then at least it would pass for a fair one. Arghatun was speaking at considerable length, but every so often he paused and the man who sat on the tail of the cart asked what appeared to be a series of questions. Rostov knew that he would not be able to understand even if he could hear, but due to the fact that Arghatun's replies were clearly either affirmative or negative he thought that probably the officer's account was being clarified at every stage.

It was not the kind of approach to the situation that the survey briefing had led him to expect, and Rostov realised that he was going to have to adjust his notions about standards of behaviour. Much of what he had

seen so far confirmed the assessment of the Imperial
survey - that the stage of development Tarvaras had
reached was equivalent to that which was thought to
have existed during the Terran medieval period.
However, there were anomalies. Arghatun's lack of
interest in the news of other settled worlds suggested
an awareness of the universe which was far in advance
of the inhabitants' theoretical evolutionary time. Military organisation was also well advanced, in spite of
the fact that only primitive weapons were in evidence.
Rostov guessed that the social hierarchy was far more
complex than anyone would have imagined. Not for
the first time he concluded that the Empire was
inclined too quickly to dismiss mutant and alien societies and to confuse technological advancement with
civilisation.

At last Arghatun seemed to have finished. He bowed
again to the man sitting on the cart, then walked back
across the clearing. Rostov searched his face for some
hint that a decision had been reached.

'The Khan will talk to you now.' Arghatun's face
was impassive.

'How should I address him?'

'Call him "Khan" or "Lord" when you speak, and
bow when you enter his presence. Tell the others with
you that they must bow and not speak unless he
speaks to them first.'

Rostov nodded.

Arghatun was shouting at the warriors who were
grouped around the clearing, and twenty or so ran at
once to one of the carts and pulled out a mass of
folded fabric. Working swiftly they erected a canopy
supported on poles and ropes.

'Come.' Arghatun gestured.

Rostov followed him; Alexei, Yuan, Zukov, Mubarak
and Vorontseff crowded behind.

116

It was cool under the canopy and there was less light than Rostov had expected. He decided that the material overhead had been treated somehow, probably to protect those beneath from the harmful effects of the sun. A floor of matting had been laid, and the Tarvarian Khan was sitting cross-legged on a carpet at one side. The fringes of the carpet had been teased out so that the individual strands could be seen.

'Bow!' Arghatun hissed the word.

Rostov took two paces forward on to the matting. Then he stopped and bowed at the waist. When he straightened again he saw that he was being examined at length. The Khan's gaze started at his feet and travelled slowly up his body so that by the time their eyes met the Khan was leaning back and holding on to his knees to stop himself falling over. He said something to Arghatun who laughed.

The others were spread out in a line behind and to either side of Rostov, and now he heard Arghatun telling them to bow. Suddenly the Khan's eyes moved left. His expression was no longer amused. Rostov turned round and saw that everyone was bowing except Alexei.

'Bow, fool!' Rostov glared.

For a moment he thought that Alexei was going to argue, but then he ducked his head quickly in the Khan's direction and stared back at Rostov, cheeks flushed, expression angry.

Rostov turned and bowed again. 'I'm sorry, Khan. This is my son and I apologise for his bad manners. Customs are different on our world and it is my fault that he does not yet understand what is expected of him.'

The Khan looked hard at Alexei. Then he gestured dismissal of the incident, and spoke.

'All men have trouble with their sons. In that at

117

least we are alike. Sit down. It hurts my neck to look at you.'

Rostov lowered himself on to his knees and sat back on his heels.

'So.' The Khan waved a hand at Arghatun. 'I have my officer's report of you. Now tell my why I should not have you killed or make you into slaves.'

The directness of the approach took Rostov's breath away. He struggled for a moment to find a proper answer.

'As to that,' he hesitated. 'I do not know what you have been told. Is it usual to kill prisoners, or have we broken your law? If so, it was not by intention.'

'Hunh.' The Khan nodded. 'Perhaps you should have been present to hear him speak. But you can believe that he is a truthful man. You are not from this world, he says, and you came here in a metal ship which flew through the air. We know of such things, but we do not concern ourselves with them. Also he says that when he saw you first there were two others with you, dressed as you are dressed. He says that they carried weapons of a kind which fire by creating a small explosion. These are forbidden by our law, which is called the Yasa, and so he killed both of them. He says that he did not kill you or your companions because you were unarmed, and anyway he thought that the two he killed intended to use their weapons on you.'

The statement was made flatly and did not seem to require confirmation. Rostov grinned in spite of the seriousness of his situation. The Khan paused, then nodded thoughtfully.

'Yes.' The Khan nodded again. 'There is a matter here which I will ask you to explain to me, although it is of no particular consequence to your situation. By our law your lives are forfeit. Have you a defence?'

Rostov thought about what had been said.

'Can a man be punished for breaking a law if he does not know that it exists?'

'An excellent point. Some say that ignorance of the law is no excuse, since any man can say that he did not know, and gain exception thereby. Is it the truth that you are not from this world, but from another far away?'

'Yes.'

'Then you could not have known our law.' The Khan seemed to consider the argument. 'Very well, I will spare you. Now tell me what I am to do with you. I have been told that your ship has been destroyed. Will your own people come for you?'

'No, Lord.'

'And you cannot be slaves. The Yasa says that we can enslave only those we conquer in battle. What else can you do?'

'In our own world we are all soldiers.' Rostov indicated Alexei and the others. 'Perhaps we could be soldiers here. Or perhaps -' He paused, unsure how to continue.

'Yes?'

'Khan, most of us have a knowledge of science which may be useful. But there may be things which are forbidden by your law.'

'Hunh. There is no law against knowledge. It is the use to which it is put which sometimes breaks the Yasa. But you would have to talk to the Sechem. It is their task to interpret Old Science and to discover the new.' The Khan eyed Rostov, then surveyed the others. 'You say that you are soldiers, but I guess that your weapons are different from ours. Can you fight with a sword, or use a bow? Can you ride long distances?'

Rostov thought about the hours which he had spent hooked up to the Naval Academy's ACSC - Accelerated Combat Situation Computer - and grinned. Like every other officer cadet he had spent three weeks with every hair shaved from his body so that he could be immersed in a tank of oxygenated fluorocarbon. Linked to the machine by electrodes, he had learned the best way to use every weapon ever invented. He had felt a spear in his hands, and a bow very similar to the type in use on Tarvaras, and he had watched his own performance with them until he was an expert. The men he had killed were only electronic ghosts, but they had seemed real enough at the time.

Non-commissioned officers like Zukov and Mubarak went through a similar but briefer course, and Rostov felt able to nod confidently.

'Yes, Lord. Maybe you have weapons that we have never encountered, but those I have seen we can use as well as any of your men. And we can ride, most of us, although we are out of practice.'

'We will see how well you fight,' the Khan observed. 'Very well, I will make you soldiers. What rank do you hold?'

Rostov indicated Yuan and Alexei. 'Those are officers, although my son has never commanded men in battle. The others have a rank which is below that of an officer but above that of an ordinary soldier.'

'Yes. In the army of the Kha-Khan they would be leaders of ten, or perhaps a hundred. But I cannot set them over others here. Will they serve in the ranks?'

'None of us speaks your language, Lord. But we will serve where you decide.'

'Well put. If there were enough of you, I would form you into a company with men of mine to supervise you. In that way those of you that are officers would have a chance to remain so. What if I give you to Arghatun, or to some other thousand commander, as a unit to fight together and act as scouts? Then you would remain as a group and could observe your own customs, those which do not conflict with our law.'

The speed of the reasoning was amazing. Rostov could only nod acquiescence.

'Good.' The Khan seemed satisfied. 'I am travelling to a place called Pesth and you will travel with me. It is our second greatest city. After that you will have the space of two months to learn our ways. Then you will ride on campaign. Learn our language quickly and things will be easier for you. I will put someone with you who will teach you. What is your name?'

'Rostov, Lord. My name is Sergei Rostov. My son is called Alexei Rostov.'

'I see. You have two names, and the second is the name of your family or clan. We use only one name here, so you will be called Suragai. Don't be offended. It isn't an insult. But it will speed your acceptance if your name sounds like one of ours. I am called Burun - Burun Khan. You are in the lands of the Yek, and I am a general in the army of the Kha-Khan of the Golden Clan - the Yek Altun. Also I am Khan of the Merkuts.'

Arghatun assigned a burly leader of ten to look after them. The man was a cheerful rogue called Kadan. It was from him that Rostov learned that under normal circumstances the whole camp would have moved about two hundred verst to the north during the late afternoon and through the night - probably all the way to Pesth - but that a full day's rest had been ordered by the Khan.

'Think yourselves lucky,' Kadan observed as he dumped the bedding and equipment that he had scavenged on their behalf on the grass and began to sort it into piles. 'From what I saw of you when you rode in, you'd have finished that journey roped face-down across your saddles, the lot of you.' He held up a pair of boots, assessed their size and tossed them to

Zukov. 'But don't worry –' His grin robbed the insult of its sting. 'By the time we ride out tomorrow, I'll have you looking like real soldiers.'

Zukov grimaced rudely behind the Tarvarian non-com's back, and Rostov grinned. He had not expected that they would be worshipped like gods, but on a world where technological ability excited only minimal interest, all of them were at a considerable disadvantage until they were able to prove themselves against local standards of performance. Kadan had digested the news that they were strangers from another star system with scarcely a raise of the eyebrows and it was clear that if the rest of the population was as phlegmatic, then the effect of the visitors on the course of Tarvarian history was likely to be non-existent.

In the evening Rostov, Yuan and Alexei were summoned to eat with the Khan and his officers. The dining area was the same canopy beneath which they had been interviewed earlier in the day, only now the matting was covered with carpets, some of them very fine, and an inverted 'U' of low square tables of some dark wood had been set out.

Burun was not at the head of the placings. Instead he was halfway down one side. He waved Rostov to an empty place at his side, and one of the aides drew Yuan and Alexei off and seated them among younger men. There were huge platters of cooked meat at intervals of every three or four settings. Rostov could see no sign of vegetables, but there were bowls of various kinds of fruits, a few of them identifiable. As soon as he sat down a slave laid a plate in front of him. It was heaped with a grain something like rice. Burun was using his short sword to cut thick slices from the meat on the platter in front of him. He dumped an enormous quantity on top of the cereal which covered Rostov's plate. The juices soaked into the white grains, staining them brown.

'Eat!' Burun commanded.

Rostov watched to see how he should behave. There were no forks, and everyone seemed to be using either his fingers or a knife. He had already observed that many of the officers, especially the older men like Burun, had fingernails which were lacquered or over-laid with silver or gold. Now Rostov was amazed to see the Khan flex his hand so that the nails extended like claws. The tips were needle sharp.

Burun impaled a piece of meat and forked it deli-cately into his mouth. Then he flexed his hand again, and the claws retracted with a flash of silver. It was the first time that Rostov had noticed the mutation and he wondered what else he had missed. It had been so easy to assume that the Tarvarians were human because they acted like men. Now suddenly he knew that he had been betrayed by the preconceptions which had been imposed by life under the Empire.

Yuan and Alexei were seated on the far side of the space which lay between the tables. The Manchu was eating with economy, and seemed oblivious to the strangeness of his surroundings, but Alexei was sitting frozen, unable to conceal his disbelief as he watched a Yek officer impaling his meat with claws which were easily three centimetres long.

Rostov saw that Burun was watching him and, unable to put the emotion into words, he lifted one hand, indicated the meat on his plate, and shrugged helplessly.

Burun laughed. 'You have no talons. Don't worry. Use your knife instead.'

He demonstrated, and Rostov followed the example.

'Does everyone have talons?'

'No. Only the Yek, the Ch'noze, and the N'pani. Everyone who lives across the northern part of this land. Khans have talons of silver like mine,' Burun flexed, and the claws flashed briefly, 'but the talons of the Altun are tipped with gold.'

The dinner became noisier as it progressed but, because most of the shouted conversation was in Yek, Rostov confined himself to his food. Now and then he was addressed in Anglic, either by the Khan or by one of his neighbours at the table, and in such cases he did his best to answer politely. Mostly they compared customs and attitudes. There was an undercurrent of curiosity which centred around Yuan's presence. Finally it was Burun who brought the matter into the open.

'Your officer.' He indicated the Manchu with a nod. 'Is he a man like you?'

Rostov was surprised that the question had not been asked earlier, and guessed that a code of manners existed which governed the kind of questions which could be asked. He pretended to consider, and then shrugged.

'Lord, he is human, as I am. Beyond that, who can say? Are all men similar in appearance on this world?'

Those who sat nearest were listening intently to the answer. Rostov saw several of the older men nodding agreement.

'And yet the Yasa is clear.' It was Arghatun who interrupted, continuing the discussion in Anglic so that Rostov could understand. 'A man who is not as other men shall be suffered to live, but not to breed to produce others of his kind.'

A gnarled hundred commander named Jenjin produced a snort of disagreement. 'Hah! The Yasa was made when your grandsire and mine both thought

124

that it was a long way from Kinsai to the Eastern Sea,' he growled. 'How was anyone to know that there were so many people in the world - or that they would all be so different?'

There was a murmur of agreement which ceased when Burun spoke again.

'The Yasa is broken every day.' Burun held Rostov's eyes for a moment. 'How many of the subject races have no talons? And yet they serve us and multiply.'

Rostov thought that it was probably the wrong moment to suggest that the qualities which defined humanity were subjective. It was startling to discover that a race which was identifiably mutant had laws for the suppression of mutations, and he guessed that the origin of cause and principle alike lay somewhere in the lost time of the isolation of Tarvaras from the Empire.

'Oh, Khan, surely that is not the same.' Arghatun turned to protest. 'For when a man who has talons takes a wife who has none, his children are taloned. The race breeds true. They are not monsters.'

'And is my officer a monster in your eyes?' Rostov enquired mildly. He saw Burun grin at Arghatun's confusion.

The thousand commander flushed. 'He does not look like a man,' he maintained stubbornly.

Burun sat back. He took two pears from a bowl and tossed one to Rostov. 'Who knows what a man looks like on other worlds?' It was clear that he was dismissing the subject.

Rostov started to peel the pear with his knife. When he looked up, Yuan was watching from his place on the other side of the dining area. Rostov wondered if the Manchu had overheard the conversation, but he gave no sign. One of the younger men with red hair was saying something to him, and Yuan answered briefly, and bowed as he sat in his place. His lengthened features were expressionless, but just for a moment Rostov imagined that the bow was intended for him, and not for the Altun. He nodded, and Yuan looked away.

When the meal was over and the tables had been cleared of everything except the wine and the cups, one of the Altun stood up. Jenjin spoke in Rostov's ear and said that the young man's name was Nogai, a grandson of the Kha-Khan.

'Be quiet, all of you!' Nogai was speaking in Anglic. He waved his arms and finally the noise of conversation died.

'We're going to wrestle.' The young Altun looked at Rostov and showed his teeth. 'To help settle the blood.'

One of Nogai's brothers shouted something in Yek and everybody laughed. Jenjin told Rostov that Burun had broken Nogai's wrist during an argument five days earlier, and that it had just been suggested that if his plan went ahead he might get the other one broken as well. There was no strapping on Nogai's forearm, but Rostov supposed that on Tarvaras a sprain or a cracked bone could just as easily be referred to as a break, depending upon the state of medical knowledge.

'Do you wrestle?' Burun looked at Rostov expectantly.

Rostov stretched so that his full size was apparent. He was a head taller than most of the men round the table, and only Burun and Jenjin were anything like as broad.

'I can,' he said. 'But would it be a fair contest?'

'Wrestle Burun,' Nogai suggested. There was a glitter in his eyes, and Rostov realised that he was trying to manoeuvre Burun into a situation where he would be either hurt or embarrassed.

126

Burun shook his head. 'I'm an old man, Nogai.'

Arghatun and some of the younger men jeered at him. Nogai only smiled.

'Oh but Khan, they say that you're in good condition for your age.'

'Do they? That's beside the point. And anyway, only Jenjin here could give me a match.'

Rostov noted that he had been excluded. He said nothing. He saw Alexei watching, and wondered what he was thinking.

'Why don't we shoot instead?' Jenjin asked.

'Shoot?' Nogai looked round. 'Where?'

'Out in the clearing.' Burun gestured.

'But it's dark outside.' A young officer at the foot of the table made the objection plaintively, and Jenjin sneered.

'You haven't ever fought in the dark?'

'No.'

'You will.' Burun made the comment drily. 'If you live long enough. Nogai, you can't wrestle with a broken wrist, and no one here is big enough to take on Suragai.'

'Yes.' Nogai agreed quickly. 'You're right. We'll shoot instead. Arghatun, tell the slaves to put up some targets.' He smiled. 'Burun, you'll shoot with us of course.'

'Of course.'

Everyone stood up and moved out into the clearing.

Most of the officers had to send orderlies to fetch their bows. While they were waiting for the targets to be set up, Burun took Rostov aside.

'Be careful of Nogai. He wants to set you against me.'

'I thought as much.' Rostov looked around the clearing. The carts had been moved to one side, and now slaves were attaching torches to the arched wooden frames. 'Would he try to shoot you?'

'Possibly. Why?'

'Well, he was pleased when you agreed to this. Maybe it was what he wanted all along.'

'Hunh.' Burun nodded. 'You're no stranger to conspiracy, that's for certain. Well, maybe you're right. But Nogai's a good shot. Maybe he just thinks he can beat me.'

Rostov shrugged, but said nothing.

'How good are you with a bow?' Burun asked.

'I may need a few shots before I find the mark, Khan.'

'I see.' Burun grinned as if he suspected an over-statement. 'I'll lend you mine. The pull's fairly heavy, but someone with your shoulders ought to be able to manage.' An orderly ran up and Burun took his bow out of the case, and strung it.

Rostov held out his hand. 'May I see it?'

Burun gave the bow to him. Arghatun came over with an aide called Hodai, and they stood and grinned and Rostov flexed the bow experimentally.

'Hah!' Arghatun elbowed Hodai in the side. 'See, I told you. He's as strong as an ox.' He took one of Hodai's arrows and offered it to Rostov. Burun shook his head.

'No, use one of mine. Hodai, your arrows haven't enough spline for use with my bow. They'll shatter if Suragai pulls it at full stretch.'

The nearest target was about a hundred paces away. Rostov nocked the arrow which Burun handed to him, and sighted on it. He loosed, and by the target a slave called out, 'Gold in the first!'

'Easy shot,' Nogai jeered. He stepped up behind Rostov, drew and shot.

'White in the fifth!' The voice of the slave beside the

furthest target came clearly.

One of Nogai's brothers slapped him on the shoulder, but Burun shouted, 'Which target were you aiming at, Nogai?'

'Huh.' Nogai snorted. 'You have a try. The light's terrible.'

'What light?' Hodai stepped up to the mark. 'I can't see the target.'

He shot well enough, however, and the slave called, 'Gold in the fifth!'

Burun shook his head. 'If Hodai can score in the furthest target, we're too close. Make another line fifty paces back. And maybe we should take down some of the torches.'

Rostov blinked. Jenjin paced off the new line, marked it, and offered his bow to Yuan. The Manchu tested the pull, nocked an arrow, and shot.

'Gold in the third!'

Jenjin slapped Yuan on the back, then took the bow and offered it to Alexei. Alexei peered down the range and shook his head.

'I can't see anything beyond the third target,' he said. He looked at Rostov. 'How can you hit something you can't see?'

Burun laughed. He took his bow from Rostov and gestured at Nogai. 'Take down the last three torches.'

'I wondered when you were going to shoot, Khan.' Nogai grinned. He trotted away.

With the torches extinguished, Rostov could see only a vague blur where each of the targets stood. He looked at Yuan, and raised his eyebrows expressively.

'Watch this,' Jenjin murmured.

Burun appeared to sight carefully. Then he lowered his bow.

'Nogai!' he shouted. 'Take down three more torches, and move the target.'

'Turn it round to face the other way!' Hodai called out, and everyone laughed.

A dim shape moved at the end of the clearing. Burun raised his bow again. 'Throw a torch!' he shouted.

A light flared briefly at the side of the furthest cart, and then a torch flew through the air over the target. Burun cursed, and Rostov saw that the straw circle had been moved back and turned sideways so that it was no wider than a man's forearm.

Burun shot, and at once the torches flared. Nogai ran over to look. Then he turned.

'Gold!'

Jenjin crowed and slapped Burun on the back. Nogai came back up range, running easily.

'My turn,' he said. He looked at Burun. 'Your choice, Khan. Move the target any way you choose.'

Burun grinned and nodded. He handed his bow to Rostov, and loped away. Rostov stepped off to the side for a better view, but already Burun was a vague outline among the carts.

Nogai stepped up to the line. He raised his bow.

'Throw a torch!'

Light bloomed, and Rostov heard Jenjin snort with amusement. Burun had set the target back in its original position, an easy shot. Nogai swore and shot swiftly twice, once at the target, and once to the side where Burun had been standing. There was a yell, and then Burun came trotting back through the trees.

'You missed the slave, Nogai.'

Several of the officers chuckled, but Nogai flushed.

'You'll insult me once too often, Khan.'

'Insult?' Burun looked innocent. 'What insult was that, Noyon?' He took wine from a slave and drank. 'Now let's put up a few of the torches again and we'll have a proper competition.' He took his bow from Rostov and smiled cheerfully.

Rostov started to feel sick in the middle of the night. He felt as if he was burning and it hurt to breathe. Kadan took one look at him, and ran for help.

'Name of God.' Burun came into the tent, knelt down, and touched Rostov's forehead. 'You're on fire.'

Rostov tried to sit up and found that he could not.

'Am I the only one sick like this?' His mouth was dry. Burun gave him water from a bowl. He shook his head.

'No. Your son and the others are the same. Don't worry. Arghatun is seeing to them.'

'You ought not to come so close.' Rostov tried to think clearly. 'Either we have caught a sickness which is native to this world and we have no immunity against it, or maybe we have brought something with us, and because the air and the temperature are different here, it grows and alters. Are any of your people sick?'

'Oh.' Burun seemed not to be perturbed. 'We never get sick.'

'Never?' Rostov was drained by the effort of conversation. At first he did not understand what had been said.

Burun shrugged. 'Sometimes a man who is wounded suffers a fever. But we don't get sick the way you are now. Maybe it was the food.'

Rostov tried to laugh, but the motion hurt his chest. 'Oh. In that case we're in real trouble. If we can't eat your food, we might as well die.'

He lay back and closed his eyes. Nausea climbed up his throat. He heaved over on to his side.

'Keep him quiet. He's going to throw up.'
'He has. Look at the mess.'

131

'Never mind. Clean him up and look after him. Keep him cool.'

One of the voices was Burun's, but Rostov did not care. He was marooned on a world full of strangeness, where nothing was predictable, and now he was sick. He remembered being sick when he was on leave on Knossos. Irina had wanted to nurse him, but the doctors had sent her away. Tears ran down his face.

'What's wrong with him now?'

'He has a fever. Wash his face.'

'No. He's crying.'

Strange dreams disturbed his mind: weird animals chased him down long dark valleys, but gradually he came to know that they were only nightmares. Somebody was supporting his shoulders so that he could drink. He spluttered, and the water went everywhere.

Burun sat back on his heels.

'You're cooler. Good. How do you feel?'

Rostov sat up. He felt as weak as a kitten, but the fever and nausea were gone.

'Better, thank you. My son and the others?'

'They recovered yesterday. I sent them on with Kadan. They'll be in Pesth by now.'

'Yesterday. How long have I been sick?'

'Oh. Four days. Your officer - the one with the yellow skin - got better first. Then the others.'

Rostov nodded. Through the open end of the tent he could see that the campsite was deserted. Hodai and Jenjin were sitting on the grass. Somewhere a st'lyan neighed shrilly.

'You waited for me.'

'Well, if I had lost you, the Kha-Khan would have been displeased with me. There was a message two days ago. He wants to see you at Kinsai. We can go there as soon as I have seen to the army at Pesth.'

'Kinsai.'

'Yes. You'd better learn some Yek in a hurry. Lie back now. If you're well enough, we'll ride when it gets dark.'

They arrived at Pesth early the next morning. It was a great walled city with a massive gate which towered above their heads.

Some of the army was camped outside the walls, but only a few sentries were stirring. As soon as the guards on duty in the gate towers saw Burun, they shouted down inside, and the gate was swung open. Inside there was a portcullis of some dark metal. It protected the entrance to a tunnel which passed through the wall, and Rostov was amazed at its length. The stones of the wall did not seem to be held together with mortar, but instead they were keyed so that each lay on the other with hardly a sign of a join.

The men operating the windlass for the portcullis cheered Burun as he rode past and, as soon as they gave tongue, more men came out of a gate-house and joined in.

Burun ignored them. He kicked his st'lyan into a trot across the wide stone-paved courtyard. At the far side was a second gate, nearly as massive as the first. Soldiers were pushing it open and Rostov saw that the whole inner yard was a clever device to protect the city. An attacking enemy could be allowed to break through the outer gates and would find that he was surrounded by walls and towers which were every bit as impregnable as those outside. A hail of arrows and other missiles could be launched on those who were trapped between the walls, and they would be decimated.

'Where are we going?' Rostov looked at Hodai. The aide was steering his st'lyan to follow Burun through the second gate.

'Oh. The Khan has a house in the city. So do most of the Altun. He'll go there first, I expect, and when he has eaten and rested, he'll see Arghatun and Wotai. They're the thousand commanders he's taking south when we go on campaign. Now that we're going to Kinsai, they'll have to supervise most of the preparations.'

'What about Nogai?'

Hodai shrugged.

'The Altun are coming on campaign. The Kha-Khan's order. But they don't hold any rank with the army unless the Khan chooses, and they command only their own guard. One of the thousands - Wotai's - is part of T'zin's tuman, but they haven't served with him for several years, and they were always a bit leery of him. Probably the Khan will give Nogai some work to do to keep him occupied until we return from Kinsai, but we could just as easily find the whole pack of them travelling with us to the capital. As long as they're in Pesth for the start of the journey south, they can do very much as they like, although none of them will be welcome at court.'

They turned in at the yard of a two-storey stone house which had a red tiled roof. Alexei was leaning out of one of the upper windows. He waved.

'Father!'

Burun grinned. 'Your son is pleased to see you,' he said.

During the ride to Pesth they had talked a great deal. Filial conduct was one of the subjects which had been touched upon. Rostov now knew that Burun's eldest son was called Jotan, and that he was married to a grand-daughter of the Kha-Khan. He wondered if Alexei would marry now that there was no likelihood that he would ever leave Tarvaras, and if he did what his children would look like.

Alexei came out into the yard as Rostov was dismounting. He had new clothes: loose grey trousers of a material which looked like silk and a grey tunic which was open at the front almost to the waist. The trousers were tucked into high boots, and Rostov saw that his son's eyelids had been stained a shade of silver-blue. Alexei turned and shouted back into the house. 'Kadan! My father's here with the Khan!'

The Tarvarian came out of the house and took Rostov's reins. Rostov stood awkwardly, aware that Hodai and Jenjin were carefully ignoring the reunion which appeared to be going on.

'You look well,' he said to Alexei at last. 'What have you done to your eyes?'

'Oh, it's a kind of tattoo. It's permanent, but Kadan says it's necessary, especially if I'm going into the hot lands. Every clan has a different colour, and they made up a special shade for us.' Alexei paused, then smiled ingenuously. 'I'm talking too much. I'm happy to see you. I thought you were going to die, you were so sick. What was it, do you think?'

'The sickness? Probably a reaction to toxins our bodies hadn't encountered before. If we're lucky it won't happen again.'

Alexei shuddered. 'God, I hope not. Do you know the Yek have no doctors? There are the Sechem, who deal with anything connected with science, and they act as surgeons if someone is badly hurt. But nobody gets sick - nobody.'

'So I've been told.' Rostov made the comment drily. 'Are the others with you?'

'Yuan's staying with Nogai. They're in a house down the street. Zukov and Mubarak are living in the camp outside the walls. They made friends with some of the Yek sergeants. Do you know that the drink they call k'miss is actually fermented mare's milk? And Voront-

135

seff is somewhere in the house. He's got some new clothes for you.'

'Good.'

'Yes. They're very fine. Do you know the Kha-Khan has sent for us? Well, not for everyone. It's you he wants to see, but I'm going too. We're going to Kinsai in a few days. Kadan says it's ten times the size of Pesth.'

'The Khan told me.' Rostov started to walk towards the door.

'They must have a very good system of communication, don't you think?' Alexei's tone was innocent, but Rostov stopped and turned. 'The Kha-Khan's message arrived the day we left camp, and yet Kinsai is four days' ride from here at least.'

'And yet they don't use machines. You've been observant. How is it done?'

'Heliograph.' Alexei made a face. 'It's very primitive. They don't have electrical power, so they can't use a telegraph.'

Rostov was suddenly sure about the purpose of his son's remarks. He sighed. 'And you think we might just take the opportunity to suggest such a thing.'

'Well. Their law doesn't actually forbid the use of machines. I checked. And anyway they could probably design a system based on the photo-electric cell. With the amount of sun they get, it's the obvious choice.'

'A telegraph, using power from a system of photo-electric cells.' Rostov summarised the idea flatly. 'Have you seen any industry at all?'

'Not much. And what there is seems to be fairly basic. I expect we could teach them.'

'It would be a lot of effort, surely, for a relatively small increase in efficiency.' Rostov made the observation with deceptive mildness. 'As you remarked

136

yourself, their communications are already quite efficient.'

'Well -'

Rostov showed his teeth. 'Electricity. Which of the dubious benefits of civilisation would you introduce them to next, I wonder? Tell me, have you spoken of this to anyone else?'

Alexei was staring at the ground. He shook his head.

'Good. Then oblige me by keeping your ideas to yourself. Apart from the fact that these people seem to possess a remarkable amount of scientific knowledge, even though they do not care to employ it, it seems possible that their ideas about civilisation and ours may be quite different.'

'Civilisation! They are primitives!' The protest was out of Alexei's mouth almost at once.

'Are you so certain?' Rostov queried. 'I grant you they don't live in a manner similar to anything we have ever encountered in the Empire. But hasn't it occurred to you that if they have access to knowledge and culture from a previous machine age, yet still continue with their own customs, then maybe they have reasons which seem at least to them to be perfectly good and sufficient?'

Alexei's expression remained stubborn. Rostov shook his head.

'Look, we have been on this world a matter of a few days. We're going to be here for the rest of our lives. Don't you think we ought to try and understand our surroundings before we try to change them?'

Rostov turned away and followed the others into the house. It was depressing to discover that the warmth of Alexei's concern was a sham, and that it had been aimed at making him susceptible to ideas which would lead to the industrialisation of Tarvaras. He was annoyed at himself for being pleased by his son's initial

137

welcome. He should have known from the first that the chasm which lay between them would not be so easy to cross.

'The man is in the field. The man was in the field. The man will be in the field.'

Rostov repeated the words, coached by Hodai. They were a day out of Pesth on the way to Kinsai and Rostov was concerned that when he met the Kha-Khan he would be able to speak enough Yek to conduct a simple conversation.

'God help the Alan against a man who learns so fast,' Hodai said. Kuchuk, the Khan's standard-bearer, laughed.

'Alan?' Rostov queried the word, although he had heard it before in connection with the campaign to come.

'Alan. The people of the land on the far side of the G'bai,' Hodai expanded. He put the new words through their paces, and Rostov incorporated them into sentences. Already Hodai was starting to adopt the mannerisms which Rostov supposed were common to teachers everywhere.

'Heh, Suragai,' Kuchuk teased. 'Now you can talk to the ladies of Kinsai.'

Rostov made a face. There had been women in Pesth, some of them attractive even by Imperial standards, but they had been the wives or concubines of Burun's officers, or else they had belonged to the Altun. In any case he was not sure that he was interested. He had been apart from Irina on many occasions - too many - but a permanent separation was something he still had to get used to.

'Maybe he's like the Khan,' Hodai said slyly. 'Burun's a great fighter because he diverts all his sexual energies into fighting and giving orders.'

'Maybe Suragai has no sexual energies at all.'
Kuchuk was grinning. 'I've heard that old men lose
their interest in women.'

Rostov cursed him in newly acquired Yek. Hodai
laughed.

'How old are you, Suragai?' he asked.

'How old is the Khan?'

'Oh, fifty summers. Are you as old as that?'

Rostov ignored the question. He looked at Kuchuk.
'The Khan has a son?'

'Several,' Kuchuk agreed.

'And his wife - is she still alive?'

'Wives. He has two. One is the daughter of Vortai
the Black, and there's bad blood from here to the
Eastern Sea over the marriage. They say he fought
twenty men, including her brothers and her father, to
win her.'

'His second wife,' Hodai sighed in a pretence of
ecstasy, 'Heavenly Name, you should see her. A N'pan
woman, beautiful, like a perfect flower. They call her
the Regal Lily. The Khan got her at the sack of T'sosei,
and when the Kha-Khan - the present one's father -
wanted her for himself, the Khan married her. He has
two sons by her, both grown, and lets no man look at
her twice.'

'I see.' Rostov smiled grimly. 'But yet he diverts his
sexual energies into fighting.'

'Oh. Well -' Hodai waved an arm, and Kuchuk
laughed.

'Hah, Suragai, you are learning our language well
enough to argue in it.'

'Not well enough yet,' Rostov answered tersely.
'Talk to me some more, Hodai.'

They rode all day and into the night. Alexei never
rode near enough to talk, but sometimes Burun
dropped back and discussed the people Rostov was

likely to meet at the Kha-Khan's court. He spoke of the feuds which surrounded the succession, and Rostov felt a small chill of worry that he had left Yuan in Nogai's house. The pace was fast; they stopped only at way stations which were situated every hundred verst or so to change st'lyan. Hodai had said that the Khan's wives were with the clan on the Merkut hereditary pastureland a day's ride north of Kinsai. Rostov wondered if Burun was in a hurry to see them again.

On the third night they stopped at an inn which was attached to a relay station. The innkeeper and the attendants were Yek, but the place was thronged with foreign traders, part of a caravan which was travelling from Kinsai to the western coast. The pack animals were large tawny-coloured beasts of a kind that Rostov had only ever seen in illustration. They had humps in which they stored fat and were capable of travelling for days without water or food. The drivers were Ch'kassians: small olive-skinned men from an island country which Hodai said was on the other side of the Inner Sea. They wore long light blue robes and smelled of strange spices.

Burun spent half the night talking with their leaders. The Ch'kassians spoke a version of C'zak, and Rostov was, with some difficulty, able to follow the conversation.

The captain of the caravan guard mentioned the Alan almost at once.

'How do they fight?' Burun asked.

'Name of God, they are invincible.' The Ch'kassian rolled his eyes. 'Each man is armoured in metal, like a fortress.'

'They carry swords.'

'Other weapons also.' The captain's eyes shifted away.

'Firearms?'

'Some, Lord. Companies of men on foot, with armour not so heavy. But they are few.'

Burun's eyes were expressionless. Rostov wondered if the scarcity of firearms indicated a shortage of the materials for making gunpowder.

'Also they use the lance,' another Ch'kassian continued swiftly. 'Heavier than those used by the Yek, Lord. They hold them locked against their sides, the points forward. On a ground of their own choosing, nothing can withstand their charge.'

Burun smiled. 'The Yek don't usually wait to be charged.'

The Ch'kassians laughed nervously. 'Everyone knows that the Yek are great fighters,' the captain said.

Burun sat back. Rostov saw that he was hiding his expression behind his cup.

'Someday we'll fight them, maybe. Then we'll see.'

After a while Rostov found that he was losing track of the ebb and flow of the conversation. He was tired, and the heat of the fire was making him sleepy. The scent of Ch'kassian was like a drug in the warm air of the common room. He rolled himself in his riding cloak, lay down upon the broad straw-covered pallet which covered the bench, and slept.

They left the inn before dawn, crossed a wide river by a stone bridge, and continued east.

Rostov was amazed at how fast they were moving. A st'lyan ate up the ground like no horse he had ever encountered, and although at first he had estimated that a verst, the basic unit of Tarvarian distance, was equivalent to about a kilometre, now he realised that it was probably more than twice that. It was common for the army to travel two hundred verst in a day's march and, with frequent changes, it seemed that the animals could be driven twice as hard.

Rostov exercised his capacity for mental arithmetic

and blinked. A Tarvarian army was capable of moving at between forty and fifty kilometres per hour, and individual units riding fast could move at twice that rate. It was a speed equivalent to that of the fastest armoured land vehicle in use in the Empire.

Kinsai was a city on a hill. It grew out of the plain like a monument. The buildings were all of red stone and many had gold roofs.

The Kha-Khan's palace was in the exact centre of everything. A river of golden water surrounded it, flowing between banks cut out of the stone, crossed by four bridges. The streets radiated away in every direction like the spokes of a wheel. There were crowds of people everywhere but, when they saw Burun's banner, they moved politely aside to let the party pass. Many of them bowed.

Hodai told Rostov that the major-domo who met them in the antechamber of the palace was a N'pani, the only foreigner with any authority at the court. The man was clad in midnight blue silk and his head was shaved except for a queue of black hair which was coiled on top of his scalp. He bowed to Burun.

'The Universal Khan will see you shortly.'

Burun sat down on a bench which was decorated with gold filigree. He unfastened the laces of his coat and yawned.

'Bring me something to drink,' he commanded.

'The Khan wishes.' The major-domo gestured to one of the slaves who knelt beside the wall. 'Would you prefer wine or k'miss?'

'K'miss!'

The N'pani's nose seemed to wrinkle. Rostov stared around the antechamber. Its silk hangings shimmered. The inside of every room in the palace was said to be roofed and walled with rich fabric, and he guessed

142

that the Yek had once been nomads. Even though they lived inside stone buildings, they furnished them like tents.

The cups in which the k'miss was brought were each cut from an individual chunk of crystal chased with gold. The bowl of Rostov's was so delicate that he felt that if he closed his hand too suddenly it would shatter.

A man entered the room, and at once all the slaves prostrated themselves. Burun only looked up idly. Then he drank from his cup and set it aside.

'Khotan. You look well.'

The Yek was dressed in silver silks so fine that Rostov thought that they would bruise if anything brushed against them. The wearer was about Burun's age, but he was much smaller and slimmer. His hair was red, so that Rostov knew that he was Altun, but there were strands of silver among the gold.

Hodai, Kuchuk and the others were bowing. Belatedly Rostov collected himself and followed suit.

Burun rose.

'Your father is keeping us waiting,' he said.

The Altun laughed. 'Not for long.'

Suddenly Rostov realised that this was Khotan the Restless, conqueror of the C'zaki and only living son of the Kha-Khan. He felt Khotan's eyes studying him.

'Are these the strangers?'

Burun nodded. 'This is Suragai, and yonder his son Alexai.'

Rostov's lips twitched at the new interpretation of his son's name. He bowed again. 'Lord.'

'Hunh. They look like men, only taller.'

'Oh.' Burun's tone was mild. 'They are quite human.'

Khotan looked once more. Then he turned away. 'How does your fighting go in the west?'

Burun sat down. 'You know the Ch'noze.' He picked up the cup. 'How can we rule a people who won't accept that they're beaten?'

'They rose again this spring?'

'They rise every spring. I put down four revolts in towns you wouldn't even notice if you rode through them. And then, thank God, your father's summons sent me south.'

'The Alan war. Yes, well, that's more your kind of fighting. Who did you leave in Ch'nozia?'

'Berke.'

'Sidacai's brother. He'll enjoy governing a province.'

'Yes.' Burun was grinning. 'He'll turn the men into Sufi if he gets the chance.'

'Huh.' Khotan snorted. 'If there are any more mystics, there won't be a Khanate. But if my cousin wants to contemplate the mysteries of the unknown, then he may as well do it in the middle of a Ch'noze snowstorm.'

'Yes.'

Khotan sat down heavily on the bench beside Burun, and Rostov realised suddenly that the Kha-Khan's son was drunk. The major-domo came quickly out of the inner chamber. He bowed to Burun. 'The Kha-Khan will see you now.'

Burun stood up. He motioned to Rostov and Alexei. Khotan subsided suddenly, but before he could fall over, the major-domo was signing to the slaves. They picked Khotan up and carried him away.

The Kha-Khan's chamber was bigger than the ante-room. The floor was made of wood which had been brushed with gold leaf so that every knot and line of the grain created a ripple in a seeming golden pool. In the centre of the room there was a raised dais, roofed with gold. The Kha-Khan was sitting in a chair which had been carved into the shape of a reclining dragon.

To one side of him there was a low couch. A woman was stretched lazily along it. She was only thinly veiled, and Rostov could see that although she was beautiful, she was old.

He stood by Burun's side, knelt and bowed, then prostrated himself. Even Alexei was awed by the splendour, and behaved perfectly.

Rostov rocked back to sit on his heels and the gold on the floor reflected his face, distorting it so that it was not recognisable. The richness all around unsettled him, for he had expected to find it accompanied elsewhere in the Khanate by signs of extreme poverty. Instead there were no beggars on the city streets of either Pesth or Kinsai, and no one in any of the towns and villages through which he had passed seemed to be poorly clothed or underfed. The existence of a noble class like the Altun was not remarkable in any way. But Rostov's experience of the Empire had not prepared him to find at the same time a complete absence of the poor and underprivileged.

Arjun the Great was white-haired. His skin was translucent with age and he had dark brown eyes like two deep pools. He said something in an undertone to the woman at his side, and she nodded and smiled.

'Burun Khan, we greet you.' The Kha-Khan's voice was strong and deep.

'Lord.' Burun had risen to his feet. Now he bowed again. 'I am happy that you are well.'

'Ho. Well, do you say? If I am well, then the desert has turned to water.'

Rostov saw that Burun was suppressing a grin. The woman laughed openly, and he stared.

'Are these the strangers?'

'Yes, Lord.'

'Then bring them closer. My eyes fail me like every other part of my body.'

145

Rostov waited for Burun's nod, then walked forward until he was a pace from the foot of the dais.

'Strange.' The Kha-Khan did not address anyone in particular as he spoke. 'The one is father to the other, we are told, yet they are not alike. See, the younger has hair the colour of freshly gathered corn, but the other, his father, is dark. Apart from his size he could be a C'zak, or even one of us.'

'Not one of us,' Burun commented softly. 'He has no talons.'

'Ah. Indeed.'

Rostov wondered how long the conversation was going to continue over his head. Suddenly he was being addressed directly.

'How many other worlds?'

For a moment he did not know what had been said. 'Your pardon, Lord. I don't understand.'

'Your people come from other worlds. How many are they?'

'Oh. I'm sorry, Lord. I don't know.'

'A thousand? More than that?'

Rostov thought. 'More.'

'And the people.' It was the woman who spoke. 'Are they like you?'

'Some are similar, many are different. Not all worlds are the same, and life upon them has strange effects upon the body.'

'Yes.' The Kha-Khan nodded. 'Your officer. We were told of him.'

'Yes, Lord. Also there are those who are not human at all - we call them aliens. Some alien races are intelligent.'

'Say you so?' The Kha-Khan seemed to digest the news. 'And the Khan of your world - how is he called?'

Rostov took a deep breath. He had dreaded this question.

'Lord, there is one ruler over all the known worlds, and he is called the Emperor. His name is Priam; he is the second of his line.'

'What's that? A Khan who claims to rule all the known worlds?' The information was not well received. Rostov wondered if he could have phrased the statement differently. But he had already said something similar to Burun, and did not know which of his words had been repeated verbatim.

'Does he claim this world?' The Kha-Khan's eyes flashed. 'What arrogance!'

'Oh. Please forgive me, Lord. The Emperor does not claim this world. In fact he has no interest in it or in any of the other worlds within your solar system. The Empire has laws which forbid contact with planets which have been contaminated by certain substances. This is one of those which is so prohibited. Excuse me, Lord, but parts of your planet are poisoned, although you may not yet have discovered that fact for yourselves. The effect of such poisons is to cause some children to be born as monsters, and the people who venture too close to contaminated land sicken and die.'

'The G'bai.'

It was Burun who spoke the word softly. The Kha-Khan nodded.

'Yes. We know of the poison. But its effect diminishes every year. Will not your Emperor send to claim this land when it is gone? Indeed,' the accusation came swiftly, 'did he not send you?'

Rostov thought that probably this one question was the reason for his summons to Kinsai.

'Lord, I came to this world by accident. If it was otherwise, surely others would have come by now to find me?'

The Kha-Khan seemed to consider.

'We are content,' he said at last. 'It seems that you would need a vessel such as that in which you came, before you would be able to return to your own world. Burun Khan may have told you that we know of such machines, but do not concern ourselves with them. It is possible that some day such concern will change. Perhaps then the Yek will meet the army of this Emperor, and on that day we will send you to him as our ambassador.'

Rostov remembered the ring of plasma weapons which ensured that Tarvaras was forever isolated, but he said nothing.

'Serve us and you will prosper.' The Kha-Khan's tone was tranquil again. 'You were a general in the armies of your Khan. No doubt you will find advancement here.'

'Yes, Lord.'

The Kha-Khan made a sign like a benediction. Then he looked at Alexei. 'Truly, this is your son?'

'Yes, Lord. He has the look and colouring of his mother. She is related to the Emperor.'

'Ho!' The Kha-Khan seemed unimpressed.

'Then the lady, his mother,' it was the woman who spoke, 'was very fair.'

'Yes, Lady.'

Rostov sorted through the physical descriptions which Burun had supplied of the principal members of the court and knew that he was addressing Va'na Khatun, once a slave and concubine, but now the wife of Arjun and grandmother to the wife of Burun's own son Jotan.

'Aah.' She nodded, satisfied.

It was born upon Rostov that he had the opportunity - perhaps the only one he would ever have - to communicate the extent of the scientific advancement of the Empire and to speak of the technology which he and his companions were capable of introducing to Tarvaras, even given the prohibitions of the Yasa. But it was as if there was a halter on his tongue.

The wife of the Kha-Khan was saying something, but for a moment the Yek was incomprehensible.

'I'm sorry, Khatun. I don't understand,' Rostov apologised.

'The Khatun observed that you would miss your wife, and suggested that it was our duty to find you another.' It was the Kha-Khan who responded.

Rostov hesitated, trying to find the words to frame a non-committal response.

'Or are our women unattractive to your eyes?'

'Oh. Lord, they are as attractive in their way as women anywhere, or so I would suppose. I am in any case no judge of beauty. But forgive me, Lord, if I say that I have no inclination towards another marriage.'

The Kha-Khan did not appear to be offended. 'As you wish. Your feelings may alter, and in such a case, you have our blessing.' He indicated Alexei. 'On this world or any other, one son is not enough.'

Rostov was not sure that these final words related to his own case. The Kha-Khan seemed to look inward as he spoke, and there was an uncomfortable silence.

PART TWO

Courtship

Orcadai's house was perched on a ledge which over-looked a sheer drop from the city wall to the plain. In reality it was not part of the city at all; the builders of Kinsai had carved away the plateau and slotted the massive stones of the defences into place around the old structure so that the marvellous symmetry of the circular layout would not be interrupted.

'Hold!' A sentry on the wall called out to Burun as he rode the narrow path below. 'Declare yourself.'

'Burun Khan. Let me pass.'

Burun kicked the st'lyan as she tried to sidestep.

'Lord.' The sentry grinned and saluted. 'I should have known you.'

Burun grunted. The silver banner of the Merkuts was flapping on a staff outside the house and, from the number of animals tethered under the lean-to shelter at one side, he guessed that Orcadai was entertaining.

The inside of the building was on two levels, constructed so that the upper portion formed a kind of balcony above the lower. Orcadai and several of the junior officers of the Kha-Khan's Guard were dicing, and they did not notice Burun when he came through the door.

Burun grinned unpleasantly. Then he grabbed Orcadai by his top knot and by the sash at his waist, dragged him to the rail, and threw him over.

Orcadai tumbled in mid air and howled. He landed on his back on the bed which was in the centre of the chamber below, and it collapsed. His guests shouted in outrage, and Burun waved them down.

'What kind of welcome is this to give your father?'

'Oh, God. It's you.' Orcadai got up out of the wreckage of the bed. 'I didn't know.' He started up the stairs, but Burun sidestepped so that he was standing in the way.

'Hah, child. You've grown fat and lazy since I saw you last.'

Orcadai looked up at him. 'Old goat,' he said, and tried to push past.

Burun caught the outstretched arm, whipped Orcadai round, and threw him back down the stairs.

'Old, do you say? Then show some respect.'

Orcadai yelled, and charged up the stairs. He dived headlong as he reached the top, but Burun stepped out of the way, caught his son's sash at the back as he passed, swung him round and threw him into the wreckage of the bed again.

The guests leaned over the rail, jeered, and shouted advice. Orcadai gestured them to silence and paced the length of the room. Burun could see that he was deciding what to do next.

'Well?' he said.

Orcadai raced up the stairs, but when he was still some steps from the top he vaulted on to the hand rail and somersaulted into the upper room. At once he was on Burun. He seized him by the waist and threw him bodily over the balustrade.

'Beloved parent.' He bowed irreverently. 'I mourn your advancing years.'

Burun charged. He shouldered into Orcadai, and they struggled at the stair head.

'Let me win,' Orcadai whispered hoarsely. 'You'll embarrass me in front of my guests.'

'Hah!' Burun snorted. He ducked his head and butted Orcadai under the chin, his hands grasping for purchase. Together they crashed to the floor, and then rolled apart.

154

Orcadai sat up laughing. The officers who were watching jeered and Burun glared at them.

'Go away,' he ordered.

They left, and Orcadai righted two stools and sat down on one of them. A female slave came from the back of the house and started to clean up the mess.

'What are you doing in Kinsai?' Orcadai straightened his robe. 'The last time I heard, you were in Ch'nozia.'

'Oh. The Kha-Khan wanted to see some prisoners who were taken near Pesth. Strangers from another world.'

'Hunh.'

'But I would have been through here sooner or later anyway. The Kha-Khan has ordered a campaign against the Alan. Siban commands, and I am to carry out the reconnaissance.'

Orcadai looked up sharply. 'You're taking Jotan of course.'

'Naturally. You as well. I have the Kha-Khan's authorisation.'

'Good. I'm tired of ceremonial. Where is the assembly?'

'Pesth. My own first tenth and a tenth of T'zin's. The bronze month.'

'That's two months away,' Orcadai objected. 'What are we going to do until then?'

'Well for a start we're going to get everyone into shape to cross the G'bai. The Kha-Khan has ordered me to take Nogai and the younger Altun.'

'Name of God. And you're taking Jotan. You know he and Nogai have a feud unfinished?'

'Yes. But they can settle it in their own time.'

Orcadai looked amused. 'Huh. I think I'm going to enjoy watching you trying to keep them apart. When do you want me to leave?'

'You can wait here until I get back from the Khirgiz.'

'Ah.' Orcadai laughed shortly. 'Let me guess. I'm to escort Zurachina to Pesth.'

'To the escarpment if she wants to travel that far. Your mother as well.'

'You're sure you don't want to make your life a little more complicated?' Orcadai made the enquiry politely. 'Jotan and Nogai on one hand, and both of your wives on the other. What a combination.' He grinned. 'Well, the journey will give my mother something new to complain about. I expect she's been bored lately.'

Burun retrieved a wine flask from the floor.

'Oh.' Orcadai looked surprised. 'Do you want a drink?'

'I thought you'd never ask.' Burun uncorked the flask and drank deeply. 'God, how can you stand this stuff? It's like taking a mouthful of honey.'

Orcadai gestured languidly. 'One gets used to it.' His tone seemed to alter. 'Everything is too sweet here.'

'Oh? And how is the court this month? I have heard some strange tales.'

'What do you expect? Khotan is drunk, when he isn't doped with hashish and, now that Nogai and his brothers are forbidden the Golden Pavilion, your father-in-law is courting everyone.'

'Hunh. I might be a drunk if I had Khotan's reasons. He always feared to inherit the Khanate.' Burun looked sideways. 'So it's to be Vortai Kha-Khan, is it? The name doesn't sit very well on the tongue. And it seems to me that there are better claims.'

'True.' Orcadai nodded. 'There's Kodai. But he's older than Arjun. How long would he reign? And everyone knows that Siban has no desire to sit on the

Dragon Throne. I'm surprised you haven't been approached to give your support.'

'By Vortai?' Burun snorted. 'He knows me better than that.' He drank more wine. 'So the Kha-Khan is really sick?'

'He fails a little more every day. Sometimes he gets better, but the improvement never lasts.'

'So.' Burun studied the wine flask absently, then laid it aside. 'Did you know that Vortai has been ordered to command the base camp on the escarpment during the campaign?'

'Ensuring that he won't be in Kinsai when the Kha-Khan dies,' Orcadai observed. 'How convenient.'

'Yes.'

'The Kha-Khan's order, do you suppose? Or is Siban trying to tell us all something?'

'Well, considering that Siban has been ordered to Kinsai, I think the Kha-Khan might be indicating a preference, don't you?'

'Hunh.' Orcadai was watching Burun shrewdly. 'And is that a preference you intend to follow?'

'God. You're all the same. The Kha-Khan isn't dead yet, so I haven't decided. Why do you think you are still unmarried?'

Orcadai said nothing. He studied the floor between his feet, and Burun guessed that the rumour was true, and he was involved with one of the Khatun's ladies-in-waiting.

'On that subject,' Orcadai spoke finally, 'I would hope to be consulted first.'

Burun grinned. If any of his sons married without his permission, he had the right to have the match annulled. He had married Jotan to the daughter of the Kha-Khan's late second son Buratai. If the opportunity presented itself he intended to marry his other children just as advantageously.

Burun took Suragai with him when he left Kinsai to ride north into the lush grassland of the Khirgiz. He was beginning to find that he enjoyed the big offworlder's company, and it was amazing how many things they had in common.

The Merkut clan was camped along the curve of a small lake, and when he saw the first yurts Burun kicked his st'lyan into a gallop, his spirit soaring with anticipation. Jotan had placed the family yurts in the centre of a clearing, part of a screen of trees which enfolded the northern end of the lake. Men were herding mares and their foals away from the water, and a few women were washing clothes beside the shore. As the riders passed they called out: high-pitched cries which startled the birds that nested in the tree-tops. Burun grinned and waved. The Khirgiz was choice pasture and, in the days before he had made submission to Daijin, the Merkuts had fought with other clans for the grazing rights. Arjun had given Burun the land for all time, and now the Merkuts occupied it in peace and prospered.

There were children and dogs around the wash tubs. The girls who were almost women practised for motherhood by taking care of the toddlers and babies, and along the water's edge whooping small boys rode their young st'lyan through sheets of spray.

Zurachina came out of the largest yurt. She was small and slim, red-haired like her Altun cousins, and her brown eyes sparkled with pleasure. She watched Burun dismount, and when he turned to face her they stood wordlessly. After a moment he took her hands in his.

'Khan. I heard you were in Pesth.'

'I was. I'm going back in three days.'

She laughed. 'And you thought I would enjoy the journey.' She nodded. 'I'll tell Anya to pack.' The offworlder was still mounted. She looked up at him and smiled. 'You must be Suragai. I've heard of you.'

Suragai was bowing from the saddle. 'Your servant, Lady.'

Burun was still holding Zurachina's hands, and she looked back at him. He knew his gaze was avid, and she blushed like a young girl and lowered her eyes.

'Did you miss me?'

'No.' She looked up and smiled, so that his heart gave an absurd bump of joy. 'But if you hadn't come, I'd have died of loneliness.'

Burun laughed. 'Woman. You always say the same thing.'

'Yes,' she agreed. 'And it's always true.'

She walked in front of him into the yurt. It had been recently re-floored, and the polished timber glowed.

'Where is Kiku?' Burun had not meant to ask so soon.

Zurachina picked up a loose cushion. 'In the other yurt.'

'And Jotan?'

'Out inspecting the herds.'

'Hunh.' He turned towards the door, but Zurachina moved in front of him.

'Have you eaten yet?'

'No.' He shook his head. 'I'm not hungry just now. Later.' He took another pace, but she did not move aside.

'I'll have the slaves prepare a feast. The offworlder - will he eat our food? He's much taller than I expected.'

Burun knew she was delaying him deliberately. 'Yes,' he answered patiently. 'He eats our food.' He grinned.

'You will be eating here?' She stressed the last word.

'Yes. But later.' He lifted Zurachina up by the shoulders and set her aside. Then he walked out through the doorway.

The smaller yurt was an ocean of coolness and quiet. Two female slaves were tending a small fire in a brazier in the antechamber, and when Burun entered they veiled themselves. Burun snorted. The floor of the inner room was of light-coloured wood which had been sanded to an unbelievable smoothness. A white rug had been laid in the centre of the floor and Kiku was seated on an ebony stool, her back to the door. She was combing her hair, her face reflected in the mirror sheet of beaten gold. Her eyes met Burun's for a moment and her hand stopped moving. Then she looked away.

Burun knelt behind her and touched her cheek with the back of his hand. She shuddered. He could see that her body was naked beneath the midnight blue silk of her robe and her scent overpowered his senses. Her hand stole up to cover his and gradually she rested herself back against him.

In spite of his desire for Kiku, he spent the first night in Zurachina's yurt. It would have disturbed the harmony of his house to have done otherwise.


'Siban wants me to scout the G'bai, the passes through the mountains, and the plain where the Moistr' River flows to the sea.' Burun took a handful of nuts from a bowl and cracked one open.

Jotan nodded. 'I've seen the old maps. There are a lot of cities.'

'Yes. We will have to siege or storm them. Or maybe we can simply cut them off from one another until they surrender.'

'Maybe. But that would be boring. What do you want me for?'

'I want you to ride east once we cross the G'bai. The land between the Serai Gorge and the southern coast is completely unknown, and I would like to be sure that we aren't going to have any surprises at our backs when we start this war.'

'Hunh. Is that all?'

'Not quite. There may be a way into the Alan country south of the mountains. I don't believe they run all the way to the sea. If there is a coastal plain you're to find it, and in that case we'll meet near that southern coastal city -' Burun gestured, searching his memory for the name, '- Ruysdal.'

'Very well.' Jotan sat back. 'I'm taking Jehan.'

Burun nodded. He had known what Jotan was going to say. 'Zurachina told me. Is there anything I can say to change your mind?'

'Nothing.'

'I won't try, then.' Burun cracked another nut and ate the meat.

'I don't know why you're so set against the idea.' Jotan sounded stubborn. 'According to Jagatan you went to war when you were ten years of age.'

'The Merkuts were fighting for their lives then. I just don't want to lose my grandson, that's all.'

'You won't. How many men are you going to give me for this work?'

'Five hundred from T'zin's fourth tenth. Also you can take Tulagai and Targoutai. Their personal guards will add another two hundred to your strength.'

'I command?'

'Subject to Siban's agreement, yes.'

Jotan made a face. 'I command, or I don't go. I've ridden with that pair before. They need authority.'

Burun thought about arguing, but dismissed the idea. Apart from anything else, he knew Jotan was right.

'I'm taking your mother and Kiku with me to Kinsai. Orcadai will escort them on from there. Are you leaving Arkhina here?'

Jotan shook his head. 'No. I'm sending her to visit her grandfather.' He met Burun's look squarely. 'I thought it might be useful if we knew what was happening at court while we were in the south.'

Burun shrugged and pretended disinterest. 'As you choose.'

He thought about the position which he was being forced to take, and decided that he was unhappy about the whole situation. In the event of the Kha-Khan's death, every Khan and every member of the Altun – even those related by marriage like Jotan – would have a vote in the election of his successor. The absence of a clear candidate was likely to result in a land torn by dispute and, because Arjun had not so far named anyone, it was to men like Burun that the others looked for indication of a preference.

Burun sighed. He had no desire to be a kingmaker.

The fire by which Jotan sat lit only half the clearing and left the rest in shadow. On a sudden instinct Burun looked round and saw that the offworlder Suragai was standing at the water's edge. He seemed to be gazing up at the night sky.

Burun wondered how long the big stranger had been there – not long, surely. Then he wondered if he was capable of putting what he must have heard to some use.

Jotan stirred the fire. 'I suppose you'll keep Nogai with you.' His tone was bland.

Burun compressed his lips. No one knew how the fight between Jotan and Nogai had started and both had the right to refuse to speak against the other except in front of the Kha-Khan. A feud was a private matter.

'Yes,' he said. 'The Kha-Khan wants me to report on his conduct.'

'Oh?' Jotan looked interested.

'I ask you not to fight with him.'

Jotan laughed softly. 'Ask? That's a sweet sound coming out of your mouth, Khan. Did you swallow honey?'

'Please. It's a fight neither of you can win.'

Jotan stirred the fire again. He grinned. 'That depends on what you call winning.'

'Damn you!' Burun was unable to rein in his temper. 'Obey me and stay away from Nogai!'

'Hah!' Jotan laughed aloud. 'I didn't think you could keep up such softness for long. But no, dear father. Saving my duty under the Yasa, that's an order you can't enforce.' He stood up. 'I'll see to Nogai in my own time and I advise you not to interfere.'

In the middle of the night one of Kiku's cats got in among the dogs and, when Burun got up to see what was causing the commotion, he found Suragai trying to save the animal. The cat was white, a Suristani with a prehensile tail, and it hung from the lower branch of one of the trees and slashed at the dogs which were clustered below. Suragai's hands were already scratched and bleeding, and he was cursing quietly in his own tongue as he positioned himself for another rescue attempt.

Burun stood watching for a moment and laughed. It was the nature of dogs to eat cats and he had never been able to see the sense of trying to stop them. Then, as the dogs started baying again, he went back inside the yurt and returned carrying a stockwhip. He shook out the coils, then reached out and clipped a piece from the ear of the largest hound in the pack. The dogs fled.

The cat howled, dropped to the ground, and shot between Suragai's legs and disappeared back inside Kiku's yurt.

Suragai looked after it. His expression was comical and Burun laughed again. Then he stopped.

'I know.' It was easy to read the resentment on the offworlder's face. 'But from where I stand, it's funny.' He inspected the scratches. They were long and deep. 'You'd better have those seen to. Come.'

Suragai followed him into Zurachina's yurt. Burun sent a slave for water and towels. The offworlder looked rueful.

'On my world a cat is a domestic pet,' he observed.

Burun was interested. 'Have your cats claws?'

'Oh, yes. And they scratch sometimes. But they're not so -' The offworlder seemed to search for a word.

'Wild?'

'Yes.'

Burun grimaced. 'Surely you don't expect our animals to be the same as yours?'

Suragai's hesitation was apparent. 'Those that I have seen are of the same basic stock,' he said at last. 'But altered. The animal you ride for instance -'

'St'lyan?'

'Yes. In the Empire they would be called unicorn. But they are -' Suragai used a word Burun did not understand, then corrected himself, '- imaginary. They exist only in stories for children.'

'Hunh. But if they are described in stories, then surely they must have lived once upon a time?'

Suragai looked doubtful. 'Well. No one is really sure. The stories originate from Terra, the birthplace of mankind, or so it is said. But if Terra exists, no one knows where it is.'

Burun tried not to let his scepticism show. 'Oh well. The st'lyan has always existed here.'

164

'Always?'

Burun shrugged and gestured. 'They are mentioned in our history and they are in the old texts. So they lived in the world before we became a people.' He visualised. 'Five thousand summers at least.'

Suragai seemed to inspect his hands. The bleeding had almost stopped. Then he looked up. 'In the Empire it is thought that the history of mankind goes back about five million years.'

Burun digested the implications of the statement. 'Five thousand thousand?' He queried the number.

'Yes. At least that, and probably more. No one knows quite for certain. But there was another Empire, about the time you say your history starts, and before that another, or something like it. Also there were the federations: groups of worlds which banded together and fought one another for supremacy.' The offworlder's eyes were troubled, as if he saw the whole past of his kind moving before him. He looked up. 'Khan, mankind has been in space for a very long time.'

Burun was silent for a moment. The fact that Suragai clearly believed what he was saying did not mean that it was true.

'You mentioned old texts,' Suragai said. 'Do they contain nothing of this? What do they say?'

Burun stared at him. 'Am I Sechem? The old texts describe the science of a time past, before we became a people. They describe our world, and speak of other worlds beyond. They are knowledge.'

The offworlder looked as if he failed to comprehend the distinction between science and history.

A slave brought hot water in a bowl. Burun started to clean the cuts on Suragai's hands. He was amazed that the wounds were still open, and that although they had ceased to bleed, they had not healed themselves.

'These will scar.'

The offworlder grinned. 'I will know better next time.'

Burun realised that the observation had been taken at face value. He flexed his hand and stroked a talon across his own forearm. Blood welled.

Suragai looked startled, then puzzled. 'Khan, why -' Suddenly he seemed to realise that the cut on Burun's arm had ceased to bleed.

Burun extended his arm for inspection. 'This will not scar.' Already the lips of the wound were drawing together.

'Does that happen every time you are injured?' Suragai appeared to be fascinated.

'To a great extent. Broken bones must be set quickly and they are weak for a time. Deep wounds must be stitched together to help the healing process and they tend to leave scars. But it is the same for everyone on this world - even for the races that have no talons.'

'And you don't get sick,' Suragai said slowly. 'I didn't understand.'

Burun nodded significantly. 'We heal differently, you and I.'

'Yes.' Suragai's expression was thoughtful. 'So we do.'

Now that the cuts on the offworlder's hands were clean and dry, Burun saw that they were not as bad as he had thought. It had been the amount of blood flowing which had made him think that they were worse. He thought about what Suragai had been saying about the origins of mankind.

'The animals on this world and on others are of common stock, you say. Surely you don't now contend that your race and mine have also a common ancestor?'

Suragai was hesitating, and Burun saw that he was trying to choose his words to avoid giving offence. He smiled softly.

'Khan, there are records which show that this world was resettled during the Second Empire, over five thousand years ago. The races without talons are similar to the inhabitants of other worlds in many respects. The C'zak language, for example, is the same in essence as the Anglic which is spoken throughout the Imperium.'

Burun weighed the argument. 'What you say may be true. Perhaps the other races on this world are the descendants of the people of this one-time Empire. But how about the Yek, the N'pani, the Ch'noze?'

The offworlder shifted as if in embarrassment. At last he responded. 'The scientists of the Empire who were responsible for examining your world from space concluded that some of the races had been altered, either deliberately or as a result of the radiation which poisoned every continent.' He looked up and met Burun's eyes. 'But of course it is possible that they were wrong.'

'Hunh.' Burun nodded. He did not think that the True People were the result of some genetic accident. More probably they were the original inhabitants of the planet, and had evolved until they were superior to the interlopers. Much of what Suragai had said suggested that all the races had been around for far longer than recorded history, but that was a possibility which had always been accepted. Only a fool assumed that the knowledge which was in his possession was the fullest extent of a man's ability to know.

Suragai was obviously relieved by Burun's reaction. Apparently he had expected that his explanation would be taken as an insult. Burun decided to mention the conversation to the Sechem at a suitable opportunity.

167

*

'Am I to be dragged halfway across the country in a cart?'

Kiku's expression was frigid, and Burun laughed. 'Tied hand and foot if you argue about it,' he agreed. 'I thought you were bored with the Khirgiz.'

She made a face and turned away. She was kneeling in front of a case of fine linen which Burun had brought for her from Kinsai. Her head was at the level of his thigh, and he laid a hand on her shoulder. Against the smoothness of her skin his hand seemed rough.

'Don't,' she said. 'You hurt me.'

Burun snorted.

He went out into the antechamber and sat with C'zinsit. The boy was eight, and still supposedly in the care of a nurse. He was dark like Burun, but his eyes held the remembrance of Kiku.

'Are you going away again?' C'zinsit asked.

Burun nodded. 'Yes. The Kha-Khan has work for me. Will you miss me?'

C'zinsit thought about the question. 'Yes,' he said after a moment. 'But you'll come back, won't you?'

'Oh, yes.'

'That's all right then.' C'zinsit had a length of string formed into a loop and he was playing a complex game with it. 'Have you seen this?' he asked Burun.

Burun looked. 'Yes.' Then he looked again. The cat's cradle had elongated so that it looked like a cone. 'No. I haven't seen that one before. How is it done?'

C'zinsit demonstrated. 'You're taking Jotan with you.' His eyes were on the string. 'And mother.'

'Yes. And you will be Khan while I am gone, and the people will come to you for justice.' Burun watched his son's face.

'Oh.' The cone collapsed. 'What you mean is that my uncle will tell me what to say.'

Burun grinned. 'That's right. Don't you like Jagatan?'

'Of course. He tells me stories.'

Burun nodded. 'I expect they're the same ones he used to tell me.'

'But -' C'zinsit paused as if he was unsure how to continue.

'Yes?'

'If I do what Jagatan says all the time, how can I be the true Khan?'

'Well you could do something else,' Burun said mildly. 'But if you made a bad decision, or gave the wrong judgement against someone in a dispute, then some of your people might suffer.'

'Hunh.' C'zinsit made a face. 'I hadn't thought of that. It's not easy being a Khan.'

'No. It's a great responsibility.' Burun smiled. 'But I think you're equal to it.'

Kiku came out of the inner chamber. 'Take me riding,' she said.

C'zinsit sat up very straight. 'Me too?' he appealed.

Burun looked over C'zinsit's head at Kiku, and she laughed at his expression. He wanted to be alone with her, to anticipate the night to come, and he guessed that she was teasing him.

'Very well.' He nodded.

C'zinsit whooped and dashed outside. Kiku's eyes were bright with mischief.

'Wait for me, Khan, while I change.' She shrugged her gown away from her shoulders. It fell to the floor at her feet.

Burun felt the heat rising through his body. Kiku was naked. She looked challengingly at him, then walked through the hangings out of his sight. He clenched and unclenched his hands, and took a long deep breath. Then he went outside to wait. The night was hours away.

Suragai was riding along the lake shore. He was schooling a new st'lyan that Burun had given him. When he saw Burun outside the yurt he guided the mare across.

'How does she handle?' Burun inspected the mare.

'Quite well, Khan.' Suragai made a clicking sound with his tongue against the soft palate of his mouth and the st'lyan backed up four or five paces. Then she snorted and dipped her head.

Burun laughed. He noticed that Suragai had not used his hands at all during the manoeuvre. 'Good. You ride like a Yek.'

'Oh well.' Suragai grinned. 'I've been practising. It seems to me that I might have my hands busy during a fight, so I've taught this one to answer to sounds, and to react to the pressure of my thighs.'

Burun nodded approvingly. 'Yes. Good.' He remembered that Suragai had said that on most worlds men did not ride, and he wondered how they managed.

C'zinsit hurled himself into the saddle and charged away. Burun nodded to a mounted trooper who galloped after the boy, guarding him like a mother hen with a chick. C'zinsit bounced out of the saddle, touched the ground with his feet, then vaulted up on to the mare's back again. He balanced with both feet on the st'lyan's withers, and Suragai stared.

'Do all Yek children ride like that?'

Burun grinned. 'No. Only the Merkuts.'

Osep brought up the piebald that Burun used for riding when he was with the clan, and Burun mounted. Kiku's st'lyan was a light golden tan and it had a pure white mane and tail. It sidestepped nervously, reared, and the slave leading it let go of the rein. Burun cursed.

'Catch that devil-damned rein!'

Already the mare was trotting past the yurt, heading for the plain beyond the trees. Half a dozen men started forward to obey Burun's shouted command, but then Kiku came out of the yurt door. She ran in front of the animal and caught at the bridle. The st'lyan tossed her head, and then quietened.

Burun guessed that Kiku had been no more than a hair's-breadth away from being impaled on the st'lyan's gilden horn. He discovered that he was holding his breath, and gulped for air. If she had been hurt, he would have had the slave bastinadoed. If she had been killed, he would personally have roasted the man over a slow fire. Kiku laughed. She was unveiled, and all the men were watching her, their thoughts plain upon their faces. The offworlder Suragai got down off his animal to help her mount, and she thanked him prettily. Then she looked across at Burun, smiled brilliantly, and lashed the st'lyan across the barrel so that it charged away through the trees and out on to the plain. Burun rode after her.

The grass was lush green and came up to the st'lyan's hocks. C'zinsit was far ahead, wheeling in wide circles which brought him every so often closer to Kiku as she now rode sedately towards the hills. The trooper in attendance kept pace, but his head was mostly turned away from his charge while he studied the occasional stands of trees or searched the land-scape for hidden folds from which an ambush might be mounted.

Burun thought that the precaution was probably unnecessary, but he approved the sentiment which resulted in its instigation. There were no enemies and only a few night-time predators on the steppe; however he was pleased to note that elementary security was not being neglected. He kicked his st'lyan into a trot and rode to catch up with Kiku.

Jagatan's yurt was set well away from the others of the clan. It commanded a rise in the ground on the eastern side of the lake, and Burun grinned at the preoccupation with strategy which appeared to have determined its position. There was a female slave working outside, but when Burun rode up she did not even raise her head. Jagatan was lying on a couch under the awning at the door. He was stripped to the waist and the scars on his chest were like a map of the battles in which he had fought.

Burun decided that his uncle was only a little drunk. There was a minstrel sitting on a stool by the yurt wall. He was singing the Ballad of the Dragon, and Burun waited until he had finished the stanza before he spoke.

'Well, uncle.'

Jagatan raised his head. 'Oh. It's you. You took your time coming to see me.'

'I did have other priorities.' Burun's reply was mild.

'Hunh. Women and children.'

'Yes. Well, I was away almost a year. And I had only a day here before I received the Kha-Khan's summons.'

'I lose track of the time.'

Burun grinned at the lie. Jagatan liked to pretend that his faculties were failing. In fact he was as sharp as a man half his age. The minstrel got up quietly and went inside. Then he started to sing again.

> '– And sank into the water's depth,
> Enfolded in his scales
> The maiden lay –
> And fast did hold in slumber safe,
> Until the dawn of time,
> And True Men came.'

172

Burun made a face, but either Jagatan failed to notice or he did not care.

'How was Ch'nozia?' Jagatan asked finally.

Burun shrugged. 'Different.'

'Oh, well. You always liked new places. But now you are returned?'

'For a short time only. There will be a war against the Alan next year. I am charged with the reconnaissance.'

Jagatan spat. 'They use you like a pack beast.' His tone was angry, almost querulous. 'How many summers have you spent with the clan since you were old enough to fight their battles?'

'Oh. Few enough.'

'And always they place you in the forefront. If they intend your death -'

Burun was alarmed to see that his uncle was becoming agitated.

'Why should they want that? I am the Kha-Khan's trusted servant, and he has given me everything I ever asked of him: this land in perpetuity, peace and security for our clan forever.'

'The land was ours by right.' Jagatan raised himself on one elbow, and Burun guessed that he had been drinking for most of the afternoon. 'I remember when we rode here, your father and I. Young and strong we were. And now -' Jagatan sank back on the couch. There were tears on his cheeks.

'I know. I know.' Burun spoke soothingly. He did not know how to react to Jagatan's distress. As a youth he had mourned his father, of course. But the memory of the man in his prime was not constantly in the forefront of his mind, and it did not cause the pain and unhappiness Jagatan always seemed to feel. The Yek had killed his father in an ambush, but he did not hate them, and had never wondered why.

Jagatan poured k'miss from a jug. He drank unsteadily. He was the elder brother of Burun's father, the son of a concubine, never acknowledged as heir. His hair had been white for as long as Burun could remember, but this was the first time his age had seemed to affect his behaviour.

'The flower of the Merkuts -' Jagatan's voice was a mumble, 'all gone. All the young men.' He wept and Burun laid a hand on his shoulder.

'I know. But we are Yek now.'

Inside the yurt the minstrel was still singing. The ballad was ancient, the kind of thing that only an old man would enjoy. It recounted the fable of the emergence of the One People from the eggs of a mythical golden dragon.

> '- All armour'd in the dragon's scales
> The young men bravely fought
> That break of day -
> And as they fell upon that field,
> Their dragon time began
> In golden flame.'

Burun went round to the side of the yurt and called the female slave he had seen working there. Together they supported Jagatan inside the yurt. The minstrel stopped singing abruptly, and went outside. Burun sneered. Jagatan seemed to be asleep.

'How often is he like this?'

The woman was middle-aged, a Keraistani. She pulled a quilt up over Jagatan's shoulders, then looked up.

'Once or twice a month,' she said finally.

'Does he get sick?'

'Sometimes. And he sees things - old battles and

people he once knew. He talks to your father.'

'Who looks after him?'

'I do.' The woman's eyes were bold, and Burun wondered if she also shared Jagatan's bed.

'Very well. Don't let him drink any more.'

'Hah.' She made a face. 'He'll beat me.'

'Tell him it's my order. Now go and make him something to eat. I'll sit with him.'

She went out. Burun sat down on a pile of cushions on the floor, and settled himself to wait. He thought that probably it would be the evening before Jagatan woke, but he needed to discuss certain matters with him before he left for Kinsai.

Because Turakina's private time had coincided with Burun's return, he had spoken to his daughter only briefly. Jotan's sister was eighteen, and Burun was constantly aware that he would have to find her a husband before the year was out, otherwise she would be entitled to go with any man she chose.

It was not that she was unattractive, or that there had not been offers for her. Turakina was nearly as tall as Burun, and she had inherited her mother's Altun colouring. Enough young men came to pay their respects, Burun was aware. But few of them were of good family or had prospects which were worthy of consideration. In any case Burun thought that there was a wild streak in his daughter's nature, and he suspected that only a mature man would be able to manage her. All the eligible mature men were married already, and it would not be fitting to contract her in a match where she was not the senior wife.

They were heading south-west along the road to Kinsai. The red ball of the late afternoon sun was low on the horizon. Both Kiku and Turakina had insisted on riding and, as they galloped along the borders of the cornfields which supplied the Kha-Khan's granaries, Turakina's unbound hair streamed out behind her so that her whole head appeared to be on fire. A wild pig started from a patch of undergrowth at the side of the road, and she whooped and rode in pursuit.

Kiku reined in beside Burun. 'She is unwomanly, that one,' she observed primly.

Burun chuckled. He had seen Kiku riding flat out along tracks where no sane man would take an animal faster than a trot - but only when she thought no one was watching.

'Hah!' He watched as Turakina caught up with the pig and rode over it. It squealed and dashed unhurt into the corn, and she trotted her st'lyan back up the road again, laughing.

Kiku adjusted her veil and rode sedately back towards Zurachina's cart. The offworlder Suragai was riding at the cart-tail and he made way and then urged his mount forward to join Burun. Turakina drew level and Suragai bowed.

'Lady.' The greeting was polite, almost formal.

Turakina ignored him. She looked at Burun. 'How much further is it to Kinsai?'

'Oh, a day's march or so,' Burun exaggerated, teasing her. 'What, are you bored already? Go sit with your mother.'

'Huh.' She tossed her head. 'Who wants to sit with women, talking women's things? Come and race with me.'

'Oh, no.' Burun shook his head. 'Not I. Race with Suragai, if you must.'

Turakina behaved as if she was seeing the offworlder for the first time. 'Can he ride that well?' Her tone was supercilious.

'Ask me, Lady.' Suragai's response was barely audible. He looked at Burun, and Burun grinned.

Turakina wrinkled her nose as if she was smelling bad meat. Her stare was openly insulting, and Burun waited to see how Suragai would react.

'Or can you only win races against men of your own family?' the offworlder finished.

Burun choked on a laugh. Turakina flushed crimson. She lashed out with her riding whip, but Burun caught the thongs.

'You asked for that,' he told her. 'Now apologise and behave, or go and ride with your mother.'

Angrily Turakina jerked her mare's head round. She galloped away towards the rear of the convoy of carts and attendants. Burun looked after her, then sighed.

'I apologise for her.' He did not know whether to be amused or angry.

Suragai shrugged. 'With respect, Khan,' he gestured dismissively, 'your daughter is no different from young women on other worlds I have visited. And no doubt she thinks me strange beyond belief. I am too tall, not handsome by this world's standards, and I don't know how to pay the pretty compliments a young woman expects. Perhaps you ought to introduce her to my son. They might get on well. He doesn't like me much either.'

Burun sniffed. He had left Suragai's son in Kinsai with Orcadai. From the outset he had decided that he did not much care for the tall fair youth who seemed to look down his long nose at everything. Alexai fitted in well enough in military surroundings, and it was apparent that he was used to that kind of ceremonial which was commonplace in the capital. However, he maintained an obvious disdain for the customs of the True People which irked Burun.

Burun thought about what Suragai had said, and finally he grinned. Now that he considered it, Turakina's expression when she stared at the offworlder was exactly like the one Alexai used when he was looking at Burun.

'I will see you in Pesth.' Burun looked past Zurachina, out into the courtyard. He hated goodbyes, and now that the women had been safely delivered into Orcadai's hands, he was urgent to be away.

'Ten days, or perhaps twelve,' Zurachina said. 'Will you be able to bear it?'

The sarcasm in her tone made Burun look back quickly, and she laughed.

'Oh, you.' He hugged her, and she nestled against his chest.

Kiku was standing beside the open window. She was pretending to look at the people who were passing in the street, but Burun was not deceived.

'Don't stare at her like that,' Zurachina whispered. 'It makes her proud.'

'Hush.' Burun buried his face in her red hair. 'You mustn't criticise her. She's not like us.'

Zurachina made a rude noise and Kiku turned.

'Don't ride while you are travelling to Pesth.' Burun addressed Kiku. 'Or if you must, have Orcadai guard you. The Ch'noze are raiding further east than usual this year.'

Kiku made a face. 'Orcadai will be too busy. And he doesn't let me ride where I want.'

'Then you will have to stay in the cart.'

'Huh.' She looked unimpressed. 'Will there be no other guards? Assign one to ride with me.'

Burun's mouth twitched. 'And who would guard the guard? They're only men, after all.'

'Oh, well.' Kiku's sigh was exaggerated. 'Of course I am only the humble second wife. I obey your command.'

Burun spluttered, while Zurachina laughed. Kiku

had never behaved humbly in her life.

'Give me the offworlder,' Kiku said suddenly. 'You can leave him behind for a few days.'

Burun stopped smiling and looked at her sharply. He had seen nothing pass between Suragai and any woman, but now he wondered if there was something he had missed.

'Well?' Kiku's face was set and determined, and as Burun tried to read her expression she turned away from him as if in dismissal. He swallowed, and went out into the courtyard.

Suragai was standing beside the gate into the street. He was talking to Jotan and a group of orderlies. Jotan said something and everyone laughed. Burun's stomach tightened. He thought about the offworlder and Kiku together.

Jotan turned. 'Have you finished your farewells? Let's ride.'

'When I am ready.' Burun stared at Suragai, fighting to conceal his feelings. The offworlder seemed to sense that something was wrong.

'Khan. Have I given offence?'

Burun looked at him hard, but the man did not flinch.

'Khan?' He repeated the query.

Burun relaxed a little. 'Do you want a woman, Suragai?'

The offworlder looked surprised. 'I made my feelings on that subject clear, Khan.'

'I didn't ask you about a wife.' Burun watched Suragai's face. 'You are a normal man. Do you want a woman?'

Suragai looked embarrassed. 'Sometimes.' He nodded. 'I'm normal enough.'

'And if I gave you one, would you take her?'

'No, Lord.' Suragai shook his head. 'It's much too soon.'

Burun stood undecided. Jotan was watching him curiously. One of the orderlies said, 'As long as you're giving away women, Khan –'

'Be quiet.' Burun silenced him. 'Suragai, come with me.'

He was sure that he would know the truth when he saw them together. He led Suragai into the house. Kiku was standing beside the window again. She turned, and when she saw the offworlder, she smiled.

Suragai bowed to her. 'Lady.'

Burun could tell that he was puzzled. Kiku was smiling again, but at him, not at the offworlder.

'Thank you, Khan,' she said.

A pulse in Burun's neck jumped, and he turned away. He was afraid that his emotions were too plain on his face. Silence hung on the air, and when he turned back he saw that Suragai was still watching as if he did not understand what had occurred. Burun took a breath, and tried a smile.

'Suragai, I want you to remain behind. Travel with my younger son tomorrow, and when my wife wishes to ride, guard her. I entrust her safety to you.'

'Lord.' The offworlder bowed. Burun nodded dismissal, and Suragai left the room.

Kiku picked up one of her cats. Her face was inscrutable. Zurachina was in the next room; Burun could hear her ordering the slaves to unpack the boxes of bed linen. He crossed the room and took the cat out of Kiku's hands.

'I am sorry,' he said. 'I cannot help what I am. Jealousy is in my nature.'

Kiku shook her head. Her eyes were closed. She moved against him and, when Burun touched her, he found that she was trembling.

There were signs of intense military preparation all

the way into Pesth. Herds of st'lyan remounts grazed the meadows above the city, and the forges were busy with repairs to weapons and mail.

Tulagai met Burun at the gates. He looked as if he had been waiting for some time.

'Where have you been?' He reined across so that Burun was forced to stop. 'We expected you days ago. Didn't you come straight back from Kinsai? What were you doing? Arghatun won't arrange the remount herds without your authority, and Wotai backs him up in everything. Nogai's fighting with T'zin, and we've been left to see to all the training and armouring, Targoutai and I.'

'So?' Burun raised an eyebrow. 'That's what you were ordered to do.'

'But you don't understand!' Tulagai reached across and seized Burun's reins. 'Listen, damn you -'

Burun kicked his mare hard; she reared and lashed out. Tulagai fell out of his saddle and someone behind Burun laughed.

'Just because we don't faint or react the way you want doesn't mean we haven't taken in everything you have said.' Burun spat. 'Now get out of my way, or I'll ride over you. There will be an officer's kuriltai at my house tonight. Sunset. Tell your brothers, and make sure they attend.' He rode on.

Nogai's house was deserted. The empty rooms echoed and there was an air of desolation about the whole place. Burun had sent Jotan on to the camp. Now he felt a gnawing feeling of apprehension in case Nogai was already there.

A clatter of hooves sounded in the yard, then three of the offworlders came into the house. The one who did not look human was in front. When he saw Burun, he bowed. 'Khan.' His tone was polite.

Burun remembered that the man's name was Yuan,

181

and that he had been staying with Nogai. He nodded curtly. Suragai had said that the race was called the Manchu and that this man was a good officer and an expert swordsman.

'I'm looking for Nogai Noyon,' Burun said. 'Do you know where he is?'

The Manchu made an odd hand gesture. 'I'm sorry, Lord. I have not seen him since this morning.'

Burun found it uncomfortable to talk to someone who was incapable of understandable facial expression. He could not interpret the hand gestures and did not know what the offworlder was thinking.

'He's not at the camp?'

'No, Lord.'

'Hunh.' Burun was relieved. He wanted a chance to talk to Nogai before Jotan caught up with him.

All three of the offworlders were dressed Yek style in tunics and loose trousers tucked into the tops of calf-high boots. The Manchu also wore a flowing cloak, and his hair had been dressed in a style which was similar to that normally adopted by the Altun. Part of the head had been shaved, however, and, instead of being fanned out across the top of the scalp, the end of the queue was simply looped over upon itself and tied. In addition to his d'jaga, Yuan was carrying a sword. Burun was amazed to see that the hilt of the weapon was almost entirely unguarded and that it was long enough to permit a double-handed grip. The Manchu's two companions were the men whom Suragai had described as non-commissioned officers. Their clothing and equipment was more functional, but they carried the same pattern of long sword.

'Who made these?' Burun asked. 'I have not seen their like before.'

'Oh. I did, Lord.' The Manchu bowed. 'May I show you?'

He extracted the sword complete with scabbard from his sash, and presented it. Burun attempted to draw the blade, but there was some kind of locking device at the hilt. Yuan had to show him how it was released.

'On my world we call this the *jusei*, Lord. The great sword.' The offworlder watched as Burun slid the gleaming blade out of its sheath. 'It is made by a special process. The metals are folded together many times before tempering. See, it has no proper point, and it is sharpened along one edge only. It is a cutting weapon.'

Burun was extending a finger to test the edge, but Yuan stopped him.

'No, Lord. Not like that. It is sharper than you think.' The offworlder pulled a hair from his queue. 'Permit me.' He brushed the single strand across the edge of the blade. It parted, and the severed end drifted to the floor.

'Hunh.' Burun was impressed. 'How do you fight?'

The Manchu seemed to hesitate. 'Lord, I cannot demonstrate well here, but I will try. Please stand over against the wall. You will be safe there.'

Burun raised an eyebrow. He did not think that swordplay was very dangerous, even when practised indoors. Yuan was saying something in his own tongue to one of his companions, the man Mubarak, who had been renamed Barakai. The fellow backed off into the centre of the room. Then he bowed.

The Manchu had replaced his sword in his sash. He stripped off his cloak. Now both men bowed together, then unsheathed. The action was curiously graceful, a two-handed movement which caused both blades to flash in the light as they revolved and reversed. Both were holding their swords double-handed, one hand above the other on the hilt, arms extended stiffly to

183

the front so that the sword blade in each case projected up and forward, cutting edge out. They seemed to bend at the knee, setting their feet apart so that they could never be off balance when they moved. Suddenly the man called Barakai gave a shout, then charged. He leapt forward and slashed at Yuan's neck, a circular cut which would have beheaded the Manchu if it had connected. Burun flinched instinctively. Then he saw Yuan duck and move aside, apparently without effort. The swords clashed once in a parry, and then both of the offworlders were circling one another cautiously.

It was clear that the Manchu was permitting his opponent to initiate all the attacking moves and, as the combat progressed, Burun began to appreciate the skill with which the mock battle was being controlled. Several times he witnessed strokes which would have killed or maimed if they had been allowed to connect with flesh and bone. He guessed that the two had fought together many times before. Barakai commenced a fury of strokes which seemed to beat down the Manchu's blade. The smaller man was retreating and it seemed that his guard was weakening. Burun clenched his fists and bit his tongue to stop himself from shouting out. Yuan seemed to turn his opponent's mightiest cut aside at only the very last moment. Then he began to advance. Clearly he was the stronger fighter now. He was striking left and right with unbelievable speed. With every stroke he shouted 'Hai!' Barakai was reeling backwards. He fell, and the Manchu's final stroke seemed to descend with unstoppable fury. Then Yuan froze. The cutting edge of his sword was a hair's-breadth from Barakai's forehead.

Burun held his breath. He had forgotten that he was watching an exhibition.

Yuan stepped back. He raised his sword two-handed so that the hilt was level with his face, then he sheathed the blade and bowed. Barakai got to his feet and bowed also. Then both men bowed to Burun.

'Name of God.' Burun could not keep the respect from his tone. 'Do all your people fight like that?'

He was not certain, but the Manchu seemed amused.

'No, Lord. Even on my own world there are only a few who earn the title of *sei-sen* - sword bearer. Those of us who now serve the Kha-Khan have practised together many times.'

'Suragai and his son also?'

'Yes, Lord.'

'And who is the best fighter?'

'Oh, I am, Lord.' The answer was given with perfect sincerity. 'Suragai is almost as good.' Yuan made another odd hand gesture. 'But I was born to the sword.'

The kuriltai at Burun's house began with a noisy argument between Tulagai and Jotan. Jotan had already countermanded a number of orders given with regard to the arming of the troopers who were to ride on his portion of the reconnaissance. Now he was criticising the discipline of the men of Tulagai's personal guard: a force of about a hundred men which was maintained by every one of the Kha-Khan's grandsons.

'Guard?' Jotan was shouting as Burun entered the room. 'A handful of Merkut children armed with stones could see them off, Tulagai.'

Tulagai was flushed and it was apparent that Jotan had been baiting him for some time. He started forward, but he was restrained by Hodai and Targoutai.

'Everyone knows that Merkut children are dangerous.' It was Nogai who spoke. He was flanked by

185

T'zin and Alexai. Yuan was sitting quietly behind him. Burun wondered what the Manchu would tell Suragai when he saw him.

Jotan looked up quickly when Nogai spoke, but he said nothing.

'Settle down, all of you.' Burun growled at them. 'I don't propose to spend all night on this, so if you can't behave, you can get out. There's a caravan leaving for Kinsai in the morning, and anyone who displeases me will be on it.'

Nogai looked amused. 'Can you do that, Khan? I think you're bluffing.'

Burun looked across the room. Then he grinned. 'Try me and see, Nogai. You're the last person who can afford to make that journey.'

Nogai tried to pretend that the threat was of no consequence, but he did not interrupt again. Burun waved his arms for quiet.

'With the exception of Orcadai, Suragai and Yoruba the Y'frike, you are the complete assembly of those who will officer the reconnaissance of the Alan country. I will command the main body and Jotan will be responsible for that part of the force which will travel west once we have crossed the G'bai.'

'The easy ride,' Tulagai jeered.

'Then you should be happy.' Burun looked at him. 'You and Targoutai travel under Jotan's command.'

At once Targoutai and Tulagai started to protest. Burun waved them down.

'Tulagai, if you don't want to go you can always stay here and run caravans of supplies down to the escarp-ment camp. No? Then I assume that you withdraw your objection. Everyone else comes with me. Once we are through the mountains and out on to the plain of the Moistr' River we may split into smaller groups, but I will decide who will be given individual commands when that arises.'

'What about remounts, Khan?' Arghatun stood up. 'I've been holding them for your decision.'

'Every man will need a string of four,' Burun said. 'What is the condition of the herds?'

Wotai was sitting at Arghatun's side. He made a face. 'Name of God, Khan. An animal we would kill for meat would look better than some of them.'

Arghatun nodded. 'That's right. Some of them are good enough, but most are returns from the tumans patrolling Ch'nozia. They've been ridden hard. I've seen splints and saddle sores that would make you blench, and you can pull the coat off some of them with your bare hands.'

Burun was perturbed. The ride across the G'bai was going to require st'lyan in the peak of condition. Since no one knew what they were likely to encounter once they entered the Alan country, the extra remounts were an absolute necessity.

'Are there none elsewhere?'

Arghatun shrugged. 'Well. There are herds belonging to your father-in-law. He has nearly twenty thousand grazing the land between here and Pantai.'

'And how many do we need?'

'Oh. A tenth of that, Khan. No more.'

Burun kept his face expressionless, but he was laughing inside. 'Very well. Commandeer from him what you require. If he protests, tell him to appeal the matter to the Kha-Khan.'

Vortai would scream bloody murder when he heard that his herds were being culled. The fact that he could do nothing about it made Burun's enjoyment of the situation all the sweeter.

'How are we to feed our animals when we are crossing the G'bai?' Targoutai asked. 'There's no grazing, and no water.'

Burun was pleased that someone had asked an intelligent question. 'We grain them. Rest up by day and travel by night. Five or six days' march if we are lucky.'

'Grain.' Sidacai was lounging in a corner. 'That means pack beasts.'

Burun glanced in his direction. Sidacai and the remaining Altun who were to ride with the command had arrived several days earlier, but since his return he had spoken to none of them.

'Yes.'

'What about the return journey?' Sodai piped up. 'If we try to re-cross the desert without water and provisions for the st'lyan, we'll end up walking.'

'Oh, well.' Burun grinned. 'I thought I would leave a few of you on the G'bai side of the mountains with the pack beasts. You can set up an intermediate camp, then bring more supplies across by caravan. Since you brought the subject up, maybe you'd like the responsibility?'

Sodai sat down quickly. There were jeers and catcalls.

Nogai chuckled. 'God, Merkut. I can see you're going to have us all counting grain sacks like traders. Is this an army or a commissariat? Surely there is another way we can do this?'

'What do you suggest?' Burun did not expect a serious answer.

'We could go down the coast from Losan,' Tulagai said. 'There's desert to cross, but it's nothing like the G'bai.'

'Don't be stupid,' Sidacai sneered. 'The land is poisoned for a day's march in every direction.'

'Not to mention the fact that the only mountain pass is probably well guarded,' Burun commented. 'No. We have to cross the G'bai where it's safe for us to do so, and where we'll be least expected. That means we have to set up supply stations, even for the reconnaissance. We might as well get used to the idea. It's going to be a hundred times worse next year when we have to move the whole army.'

'You made them think.' Arghatun poured wine.

Burun nodded. 'Yes.' Until the kuriltai most of the Altun had entertained no notion of the problems presented by the campaign. To the majority of them the Alan country was just another part of the continent. They failed to appreciate the fact that the G'bai turned it into an island.

'Why can't we avoid the G'bai?' Arghatun asked. 'We took Y'frike by sea.'

'We landed unopposed,' Burun pointed out. 'Five tumans by sea from X'nadu, with remounts.'

'God, yes.' Arghatun laughed reminiscently. 'I was sick the whole way.'

'But once we landed, we had grazing in plenty.' Burun reached out and took a cup. 'It was just another campaign. But this time will be different. We're fighting cities. We don't know the country. And the Alan use firearms.'

'Even so -' Arghatun started.

'No.' Burun shook his head. 'Besides, the Alan trade with Ch'kasia. They would scarcely need spies to discover that we were preparing the kind of fleet we would need to land an army across the Inner Sea. They would be waiting for us.'

Sidacai came quickly into the room and Burun looked up.

'Nogai and Jotan are fighting in the stables,' Sidacai said.

Burun leapt to his feet and charged out of the door. Sidacai and Arghatun were close behind him as he descended the stairs. The stables were at the back of a courtyard and there was a crowd outside the door. Tulagai and Targoutai were holding everyone back so that they could not push inside.

'Get out of my way, damn you!' Burun forced his way through the press, using his elbows.

The interior of the stable was lit by lanterns which hung from the rafters above the central passage. T'zin was standing at the far end, and Jotan and Nogai were circling one another in the wide space of one of the loose boxes. They had pitchforks.

'Come on, Merkut,' Nogai invited. 'You want me - come and get me.' He slid quickly aside as Jotan charged, and the bright steel tines of his fork flashed.

Somewhere outside Burun heard the high-pitched cry of a boy, and knew that it was Jehan. He turned to Sidacai.

'My grandson. Keep him out of here.'

Sidacai nodded, and pushed back through the crowd.

Jotan's tunic was hanging in tatters, but he did not seem to be badly injured.

'Come on, Jotan,' Nogai urged. 'You can do better than that.' He backed away as Jotan moved forward again, missed his footing on the straw, and stumbled. Jotan's fork flashed twice.

'Yes.' He laughed harshly. 'So I can.'

There was bright blood running down Nogai's left arm as he rolled out of the way and, when he scrambled to his feet again, his expression was less confident. Burun sensed a movement at his back and turned. Yuan had worked his way through the crowd and now he ducked under Tulagai's arm.

'Lord,' he said. 'We can stop this.'

Targoutai snorted. 'And get ourselves spitted in the process. Let them fight. We can stop it before they kill one another.'

Nogai backed out into the passage. He spat over his shoulder. 'Come and try,' he said.

Yuan ignored them both. His eyes were steady on Burun's face. 'Lord?'

Burun shook his head. It was time for Jotan to learn. 'No. Not yet.'

In the passageway Nogai seemed to stumble again and Jotan leapt forward. But the move was a feint. Nogai rested on one knee and brought his fork up so that Jotan almost ran on to it. When he moved back there was blood running down his chest and soaking into the waistband of his trousers.

'They're playing,' Tulagai observed. 'They're trying to cut each other to ribbons. Look at the blood.'

'God. I suppose we'd better stop it,' Targoutai said. He sounded reluctant.

'Try.' Jotan darted forward, slashed at Nogai, and backed away. Nogai went after him.

Jotan stepped round the side of a loose-box door and swung it hard. The wooden end caught Nogai in the face, and he pitched over backwards. At once Burun nodded to the Manchu. 'Now,' he said.

The offworlder seemed hardly to move. A black metal ball flew from his right hand. It caught Jotan on the forehead and he collapsed without a sound. The ball was attached to a length of thin chain; the Manchu reeled it in, then tossed it idly in his palm. There was a sudden silence. Then Targoutai laughed.

'Surprise,' he said.

T'zin was kneeling beside Nogai. He looked up. 'Out cold,' he reported.

Jotan was in a similar condition.

'They'll have to be bandaged,' Tulagai said. 'Some of the wounds are deep.'

'Yes.' Burun nodded. 'Use horse blankets to carry them.' He nodded to the Manchu. 'Thank you.'

The Manchu bowed. Targoutai was examining the metal ball and its attached length of chain. 'Clever,' he said. 'Very clever.'

Arghatun and Tulagai carried Jotan back to the house. T'zin stood by as two officers rolled Nogai in a blanket so that he could be taken down the street.

'They'll kill each other next time.' He glared at Burun.

'If we let them,' Burun agreed. He looked around. 'Where's my grandson?'

'He ran into the house,' Sidacai said. 'When they brought Jotan out, he thought he was dead.'

Burun cursed. 'Damn it. Couldn't you have kept him out of the way?' He went across the yard and the trooper guarding the door saluted. 'Which way did my grandson go?'

'Upstairs, Lord.'

Burun ran up the stairs and started to search the rooms. He called Jehan's name, but there was no answer. Then he looked up. Jehan was sitting among the rafters.

'Jehan, come down.' Burun gestured.

Jotan's son was a copy in miniature of his father. His face was white and his lips were trembling. 'My father's dead!' he accused. 'You let them kill him!'

Burun shook his head. 'He's alive, Jehan, I promise. Come down.'

Jehan slid off the rafter and jumped into Burun's arms. 'He's dead,' he said. 'I saw him.'

Burun hugged him. 'No. Nogai made him bleed a little, that's all. Then he got knocked out. But he's all right.'

Jehan looked doubtful. 'You're sure? Nogai was trying to kill him.'

Burun laughed. 'Maybe. But your father doesn't kill that easily. He did some damage to Nogai, and now they'll know to keep away from one another.'

'Hunh.' Jehan buried his face in the fur of Burun's collar. 'He's really not dead?'

'Really. We'll go and see him in a while.'

'Now. I want to see him now. And I want my mother.' At last Jehan began to cry, and Burun rocked him and held him close.

'There,' he said. 'Don't cry.'

He carried Jehan back downstairs, and together they waited while Jotan was bandaged.

Orcadai arrived eight days later. When the scouts reported that the caravan was approaching the city, Burun rode out with Jehan to meet them.

'Will my mother be with them?' Jehan asked.

'No.' Burun shook his head. 'Your father arranged for her to stay in Kinsai. I told you.'

'Oh.'

They rode at a gentle trot. Ahead Burun could see the dust which hung in the air above the moving carts. It had been dry for weeks, but there were thunderheads over against the mountains and the atmosphere was heavy with the hint of rain. A pair of riders breasted the rise ahead, and Jehan yelled and spurred forward. Kiku rode sedately down the slope towards Burun and Suragai followed her like a shadow. Burun saw that his bow was uncased and ready to hand.

'Well, Khan?' Kiku reined in.

'Very well, thank you.' Burun grinned, and Kiku answered with one of her rare smiles.

'Jehan,' she said. 'Your grandmother is in the second cart.'

The wagon was drawn by a team of matched oxen. Jehan rode up beside it, stepped out of the saddle, and ducked inside the cover.

Burun shook Suragai's hand. Then he indicated the bow. 'Trouble?'

Suragai shook his head. 'Not really, Khan. I was just being careful. We were raided two nights ago - nomads, your son said. They tried to drive off a pair of pack beasts.'

'Hunh.' Burun did not bother to ask about the fate of the raiders. 'So where is he? My son I mean.'

'About a verst to the rear.' Suragai gestured. 'One of the baggage carts has a loose wheel. It's been holding us back since yesterday.'

'You made good time.' Burun raised an eyebrow. 'But then Orcadai doesn't like to travel slowly.'

Suragai laughed. 'Oh, Khan, I think if we hadn't been so near the city, he would have burned the cart. I didn't know your language had so many swearwords.'

Burun chuckled.

Kiku was wearing cloth of gold. She twitched her reins abruptly and started to ride towards the caravan. The red sunlight made her garments glitter. Burun watched her for a moment, then he looked back at Suragai.

'Thank you for guarding her.'

'An honour, Khan.' The offworlder bowed. He seemed to hesitate, then spoke again. 'She - the lady, your wife - explained to me the reason for your behaviour the day you left Kinsai. Thank you for trusting me.'

Burun grunted non-committally. He rode after Kiku.

Zurachina was seated in a nest of silk cushions. She had one arm round Jehan. 'I gather my son's been fighting,' she said.

Burun stepped off the back of his st'lyan into the cart. He hugged her, and Jehan burrowed in between them.

'He lost some blood.' Burun caught at his st'lyan's reins and attached them to a hook on the cart tail. 'With any luck he'll stay away from Nogai for a while. I sent him out to command the men culling the remount herds as punishment. He'll be back tomorrow.'

'He wasn't badly hurt, then.'

Burun shook his head. 'No. His pride suffered more than anything. He didn't beat Nogai. He just knocked him out.' He stood up and looked at the following wagon. 'Where is Turakina?'

'Oh.' Zurachina nodded at Suragai as he wheeled in behind Kiku. 'Wherever that man is, look in the opposite direction. She's probably with Orcadai.'

'Ah.' Burun nodded understanding. 'I thought she might have learned to behave.'

'Behave?' Zurachina laughed. 'Khan, if looks could kill, Suragai would be stone dead and our daughter would be on trial for her life. She hasn't exchanged two civil words with him since we left Kinsai, and the fact that he lets most of her insults pass over his head just makes matters worse.' She grinned. 'She's wearing herself out getting him to notice her so that she can pretend to ignore him.'

'Hah.' Burun snorted. 'It sounds as if she's in love.'

It was a joke, but Zurachina's face became thoughtful for a moment. Then she shook her head. 'Unlikely,' she observed.

Burun was taken by surprise. He liked the offworlder well enough, but it was ridiculous for Zurachina even to consider the suggestion. Apart from the fact that Suragai had no rank, it was doubtful if he was human.


'Don't fight with Jotan.'

Nogai stood in his stirrups to see where the outriders had been placed. Then he sat down in the saddle again and looked at Burun.

'The dispute I have with your son is a private

195

matter, Khan.' He spoke calmly. 'You can't interfere.'

'The next time you may not be so lucky,' Burun pointed out. 'He could have killed you.'

'Or I him. Under the Yasa I don't have to discuss the subject with anyone other than the Kha-Khan.' Nogai turned his head, then looked back. 'Have you asked Jotan if he wants to yield?'

Burun made a rude noise. 'All right then,' he tried another approach, 'if you have to fight, don't do it with pitchforks, or knives, or swords. I need both of you. The Kha-Khan needs you. Call a truce until the war is over.'

The under-officers of the exercising thousand galloped up. Nogai gave them fresh orders and sent them away again.

'As everyone is so fond of reminding me,' Nogai met Burun's eyes, 'my death would not cause a ripple in the affairs of the Khanate. It might even be welcomed. And as for Jotan –'

'I need Jotan,' Burun said quickly.

'Oh? What on earth for?'

Suragai rode up into the grove of trees. He exchanged a few words with Hodai, then rode away again. As he passed Burun he nodded respectfully. Nogai ignored him.

'I asked you why you need Jotan.'

'He commands my scouts.'

'So he does.' Nogai sounded amused. 'No doubt he could be replaced.'

Burun compressed his lips. He had already tried to talk sense into Jotan, and had got nowhere.

Yuan rode up the slope. He saluted Burun.

'Lord, there is a body of riders approaching from the west. Their banners are black.'

'Vortai.' Nogai was suddenly alert.

'Maybe.' Burun considered the possibility. He was

196

sure that Vortai was still in Kinsai, which was in the east. The only other person who was likely to travel under the banner of the Gaijin clan was Sipotai, Vortai's son, Burun's brother-in-law. 'How many men?' He looked at Yuan.

'Over a thousand, Lord.'

'So many.' Burun experienced a feeling of anticipation. It would be just like Sipotai to attempt overwhelming force, and he had been expecting some kind of reaction ever since he had issued the order for Vortai's herds to be culled.

'Hodai!'

'Yes, Khan?'

'Send to Jotan. He is to bring the men under his command in from the west. Tell him Sipotai is coming. He will know what to do.'

'Yes, Khan.'

'And tell him to leave Tulagai and Targoutai behind. They can't be involved in this.'

Hodai nodded. He galloped away downslope. Burun picked up his reins.

'You're preparing to fight.' Nogai sounded surprised.

'Only if I'm attacked.' Burun snorted. 'Don't worry. You won't be involved.

He saw Nogai flush. The insult was a mild one, but explicit.

'That wasn't what I meant,' Nogai protested. 'But you can't make war without the Kha-Khan's permission.'

'Oh, I don't think it'll come to war.' Burun grinned. 'But if Sipotai is fool enough to offer me the chance, then we have a score to settle, he and I.'

'God. He'll claim provocation, surely.'

'Let him,' Burun said shortly. 'Besides, dead men can't complain. He looked over his shoulder. 'Kuchuk!'

'Yes, Khan.' The standard-bearer urged his st'lyan forward.

'Signal the hundred commanders under my banner. And bring in the outriders.'

'I can do that, Khan.' Yuan spoke.

The scouts and outriders were part of a growing band which had started to acknowledge the unofficial leadership of Suragai. Burun nodded.

'Yes. And find my other son.'

'The Khan wishes.' The Manchu saluted. He charged away.

Four of Nogai's guard rode into the grove. They were all Altun family retainers of long standing - men whose first and only concern would be to protect the interests of the Kha-Khan - and Burun watched them out of the corner of his eye in case it occurred to Nogai to send Sipotai warning.

'Please,' Nogai said. 'If you have a quarrel with Sipotai, let me mediate it.'

'Did you permit me to interfere in your feud with Jotan?' Burun asked. 'Thank you, but no.'

'But you're breaking the Yasa!'

'Not yet. I will fight Sipotai only if he attacks me first.' Burun thought that the objection was foolish. 'Do you expect me to make no preparation? He's the most treacherous member of his family, and that's saying a lot.'

'Then let me arrange for the two of you to meet.'

'Oh.' Burun showed his teeth. 'We are going to meet, certainly. But it will be on my terms.'

Suragai came up through the trees. 'The outriders are all in, Khan.'

'Good.' Burun turned aside from Nogai. 'How well do you know the land to the west of the city, Suragai?'

The offworlder shrugged. 'Well enough, Khan. It is

full of little valleys and defiles. We have used it for scouting exercises.'

'Very well.' Burun looked at the sun and estimated the time. 'The riders who are approaching. Locate them, and find out if there are any more. There could be a second group riding behind or parallel. Send to me in any event. I'll be on the plain before the city gates. Hurry.'

'Yes, Khan.' Suragai nodded. 'And if I run into their outriders?'

'Oh. Well, if you have to kill them, they must not be found.'

A few weeks earlier, Suragai would have betrayed his misgivings. Now he seemed undisturbed. He saluted and rode away.

Orcadai arrived. He was accompanied by Arghatun and Jenjin.

'Sipotai?' he asked.

Burun nodded. 'It can't be anyone else.'

'Well. You must be pleased.' Orcadai sounded amused.

'You think I like the idea of fighting my in-laws?' Burun scowled fiercely.

Orcadai laughed, unabashed. 'Not especially, I'm sure. But I imagine the fact that it is Sipotai who is charging into the net must provide you with certain gratification.'

Burun ignored the sarcasm. He looked past Jenjin at Arghatun. 'Well?'

'Oh! I'm sorry, Khan.' Arghatun grinned. 'We're ready to ride whenever you command.'

'God, I should hope so.' Burun snorted. He could not understand why everyone was suddenly so cheerful. 'In that case let's go. If I stay here any longer, I will choke on all the good humour.'

*

'Khan.'

'I know. I saw their dust ten minutes ago. Is there any word from Suragai yet?'

'No, Khan.' Hodai shook his head. 'Shall I send to look for him?'

'No. Either he's coming, or he's dead.' Burun thought about that possibility, then stood in his stirrups. 'Is everyone in position?'

'Yes, Khan.'

'And Jotan?'

'As I told you, Khan. We have heard nothing from him since he acknowledged your order.'

Burun chewed the end of his moustache, then spat it out again. Even without Jotan's five hundred, he could deal with Sipotai, but he preferred the edge that would be provided by Jotan's presence in Sipotai's rear.

The grass on the plain was short, sharp-bladed stuff, no good for grazing. Most of the hundred or so men who were waiting with Burun had dismounted, but their st'lyan stood heads up, waiting patiently. Kuchuk was sitting cross-legged behind his saddle. He was filing arrow heads, and the sound of the metal on the whetstone set Burun's teeth on edge.

The dust cloud was closer now: about half a verst away. Burun estimated that the party of riders beneath it was coming through the last of the little valleys which led out onto the plain.

'Rider, Khan.' Hodai pointed.

'Yes. I see him.'

It was Suragai, riding flat out. When he saw Burun, he reined in so hard that his st'lyan sat down on her haunches.

'Report.' Burun's eyes were on the nearing dust cloud.

The offworlder was breathing almost as hard as his

200

mare. It was a moment before he answered, and Burun saw that he had an arrow embedded in the edge of his shield.

'Khan, as you ordered, I scouted the intruders. There are only the men whose dust you can see. I estimate twelve hundred. They have scouts, but only in front, and they are riding too fast to see much of the ground.'

'Hah.' Burun was pleased. 'How close did you get? Did they see you?'

'I ran into one of their forward scouts.' Suragai gestured at the arrow in his shield. 'But we were in some trees, and so -' He made a motion with one finger across his throat. 'No one else saw me.'

'Good.'

'And I got close enough to count them as they rode past. Their leader is a small man on a black st'lyan with white fore-hooves. He has dark hair and wears a gold helmet with a crest. His banners are black and his standard-bearer carries a totem - a skull cased in gold on top of a golden lance.'

'So.' Burun was impressed. It was clear that Suragai had a talent for fieldcraft. 'Well done. Now let's pretend that we are taken by surprise. Hodai, get everyone mounted. We'll ride away from them at the walk.'

Burun led the troopers north-east, a diagonal path across Sipotai's projected route towards Pesth. He wondered if the fact that there were no tracks in the direction from which they were supposed to be coming would be noticed, and thought not. Once Sipotai's scouts saw the small party under Burun's silver banner, they would forget everything else. The whole horde would come charging across the plain to intercept. Straight into his trap.

'They're out on the plain, Khan.' Hodai shaded his

eyes as he looked back. 'I can't see any detail yet, but I think - yes - they've seen us.'

'Good. Keep riding.' Burun uncased his bow.

'Name of God,' Kuchuk muttered. He sounded elated. 'I feel like a piece of bait in a snare.'

Suragai laughed. He looked back over his shoulder. 'They're splitting into two groups to surround us, Khan. Here they come.'

A screen of black-clad riders was spreading out on both sides. Burun reined in and sat waiting while they circled and closed in. Few seemed to have weapons drawn or shields unslung.

'They're confident.' Hodai's voice came softly.

'They ought to be,' Kuchuk answered sourly. 'They outnumber us about twelve to one.'

'Oh well, if you're worried about the odds -'

'Be quiet, both of you,' Burun growled. 'At least try to look serious. See, here comes Sipotai.'

There were perhaps six or seven men under the skull totem. The leader wore a golden helmet. When he saw Burun he smiled unpleasantly.

'God is good to me today. I swear, Merkut, I never thought to come on you so easily.'

Burun showed his teeth. 'Indeed, brother-in-law. You never could find your way without God's help.'

Kuchuk sniggered.

At the edge of the plain a new dust cloud hovered. Burun wondered if anyone else had noticed it, and he spoke again to divert Sipotai's attention.

'And is this a social visit?' He made his tone deliberately insulting. 'Or do you have some serious purpose?'

'Oh.' Sipotai laughed harshly. 'I'm hunting thieves. Merkuts, they would be.'

Burun ignored the growl of anger which went up from his men.

'I am sad for your loss,' he said mildly. 'And what did

they steal, these thieves? Apart from your sense of direction, that is.'

'Merkut pig!' Sipotai spat. He gestured, and the men on either side of him lowered their lances and charged Burun.

Burun was prepared. He ducked and turned his st'lyan into a sidestep. Both attacks missed. The man on the right surged past, then wrenched his animal's head round to charge again. At once he was feathered with arrows like a pincushion. He pitched out of the saddle.

Yuan intercepted the man on the left. The offworlder seemed to unsheath and strike in one fluid movement. The Gaijin rode on for a moment. Then his head toppled from his body and bounced in the dust. There was a roar from men on both sides. Burun flung up a hand.

'Look behind you, Sipotai!'

There were mounted men spilling out of the defiles and patches of dead ground on both sides of the plain. They rode forward at the walk, but their weapons were ready. To the Gaijin rear Jotan's five hundred were a solid mass cutting off the line of retreat. The silver banner of the Merkuts waved everywhere.

Sipotai's st'lyan reared. He was looking for a gap in the net which enclosed him and his men. 'Dog!' he screamed.

Burun was amused. 'Name of God, Sipotai. Did you think I would sit here and wait for you to kill me. Yield now. There are half a dozen bows drawn on you. If we fight, you will be the first to die.'

Sipotai's face was suffused with rage. 'Then we die together!' He gestured at the Gaijin around him. 'You think you will live long after me?'

Burun looked, but he could see only unprepared men who had not even drawn their bows because they were so confident of success.

'It is possible,' he said. 'Can you tell me that your men will fight on after you fall? Will they avenge you, knowing that they must die?'

He raised his voice so that it carried, and saw that some of the men in black were already raising their helmets on lance or sword points, the universal token of surrender.

'We outnumber you.' Burun addressed Sipotai cheerfully. 'But if it is your wish to die, then by all means let us set to. Come, give the word.'

Sipotai's hand went to the hilt of his sword, then withdrew again. Burun could see the seed of doubt blossoming in his eyes.

'The next time, Merkut,' he said. 'The next time.'

'Oh?' Burun laughed. 'And what makes you think there will be a next time?'

Sipotai stared back. He said nothing.

Jotan rode up. 'What are we to do with them? I never saw men with such a small desire to fight.'

Burun had intended Sipotai's death. Now he saw that it was not the right time.

'Disarm them and release them. Escort them away from the city.'

'Eh?' Jotan gaped.

Even Sipotai seemed surprised. Then he seemed to anticipate a possibility. He smiled bitterly.

'Such mercy,' he sneered. 'You send us on our way weaponless, so that we can be slaughtered from ambush. Do you lack the courage to kill us cleanly?'

'What, don't you trust me, brother-in-law?' Burun said innocently. 'Leave a few men behind when you go. They shall load your weapons onto carts and follow you. Only be sure you ride back to Pantai. You have seen that we were waiting for you. Don't try again.' He kicked his st'lyan into motion and she trotted out on to the open plain. The Gaijin who were with Sipotai had melted away from his side so that he was left alone in the middle of an escort of Merkuts.

'I can't believe you're letting him go.' Jotan caught up and rode alongside. 'Have you gone soft?'

'You should have taken him when he sent those two against you, Khan.' Hodai came up on Burun's other side. 'That was the right time. God, when those lances passed over your head, I swear my heart stopped beating.'

'You're making a mistake.' Jotan ignored Hodai's comment. 'What if they arm, then turn round and try again? Sipotai can add nearly a tuman to his strength whenever he wants, and most of them are no more than two days' ride from here.'

'Well.' Burun considered. 'Perhaps we ought to make sure that they keep travelling towards Pantai. We could send them on their way with the odd arrow, maybe. Once they get used to running, they'll find it hard to stop. Who knows,' he pretended that the thought had only just occurred to him, 'they might be attacked by bandits.'

Jotan looked at him sharply. 'Bandits. I see.'

Burun guessed what Jotan was thinking. He thought seriously about having Sipotai ambushed on the road, and remembered Sipotai's eyes on Kiku, desiring her. He burned for revenge. But even if he denied involvement, no one would believe that he had not arranged matters so that Sipotai was killed.

'I am sure you do,' he said after a moment. 'But I want Sipotai to reach home safely.'

Jotan looked disbelieving. Burun searched for a convincing argument.

'Consider,' he said. 'Sipotai can only die once. But why should it be soon? In the meantime he will have Vortai to face.'

'Name of God, yes.' Jotan grinned. 'I hadn't thought of that.'

Burun was easily able to imagine his father-in-law's reaction. The news that Sipotai had tried to recover by force the st'lyan which had been commandeered under the Kha-Khan's warrant would be bad enough - especially since the attempt had failed. But when he heard that Sipotai had tried to kill Burun in front of an army of witnesses, he would spit blood. No matter how the outcome of the incident was considered, it was a victory for Burun. Sipotai was shamed and Vortai was embarrassed.

In spite of everything, Burun felt depressed by the whole affair and could not understand why.

He stood in the stirrups and looked around. The Gaijin were piling arms in an orderly fashion. Along the edge of the plain the outriders that Burun had planted were galloping back to join the main body. It was strange to see Yek surrendering, but it had been Sipotai's mistake to involve troops in a private feud. Faced with an enemy such as the Alan, no warrior of the True People would ever yield. But with the possible exception of the Gaijin family retainers, most of the men following Sipotai would have been reluctant from the start. He was an ill-starred leader, and no one liked the risk of being caught breaking the Yasa.

'What would you have done if Sipotai had decided to fight to the death?' Jotan asked suddenly.

'Oh.' Burun considered. 'Probably I would have died.'

Jotan nodded. 'So you were bluffing after all. You knew they wouldn't fight.'

Burun grunted sourly, but he said nothing. There were times when Jotan was too perceptive for his own good.

Burun opened his eyes in darkness. It was the middle of the night. Kiku was lying beside him, separated from him by the space of no more than a hand span. He could smell her perfume and sense the delicate warmth of her body. If he reached out and touched her, she would wake at once.

The house in Pesth. Now that Burun knew where he was, the detail of the room became familiar. He guessed what had wakened him and strained his ears to hear it again. Obligingly it came, a long low cry like the call of an animal or the sound of a lost soul howling in the wind. It seemed to be just outside the window, and Burun relaxed. The first time he had heard it he had been a child on the Khirgiz, sleeping in bed with his father and mother, and it had wakened him and Sebu both. Then Sebu had told him that no one but a true lord of the Merkuts ever heard the sound.

Noiselessly Burun got up and went to the door. When he went out into the passage the sentry started to rise. Burun waved him down.

'Peace, Kalai.'

'Yes, Lord. Are you all right?'

'Yes. Give me something to drink.'

The sentry offered a flask of k'miss. Burun took a mouthful. Then he padded barefoot down the passage. The sentry at Zurachina's door raised his head.

'Khan?'

'Who else? Be still. I'm only going into the ante-chamber. Is there a fire?'

'Yes, Khan.'

'Good.'

Burun went inside. The fire was burning in a brazier which was cushioned in a bed of sand in a box. He laid some coals on it, then knelt to open the chest where the parchments and inks were kept. While he was trimming a pen, a slave came in quietly and laid a flask of wine and a cup at his side.

'Thank you.' Burun nodded. 'Is my wife awake?'

'No, Lord. She sleeps.'

'Good. Don't disturb her.'

Burun unstoppered a jar of ink and dipped the pen.

'To Siban the White, General of the Army, from Burun Khan, greetings.'

He wrote carefully, absorbed in the task of composition. He had almost forgotten the sound which had awakened him.

'I am now returned from Kinsai. The tenth of my own tuman and the tenth of T'zin Bahadur's that I am to take with me on the reconnaissance to the Alan country are assembled, and their training is continuing. Necessity required me to order the herds of your brother Vortai to be culled to supply remounts.'

Burun dipped his pen into the ink again and thought how best to phrase what he was going to say next. The bare statement of fact was likely to be enough. He knew that Siban would appreciate the motive behind his actions and would accept that, even though Vortai was sure to view the order as deliberate provocation, Burun had at least justification as his defence.

'Your nephew Sipotai made an attempt to recover by force those animals which had been gathered, but I was able to forestall him. I suspect that he will try to discredit me with the Kha-Khan. For our friendship, and remembering your relationship with my wife, I ask you to watch over my interests whenever you are at Kinsai.'

Siban would probably take Burun's part in any case, since he was no friend to Vortai, but it did no harm to remind him that he was Zurachina's uncle as well as Sipotai's.

'Sealed at Pesth by my hand and in the Name of God.' Burun dripped molten wax on to the parchment and sealed it with the ring from the chain round his neck.

The coals on the fire were burning brightly now, and he got up and moved away from the brazier. Three weeks remained until the time when he planned to move the reconnaissance force south to the escarpment prior to crossing the G'bai. Since Siban had indicated that he was expected in Kinsai about the same time, it was by no means certain that they would meet.

'Father?' Orcadai came softly into the room. 'I heard that you were up.'

'I couldn't sleep. Sit down.'

Orcadai folded himself on to a cushion near the brazier. 'What are you doing? Are you working?'

'I was writing a letter to Siban. Are you commanding the guard tonight?'

'Yes.' Orcadai reached for the wine flask. 'With Suragai as deputy. I might as well sleep. He can do the job with his eyes closed.'

'Hunh.' Burun took the flask out of Orcadai's hand, poured some wine into the cup, and drank. Then he raised his eyes. 'You like him, don't you?'

'Suragai?' Orcadai seemed surprised by the question. 'Yes. He reminds me of you.'

Burun swallowed the wrong way and spluttered. 'Of me? I hope that's a compliment.'

'Oh.' Orcadai grinned. 'I think so. He's competent, reliable, efficient - all the best qualities. He's so good at everything he does, just like you. You know, I always envied you that when I was a boy; yet, at the same time, it made me feel safe.'

Burun drank again. He looked into the fire and wondered if it was inevitable that sons should resent the strength and influence of their fathers, and struggle to be free of it.

'The world Suragai comes from must be very strange.' Orcadai spoke thoughtfully.

'No stranger than ours,' Burun observed mildly. 'Does he speak of it much?'

'No.' Orcadai shook his head. 'It's as if his past belongs to another life. He doesn't believe that he will ever return to it, so he behaves as if it does not exist.'

'Hunh. Maybe.'

Burun thought that there were other reasons for Suragai's unwillingness to speak about his life in the Empire, but he doubted if Orcadai would appreciate them. With the possible exception of Alexai, who was still something of a misfit, the offworlders had settled in very well. Only their size and the different set of their features now set them apart. The under-officers were good soldiers, and if they had not been more useful as scouts, Burun would have made them hundred commanders to fill the vacancies in his own tuman. The Manchu was the best fighter Burun had ever seen. He raised the profession of arms to an art form, and more and more Burun employed him as a bodyguard and companion.

He had intended to employ Suragai in a similar fashion, but as training progressed, it had become clear that the offworlder was so used to command that he was wasted in any other capacity. The scouts whom he now commanded often operated more than a day's ride ahead of the line of march. As a result Suragai had roughly the same rank as a thousand commander, and had risen to it in an incredibly short space of time.

'Has Suragai ever told you that he learned to fight from a machine?' Orcadai stretched.

'Yes.'

'Do you think it's possible?'

Burun shrugged. 'The offworlders come from a civilisation which appears to use machines for every purpose. Their soldiers are not required to fight as we do, yet those who are in our service seem to manage as well in the Kha-Khan's army as in their own. Probably it is true. Why should Suragai lie?'

Orcadai shook his head. 'It just seems strange to think of a man's mind storing memories of doing certain things - like riding or using a bow - when his body has no experience of them. Do you think the offworlders learn everything the same way? They really aren't like us at all.'

'Yes.' Burun nodded. 'And yet it is easy to forget that they are strangers.'

It was something which worried him whenever he thought about it long enough. Apart from anything else, he was not sure that he would have managed to find advancement if he had found himself in Suragai's situation - abandoned by his people on a world which was alien to his experience. Burun guessed that Suragai's ability to fit into the environment in which he found himself meant that he was far more intelligent than anyone suspected. Perhaps all the members of his race were.

'This chest is very fine,' Zurachina said. 'Does it come from Ch'kasia?'

Burun squinted sideways to see which chest she meant. He was sitting cross-legged on the floor so that Kiku could kneel behind him on a cushion to dress his hair. She had drawn the strands back tightly and was starting to weave them into a queue. Every time he moved his head she was forced to begin again.

'No. That one's from Suristan.'

'See how the carving runs with the grain.' Zurachina traced the frieze around the lid with her fingers.

211

Jehan came into the room. He wrapped himself around Zurachina and pushed his head up into the curve of her arm so that she was forced to stop what she was doing to pay him attention. She bonked him on top of the head with her elbow and he giggled. In the mirror Burun saw Kiku's mouth turn down, and he grinned. She saw the reflection of his expression and tugged sharply at his queue.

'I don't know how I can bear to look at you,' she said softly. 'You are so ugly.'

Zurachina turned to look. 'Yes,' she agreed. 'But ugly men are always interesting.'

'Indeed.' Burun spoke drily. 'I always knew I had some good quality that you found attractive. But I wish you wouldn't discuss me, the pair of you, as if I was a piece of meat.'

Turakina was sitting in the corner sorting through a heap of linen. 'Every woman thinks her husband is handsome,' she observed primly. 'But in reality there are few attractive men in the world.'

'Oh?' Burun grinned. 'And are you so suddenly an expert on husbands?'

Turakina flushed, but Zurachina only smiled. She took some of the folded linen and placed it in the box.

Burun settled again and let Kiku turn the fan of his queue so that it was spread out against his scalp. He guessed that Turakina was once again in love with some young man who was paying her court. It would have to be someone with no title or lands, otherwise he would have declared himself.

'No.' Kiku shook her head. 'Every woman thinks that her husband is ugly. Then she tells herself that she does not mind, that she loves him in spite of his faults and his ugliness. That way she always feels superior.'

'I see.' Burun turned so that he could admire

212

himself in the mirror against the wall. 'And if he really is ugly?'

'Oh.' Kiku laid the comb aside. Then she looked at Turakina and spoke again. 'In such a case her pride is justified. For every other woman applauds her sacrifice, that she remains tied to a man who is ill-favoured. But Turakina was right. There are few really attractive men in the world.'

'And yet it is said that ugliness of the face may hide true beauty of the soul,' Zurachina observed softly.

Kiku considered. 'Yes.' She nodded finally. 'Even so.'

Burun suspected that the conversation centred upon a matter which was less than abstract. He wondered if Turakina would mention the name of her ill-favoured admirer, but she said nothing. Kiku and Zurachina both knew who he was, of course.

'Tell me how I should arrange your marriage.'

It was the afternoon of the following day and Burun had waited until he knew that Turakina was alone in the garden. She was playing with one of Kiku's cats, and he squatted cross-legged in the shade near her.

Turakina's hands stilled. The cat twisted free and ran across the grass.

'Have you had an offer for my hand?' Her tone was disinterested, but Burun was sure that her reaction was a pretence.

He plucked a stem from a tuft of grass at his side and chewed at it. But it was not sweet like the grass of the Khirgiz, and he spat it out again. 'Several,' he said easily. 'But none that I would countenance.'

All the men who had offered seriously for Turakina were either old, with established marriages, or else they were not of comparable rank and their prospects were doubtful.

'I will not be the junior wife of some grey-beard.'

Turakina did not look up, but her shoulders were stiff, her whole attitude stubborn. 'And I am not a chattel to be traded to the Altun for the sake of an alliance.'

'I agree,' Burun said. 'It would not be fitting.'

She looked quickly as if she mistrusted the sincerity of the statement. Burun stared back at her candidly, and after a moment she seemed to relax.

'In any case the Yasa says that you cannot marry me without my consent.'

Turakina had appealed this point before. Burun smiled.

'The Yasa also says that a daughter is subject to the will of her father until she is married,' he countered. 'Don't try me with the law. You will fare better if you appeal to my good nature.'

Turakina snorted.

Burun sighed. 'Heed me.' He tried to maintain the reasonable tone of voice, but it was hard. 'I mean to see you married and I will consider your wishes. We both know what would be fitting and what would not. But how can your desires be accounted if they are not known?'

He saw that she was considering the argument. She was so reluctant to speak that she must be sure he would disapprove of her choice. Burun was almost ready to say that whoever she loved, he would give his consent. But if the man was so unsuitable that Turakina was afraid to say his name, then probably he would make a poor husband and in the long run she would be unhappy. So he said nothing, and in a while she got up quietly and went into the house.

The Sechem from Kinsai was called Parin. He had arrived shortly after first light, disturbing the peace of Burun's house with his entourage of scribes and assistants. It was now a little after midday, and there was no

214

sign of a break in the onslaught of polite but persistent questions which were being directed at the assembled offworlders.

'Then how is it that the water is raised from the lower level to the higher?'

Every time he received an answer to a specific question such as this, the Sechem's assistants muttered quickly to their accompanying scribes the particulars of new areas of knowledge which had been revealed or suggested. When he had exhausted one topic, the Sechem consulted the list which had been compiled by this process and moved on to another. Most of the time it was Suragai who spoke for the whole group. Often he conferred briefly with the others but, so far as Burun could tell, this was only so that some matter could be explained fully, not for any purpose of evasion or concealment of what was known.

It was the youth, Suragai's son, who tired first of the Sechem's tireless attempts to unravel the strands of offworlder knowledge about every subject under the sun. He rose quite suddenly to his feet, crossed the room, and stood stretching in the open bay of the window, where Burun was sitting on the broad ledge, his legs outstretched, his back supported by the stone pillar which was one side of the window recess. Burun inspected the toes of his boots, then glanced back into the interior of the room and cocked his head to listen. The Sechem was still examining the subject of water power.

In spite of the fact that he now dressed like a civilised man, the young offworlder's appearance was still impossibly alien. He was far too tall, and his skin and hair were the wrong colour. He resembled nothing that was to be found in the known world.

'Such persistent questioning is wearisome.' Burun made the observation out of courtesy only.

'Yes, Lord.' The honesty of Alexai's response was disarming.

Burun grinned. 'Oh, well. Think of it as a penalty which must be paid for the possession of so much knowledge.'

The youth snorted softly. Burun grinned again. The trouble with the Sechem was not that they wanted to know everything that ever was or could be known, it was their total disregard for even minor amenities like food and sleep which people usually found most irksome.

A Sechem's mind was like a sponge. It soaked up information until a connection could be made between apparently unrelated pieces of scientific fact. Often there was no useful purpose, subject to the prohibitions imposed by the Yasa, to which the knowledge so obtained could be applied. But that did not matter to the Sechem, for whom the pursuit of information was an end in itself.

'I think that I would consider the time well spent,' Alexai commented, 'if our knowledge was destined to be put to some use. But the Yasa forbids so much!'

Burun shrugged.

'I have not visited other worlds as you have. But as to that, I would expect to discover that all civilised men have laws which govern the conduct of life. And the Yasa can be changed if it is the will of the people.'

'Of all the people.'

'Yes.'

'A process which can take years.'

'Even so,' Burun agreed.

'And so the process halts progress -'

'You must forgive us -' Burun spoke as if he had not heard the protest, 'if we do not accept that science is good simply because it permits a thing to be done faster or with less effort. The Yasa is a good law. It was

216

handed down to us so that we would always have the choice: to use that which we found to be necessary for the continuation of life and the survival of the True People; to reserve for another time that upon which we cannot agree, or are undecided, or mistrust for reason of its nature.'

'But the Yasa governs *every* aspect of life.'

'Of course.' The observation surprised Burun. 'Should it be otherwise? I have no doubt the law differs on other worlds. But law there must be, or how can there be order?'

There seemed to be something about the issue which Alexai did not understand. Burun was perplexed. Surely the matter of law was the most clear cut of all. A law was, or was not, and that was the end of it.

'The Yasa makes no differentiation between natural law and moral law,' Alexai said.

It was clear that he was attempting to make a point based upon the idea that the two were not necessarily capable of reconciliation with one another, but Burun was unable to imagine a situation where disparity might be found to exist, and he allowed his facial expression to demonstrate the fact.

Alexai spoke again. 'Moral law is often derived from a belief in God - at least on other worlds. It is an ideal-ised code of behaviour. But your law is different. It embraces the whole of life, but it is not part of your belief in the existence of God.'

'God?' Burun laughed incredulously. 'What does God have to do with the law?'

'Well, people of many civilisations believe that moral law is sanctified by God. In some societies there are men who are charged with the interpretation of the will of God as it relates to earthly life.'

Burun snorted. 'Why should God be concerned

with life on earth? Is He not the Lord of Heaven?'

'Yes, but -'

'And do not all men accept that the earth is an imperfect world?' Burun ignored the interjection. 'Whereas Heaven, as all men know, is a paradise. Why then should God concern himself with the doings of men on earth, and with the law?'

Alexai appeared to be trying to muster a counter-argument. At last he gestured hopelessly. 'I don't know, Lord. I am not a priest, and I think that only a priest could answer your arguments.'

'Hunh.'

Burun sat back, nodding. He was satisfied that he had made his point, and that there was no answer to it.

The period of training was by now almost at an end. Burun was fairly satisfied with the progress which had been made. The Altun were beginning to think like soldiers again, and the whole reconnaissance force was starting to mould itself into an effective fighting unit.

It was two days after the departure of the Sechem, and Burun was engaged in issuing orders for Suragai's scouts to carry out an extended exercise north-west into the mountains which formed the border with the province of Ch'nozia. He had already detailed Nogai to act as an observer, deciding that if his report was favourable, he would invest Suragai with the rank of Amir. If the offworlder could impress the son of the son of the Kha-Khan, then it was probable that he was capable of dealing on equal terms with any of the other Altun who crossed his path. In any event, it was Burun's instinct to secure Suragai's permanent and recognised fealty, and an Amirate - a fief granted by a Khan to a favoured vassal - ensured that the offworlder would recognise that whatever he now possessed, he owed to Burun.

Even with the addition of Nogai's retainers, Suragai's party was still only just over a hundred strong. Burun was concerned in case the offworlder felt that he had to prove his ability to command against an enemy.

'There are Ch'noze raiding parties all through the foothills.' Burun kicked at a loose turf as he spoke. 'Don't engage them unless you can beat them at the first attack.'

Suragai looked as if he thought that the advice was superfluous, but he nodded. He was wearing a mantle over his tunic, and it had been stained with green and brown dyes so that, against the trees and undergrowth at any distance, the wearer would merge with his surroundings. Jotan had mentioned the idea, but it was the first time that Burun had witnessed its use.

'You'll encounter Berke's patrols.' Burun was trying to think of every eventuality. 'Don't let them try to use you as an addition to their strength, and don't accept orders from their officers, no matter what rank, if they countermand mine.'

Nogai was perched on a stool a little way off. He muttered something to Targoutai, who laughed. Then he looked at Burun. His expression was insolent.

Deliberately Burun raised his voice. 'And don't let Nogai interfere in any matter which bears upon your command. He is only an observer.'

Suragai looked over his shoulder at Nogai. The noyon cursed him cheerfully.

'Can he piss when he wants to, Khan?' Nogai called. 'Or do you have orders to cover that eventuality as well?'

Burun compressed his lips. Suragai was trying not to grin, and suddenly Burun knew that the comment was justified. The offworlder had already proved that he could look after both himself and his men.

219

Suragai's son came through the tent lines and, before Burun could think of a suitably crushing reply, Nogai and Targoutai were crossing the grass to join him. They turned away between two of the larger pavilions, and were lost to sight.

Burun scowled and threw up his arms. Suragai laughed.

'I know.' Burun glared. 'I'm behaving like an old woman. Why don't you say it?'

'I'm honoured by the Khan's concern, naturally,' Suragai said formally.

Burun tugged at his scalp lock. He shook his head in annoyance at himself.

'Once when I was a boy,' he said, 'my father told me that the greatest gift of a man was the ability to know himself. Do you know what you are, Suragai?'

The offworlder seemed to consider the question.

'Khan, what can I say? I am a man. Not quite as you are, perhaps, but a man nevertheless.'

'Hunh.' Burun nodded. 'That was the answer I knew you would give. And yet, although we are alike in many ways, there is much about one another that we will never be able to comprehend.'

Suragai's expression was suddenly wary, but he said nothing. Burun nodded again, as if he had heard the unspoken acknowledgement that what he said was true.

'I ought to fear you, I think.' He watched Suragai's face for a reaction, but found none. 'You ought to be a slave, or dead, but you are not. Instead, I find myself giving consideration to your ennoblement.'

Suragai's eyes opened wide for a moment. Then, as if he realised he had betrayed emotion - surprise or shock perhaps - he looked away.

'I am not deserving, Khan,' he said quietly at last.

Burun considered. 'Perhaps you would not be,' he

220

said, 'if you were an ordinary man. But you are not; I sense the difference in you.'

Suragai was gazing blindly into the middle distance. Burun wondered what he could see.

'Can you understand my thoughts, Suragai?'

Burun asked the question quietly, calmly, aware that he might not believe the answer, unsure that he wanted a response at all.

The offworlder produced a tired smile.

'You mean, can I read your mind, Khan, and can I influence you to think about me in a certain way? No. In that at least, I am a man as you are.'

Burun tested the reply in his mind. But he could see that there was no way that he would ever know if he had listened to the truth. He made a face.

'Then perhaps you are under the hand of God.'

The words were a formula, nothing more. But even as he spoke, Burun was remembering what Alexai had said about the belief of some civilisations that God was concerned with the activities of men, and suddenly he wondered if it could be true.

'Tell me who has been courting Turakina.'

Burun lay on his back and looked up at the silks which were draped above the bed. Kiku lay against him. She had been stroking the inside of his leg with her foot, but now she stopped. She raised herself on one arm, and at once her hair flowed like a dark torrent to the side so that it covered one shoulder. She stared at Burun innocently, but he met her eyes, and at last she looked away.

'Tell me.'

He reached out and stroked a hand down her neck and across the curve of the shoulder which had been exposed by her movement. Kiku's eyes closed, as if she savoured his touch. Then suddenly they opened again.

221

'I am not your spy, Khan.' She caught his wrist with her hand, and moved his arm aside.

'Very well.' He shrugged. 'It is of little importance.'

She traced the outline of his pectorals with one talon. 'Perhaps not,' she said, 'but if she wishes to marry?'

Burun had allowed his head to fall back on to the cushions again. Now he glanced sideways. 'Does she?' he asked casually.

Kiku did not answer. Her hand moved idly lower, and Burun's muscles tightened as the exposed talon brushed his stomach.

'Among his own people,' Kiku observed, 'it is said that he is a prince of the blood.'

'A prince?' Burun pretended to be impressed. 'Then he is a foreigner. Well, that may not be a problem.'

Turakina had not been at Kinsai for over a year. He was sure that none of the embassies from the subject states sent to pay homage to the Kha-Khan had contained any person of very much more elevated rank than his own. Mentally he examined a list of the men with whom she might have come into contact. She would not have degraded herself by falling in love with a slave, and none of the foreigners serving with the army were the sons of anything more exalted than minor noblemen. In any case he was almost certain that Turakina's current infatuation was a recent event. There was no one else, except -

'Name of God!'

Realisation struck Burun like a blow. He sat up so suddenly that Kiku's talon scored his chest and blood welled.

'The offworlder, Suragai's son!'

Burun ignored the wound. It was only minor and would soon close. Kiku said nothing. Burun wondered if she had revealed Turakina's secret deliberately, or if she had supposed that he would fail to make the connection. She pulled back to her own side of the bed, and reached for the comb which lay on the chest at the bedside. He could not see her eyes when she was combing her hair.

'Arvid!'

Burun shouted, and the door to Kiku's chamber opened a fraction so that the guard outside could answer.

'Yes, Khan?'

'Send someone to find Jotan Bahadur. Ask him to attend me.'

'The Khan wishes.' The door closed again.

Kiku was still combing her hair. She looked up, met Burun's eyes, and her hand faltered. Then she regained her composure once more. Her silence was like an accusation.

'I know.' Burun glared at her. 'It is the third hour of the night watch and I could at least wait until morning. Do you think I would sleep?'

He rolled off the bed and stood up. His chest had stopped bleeding and he splashed some water from a bowl to remove the dried blood. Then he dried himself with a piece of linen from the bed chest.

Jotan would not know what to do, but it would help to talk the matter out with him. Burun's first instinct was to have the young offworlder dragged back to the city and to confront Turakina with him. But that would solve nothing. Indeed if it had any effect at all, it would probably be to stiffen her resolve.

Burun wondered if Suragai knew about the courtship, and guessed not. Then he realised that he was facing a double problem. He could scarcely honour the father, if at the same time he was inflicting punishment on the son for his presumption in paying court to the daughter of a Khan.

Burun heard Jotan's footsteps in the passage, then

the sound of his voice as he greeted the sentry. He glared at Kiku.

'Cover yourself.'

Kiku hated any man to be permitted access to her chamber. It did not matter that Jotan was family. She stared frostily at Burun, then rose and put on a silk robe. Climbing back into bed she picked up the comb once more and studied herself in the mirror, ignoring him.

The door opened a little way.

'Khan?' the sentry called. 'Your son is here.'

Burun grunted acknowledgement. He stepped into trousers, went to the door, and pulled it wide. Jotan looked as if he had been in his quarters. He was wearing a loose tunic and trousers of silk, and they contrasted oddly with the half boots which he must have pulled on in order to answer Burun's summons. He surveyed Burun up and down.

'Name of God, Khan. I expected to find you sick or dying. But now I see that you are only a little wounded.'

Burun growled wordlessly. It was not a time for jokes.

Jotan grinned crookedly. He walked past Burun into the bedchamber. Kiku glanced at him, then turned ostentatiously so that she was presenting him with a view of her back. Jotan laughed and looked at Burun again.

'So tell me why you summon me at this hour. Do you have a good excuse for interrupting my leisure, or is it simply that you need help to master your unruly women?'

Burun scowled at him. 'The day I need help for that, they can grave me. I need to talk to you. One of the offworlders, Suragai's son, has been paying court to your sister.'

224

Jotan snorted. 'Huh. I wondered when you would find out about that.' He sat down on the bed chest.

Burun gaped. 'Are you telling me that you knew and said nothing? Do you have pig's droppings for brains?'

'What should I have told you?' Jotan was amused. 'It is nothing serious.'

'Nothing serious?' Burun paced the length of the chamber, turned, and paced back again. 'She's in love with him, damn you. She probably thinks she wants to marry him. And you tell me it's nothing serious?'

He was appalled at such a betrayal, astounded that Jotan was unable to comprehend the seriousness of the situation. It was as if everyone had conspired to keep the secret from him. He glared at Kiku, but she ignored him.

'Aaah!' Jotan gestured. 'How many times has Turakina been infatuated? Dozens that I know of. Why should it be more serious this time?'

Burun wanted to spit, or to kick something. Jotan's observation was sound enough, but there remained Turakina's preoccupation with an alien. It was beyond comprehension.

Jotan stood up. 'Khan, if you don't want me for anything more important than this, I'm going back to my quarters. Talk to me in the morning, if you must.'

Burun waved a hand at him.

'Go. Go on. You are no help to me.'

Jotan turned towards the door. Then he stopped and bowed deeply, insolently, in Kiku's direction.

'Stepmother. An honour as always to be in your house.'

Kiku turned her head and looked down over her shoulder. Her expression was frigid.

'Jotan.' She pretended that it was the first time she had known he was in the room. 'Go away. Your presence offends me.'

225

Jotan laughed harshly. He walked past Burun and out into the passage. Burun flinched at the aura of restrained violence which his son gave off as he brushed past. It was the first time that he had realised that Jotan and Kiku were enemies.

He sat down on the end of the bed. Somehow he had started to chew his moustache again and he spat it out. Zurachina always complained that one end of his moustache was more sparse than the other because of his habit of biting at it whenever he was thinking. He pondered his new knowledge of the identity of Turakina's courtier and knew that his reaction had been unbalanced. He had given Kiku an opportunity to make trouble. In any case probably Jotan was right; the infatuation was not serious. It emphasised however the fact that a husband would have to be found for Turakina - and found soon.

It was foolish to fear the offworlders because of their strangeness. They were few and alone in the midst of a world about which they knew almost nothing. It would be a pity, perhaps, but they could always be killed.

Burun pitched back onto the bed. He was too disturbed now to sleep, and too aggravated to take revenge on Kiku for perpetrating the upset. He was used to a feeling that he was in command of every situation but, ever since the arrival of the offworlders, events seemed to have been running out of control, like a driverless cart running downhill.

Orcadai was working in the courtyard when Burun came out of the house. He was stripped to the waist, wrestling a new crown pin into the yoke for Zurachina's cart.

He looked up briefly when Burun appeared, then bent to his task again. Jotan was sitting on the end of the yoke to keep it steady, and Burun saw the look which passed between them. He guessed that they had been discussing Turakina before he had emerged from the house, and now Jotan was warning Orcadai to silence.

Osep led a bay with black points round from the stables and stood with her. The st'lyan was a new addition to Burun's string of remounts, and he was riding her every day in order to accustom her to his touch.

'Don't we have slaves enough, that my son has to become a carter?' Burun pitched his voice so that it carried across the courtyard.

Orcadai looked up. 'If I left the job to a slave, you would demand to know why I had not given it my personal attention. Go spill your anger at another target, Khan.'

Burun was conscious of a flush of anger which spread until it seemed to encompass his whole body. The distance across the courtyard was only a few paces; he itched to seize Orcadai by the neck and to throw him bodily over the low wall into the street. It was contrary to reason for a father to permit his son to speak to him in such a fashion. But then they would have to fight, and Jotan would only sit and laugh, and Burun had no wish to appear small. Instead he twitched the reins out of Osep's hand and pulled himself into the saddle.

Turakina was standing at the window of her chamber. When she saw that Burun was looking up at her, she stepped back quickly and slammed the shutters. Burun turned to see if Jotan and Orcadai were watching, but they seemed to be engrossed in the task of separating the split ends of the crown pin. Jotan was holding the prongs apart so that Orcadai could hammer them flat, a process which would prevent the pin from being withdrawn once the harness was attached. They did not look up, and Burun guessed that they had warned Turakina that he knew about her love for Suragai's son.

Burun snorted. He gigged the st'lyan into a sidestep, then wrenched her head around and galloped her out through the gate. The troopers lounging in the deep shade of the wall outside were taken by surprise when he rode past them, and by the time they were mounted he was already turning into the next street.

Tulagai and Targoutai were walking their animals sedately out through the archway which led to Nogai's house. Burun sat his mare down hard to avoid running into them. Tulagai's st'lyan reared, shrieking, and he fell onto the cobbles.

'Name of God, Khan! Are we being attacked that you ride in such a set?'

Targoutai attempted to divide his attention between the sight of his brother as he lay cursing, and the madness which he could see in Burun's eyes.

'Get out of my way, damn you!'

Burun kicked his st'lyan into motion again. She shied, then settled as he started to urge her past Targoutai's grey.

'Hold, Khan!'

Targoutai reached out and grabbed Burun's rein. Burun was aware that the first members of his escort were entering the street at his back. He sidestepped his mare, disengaged one foot from the stirrup, and kicked Targoutai's animal hard in the barrel. She reared, and Targoutai landed in the street beside his brother. The commander of Burun's guard reined in and surveyed the confusion.

'Khan?' He spoke nervously.

Burun's anger departed as quickly as it had arrived. He closed his eyes for a moment, then opened them again. Tulagai was getting to his feet and a male slave was running down the street to catch his st'lyan.

Targoutai sat up. He tested his limbs one by one as if he expected to find them damaged by the fall, then launched himself at Burun. One of the troopers of Burun's guard had leaned down to catch the reins of Targoutai's grey and as he secured them he pulled at the animal's bridle. The st'lyan swung round and got in the way of Targoutai's attack. He ran into her broad flank, cannoned off, and sat down hard.

Someone laughed.

Burun got down from the saddle, reached down, and pulled Targoutai to his feet.

'Noyon, I ask your pardon for my ill manners.' He bowed formally.

'Eh?'

An apology was clearly the last thing Targoutai expected. He was nonplussed.

Tulagai laughed harshly. 'Brother, your mouth is flapping open. Close it before the wind changes. And accept the Merkut's apology before he changes his mind.'

Targoutai glared. Then he collected himself. Burun's words had been uttered in a precise form which was dictated by the Yasa to avoid the onset of casual feuds. Since he had suffered no injury, he was obliged to accept them at face value. He bowed.

'Khan, I accept your apology. I have suffered no hurt, and I excuse you.'

Burun bowed again, then remounted. The action took Targoutai by surprise.

'But, Khan -' His words were the beginning of a protest.

Burun sidestepped his st'lyan so that he was looking directly down at Targoutai from the advantage of height.

'What is it, Noyon?'

He was amused now, because Targoutai was having trouble finding the words to say what was on his mind. The Yasa provided a formula for apologies, but said nothing about explanations. He stared innocently.

'Name of God, Noyon. You've had your apology. You want an excuse as well?'

Targoutai went crimson, but Tulagai only laughed. Burun glared at him. Then he kicked his st'lyan into a trot, and made no attempt to look back to see if his escort was following until he was riding out into the square which lay just inside the city gates.

Exercising troopers streamed across the plain. The grass near the camp had been grazed down to the roots. Even the bark of the young trees and the leaves on the bushes had been stripped by foraging st'lyan and, with little to hold the soil, the ground was being pounded into dust every time animals moved across it.

There were banks of heavy clouds gathered over the mountains to the east, but they did not signify rain; the air was dry and heavy. When the rain came, it would be suddenly. The clouds would be blown in from the south-west by the harsh *khamsin* wind and would empty themselves in a downpour which would soak everything in minutes. Whole fields of unharvested grain would be battered flat and the arid plains turned into a morass across which nothing could travel for several days. Burun had seen the phenomenon many times and planned to be away from Pesth long before it occurred.

'Here they come, Khan.'

Hodai was standing in the stirrups. Now he pointed north.

'Hunh. I see them.'

Burun nodded. He wanted to talk informally with Suragai, without giving the offworlder warning or the time to prepare himself. It had not been hard for Burun to place himself in the way of the returning scouts. He thought that even Hodai could only suspect that there was more to the incident than military interest.

'Either they've managed a feat of multiplication which is quite remarkable, Khan,' Hodai shaded his eyes, 'or they've picked up some prisoners.'

Burun held up his hand to block out the glare of the sun, but he could not make out any detail in the haze. He gestured at Kuchuk.

'Double red, Khan?'

'Yes.' Burun nodded.

The standard-bearer attached a pair of crimson pennants to the end of his signal pole, and rode forward waving it in great circles above his head. At once the oncoming column swerved to meet him.

Suragai was in the lead. When he saw Burun he bowed in the saddle. There were about fifty Ch'noze prisoners riding between the files of the scouts, and a middle-aged man who bore the facial tattoos of a war-leader was riding at the offworlder's side. It was obvious that he was a captive, but his hands were unbound, and he met Burun's stare with a mixture of defiance and pride.

'Well, Khan.' Suragai eased one foot out of the stirrup, and crossed the free leg over his saddle. He looked tired. His mantle was covered with a film of red dust, but there was a light in his eyes which Burun had not seen before.

'Well indeed.' Burun had intended to draw Suragai aside. But now he saw that it was not the time.

Nogai was riding at the rear of the column. He was accompanied by several of his own retainers, and the youth Alexai was riding among them. Burun felt as if his face was frozen into the rictus of a smile, and he was sure that he was betraying his feelings. He nodded to Nogai, and Nogai swung down from the saddle.

'Well met, Khan,' he said.

Suragai's son bowed politely, but Burun turned away, pretending that he had not noticed. He looked for Jenjin among the officers who were gathered to watch, and signalled to him.

'Yes, Khan?'

'Take some men and escort the prisoners into the city. Hold them for my disposal.'

'Yes, Khan.' Jenjin saluted. Then he whirled away, shouting instructions at the under-officers of the nearest company of exercising troopers.

Shrill commands echoed down the lines and, as Jenjin's men rode up on each side of the Ch'noze, the scouts who had been guarding them peeled off and dismounted.

Jenjin came riding back. He leaned forward to take the head-rope which was attached to the bridle of the Ch'noze war-leader's mount, and at once the man turned to look anxiously at Suragai.

'Jenjin, wait.' Suragai looked at Burun. 'Khan, this man is called Teng. He is war-leader of the Ching clan of the southern Ch'noze. He gave his word to me personally and I claim him under the law.'

Burun wondered who had told Suragai about that particular privilege, and guessed that it had been Nogai. 'I see.' He nodded. 'Very well. He is yours.'

'Also -'

'Yes?'

'Khan, the man's son is with the other prisoners. Nogai Noyon has given his word that the youth, who is called Fong, will be lodged at Kinsai in a manner which befits his rank, so that he may serve as a hostage for the good behaviour of his father.'

'Indeed.' Burun looked at Nogai. 'You confirm this?'

'Yes, Khan.' Nogai's expression was inscrutable.

Burun thought that probably he was still examining the ways in which he could take advantage of the situation. Usually a Ch'noze promise was good only until the first time his captor's back was turned. But so long as the war-leader's son was secure in Kinsai, the man would follow Suragai to the death. Perhaps Nogai imagined that he could use the son as a lever on the father, possibly in some plot.

'Then of course I confirm the arrangement. Send to Jenjin later and he will have the youth released into your custody. Jenjin, you have leave to go.'

Jenjin saluted again and turned away.

Nogai inclined his head. 'Thank you, Khan.' He looked as if he had expected Burun to dispute the matter, and Burun's suspicions about his motives hardened into certainty.

The scouts looked tired but fit. There was a spirit of elation which had been absent before, and Burun was surprised that a few days away from the main command had made such a difference. He tossed his reins to Kuchuk and slid out of the saddle. At once Suragai dismounted. He let his st'lyan's reins hang loose, and the animal tossed her head once or twice. The offworlder turned and seemed to speak softly to her and at once the mare quietened.

'You took fifty prisoners,' Burun said. 'How many did you kill? And how did you fall in with an enemy so numerous? I thought I told you to avoid contact with any large force.'

Nogai laughed. 'Ah, but Khan, we didn't kill any.'

A group of dismounted scouts was standing nearby. They were listening to the exchange, and grinned with the kind of reckless elation which Burun had recognised in Suragai's eyes.

He looked at the offworlder. 'You didn't kill any. I see.'

The whole thing seemed unlikely, given what Burun knew of the Ch'noze attitude to surrender.

'Khan, let me explain.' Suragai was stretching to ease the stiffness from his back and legs. 'We came on their sign the first day out. They were very careless. I thought it would be good practice to scout them for a time, and we did that for a day and a half. Then they got really careless. They set up night camp in a hollow. So we surrounded them, and in the morning they surrendered.'

It was a simple enough statement, but all the scouts who were listening laughed. Suragai looked over his shoulder at them. His expression was frosty, as if he was tired of a particular joke, and they subsided at once. Nogai was laughing also, and when Suragai glared at him, he only laughed louder.

'Now I'll tell the Khan the real story,' he said. He slapped Suragai affectionately on the shoulder.

Burun had never seen Nogai so friendly towards anyone who was neither a vassal nor a trusted ally. He wonderd if Suragai had pledged himself to Nogai, but thought not. Although Nogai did not seem to sense the fact, the offworlder was radiating hostility towards him.

'We had the Ch'noze surrounded,' Nogai said. 'That at least is true. Their sentries were half asleep and, when we took them prisoner, we found out that the whole bunch had not eaten for days. The whole area has been raided out by other bands. When we came up with them they had travelled for over a week without finding a settlement that was inhabited, or an animal they could slaughter for meat.'

'You met none of Berke's patrols?' Burun queried.

It was Suragai who shook his head. 'No, Khan. Nor saw any sign of them. That whole part of the country is like a wasteland, and if there are people trying to live there, we never saw them.'

'Hunh.' Burun nodded. 'Go on, Nogai.'

'Well, it was the morning.' Nogai gestured. 'We had the Ch'noze under our bows. We could have killed them while they slept, I swear. But this, this insane man, he would not give the order. And then when it was light he went into their camp alone to demand surrender.'

Burun raised an eyebrow. Suragai shrugged.

'Khan, it seemed like a good idea at the time. Few of them would have survived our first volley. I thought I could reason with them.'

'Reason.' Nogai sniggered. 'That's one word for it.'

'It seems that they agreed, however.' Burun spoke mildly.

'Hah. I think they would have tried to take Suragai. Although there were half a dozen of us with our bows drawn to cover him.'

Burun was not sure that he would have trusted Nogai under similar circumstances, but he made no comment. Then he looked at Suragai again. 'How did you compel them?' he asked.

Suragai was looking at the Ch'noze war-leader as he spoke. 'Khan, I simply told that man that I would take either his word, or his head. And since the edge of my sword was resting against his throat at the time, he chose to believe me.'

Burun was struck by the ruthless quality which was exemplified by the act. There was no doubt that the scouts now believed that the offworlder was favoured or lucky because he had emerged unscathed. Luck was important to a soldier, and men often followed someone who was possessed of it in preference to the man who was simply a good commander. But Burun was troubled. He wondered how the scouts would feel if they knew they were following a man who did not care if he lived or died.

'Dismiss your men,' he said finally. 'Then come to my tent. I want to talk to you.'

'Your son has been paying court to my daughter.'

The offworlder was sitting down, but it was as if he had received a blow. His eyes closed, then opened again.

'I'm sorry, Khan. I didn't know. What has he said to her?'

It had occurred to Burun to harbour the suspicion that Suragai had encouraged Alexai, as a means of insinuating himself into the ranks of the ruling class of the Khanate. But the offworlder's response was too dismayed to be anything but genuine.

Burun shrugged. 'Probably the same things that young men find to say to women anywhere. I did not make specific enquiry. But you should know that there are certain forms of words which we regard as an indication of feelings which go beyond casual flirtation. Maybe your son is not aware of this. Or perhaps he has spoken in your hearing of a more than casual interest in Turakina.'

Suragai shook his head. 'We do not speak much, my son and I. Though if Alexai wished to court your daughter formally, I believe he would have told me.'

'So.' Burun took wine from the table, and poured it into two cups. 'Love play then - nothing more.'

'Yes, Lord.' Suragai nodded. It was apparent that he appreciated the escape from the situation which was being offered. 'I suppose so. I apologise, of course, for the offence.'

Burun grunted. He was still inclined to have Alexai bastinadoed for his impudence, but on reflection he guessed that the fault lay as much with Turakina for her ability to fall in love with courtly manners and pretty attentions.

'Hunh.' He gave Suragai one of the cups and drank from his own. 'I'm not offended, Suragai. Though I do not think your son is a suitable match for my daughter.'

'No, Lord.'

'No.' Burun paused delicately. 'She needs an older man, who is capable of her.'

Suragai seemed to hesitate. His eyes were wary. The qualities required by a suitable candidate for the hand of Burun's daughter was not a subject upon which he would expect to be asked to offer an opinion.

'Yes, Lord,' he said finally.

The parchment upon which the grant of the Amirate had been recorded lay upon the table. Burun picked it up and held it out. 'This is yours now.'

The offworlder read the Cyraic script slowly. It was clear that he was surprised that he was still being honoured. Burun was pleased that he was able to keep him off balance.

'I will announce your elevation before tonight's meal. You can swear fealty to me then. It is customary for a person who is being raised to nobility to have a second or sponsor. Is there someone of rank whom you would like to act for you?'

Burun wondered if Suragai would nominate Nogai, but the offworlder only shook his head. 'No, Lord.'

'Then I believe that either of my sons would be pleased to stand for you.'

'Lord, whatever you decide.' Suragai was looking at the parchment in his hands. He laid it aside. 'Khan, I do not deserve this.'

'Nonsense.' Burun dismissed the objection. 'I am pleased with you. The Kha-Khan will be pleased. While it is unusual for someone who is not a True Man to be elevated, it is not unknown. And anyway, am I not the best judge of your worthiness or lack of it?'

Suragai looked up. Burun was unable to interpret the expression on his face.

'Yes, Khan.'

Burun considered what he was going to say next. He had discussed the matter with no one and had been unable, as a result, to obtain the benefit of an alternative point of view.

'Is there some duty to your Empire, or to God, which I must consider when I administer the oath of fealty to you? You must swear some form of allegiance, but you may do so in a manner which provides that you will serve me, saving only your duty already given to another.'

Burun wondered if Suragai realised that he was being offered another test. No man was capable of serving two masters, and the provision which he had mentioned applied only when a person of noble rank swore fealty to a feudal overlord who was not his father, to avoid a breach of the Yasa.

The offworlder's expression was remote. Burun experienced a moment of trepidation. It was impossible to know if he had judged his man correctly.

'No, Lord.' Suragai shook his head. 'Although the Empire is only on the other side of a barrier which is placed around this world, I do not think that it will be crossed in my lifetime.'

Burun had heard the offworlders mention the phenomenon, but since he was unable to visualise such a thing he remained unconvinced. Anything which had been made by men could be destroyed by men. So far as the power of the Empire was concerned, Burun would pay heed to it when it became necessary, and not before. He nodded wisely.

'You are right to forget your other life. For what choice have you? You will live out your days with us, and prosper. No man can ask for more.'

238

The wine which they were drinking was light but strong. Experience had shown that Suragai had a tremendous capacity, but he was tired, and had not eaten. Burun refilled both cups.

'Will it please your son that now you are of rank among us?' Burun phrased the enquiry carefully, as though it was a politeness.

Suragai drank, then laid the cup aside. He seemed to be disturbed by the question.

'Khan, I do not know. My son finds it hard to forget his other life. He regards this one as a poor substitute.'

'Ah.' Burun nodded. It was the kind of answer he had expected. He reached for the wine jug, but Suragai covered the mouth of his cup with his hand. 'Sons are important to any man,' Burun said softly.

The offworlder looked up. Then he laughed quietly.

'The Khan thinks that I should marry. Who does the Khan think that I should marry?'

It was Burun's instinct to pretend innocence. Then he saw that he was more likely to achieve the result he desired by directness. Even so he was troubled that Suragai had divined his intention so easily.

'I am of the opinion that you should marry.' He nodded. 'On this world at least, you have no wife. And no man who is noble should be unmarried. It is contrary to nature. And though you have a son, by your own admission you are estranged.' Burun paused. Then he posed his question gently. 'For whom will you prosper,' he asked, 'if not for your children?'

If the offworlder was dangerous, then Turakina would disarm him. And whether he was or not, the bond of a family relationship was the best security after blood.

Burun considered again what he was going to say next, and wondered again if the offworlder was capable of influencing the mind of another.

239

Turakina was in the garden. She was sitting in the shade of a tree which had broad, light-coloured leaves. Its branches curved over and brushed the ground in a circle around the base of the trunk, and she had chosen to sit within the overhang. When she saw Burun, she started like a wild animal about to flee.

Burun gestured easily. 'Peace, daughter. I need to talk to you.'

He lowered himself on to the grass at her side, sensing her tension.

'I am told you are mooning over that young Alexai, Suragai's son.' Burun saw Turakina flush, as if she was standing in front of a roaring fire. He took her hand and opened the fingers from the fist which they made. 'It is time you were married,' he told her.

Turakina turned her head quickly. 'Married? To Alexai?' She smiled.

Burun shook his head. 'That isn't what I had in mind.'

Turakina sat back on her heels. 'What?' she said.

'I thought Suragai.' Burun waited for her reaction.

She laughed in disbelief. 'The father? You want me to marry him? Never!'

If they argued, he would be unable to persuade her. Burun contemplated his hands until the silence between them seemed to be ready to explode.

'I won't do it.' Turakina spoke at last. Her tone was subdued, and somehow Burun was sure he would be able to reason with her.

'Listen to me. Suragai is older, yes, but he is also able to take care of you. And you need a man, not some boy who can give you only pretty words.'

She stared out across the garden, then turned. 'Among his own people, Alexai is a prince.'

Burun pursed his lips. 'On this world he is only the son of his father,' he said. 'Marry Suragai. Today I gave him an Amirate. Next year or the year after, if the war goes well, he could be a Khan.'

It was perfectly possible. Success in the war would create a number of new Khanates and someone had to rule them. Suragai would be in the forefront of the fighting and would attract notice.

'I'll wait for Alexai,' Turakina said.

There were crickets in the grass, and suddenly their noise was the only thing carried on the still air. Burun thought about appealing to Turakina's sense of family. But the notion that she should marry to provide him with grandchildren, to secure the line, would mean nothing to her. She had been herself too recently a child.

'Does Suragai desire me?' Turakina asked suddenly.

'He needs a wife.' Burun avoided the question. He thought about the offworlder's reaction to the proposal that he should be betrothed to Turakina. It had not occurred to him to ask if Suragai had any feeling for Turakina, and now he wondered about the possibility. 'You need a husband. How often have you talked with him?'

'Oh.' Turakina frowned. 'We don't like one another.'

'Oh well.' Burun grinned. 'Some of the best marriages start that way. Trust me. I'll watch over you.'

Turakina stared at him, troubled. 'Don't you care if I am happy?' she asked.

Burun sighed. 'Child, of course I care. That is why I won't let you marry Alexai. You could never be happy with him.'

She met his stare stubbornly. Then her eyes dropped.

'Very well,' Burun said persuasively. 'Maybe Suragai can convince you. I'm sending him ahead to the escarpment tomorrow. It will be some days before you see him again - time enough for you to think about the idea. Will you let him talk to you then?'

'I won't marry him.'

'Only talk to him.'

'All right,' she said. She looked away.

From the look on her face, Burun guessed that she meant to talk to Alexai as well, and he wondered if he should have sent the youth to the escarpment with his father.

# PART THREE

# Amir

Rostov sat cross-legged on the straw tatami which had been placed in front of the door of his yurt.

*Suragai*, he thought. *I am Suragai now.*

The sword which Yuan had forged lay close to hand, and his great compound bow, a gift from Burun, was in its case on a stand which had been placed just inside the antechamber. He turned his head and watched the slave who was walking his st'lyan back and forward near the edge of the escarpment.

*I should feel strange, living like this. But I do not.*

'Will you drink, Lord?'

'Thank you.'

Rostov accepted the cup of k'miss and drank from it. Teng had been a Ch'noze war-leader. Now he was body servant and personal guard.

The k'miss was light and sharp, and Rostov savoured the flavour of the liquor. Apart from the wine which the Yek accepted in tribute from conquered nations, there were three principal alcoholic drinks: k'miss, which was made from fermented mare's milk; k'vass, a light ale produced by brewing the k'va grain, which was a staple similar to rice; and tr'van, or rice wine. The k'miss which was made from the milk of the mares in the great herds belonging to the Kha-Khan was supposed to be the best but, so far, Rostov was unable to discern any difference between one fermentation and another.

'Amir?'

The Ch'noze was placing a low laquered table within reach. Rostov placed his cup upon it, then nodded.

'Thank you, Teng. Go inside now. I will call when I want you.'

'The Amir wishes.' The Ch'noze bowed. He retreated into the shadow of the door hangings.

Rostov smiled. The formula which Teng had employed was one normally used to acknowledge the orders of a Khan. The Yasa did not provide for the wishes of lower orders. An Amir existed to do the bidding of his Khan.

It was nine days since he had led the scouts south from Pesth, and the arrival of Burun and the main part of the reconnaissance force was expected at any moment. According to Kadan, the escarpment camp had been in existence for more than half a year, but now it was being expanded to hold not only the expeditionary force but also the commissariat and logistic support which would be required by the army which would assemble the following year. Large areas had been covered with awnings of treated linen, much heavier than the linen in ordinary use. The tent-like structures were remarkable, and reminded Rostov of the kind of shelters which were used by an Imperial circus. They were supported, between thirty and forty metres off the ground, by an intricate network of stays and cables, so that beneath them, the occupants of the camp were able to live and work through the very worst heat of the sun. Parts of Imperial Knossos were covered by huge permaglass canopies which floated on contragrav and, in spite of the fact that these Tarvarian covers were held up only by strategically placed poles, the similarity in structural design was amazing.

The heat of the sun was incredible. The native Yek in his scout company had told Rostov that this was the start of the coolest part of the year, but even so he was finding it hard to breathe and function during the hours of the day when the solar intensity was at its height. Only the races which everyone referred to as the True Men - the Yek, N'Pani and Ch'noze - appeared to be capable of disregarding the remarkable extremes of heat and cold to which Tarvaras was subject, and of all of them, the Yek were the best adapted.

Mentally Rostov chided himself for employing the planet's Imperial name. The Yek used no word in particular. When they spoke about the earth or the world it was possible for them to be referring to either the whole planetary mass or only a part.

It was important for the native inhabitants of the planet to forget that Rostov was an alien. To that end he was training himself never to speak, or, as far as possible, think in terms which related to his service with the Empire.

An Amirate was only the first step.

*Every day they must accept me a little more. Until they forget that I am not one of their own.*

The physical transformation had been the easy part and it had not been difficult to make Alexei and the others follow suit. Yuan had adopted Yek dress and customs quite naturally. They were not, after all, very far removed from those which were normal to Manchu, and those adaptations which he had made to suit his personal preference had excited no comment because, so far as the Yek were concerned, his physical appearance was in any case inalterably strange. Rostov's size made him stand out in any crowd, but he was not the only big man in the army. His kulak colouring and natural swarthiness was a minor advantage. As soon as he exposed his skin to the rays of the red sun, it altered to a tone which was almost normal for the planet.

The golden skin tint which was the result of the

prolonged use of Longivex was already vanishing.

*How many years will I live? Fifty? Less?*

It was impossible to be certain of the answer. All he knew was that once the longevity treatment was withdrawn, his body would begin to age at a progressively more normal rate.

*What age am I? I received my first treatment when I was in my early thirties, more than thirty years ago, and I have the appearance of a man of maybe forty or a little older.*

The first sign would be greying or perhaps whitening of the hair. A clean-shaven style was popular among younger officers, and it was no accident that Rostov had chosen to adopt it, even though moustaches and beards were normal among mature men. Fortunately the manner in which Yek nobility dressed their hair was one of the means by which rank was indicated. As an Amir, the forepart of Rostov's scalp was shaved clean, and the rest of his hair was drawn up and back into a stiff queue which was folded forward and secured with dark braid. Even if he began to go grey, the change would not be particularly noticeable.

People on the far side of the camp suddenly started to cheer and at once the troopers of Rostov's personal guard got to their feet. They looked expectantly at him. Rostov deliberately counted silently to fifty before he moved. Then he rose in the single elastic movement which he had copied from Burun. He inserted the scabbard of his sword into his waist sash, adjusted it to the precise angle, and strode towards the awning which had been set up to accommodate scout briefings. The guard commander hastened forward. He bowed and then gestured frantically at the slave who had been walking Rostov's st'lyan.

'Quickly, dunghead! Are you blind? Do you expect

your master to greet the Khan on foot?'

The slave rushed to lead the animal to the front of the canopy. Like most of the general servants he was a Y'frike, and now the pallor beneath his dark skin betrayed his fear.

It was a reaction which still troubled Rostov. Somehow, a rumour had spread that the offworlders possessed supernatural powers. The story was not taken seriously by civilised races like the Yek, but the Y'frike still adhered to many of their ancient tribal customs, among which were belief in magic and wizardry.

Rostov frowned as he took the st'lyan's rein and at once the slave prostrated himself.

'Jamil, get up.' Rostov realised that his frown had been taken for an expression of displeasure, and he sighed. 'Get up. I'm not angry with you.'

'No, Sidi?' The slave got to his feet. His eyes were wary.

'No.' Rostov showed his teeth.

It was the wrong response. Jamil backed off hastily. Then he turned and ran.

Rostov snorted.

The st'lyan was a chestnut with a light mane. Her single horn had been gilded with silver. The sound of renewed cheering made her start, and she pranced nervously.

Rostov stepped in under the sweep of the great horn, caught at the bridle, and blew gently into the widened nostrils.

'Hah. Easy, you devil spawn. Easy now.'

The animal whickered softly and tried to butt him. Rostov laughed, caught up the reins, and pulled himself easily into the saddle. Some of the troopers of the guard were already mounted and now the rest dashed for their tethered animals. The guard commander was a Yek called Y'zan. He leaned down to snatch up the guidon which had been standing outside Rostov's pavilion. The silver-blue flag unfurled lazily in the heavy air to reveal the insignia which Rostov had chosen as a totem - a black bear standing at bay on a silver field.

For no reason that he could have explained in words, Rostov was filled with a feeling of fierce exultation. He reined the chestnut into a tight curvet, and she reared and screamed.

The baggage train was stretched halfway across the plain, and Rostov began to believe that Burun was serious about his intention to treat the escarpment camp as a permanent base during the Alan campaign. He looked for the totem of the red ox among the flags of the vanguard and rode towards it.

'Good morning, Khan.'

Burun was riding alone. Rostov reined in until the chestnut and Burun's grey were walking shoulder to shoulder. The Khan stood in his stirrups, looked back over his shoulder, and spat.

'Good morning be damned. I'm in a bad mood, Suragai.'

'Really, Khan?'

'Yes, really.' Burun scowled. 'We've been eight days getting here, and I think half of the baggage is still in Pesth.'

Rostov suppressed a smile. 'You surprise me, Khan. I'm under the impression that you have commandeered every cart in the province.'

'Hunh.' Burun nodded sourly. 'And every pack animal. But I don't think anyone ever tried to move the whole contents of a city before.'

'Well, Khan, you could have organised the move in several stages,' Rostov observed mildly. 'The reconnaissance only involves two tenths, after all.'

'True.' Burun nodded. 'But I would have needed three full tumans to ride patrol between here and Pesth. Otherwise every bandit and vagabond from here to Ch'nozia would have been feeding off my supply train. Suragai, you look fit. Nobility must suit you.'

Rostov sat back in the saddle. 'Thank you, Khan. It's a condition to which I intend to grow accustomed.'

'Hah.' Burun's eyes narrowed. 'You're honest.'

Rostov shrugged. Suddenly he wondered if he had said too much.

'I doubt if I could deceive you, Khan.' He kept his tone matter-of-fact. 'Would you believe me if I pretended humility?'

'No.' Burun shook his head. 'No, I would not. We are alike in that at least, Suragai. There are few heights to which we would not aspire.'

Rostov was sure that he was betraying his thoughts upon his face. He looked away quickly. Nogai and his brothers were cantering past in line abreast. When they saw that he had turned in their direction, they waved.

'Greetings, Amir.' Nogai reined across.

'Good morning, Noyon.' Rostov nodded politely, but Burun only growled deep in his throat.

'Get back with your brothers, Nogai,' he said.

Nogai laughed. 'Name of God, Khan. I wouldn't wish a humour like yours on any man.' He looked at Rostov. 'Suragai, I would speak with you later.' He kicked his st'lyan into a trot, and pulled back into the column again.

Rostov let his mare find her own pace. The head of the train was dispersing into the camp now, although it would be an hour before the main body had finished crossing the plain.

'Beware of Nogai.' Burun spoke softly. 'He will try to involve you against me.'

251

Rostov was perfectly aware of the unofficial feud which was going on between Burun and Nogai, and he had already vowed that he would not be involved. He said nothing.

'Heed me,' Burun said. 'You are my vassal.'

'Is Nogai your enemy then, Khan?'

'Hah.' Burun grinned suddenly. 'A good question that. No, probably he is not. But he wants me to bow to him, which at present amounts to the same thing. Nogai intends to be the next Kha-Khan, for which, among other things, he thinks he requires my support. He reasons that if I am not for him, then I am against him. Thus he uses every opportunity to try to humble me. He will use you if he can, and so you must beware him.'

The command post with Hodai at its head was moving slowly past. It turned off into one of the covered areas of the camp. Slaves ran out to take the lead ropes of the st'lyan and others began to pull bales and boxes off the first of a line of two-wheeled carts. Rostov was aware that Burun was watching him intently. Suddenly Jotan rode up.

'Suragai.' He spoke as if in surprise. 'I expected you to be searching the baggage train for my sister. Are you such a cold suitor?'

Rostov was unable to conceal his dismay at the remark, and Jotan and Burun both laughed.

'My father tells me everything sooner or later,' Jotan observed smoothly. 'You should not be surprised that I know of his plan for you.'

Rostov felt himself flush under the younger man's scrutiny. It made sense for Burun to have discussed with someone the notion that Turakina should be married to an offworlder, but the fact remained that if she now refused the match he would be doubly embarrassed.

'As to the matter of courtship,' Rostov spoke to give himself time to recover, 'I have as yet no reason to suppose that my suit will be welcomed.'

'Well answered,' Burun said quickly. 'Jotan, go away. This marriage is none of your affair unless I choose. I will arrange matters as I see fit.'

'Oh, Khan.' Jotan shook his head. 'If I disapproved, I would make it my affair in spite of you. But since I do not,' he grinned at Rostov, 'you may plot and scheme as you please.' He nodded and rode off towards the nearest group of yurts.

Burun watched him go. His lips were compressed. After a moment he spoke. 'Sometimes my son is too perceptive for his own good. But what he says is true enough. For reasons which I do not understand, he is in favour of your match with Turakina.'

Rostov hesitated. It was important to choose his words with care. 'I suspect that the final decision lies with the lady, your daughter.'

'Hunh.' Burun nodded. 'You are right, of course. Still, she has agreed to speak to you.'

Rostov was surprised. 'She has?'

'You did not expect her to agree.' Burun grinned. 'Neither did I, or at least not so easily. Have you spoken with your son yet?'

It took Rostov a moment to adjust to the shift of topic. He shook his head. 'No, Khan.'

He had seen no point. Alexei would never accept the idea. It would mean accepting that they were on Tarvaras to stay.

'Hunh.' Burun looked thoughtful. 'Maybe you are right. Very well. Speak to Turakina tonight, after the command kuriltai. We leave in six days and I want you married by then.'

'Name of God, Khan!' Rostov spoke before he could stop himself.

253

Burun looked at him, then chuckled. 'Suragai, either you want to marry my daughter, or you don't. Either she will accept you, or she will not. But even if the G'bai turns to pure water, we leave in six days, and we will not return until the red month.'

Rostov calculated. A Tarvarian year consisted of ten months, each of nearly forty days standard. The calendar started with the black month, and ended with the bronze, and colours were related to some extent to the intensity of the sun. The red month was two hundred days or so hence, at a time when the sun would be at its height.

The command kuriltai was held in Burun's pavilion in the centre of the camp. The walls were hung with silk and the carpets were very fine. Low couches had been laid out in a rough circle and Rostov found a seat several places to the left of Burun.

Nogai and his brothers were crowded on to a single couch which was situated almost directly opposite. They had been drinking, but Burun had ordered the slaves to remove all the wine until the meeting was ended. One of Kiku's cats had found its way into the tent and T'zin was trying to persuade it to drink the lees from his cup.

'Have you had much time to scout the G'bai yet?' Jotan sat down on the couch at Rostov's shoulder.

Rostov nodded. 'I took a patrol ten verst south yesterday. It's brutal country.'

'It gets worse.' Burun was studying a copy of one of the old maps. Now he looked up. 'And there are things out there in the sand - creatures like nothing you have ever seen.'

'Afraid, Khan?' Nogai's voice was mocking.

Burun looked at him. 'Why should I be afraid, Noyon?' He showed his teeth. 'I don't know if there is

254

anything big enough to give us trouble out there, but if there is, you will encounter it before I do.'

'I see.' Nogai sat back. 'I'm riding vanguard, of course.'

'Of course.'

T'zin had succeeded in tempting the cat onto his lap, but now he scooped it up and dropped it on to a nearby cushion. 'In that case I'm riding vanguard too,' he said.

'And I.'

'And I.'

Tulagai and Targoutai spoke simultaneously.

Burun studied them for a moment. He seemed amused. 'Very well. But Nogai is in command.'

Nogai looked satisfied. 'Thank you, Khan. I might be honoured by your trust were it not for the fact that I know you hope I will fail in command and suffer disgrace.'

Burun looked innocent. He said nothing.

'Spare a thought for Suragai,' Jotan commented. 'If anyone runs into trouble first, it will be the scouts.'

Everyone turned to look at him and Rostov pretended a calmness he did not feel.

'Scouts are expendable.' Nogai showed his teeth. 'The good ones survive and the rest can be replaced if necessary.'

Rostov stared back at him. He knew that Nogai was trying to place him at a disadvantage, probably so that he could exert some kind of pressure in his struggle with Burun. 'I will scout for you, Noyon. But don't expect me to die unless it is quite unavoidable.'

Burun snorted. 'On this expedition, no one is expendable,' he said.

Turakina was in the small antechamber of the yurt which Burun occupied with his first wife, her mother.

She looked up once when Rostov entered, then dropped her eyes again.

It was the first time that Rostov had thought that she was truly attractive. She was taller than her mother, but she had the same red-gold hair which was common to Yek of Altun birth, and her eyes, though downcast, showed green in the light of the lamps which hung in the centre of the chamber.

'Your father says you don't want to marry me.' Rostov watched her face for a reaction.

She looked up. 'I love another.' Her stare was cold.

Rostov nodded. 'My son.' He caught up a stool and placed it so that he could face her. Then he sat down.

Turakina started. She began to rise, and Rostov caught her wrist with his hand. He was surprised how delicate the bones of her arm were, how soft the skin.

She jerked her arm out of his grasp.

'Name of God, you are a sorry courtier,' she gasped.

'I know it.' Rostov shrugged. He took her hand, and this time she did not try to pull free. 'My son is far better at this game than I. He has the experience of the court. He charms every woman.'

He saw her blink. Clearly this was an aspect of Alexei's character she had not considered before.

'I will always love him,' she announced stubbornly.

Rostov could not suppress a smile. 'Always is a long time.'

Turakina frowned, and he realised that she thought he was condescending to her. Her hand tightened into a fist, and then relaxed gradually again.

'Why do you want to marry me?' she demanded. 'I don't understand. Is it to spite your son?'

Rostov snorted. 'No, Lady.' He shook his head. 'Though if you accept me he'll be displeased.'

'Because he loves me,' she said at once.

'No.' Rostov let go of her hand. 'Alexei just wants to

256

play with you. He courts any woman, especially the pretty ones. I want to marry you. Surely you can see the difference.'

'But why?'

'Why do I want to marry you?' Rostov hesitated. He had spent an hour preparing the arguments he would present to support his suit, but now that he surveyed them, they were meaningless. He lifted his hands, and then let them fall. 'I doubt if you would understand.'

'I will.' This time she caught his hand. He started, surprised. 'Tell me,' she said.

He looked at his hand held in hers, then met her eyes. There was interest in her face, and the hostility was gone. He wondered if this was the first time she had received a serious proposal which was not shrouded with protestations of love and pretty speeches.

'Well, for one thing, I am the kind of husband you ought to have,' he said simply. 'I am a stranger to this land, an incomer, but that makes no difference. In any case there is a war coming, and there will be opportunities for someone who knows how to command men. You are the daughter of a great Khan, and you should not marry anyone who does not aspire to be a Khan as great.'

He could see that what he had said caught her imagination, and wondered if he should say also that her father desired the match.

'You are not human.' Her expression was doubtful.

Rostov showed his teeth. 'That is a matter of opinion, Lady. We are both of human stock, you and I. Will you define humanity?'

'No.' She shook her head. 'I believe you are a man, Suragai.' She smiled suddenly and he was surprised.

'Shall I court you?' he asked. 'What kind of things does Alexei say to you?'

Turakina shook her head and he waited for her to speak. Suddenly she stood up and he was sure that she intended to leave. 'I will marry you.' She looked down at him.

He got to his feet. The top of her head was level with his shoulder. Now that she had accepted him, Rostov felt absurdly pleased.

'I am a poor lover,' he said. 'But I'll be a better husband.'

Turakina said nothing and Rostov wondered if he ought to offer to kiss her. He had never seen a Yek kissing and did not know if perhaps it was contrary to custom.

'Tell my father I have accepted you.' Her expression was remote.

He nodded, and she turned away abruptly and left the chamber. Rostov went outside. Burun was standing waiting with Jotan and Orcadai, and behind them in a group were most of the Altun. When they saw him they swarmed forward.

'Well?' Burun demanded.

Rostov nodded, and at once Orcadai let out a yell of triumph.

Jotan slapped Rostov affectionately on the shoulder. 'Brother,' he said. At once everyone began to offer their wishes for the good fortune of the marriage. Rostov looked over the heads of those who were around him. Alexei was standing alone at the back of the crowd. For a moment their eyes met, and then his son turned away.

Burun took charge of everything, but even so it was four days before the ceremony of marriage took place. Plans for the reconnaissance expedition were almost complete, but whenever Rostov was not commanding a scout patrol he was kept busy with the minutiae of military preparation. Every animal, weapon, and piece of equipment was inspected at least twice. Every man of the expedition force was required to undergo a physical examination at the hands of a Sechem who had appeared in the camp.

Because Turakina was to be Rostov's chief wife and he had no male relative to whom the task of negotiating the contract of marriage could be delegated, Wotai, the commander of the fourth tenth of T'zin's tuman, was appointed by Burun to act as representative of the groom. The Yek lieutenant was tall and lean, his skin burnt almost black by constant exposure to the southern sun. He at once immersed himself in the endless technicalities surrounding the provisions for dowry and the portion of Burun's estates to which any children produced by the marriage would be entitled. Every time Rostov walked into a conference tent he found Wotai locked in heated argument with either Burun or one of his sons and he began to think that the wedding would never take place.

On the evening before the expedition was due to depart, everyone assembled under one of the huge canopies which had been erected to cover whole portions of the camp. Rostov stood in front of Burun and vowed to take Turakina as his wife. The bride was shrouded in golden veils and Rostov fleetingly wondered as she stood beside him if it really was Burun's daughter he was marrying and not a last-minute substitute. Her hand trembled when he took it in his to make the formal vow.

Custom did not require Turakina to speak. Burun asked her if she assented to the marriage and she nodded once.

With Burun on one side and Wotai on the other, they were conducted to a place of honour at the long table which had been set up along one side of the area.

Turakina sat down and her maids lifted back the veils. She was wearing a gown which had been sewn with myriads of pearls and gold droplets and her hair had been woven through with silver threads. She looked once at Rostov and he was struck by her beauty as if by a thunderbolt.

Everyone sat down, and the feast began. Representatives of all the Altun houses brought gifts to the table and soon there was a pile as high as a seated man and four times as broad.

Burun made a speech which was interrupted at frequent intervals by wicked jokes which were shouted from every part of the table. Rostov looked for Alexei and saw him sitting between Tulagai and Targoutai. The Altun were plying his son with drink and when they saw Rostov watching they laughed and winked. Yuan, Zukov and the others who had been with Rostov on the *Simonova* came and knelt in front of the table and swore to serve Burun as his vassals. Each of them kissed Turakina's hand, and Yuan gave her a *hiranu*, a Manchu dagger suitable for a woman, which he had forged.

One by one the Altun and the officers of the army were standing up before Rostov and Burun and offering to drink with them. Rostov mixed water with his wine and saw that Turakina was doing the same.

Alexei came before Rostov and saluted him with his cup. The youth was drunk, but he stood tall and straight. His hair was gold in the light of the lamps, rather than blond, and Rostov saw that people were marking the differences between them.

'Good fortune, Amir.' Alexei's voice was only slightly distorted by the amount he had been given to drink. He bowed, straightened and turned, then toppled like a falling tree. Tulagai laughed, and bounded over the table in a single leap. He draped one of Alexei's arms over his shoulder and supported the youth back to his place. The Altun cheered.

There were dozens of different dishes on the table, but Rostov had no appetite. He accepted a plate of a light-coloured meat which had been seasoned with the spice ch'min, which was a cross between pepper and coriander, and ate sparingly. Turakina was still refusing to look at him. Kiku and Zurachina came up and drew her away from the table and Burun reached across and poked Rostov in the side.

'Suragai, don't you want my daughter?' He laughed.

Rostov got to his feet and at once there was a yell from the people watching which tore the evening sky. A crowd of women were bearing Turakina away towards the yurt which had been built according to Yek custom on previously unbroken ground at the edge of the camp and now Rostov found himself being picked up by a group of young men led by Nogai. When they were only halfway down the beaten path to the yurt, they were loosening his tunic and pulling off his boots, and in the antechamber they ripped off his clothes as if they were skinning him. On the other side of the hangings which gave access to the main chamber Rostov could hear the excited laughter of the women. Then several of them ran past him carrying the gown which Turakina had been wearing at the ceremony.

The men stripped Rostov naked and pushed him through the door hangings. There were still women in the chamber, among them Kiku and Zurachina. When they saw him they screamed with laughter and ran out. Suddenly it was quiet.

Turakina was sitting in the middle of the bed. Her knees were drawn up, and she was clasping them with her arms. Her unbound hair was like a curtain across her shoulders. When she saw Rostov she moved to one side. Her breasts were small, the nipples salmon pink.

Rostov's mouth was dry and he wished that he had accepted one of the cups of wine which had been thrust at him in the antechamber. He sat down on the side of the bed.

'Which side of the bed do you want?' Turakina's voice sounded strange.

He hesitated, then shrugged. 'It doesn't matter.'

Outside the yurt someone shouted something, and Rostov cursed silently. There was a heap of silk sheets at the foot of the bed. He drew one up, then moved until he was beside Turakina. He slid one arm under her shoulders and she turned until she was against him. His heart pounded in his chest.

'I am a virgin.' Her voice was muffled.

Rostov drew back so that he could look at her. Turakina's mouth was drawn into a tight line and her eyes were blank.

'Yes,' he said. 'I know.'

He kissed her cheek and then her mouth, but she did not respond.

'Take me then,' she said. 'Everyone will know if you do not, because there will be no stains on the bed linen.'

The heat which had started to expand through his loins dismayed him. He was shocked to find how much he desired her, but now she was offering herself coldly, for no other reason than the fact that it was expected. He moved away from her and sat up.

'Don't you want to?' she asked.

Rostov closed his eyes, then opened them again. 'Of course I do not know your customs.' He did his best to speak without emotion. 'But among most civilised races it is accepted that it is wrong for a man to take a woman who is unwilling.'

'Did I not offer myself?' She stared at him but her expression was remote.

'Indeed you did.' Rostov considered her. 'And in such a fashion that it was clear that it was a matter of duty only.'

'What did you expect?' She seemed amused.

Rostov sighed. 'Lady, I expected nothing. I hoped that we might be friends and that in time you might feel more for me than friendship. As to desire, I admit the sight of you arouses me. But I will not take you, save that you wish it as I do.'

'Hah.' She shook her head scornfully. 'Then you are a fool. How could I desire you? But come, I will lie with you, for I am your wife, Suragai.'

Rostov was stunned by the power of the temptation which was being offered. It would be necessary for him only to touch her again to obtain her submission.

'You must take me.' Turakina's tone was objective. 'Otherwise I am disgraced. What must I do to arouse you? Show me.'

She put her hands on Rostov's shoulders, but he shook her off. The *hiranu* which Yuan had given her was lying on the table beside the bed. He picked it up. Her eyes widened and she moved back out of range, but he only used the blade to gash the palm of his hand. Blood welled, and he stirred briefly at the bowl of water on which the petals of some fragrant flower had been floated to assist their scent to permeate the air. Then he wiped his hand across the sheet, staining it.

'That for your maidenhead,' he said. 'Is that blood enough?'

Turakina looked as if she had been turned to stone. Rostov gathered a sheet around his waist for the sake of modesty, and went out into the antechamber.

The scouts left the escarpment camp before sunrise. Rostov had not spoken again to Turakina. The troopers of his guard seemed to sense the blackness of his mood and avoided him.

The G'bai was a desolate wilderness of rock and sand. There was almost no vegetation, nor any sign of animal life. The air was heavy, but there were winds which arose every so often apparently out of nowhere. They whipped the black sands into a choking mael-strom which blotted out the sun and made travel impossible. The Yek scouts cursed, but the savagery of the place matched Rostov's feelings to perfection.

Every scout carried a disc of baked white clay. Usually it was inserted in a leather holder which was fastened to saddle harness. The blend of chemical constituents in each disc was such that it would at once discolour if it was exposed to gamma radiation, and the incongruity of the use of such advanced tech-nology in these primitive surroundings caused Rostov to reflect anew on the unusual approach which the Yek adopted towards scientific knowledge.

Prior to the journey to the escarpment, he had directed Zukov and Mubarak in work to improve the heliograph which was used to communicate messages from province to province. The instrument which had been designed by the Sechem was large and cumber-some, and had been installed in a series of permanent stations which were situated on strategic hilltops. Although the Yek possessed an amazing amount of knowledge about optical science it had not occurred to anyone to construct a device which was portable, and the method of aligning the mirrors was primitive in the extreme. On a world where the light of the sun was red-shifted, glass appeared to be little more than a curiosity. Even in the cold lands of the north it was employed principally for decoration, and the fact that it could be manufactured in a transparent form seemed to excite no interest at all. The Sechem had been only politely curious when Zukov had started to hand-grind a series of lenses using small circles of clear glass and a quantity of fine sand. It was not until the first sighting telescope was completed that everyone seemed to grasp the implications.

The new heliograph was a tripod upon which was mounted a double mirror equipped with a shuttering device. Tests had shown that in the relatively flat country of the G'bai the instrument could be assembled, sighted in, and that messages could be transmitted over distances of ten verst or more. Broken down into sections, the heliograph was capable of being carried on a single pack animal, and Burun had at once agreed that every forward patrol should be equipped with one.

The alacrity with which the device had been accepted still surprised Rostov. In the early days after he had been marooned on the planet he had assumed that the Yasa was a series of absolute directives. Now he had begun to understand that the parameters which were set by the law were complex, and that there were degrees of behaviour.

*The Yek are not environmentalists.* The thought came unbidden into Rostov's mind. *Although they might as well be.*

In the Imperium there was perhaps an over-concern with environmental issues. But then again the evidence of the damage which could be done by the uncontrolled use of technology on planets where the natural resources were not inexhaustible was everywhere in the universe. Many of the worlds which had been populated during the Second Empire were now uninhabitable.

It was not simply expediency which governed Tarvarian use of scientific knowledge, although expediency was a code which the Yek understood and appreciated. Rather it was as if they had an almost faultless perception of what technology was right for their time and place. The science which supplied the reconnaissance force with a means of detecting lethal radiation subsisted alongside a quite primitive approach to the waging of the war, and yet the Yek perceived no contradiction of one by the other.

*It is as if someone took the trouble to predict the exact dangers for them and their environment inherent in the employment of every aspect of scientific development.*

Rostov had seen the codex in which the Yasa was contained. The entourage of every Sechem in the land incorporated the required number of carts or pack animals to carry the thousand or so volumes which delineated the law relating to every aspect of Yek life. The Sechem were not only the custodians of scientific knowledge, they also spent their lives learning to interpret the content of the Yasa and were the sole judges of its meaning and intention. Occasionally re-examination revealed a contradiction between one element of the law and another, and where the issue was complex the principal Sechem met in a kind of synod. Important decisions were sometimes years in the making and had to be confirmed by plebiscite.

According to Yek tradition the Yasa had always existed. They believed that the law came from God and was given to the True People so that they would prosper in the world of men.

*They have no religion and an almost complete absence of the kind of superstition which usually accompanies the development of a code of religious belief.*

The Yek had an unshakeable belief in the existence of God, but no system for worship. The Shamen, who were the nearest thing on Tarvaras to a priesthood, were concerned with the conduct of cremations and with the ritual cleansing of those who found themselves under a roof with or in the same room as a person when he died. It was generally accepted that the spirit of any deceased, which was released by the act of cremation, travelled to Heaven and dwelled there. There was however no word in the Yek tongue to communicate the notion of hell, save as a vague concept for a limbo into which a spirit might descend after death as a result of failure to observe proper rituals. The Yek did not connect behaviour on earth with the right to ascend to Paradise and as a result they were openly scornful of the notion that God was concerned with earthly conduct.

The clue to the origins of the Yek clearly lay in the Yasa. If it was not God's law, then it was the gift of a beneficent and far-seeing progenitor.

*Horse collars.*

According to the myth of Terran history, the development of the horse collar was the single most important element in moving mankind from primitive civilisation towards agrarian and technological reform. Certainly it seemed to be true that progress was related to the use by man of animals for the performance of heavy tasks like ploughing. Rostov had observed the phenomenon on a number of worlds in the Imperium. The fact that machines were later developed to carry out the same work tended to be simply another step in the progression towards what was classed in the Empire as civilised society. Except that on Tarvaras the progression did not exist. The earliest carvings depicting the tilling of the soil showed animals wearing collars which spread the load, allowing them to do ten times as much work as a man. It was Rostov's conclusion that someone had made the Yek a present of all the technology necessary for the development of a managed civilisation, along with sensible advice about the traps and pitfalls which had to be avoided along the way.

Rostov mentally doffed his cap to the unknown space wanderer who must have found his way to Tarvaras after the collapse of the Second Empire.

The pack beast that Zukov was leading on a long head-rope was called a p'tar. The animal possessed many of the physical characteristics of a st'lyan, although it was much bigger boned and lacked a horn. Its mouth was full of large yellow teeth, and its breath and temper were both foul. Every time the patrol halted, it promptly sat down. A goad, a metal-tipped length of hardwood, had to be employed on its rump before it would rise again.

A scout rode up and saluted.

'Amir, there are caves in the rocks ahead.'

'Good.' Rostov nodded. 'We'll rest there at least until nightfall.'

Orcadai had chosen to ride with the scouts. He looked surprised. 'We have travelled only a hundred verst. Why are we stopping?'

'We've come far enough,' Rostov said. 'Don't forget that your father won't leave the escarpment camp until it gets dark. Even the vanguard has not departed yet.'

Orcadai considered. 'In that case I don't understand why we have come this far.'

'Oh well, if you want to scout this territory at night, Noyon, you're welcome to try.' Rostov stood in the stirrups and surveyed the ground ahead. 'Personally I prefer to be able to see a trap before I ride into it.'

Orcadai looked as if he thought that over-caution was the prerogative of old men, but he said nothing.

The caves were really hollows which had been roofed over when the slabs of basalt which rose up on either side had split and collapsed until in some instances they met at the top. One of the covered depressions was occupied by a reptilian creature which looked like a cross between a crocodile and a monitor lizard. It rushed the troopers who disturbed it and had to be killed.

Zukov examined the metre-long mouth full of razor-sharp teeth with respect. 'By the Sack. I would be happier not to meet this in the dark,' he commented.

Rostov nodded agreement. It was the first sign of animal life the patrol had encountered, and he guessed that anything which could survive in the G'bai was likely to be equipped with either teeth or fangs.

Orcadai had climbed on the roof slabs. Now he came sliding back down the basalt again.

'I don't see how we can establish a regular caravan route across this country. The land is identical in every direction, and there are no features worth the trouble of mapping. I can only tell which way we ought to be travelling because I can see the mountains on the horizon.'

It was a point which had already occurred to Rostov.

'Yes. Every staging post will have to set up a beacon. The supply trains can travel at night, so the lights will serve as markers.'

'Beacons?' Orcadai looked perplexed. 'There's nothing to burn.'

'I had noticed.' Rostov tossed his reins to an orderly. 'Every caravan will have to pack oil. Mix it with sand and contain it in a shallow tray and it will burn for quite a time.'

'More weight to carry.'

'Well. No one said it was going to be easy to cross this wasteland.'

'And yet you treat each problem as if it were nothing.' Orcadai sounded envious.

Rostov shrugged. 'Military problems are much the same on every planet. A commander's aim has to be to move men and equipment to the right place on time, to ensure that his forces are in a condition to fight, and to maintain an adequate supply chain.'

'Hunh.' Orcadai started to strip away the cloths which were wrapped around the lower part of his face as a screen against the sand. 'I had forgotten. You're used to this.'

Rostov was amused. All he had seen since he had come to Tarvaras was military preparation being carried out by men who seemed to soldier as if by pure instinct.

He had left small patrols at intervals along the way, and late in the afternoon the signal chain which had been so established made contact with the vanguard of Burun's advance.

'Nogai Noyon wants to know what the ground is like.' Mubarak clattered the shutter of the heliograph in response to the signal flashes which were visible in the distance.

'Tell him it's all the same.' Rostov grunted. 'Suggest that he establishes a line of way stations with signal lamps. The main body will need something to follow tonight. They will lose Nogai's tracks as soon as a wind blows up.'

Mubarak nodded. He worked the shutter energetically.

'My father did not envisage this kind of difficulty.' Orcadai looked worried.

Rostov doubted if that was the case, but even if it was it did not matter. 'So we will improvise, Noyon. That's what soldiers do.'

The G'bai was not entirely featureless, but the

270

problem was to move men and animals along the same route every time so that supply dumps could be set up and maintained. If every tuman was not to be burdened with a huge load of water and grain - in theory sufficient to provide for a journey in both directions across the desert - then pack trains had to be organised, camps set up, and a mammoth logistical exercise undertaken to prepare for the movement of a full army the following year.

'Maybe we'll locate water,' Orcadai said.

Rostov did not answer. He was already fairly sure that the G'bai was not a natural geological feature, but rather the weathered and wind-eroded remains of a large radioactive basin, possibly the result of the detonation of a considerable number of atomic weapons, or perhaps a volcanic outflow produced by a massive nuclear accident.

The mountain peaks to the south shimmered white in the heat haze which was rising off the desert plain, and Rostov stared towards them. Until Orcadai spoke Rostov had forgotten that he was younger than Alexei, and that this was his first real campaign.

They were attacked on the fourth day. The first file of troopers was starting to cross an apparently deserted wadi when shapes rose up out of the sand all around them. A st'lyan screamed and fell, and suddenly there seemed to be half a dozen scouts each with a cluster of assailants dragging on harness or leaping to topple a rider from his saddle.

Several more men rode downslope before anyone could stop them, and Rostov cursed steadily as they too were overwhelmed.

'Use your bows!' He gestured. 'You can't fight them hand to hand. Pick your targets and shoot.' He ripped his own bow from its case, nocked an arrow and loosed into the mêlée.

More of the attackers were pouring into the wadi from both ends. They did not seem to be armed with anything more than knives, but already they were racing up the sandy incline towards the bulk of Rostov's command.

'Kill the leaders first!' Orcadai screamed. He rode along the crest directing fire.

Arrows hummed downslope and the first wave of the assault withered into nothing. The remainder wavered for only a moment. Then they came on.

Rostov concentrated on the bitter task of slaughter. He tried to aim each shaft mercifully, but there were too many targets and they were coming much too fast. The troopers of his personal guard were lined up on either side of him, and they too were shooting without a pause.

None of the attackers reached the top of the slope. The scouts started to yip triumphantly as they sensed that they were gaining the upper hand. Rostov switched his aim down into the wadi, and he began to pick off the shapes which still clustered round the fallen. The raiders were easy targets now because they were stopping to pillage even their own dead before they tried to escape out of range. The sand which had been churned up hung in the still air like smoke, and troopers moved along the crest so that they could see to shoot down at the figures now running to find cover. The action petered out as suddenly as it had commenced and there was silence.

'Name of God.' Orcadai sat slumped in the saddle. 'Name of God,' he said again.

There were eleven Yek dead, and in the short time since they had been killed they had been stripped of everything. Their robbers had not gone far. Still figures lay in clumps everywhere, and even the rags they had worn had been torn from their backs by others.

Rostov allowed his st'lyan to find her own way through the carnage. The physical appearance of the attackers was only marginally human. No two of them exhibited a similar mutation. The troopers who were recovering their arrows made no attempt to hide their distaste for the task.

It was now clear why the advance party of scouts had failed to notice that they were riding into danger. The wadi was really only a dry depression in the desert plain, and shallow pits had been excavated all over the hard-packed sand of its floor. Each foxhole was just large enough to contain a man. The strips of proofed material which had been thrown aside demonstrated how the occupants had avoided suffocation once the sand had been heaped back to cover every hiding place. The complete absence of tracks in the sand before the incident suggested that the raiders had been lying in concealment before the most recent windstorm, if not even earlier. It occurred to Rostov to wonder if the ambush had been planned or if the sheltering horde had simply reacted to the disturbance of their temporary domicile.

'Should we bury them?' Orcadai gestured at the dead lying everywhere.

The bodies of the fallen troopers had already been recovered, and they were being secured across the backs of spare mounts, even though it was not clear when it would be possible to cremate them according to Yek custom.

The commander of Rostov's personal guard spat once in the direction of a huddle of rags which appeared to possess claws in place of hands and feet.

'The G'bai will do the job for us soon enough,' he said.

Rostov nodded. The next windstorm would cover the bodies with sand, and before long there would be no indication that they had ever existed. He urged his st'lyan up the incline and out of the depression.

'You did well,' Burun said.

The vanguard was already out pasturing st'lyan in the lush grass which covered the plain at the foot of the mountains. Rostov sat in the shade of a tree which had broad leaves the colour of oxidised copper.

'Thank you, Khan.'

'Although you lost a man or two.'

'We were ambushed. Did your son tell you?'

'Yes.' Burun nodded. 'Probably you were lucky to lose so few.' He sat down on Rostov's saddle.

'We were careless.' Rostov had been sharpening arrows, but now he laid his quiver aside. 'They were among us before we knew what was happening. We should have pulled back from contact at once. Instead I lost more men because some went to help the others.'

'We will know better next time, all of us,' Burun said. 'Have you scouted the foothills yet?'

'Twenty verst in either direction.' Rostov nodded. 'We haven't located the pass yet, but Yesugai is still out on patrol. His last message said that he had found a river. Maybe if he follows it back he will find the gorge.'

'The old maps show a river which runs through to the plain on the other side of the mountains.' Burun pulled off one boot. He was wearing silk hose and when he pulled at a loose thread a great hole appeared at the heel.

'Yes, I remember. It could be the same.'

Two orderlies ran past with haunches of meat over their shoulders and Rostov turned his head to watch them. The meat was fresh, and he wondered which of the officers had been enterprising enough to organise a hunt.

'This is a good place.' Burun eased off his other boot. There was a hole in the heel of the stocking on that foot as well.

'Yes.' Rostov agreed. 'There are scores of small mountain streams feeding the plain. I think that is why it is so fertile, but even so it's a remarkable contrast to the desert. The land here has never been poisoned, I think.'

Burun looked interested. 'Could we set up summer camp here?'

'I don't know, Khan.' Rostov pondered. 'How much pasture does a st'lyan need? And would the Alan not attack us once they were aware of our presence? I imagine the G'bai represents as much of a barrier to them as it does to us.'

'Hunh.' Burun nodded. 'You are right, of course. And we would have to move everything from the escarpment. The sand I saw was too soft for carts.'

Rostov picked up the arrow file again. He selected an arrow from his quiver. Burun was only thinking aloud, and his mention of the possibility was not serious.

Jotan and Orcadai rode up. An orderly took charge of their st'lyan and led them away on a head-rope. No one was bothering to set up shelters or tents. Nogai and T'zin walked suddenly out of a patch of tall grass and Rostov saw Jotan tense.

'The perimeter guard is set,' Nogai announced.

'Good.' Burun did not look up.

Nogai squatted on his heels. He nodded to Rostov but ignored Jotan's presence. He was wearing a flowing sleeveless coat of some golden fabric over his tunic, and the material was bruised and tarnished

275

where it had been in contact with weapons and harness.

'How long do we remain here?' Nogai addressed Burun.

'Oh.' Burun selected a grass stalk, pulled it, and chewed thoughtfully. 'A night and a day. No more.'

'Hunh.' Nogai straightened abruptly.

Jotan jumped. His talons flashed, and at once Nogai moved into a fighting crouch. His hand stole towards the d'jaga at his waist.

'Go away, Nogai.' Burun spoke softly.

'Oh, Merkut.' Nogai showed his teeth. 'Make me.'

He started to circle to his left. Rostov whistled idly through his teeth. Then he reached out and tripped Nogai neatly with the arrow which he had been filing. Jotan jumped forward, very fast, but Burun was already on his feet. He caught his son by the arm, swung him in a half circle, and threw him headlong.

'I said go away, Nogai.' Burun looked back over his shoulder.

Nogai scrambled to his feet. He glared at Rostov, then looked back at Burun again. His face was flushed. Rostov saw that T'zin had not moved.

Suddenly Nogai seemed to relax. He laughed harshly. 'Name of God.' He threw one arm round T'zin's shoulder. 'The father is as poisonous as the son. Come on, brother.' He walked a few paces.

Jotan began to get to his feet. He appeared stunned.

Suddenly Nogai stopped and turned. 'I made a mistake,' he said. 'Merkuts are like oxen, slow and stubborn. But one should never try the strength of an animal before it has been broken.' He was not laughing any more. He turned away.

Burun sat down on Rostov's saddle again.

Jotan shook his head as if to clear it. 'Why did you stop me?' he asked.

276

Burun snorted. 'You don't learn, do you? He was only trying to provoke you.'

'I could have beaten him.'

'Maybe.' Burun smiled mirthlessly. 'But he was counting on me to protect you.'

'Hunh.' Jotan seemed to consider. He looked at Rostov. 'If my father is right, then you did well to interfere. Thank you.'

'I'm not sure that it was such a good idea.' Rostov picked up the arrow again. 'I gave Nogai an easy way out, didn't I?'

Burun nodded. 'He had forgotten about you at his back. Now that he knows which side you are on, he will be more careful.'

It had not occurred to Rostov that when he tripped Nogai he was also declaring himself. A squad of troopers carrying saddles and other equipment marched past. Jotan's son Jehan was with them.

'Hello, grandfather.'

Burun turned his head. 'Good day, Noyon.'

Rostov guessed that Jehan was perhaps eleven or twelve years of age. The boy was lanky, with the kind of awkwardness and lack of coordination which was the product of sinew and muscle development which was unable for the moment to keep pace with physical growth. His hair was Altun red, but his eyes were dark like Jotan's.

'I saw my cousin here.' Jehan sat down on the grass beside Burun.

'Who?'

'Nogai.' Jehan was watching his father's face as he spoke. 'He's my cousin, isn't he?'

'Oh.' Burun considered for a moment. 'A kind of a cousin, yes. He's the son of the half-brother of your grandfather.'

Jotan snorted. 'Not a relationship you should place

any trust in,' he observed. He ruffled his son's hair.

Jehan looked up. 'Oh, I don't. Besides, you're fighting with him.'

Jotan spluttered, but Burun only laughed.

'Well,' he said. 'He's certainly trying to.'

'I spoke with Turakina.'

Jotan came up silently and sat down at Rostov's side. The sun had set, but the two moons were both visible. They illuminated the grass of the plain so that it looked like a silver sea. Rostov closed his eyes, willing Jotan to go away.

'She is unhappy,' Jotan said.

Rostov opened his eyes. He had not thought that Turakina would confide in anyone. She was much too proud. He smiled grimly. 'Has she made complaint, Noyon?'

Jotan ignored the question. He laid a hand on Rostov's arm. 'Let me intercede between you,' he said. 'Are we not brothers?'

It was not an appeal which was designed to penetrate the barrier which Rostov had long since erected around the subject. He lifted Jotan's hand from his arm and laid it gently but firmly aside.

'What does the Yasa say about interference between husband and wife?' he asked coldly. 'Surely there is something to cover such a situation?'

Jotan sat back on his heels. He surveyed Rostov's face, then shrugged. 'It is forbidden for anyone to interfere in a private quarrel between husband and wife. Breach of the law is punishable by - I've forgotten the penalty - a fine, I think. I will pay it. The Khan, my father, will pay it for me.'

Rostov sat silent. Then he shook his head. 'Jotan, let it be,' he said at last. There seemed to be nothing more to be said, and after a while Jotan got up and went away.

*

Rostov woke early. It was cold before sunrise. A few troopers were already moving about. They fumbled with harness and equipment like men whose fingers were clumsy and sore.

Teng was heating a pan over a fire. When he saw that Rostov was awake he came over, a bowl in his hand. The meat in the bowl was hot and tasted of the spices in which it had been cured.

Burun was sitting on the other side of the fire. He wore a fur robe and Rostov wished that he had thought to provide himself with something warmer than the long overmantle which was inside his saddle roll. He had not expected it to be so cold.

Y'zan came from the direction of the pasture. He was leading Rostov's riding st'lyan. Other troopers were starting to cut their animals out of the grazing herd. Rostov scooped the last of the meat from the bowl into his mouth. He lifted one hand and caught the st'lyan's head-rope as his guard commander threw it. Then he tucked the end of the rope in his belt and bent to pick up his saddle.

The st'lyan reared suddenly. Its forelegs thrashed the air. Rostov dropped the saddle. He wrapped an extra turn of the rope around his forearm and pulled back, bracing his feet apart. The st'lyan crashed back on to all four hooves and Burun came up and grabbed a handful of her mane.

Someone was laughing. Rostov looked round. Nogai was standing on the far side of the fire. He was tossing a stone idly in his hand. He cocked his arm to throw again just as Jotan rode up. He caught Nogai's arm, swung him, and dropped him in the long grass. Nogai sat up cursing.

Burun picked up Rostov's saddle and threw it

across the st'lyan's back. 'I told you,' he said. 'He knows whose side you are on now.'

The river which Yesugai had located led to a gorge which ran all the way through the mountains. According to the old maps the river was called the Moistr', and it joined the sea beside an Alan town called M'skva.

There were no trails and no signs of human habit-ation. The mountains on either side of the pass were too steep to be climbed without difficulty. Rostov thought that if the Alan knew the route existed, they assumed that the G'bai was still an adequate barrier to the north-east. He led scouts as far as the plain onto which the river meandered, then sent men back to act as guides for the rest of the reconnaissance force. After that, Rostov ordered the men who were with him to make camp. He rolled himself in his overmantle, and went to sleep.

'I sent your son with Jotan.' Burun surveyed the camp-site.

A command post was being established beside Rostov's sleeping place. One of the tenths was already occupying a rise which overlooked a bend in the river.

Jotan had been detailed to scout along the foot of the G'bai side of the mountain range as far as the sea. No one knew what lay at the desert's southern edge. Even the maps were vague. There was a river running through the Serai Gorge which was to the eastern end of the escarpment, but the land where it crossed the G'bai was poisoned and no one was sure where it reached the sea.

Rostov sat up. The second tenth - part of Burun's own tuman - rode past and disappeared into the screen of trees which followed the line of the hillside.

He wondered if Jotan had spoken to Burun about his approach on Turakina's behalf and thought not. Burun was mentioning Alexei only because he was spending an increasing amount of time in the company of Nogai and his brothers. Sending him off with Jotan was calculated to remove him from association with the complex plots with which Nogai occupied his spare time. Rostov nodded, but said nothing.

'This is good land.' Burun was shading his eyes to look out across the plain over which the river flowed. 'I wonder why no one lives here.'

The same question had occurred to Rostov. The land was clearly fertile, yet there was no sign that it had been cultivated.

'Are the Alan a numerous people? Maybe they don't need to grow crops here.'

'Maybe.' Burun turned. 'They are city dwellers, of course. But they have to eat. I expected farms. There are two cities within a day's ride.'

'Within a day's ride for a Yek.'

'Well.' Burun grinned. 'Yes.'

Rostov visualised the land as it was depicted on the old map which he had seen. Apart from M'skva there was a place called Ruysdal on the coast to the south. If there was a way south around the end of the mountains, then probably Ruysdal guarded access onto the plain.

'How do you intend to scout this land, Khan?'

Rostov was having difficulty with the concept of reconnaissance in strength. The Yek were riding through the Alan country with a force of more than two and a half thousand men. It seemed to be common sense to assume that as soon as the occupants of the cities became aware of their presence, they would sally out to deal with the invaders. Burun's scouting expedition was too large to escape detection, yet it was too small to win any kind of battle.

The question seemed to amuse Burun.

'How? Why, with circumspection, of course,' he replied, and showed his teeth.

Ruysdal was surrounded by only a low stone wall. A man standing on the back of a st'lyan could have reached the top. The builders of the place had secured it by making it into an island. There was a moat around the wall and this was connected to the sea by a short canal. A bridge across the canal gave access to a single gate and the causeway up to the bridge was long and exposed.

As soon as the Yek rode out on to the open ground which led to the causeway, the townspeople closed the gate and raised the bridge. Boats which had been tied up along the length of the canal raised their sails and put to sea.

The people who lined the walls shouted insults at the troopers who rode up to the head of the causeway. Someone fired a gun and soon there was a regular barrage of weapons going off all along the wall. None of the shots even came close, and Rostov estimated that the range of an Alan musket was only a hundred metres or so.

Nogai rode over. 'What are they shouting?'

Burun turned. 'They are calling us T'tars. It's their word for barbarian.'

'Hah.' Nogai spat into the moat. 'When we take the place I will skin them all.'

Burun did not answer. He rode down off the causeway and along the edge of the moat. A thing like a hackbut boomed on the wall and the ball ploughed into the turf beside Rostov. He ducked instinctively, then straightened again. None of the troopers had moved and they seemed amused by his reaction.

Rostov was amazed at the casual manner in which everyone on the reconnaissance was behaving. They were riding up and down within gunfire range of a fortified town which had to be occupied by at least ten thousand people as if there was no cause for concern. Burun was inspecting the ground like the captain of a ball team before a match and it seemed to have occurred to no one that if the defenders chose to sally out in force they would be outnumbered.

Burun had stopped opposite a section of the bank which had been shored with stones and timbers. Rostov rode down to join him. The timbers on the other side of the canal had been painted black and he wondered if the Alan knew about pitch. The wall looked as if it was broad enough on top for a cart to be driven from one end to the other. There was only a low parapet and the stones on the exterior of the wall were stained with salt to show the height to which the water rose at high tide.

Nogai shouted a command at some troopers at the head of the causeway. They started to shoot steadily at the people who were clustered on the wall on either side of the gate and, as the hail of arrows increased, the sound of gunfire ceased abruptly.

'Could we fill the moat, do you think?' Burun stood in his stirrups and peered over the edge of the bank.

'I don't know, Khan. Probably.' Rostov looked around for trees, but there were few on the plain. 'We would have to collapse our side of the bank to fill the gap. That would make crossing under fire hazardous.'

'Yes.' Burun nodded. 'Maybe we could capture one of the boats.' He indicated the small fleet which was still circling in the bay. 'We could turn it across the channel to make a bridge.'

A single hackbut boomed again. Rostov managed not to duck. He was amazed at his own composure.

A rider spurred across. Rostov saw that it was Yesugai, an officer of the scouts.

'Khan, there are mounted men coming in from the west.'

Burun reined in. 'Good. How many?'

'Oh. Perhaps two hundred.'

'Excellent.' Burun uncased his bow. 'Now we can give these people a demonstration. I want them to learn to fear us.'

The tenth of Burun's tuman was already in motion across the plain. Rostov watched as its formation altered until it was a line of troopers two hundred or so abreast and about five deep. Burun waved at his standard bearer.

'Black flag, Khan?'

'Yes. But signal Wotai first. I want the tenth of T'zin's tuman to hold station along the causeway. The townspeople may consider sallying out when the fighting starts.'

The standard bearer nodded. He was unlatching his panniers of signal flags as he rode away.

'Right.' Burun urged his st'lyan off the side of the bank. 'Let's gallop.'

He sped after the extended line of T'zin's men. Most of the Altun were already following, and their personal guard were spread out so that they formed a second thinner line abreast which supported the thousand in front. Rostov uncased his bow. The st'lyan all around him were gathering speed. The ground rose at the point where the moat curved around the furthest extent of the wall. His mare charged upslope, gathered herself, and galloped flat out down the other side. The extended line of Burun's thousand was only metres ahead now and on the level ground beyond waited the enemy.

The Alan were wearing plate armour. Some of them

284

bore lances, but the majority seemed to be equipped with the heavy short-barrelled weapon which Rostov had mentally designated as a kind of musket. The Alan appeared to be disciplined and in good order. They were dismounted and their animals had been moved to their rear. Now they formed up in a screen across the path of the oncoming charge. There was a pause, then smoke bloomed along their line, and Rostov heard the noise of gunfire.

The Yek screamed. A single st'lyan fell and then it was as if the whole charge had accelerated. No one shouted a command, but the space between the two groups of opponents was momentarily black with arrows. Then there was a crash as the Yek rode over the musketeers and trampled them.

'Yaaaiyah!'

The yell of triumph carried clearly over the sound of battle. When it died away Rostov looked around. Nothing moved on the plain over which he had passed, and on the wall of the town the people who were watching gave a shout of dismay.

Nogai reined over. 'If they all fight like that, we'll soon conquer them.'

Rostov cased his bow. He could not remember using it, but the arrows which he had taken from his quiver were gone. Now that the Yek were forming up again he could see that the Alan had been slaughtered where they stood. The litter of armoured figures in the grass was in almost perfect formation.

'Nothing could have withstood such a charge,' he said.

Burun was sitting his st'lyan in the middle of the command post. Arghatun had commanded the charge, and now he rode up and saluted.

'We lost seven men, Khan.'

'Very well. And the Alan?'

'We're still looking for survivors, Khan.'

Nogai urged his mare forward. 'Kill them all,' he said. 'The weapons they use are contrary to the law.'

Rostov opened his mouth to protest, but Burun only laughed drily.

'Perhaps we ought to teach them the Yasa before we punish them for breaking it. Arghatun, if you find any alive, they may be taken prisoner. But destroy the weapons. Break the barrels, and then build a fire and burn them.'


'How can we lay siege to such places as these?'

They had just passed M'skva. It was another walled town like Ruysdal, but this time it had been built on an island in a river delta and no moat was necessary.

Rostov said nothing. He had already discussed the subject at some length with Burun.

'We can't.' Burun was riding at ease, one foot out of the stirrups, the free leg hooked across the pommel of his saddle. 'Or not for long, at any rate. If we have to camp round a town or city for any length of time, we'll need to be in control of large areas of the country. Otherwise we will starve before they do.'

'There are farms,' Orcadai objected.

'Yes. And each farm is a small fortress. These people were fighting one another long before we came along. That's why they shut themselves up behind stone walls.'

A courier galloped back along the column and Rostov stood in the stirrups to see where he was going. Burun had sent Nogai and T'zin to scout two cities which lay to the north and there had been no word from them for a day and a night.

'How can we beat the Alan if we cannot capture the towns?' Orcadai sounded puzzled.

'I didn't say we couldn't take them. We can't main-

286

tain a siege, so we will have to storm them. And we will have to tempt their army on to ground of our choosing so that we can destroy it. Once they get used to being beaten, they will run from us. The farmers will be isolated and it will be easy for us to exercise control.'

Hodai was riding on Orcadai's other side. He laughed softly. 'Of course if you say it, Khan, it must be so.'

Burun snorted and everyone laughed.

Yesugai rode in from the flank. He was accompanied by Tulagai and Targoutai.

'Well.' Burun looked at Targoutai. 'Tell me about M'skva.'

'Oh.' Targoutai was taken by surprise. He seemed to make a conscious effort to remember what he had seen. 'Well, it's bigger than Ruysdal.'

'How much bigger?'

'Oh. The walls are straight, so it's hard to tell, Khan. But it's definitely bigger.'

'Hunh. Half as big again, I would say.'

'Er - the walls are stone. They are about ten times the height of a man. There must be a rampart. I saw men standing on the top.'

Burun showed his teeth briefly. 'An excellent deduction, Noyon. What else?'

'I saw only one gate.'

'Did you look at every wall?'

'Oh. No, Khan.'

'How deep was the water surrounding the walls?'

Targoutai looked perplexed. 'Khan, it was impossible to tell.'

'Oh? Were there boats? A bridge? Do they drive carts across the river? They don't walk on the water.'

Targoutai flushed, then seemed to collect himself. 'There were cart tracks, so there must be a ford. Probably the water is not very deep.'

'Good. Were there any people outside the wall?'

'No, Khan.'

'Very well. There was smoke coming from the place when we rode past. What were they burning?'

'I don't know.'

'Wood? Rubbish? Dead bodies?'

'I don't know.'

Burun snorted. 'Use your nose next time. Were there soldiers on the walls, or only townspeople?'

'How could I -'

'Soldiers wear armour. Were the men on the wall wearing armour?'

'Some of them were.'

There were clouds scudding across the horizon. Rostov wondered if it was going to rain. There had been one downpour already that day and, although he had spread his mantle out behind his saddle, it was not yet dry.

Burun rode on a little way. 'Very well,' he said finally. 'Targoutai, next time try to think about the things you might want to know if you were planning an attack.'

'Yes, Khan.' Targoutai was clearly relieved that he was not to be criticised further. 'I'm sorry.'

'You should be. You'll learn.'


Messengers from Nogai came in during the night. They had ridden past both Shermetyev and Suslev.

Rostov remembered the map. Shermetyev was a city in the centre of a plain. Suslev was the port at which Yek envoys had been detained the previous year. Burun only grunted when he was told. The reconnaissance force was now roughly halfway between the mountains and the sea coast to the west. So far the information provided by the old maps had been accurate, and only a few small settlements had been located which were not marked.

A number of prisoners had been taken. Mostly they were Alan scouts who had been intercepted as they tried to keep pace with the fast-moving Yek column. They spoke freely when they were questioned and confirmed that the Alan capital was a city called T'ver. According to the map, it was four or five days' ride to the west, at the head of a gulf which gave access to the Y'rabe Gulf.

The roads between the towns and cities were narrow and poorly maintained. Rostov thought that probably little cooperation existed between individual communities. Every stronghold appeared to serve as both the headquarters of local government and as the centre for trade. Outlying areas relied upon their own resources for continued survival and the most prosperous farming land was that which was closest to a principal fortification.

The column turned on to a road which was so narrow that only two men were able to travel on it abreast.

'These must have been city states not so long ago.' Rostov reined over, dismounted and bent to examine his st'lyan's hooves.

Burun stopped beside him. He took both feet out of the stirrups and flexed them to restore the circulation. 'Yes. Some of the prisoners we took are men from M'skva. They were fighting for Ruysdal only because they were paid. The two places are not allies.'

'I did not know that you had spoken to them, Khan.'

Rostov had been astounded to discover that Burun spoke nearly every known Tarvarian language. Alan was a little like the colonial argot which was spoken in the Imperium, but the vowels were different and the meanings of some of the words were incomprehensible to Rostov.

The hooves of his mare were full of compacted earth and stones. He lifted each in turn to clean them.

'They are a barbarian people,' Burun said. 'They have no notion of order.'

Rostov was still becoming accustomed to the Yek attitude towards civilised behaviour. Barbarity on Tarvaras seemed to be a matter of degree. He grinned.

A courier was forcing his way along the road past troopers of Burun's guard. When he saw Burun he pulled over and saluted.

'Khan, I have a message from Jotan Bahadur.'

'Go on.'

'He has found a way past the mountains south along the coast. Also he followed the edge of the G'bai east until he encountered the mouth of the Y'ntze River. He found a city there, but it was empty. The land beyond the river is poisoned. Nothing lives there.'

'Very well. Where is my son now?'

'Khan, he was at Ruysdal two days ago. He said that he would find you.'

'Hunh.' Burun nodded.

The courier saluted again and turned away.

The column was moving suddenly faster. Rostov guessed that the vanguard had reached a wider place in the road, probably where it left the forest. He had scouted the route the previous night, encountering no one.

Burun was inserting his feet in his stirrups again. 'Now we can go and find T'ver,' he said. He sounded pleased.

They camped that night beside the ruins of a small town. Much of the stone and all of the timber had been removed by scavengers, and the scouts who explored the place expressed the opinion that it had been deserted for years.

The troopers of the guard lit fires and everyone clustered round them. Only one moon was visible, partially obscured by cloud, and the night was very cold.

'Where do you suppose the people went? Did they die?'

At first Orcadai had rolled himself in his riding cloak, but every time someone wanted to get in to the fire he was forced to move aside and now he was huddled shivering at the base of a fallen tree.

Burun drank from a leather bottle which he had taken from Hodai's saddlebag. He swallowed, then tossed the bottle to Rostov.

'Probably they were forced to move to one of the cities. A settlement this size wouldn't be big enough to protect itself.'

'Maybe there was a famine.' Arghatun fed a log into the fire.

'Maybe.' Burun shrugged. 'But I think that to survive in this land, a community has to be self-sufficient. It has to be big enough to defend itself. They were fighting one another before we came. Every city has a duke and they all try to steal one another's land. The duke who controls the most becomes king.'

'Hunh.' Orcadai edged closer to the fire. 'That's good for us, isn't it?'

'It could be. One city won't rush to help another when we attack. The army is controlled by the king. But if every duke is trying to be king, then probably the army only fights to protect the king's land. Maybe the army has trouble with supplies if it travels very far from the capital.'

Rostov sniffed the contents of the bottle, then drank cautiously. The k'miss was almost clear spirit and it had been distilled and re-distilled for maximum strength and purity.

'Maybe an attack will make the Alan forget their differences,' he said.

Burun looked up sharply. He waited until Rostov had finished drinking, then took the bottle again. 'Maybe,' he said. Then he upended the bottle and drank.

Rostov followed Yuan down into the hollow. The Manchu's st'lyan was a bay with white forelegs and he managed her with an economy which even the Yek had trouble equalling.

The grass was bright green, and the trees were tall and straight. Their bark was flesh-coloured and instead of leaves they sprouted huge growths like fungi at various points up the trunk. Zukov and Mubarak were waiting in the shade of the largest.

When they saw Rostov, they saluted. A Yek trooper saluted by bringing his right forearm up, fist clenched and more or less level with the left eye so that the arm was diagonal to the body. The non-coms were employing the familiar Navy version and Rostov guessed that the choice was significant. Alexei was off with Jotan and Vorontseff was in Pesth, but he saw and spoke to the other *Simonova* castaways on a more or less daily basis.

It was Yuan who dismounted first. The Manchu looped his st'lyan's reins over one arm. Then he squatted on his heels. Rostov looked at the sky. It was difficult to tell what time of day it was and he was still getting used to the fact that on Tarvaras the redness of the sun always tinged the clouds.

He kicked one foot free of the stirrup and crossed the free leg over the saddle.

'Well?'

Instinct made him wary and he watched the faces of the non-coms with suspicion.

The months had been good to Mubarak. The ex-gunnery sergeant was the member of the group who most resembled a native Tarvarian in height, features and skin colour; he had made the transition to his new life with ease. As a scout for Burun's tuman and as the acknowledged liegeman of an Amir, the one-time marine was well provided for by the Khanate's feudal system. He owned property and mastered slaves. In due course of time his military skills would guarantee him advancement. Zukov, on the other hand, had changed little. The Master-at-Arms was still grizzled and burly, and needed only to resume Navy coveralls to be recognisable once more as a servant of the Empire. He spat to one side, then dismounted. Mubarak followed after a moment.

Rostov felt as if he was facing strangers. The non-coms had the look of conspirators. Their expressions were closed, as if they had a secret to protect, and they watched Rostov as if he was a potential obstacle to their plans. It was a development which took him by surprise. He had always taken his relationship with them for granted and now he was unable at first to comprehend how it could have changed.

'We scouted south yesterday.' Mubarak spoke without preamble. 'A city called Pereislav.'

'I know.'

Pereislav was on the coast. It exercised nominal control over the area through which the reconnaissance force was passing, and it possessed a fleet which apparently ruled both of the almost land-locked arms of the sea, which penetrated the mainland east to M'skva and west to T'ver.

'Oh yes.' Mubarak nodded. 'We reported.' There was a sense of reservation in the remark.

Rostov looked up sharply. He was sure that there was more. He was also certain that it would be a mistake to display too much interest.

'So?'

It was clear that both Mubarak and Zukov were disappointed by the lack of reaction. They glanced at one another, then, as if they had arrived at a decision, Zukov nodded.

Mubarak met Rostov's eyes. 'The duke of Pereislav is called Yuri,' he said simply. 'We have spoken to him and he offers you a dukedom if you will join him, and help him to become king.'

Something moved in the long grass on one side of the hollow. Yuan's st'lyan tossed its head, tugging the reins from the Manchu's grasp. Rostov wondered if the meeting was being spied upon by the Yek, but when he looked he saw only the flash of a brown speckled hide as some unidentifiable animal scurried over the crest of the rise and out of sight.

'A dukedom,' he said. 'I see.'

They would not have transmitted the offer if they did not think he ought to accept. Suddenly Rostov wondered how much Yuan had known before the meeting.

'We could make ourselves the masters of this land.' Mubarak seemed to assume that in the absence of an outright rejection there was at least a measure of interest. 'These people use guns, not like the Yek. And they're not all that far from industrialisation. With our help, who knows what they could become?'

By pooling their knowledge and skills, the *Simonova* castaways could probably advance Alan military science by several centuries. Improved fire-arms would make a tremendous difference to the defensive capability of the cities and industrial development would quickly erode their isolationist tendencies.

'The Yek don't want what we can show them,'

Zukov commented. 'They've made that clear enough.'

Rostov was recalling the careful extraction of every particle of scientific and technical knowledge by the Sechem Parin. Their understanding of law, philosophy and religion had been investigated - even the games the people of the Empire played. He said nothing. It was true that the design of an improved heliograph and the introduction of camouflage scarcely rated as recognised technological advancement. It was fair comment to observe that the Yasa seemed to have been drawn up with the specific purpose in mind of impeding scientific progress. He was in any case dismayed by the whole turn of events. Mubarak and Zukov had certainly entered Pereislav. They had spoken to the duke and so they must have been seen by scores of people who might survive as captives to remember the incident when, next year, the city was taken by the Yek.

'The Yek will conquer the Alan next year.' He watched Mubarak's face.

Mubarak's eyes became shifty. 'Not if the cities are prepared,' he said. 'A year is a long time.'

Rostov guessed that the ex-marine had already betrayed everything he knew of the Yek intentions to Pereislav's duke.

'Oh?' He raised an eyebrow in deliberate sarcasm. 'You think you can support and equip this duke, make him powerful enough so that he can impose his will on others and still have time to prepare a defence against invasion?'

Mubarak flushed.

The whole thing was possible, of course. A Yek attack could be halted at the mountain passes, provided that all the cities cooperated.

'It could be done.' It was as if Zukov was reading Rostov's mind. 'You could do it.'

The observation was made in a matter-of-fact tone, and Rostov remembered how often the Master-at-Arms had followed his lead blindly into a variety of seemingly hopeless situations. Then he shook his head.

'Maybe I could. But I won't.'

They had sworn fealty at his wedding, but now Rostov thought that at least for Mubarak the words had been simply a matter of form. A divide had come into existence between them. Or perhaps it had always been there. It was clear that Mubarak was prepared to argue the decision, but Zukov drew him away with no more than a muttered word. He nodded to Rostov, and together they mounted and rode up out of the hollow.

Yuan stood up. He had remained silent throughout. Now he caught up his st'lyan's reins and pulled himself into the saddle. Then he met Rostov's eyes.

Rostov made a face. As on a variety of occasions before it was easier to convey the sense of his feelings in Manchu.

'*Nan-ja?*' - What now? -

He was aware that his tone was a challenge. Yuan seemed to consider. When he responded, his accompanying hand gesture displayed his concern.

'*Shigata ga nai, Sama.*' - There is nothing to be done, Lord. -

The reply took Rostov by surprise. He had expected a more positive observation. Now he shook his head.

'*Ogoku na.*' - I don't agree. -

Mubarak and Zukov had to be watched, and somehow Burun had to be told before he found out. Suddenly it occurred to Rostov that he was thinking like a Yek.

The Manchu bowed from the saddle. For the first time since Rostov had known him, he appeared flustered.

'*Hai. Gomen nasai, Sama. Watakshi wa kuru kumoko.*' - Yes. I am sorry, Lord. I will place a watch on them. -

'*Yoi.*' - Good. -

Rostov nodded as if he was satisfied. He was not sure that the Manchu had not been party to the idea, but there was no way to be certain. Yuan would know at once if he was being watched.

He nodded again, but this time he could not meet Yuan's eyes.

'*Taihenyoi.*' - Very good. -

He put his free foot back into the stirrup. Then he lashed the reins angrily across the barrel of the st'lyan and charged up on to the plain.

The closer the reconnaissance got to T'ver, the more time the Yek spent riding through the forest to avoid Alan patrols. They were at full strength again, now that both Nogai and Jotan had rejoined, and it seemed incredible to Rostov that a force of over two thousand men could ride through a country without detection.

The forest here was dense. Rostov could see only the riders two or three abreast of him. The ground underneath the trees was covered by a thick blanket of fine needle-shaped leaves and the st'lyan made almost no sound as they moved. Someone rode silently in and out of a patch of light-coloured saplings off to the right, and in the distance a patch of lake glittered, revealed momentarily by the contours of the landscape. Then it was lost to view again.

Burun came up. He drew level with Rostov so that they were riding practically toe to toe. Somewhere ahead a voice called out, and Rostov stiffened.

'That wasn't Yek.'

'I know.' Burun uncased his bow.

The ground started to slope downhill. Rostov's

st'lyan was stretching out and he tried to rein her in. A trooper yipped, and Burun cursed savagely.

No one was sure how close they were to T'ver. The Alan capital was supposedly situated at the head of a branch of the sea which penetrated north-west into the land mass. The reconnaissance was coming in from the east, but no one had seen anything except plain and forest for a day and a half.

Another shout sounded, much closer this time. Hooves beat on the slope, and a bunch of troopers broke through the screen of trees to the left. They pulled up when they saw Burun.

'Khan, there are men on foot ahead,' one of the riders shouted. 'I think the vanguard needs help.'

'Damn these trees!' Burun gestured at Rostov. 'Come on. If Nogai is in trouble it must be the Alan army.'

He kicked his st'lyan into a gallop and Rostov followed.

It was impossible for cavalry to fight properly in a forest this thick. If the enemy were in any kind of strength there would be chaos. Rostov uncased his bow and selected an arrow. His st'lyan leapt over a windfall, staggered, then gathered herself once more. Troopers yipped steadily. They were using the sound to maintain contact with one another, but the noise made it impossible to determine exactly where the action, if there was any, was taking place. Suddenly a different voice bellowed. Rostov saw men fighting on the ground among the trees ahead. The strangers were not trained soldiers, and they were clothed in padded garments in a variety of drab colours.

'Wood cutters.' Burun sounded relieved. 'We must be close to T'ver.'

The Alan were swinging axes. The low branches of the trees were getting in the way of the troopers who were trying to deal with them and Rostov saw someone swept out of the saddle.

'Surround them, damn you!' Burun stood in the stirrups and shouted. 'Don't let any of them escape!'

Already a few of the men on foot were running off through the trees. An arrow caught one of them between the shoulder blades and he pitched forward on his face.

'Don't kill them all!'

Burun wanted a prisoner from T'ver. Troopers dived out of the saddle on to one of the runners and he was wrestled to the ground. A horn blew somewhere and at once all the woodcutters tried to run towards the sound.

The prisoner was being roped to the saddle of a spare st'lyan. Burun watched, then gestured to Yesugai. 'Take everyone and go. Head east. Move.'

'Yes, Khan.' The officer saluted.

Nogai rode up. 'What's this? We're running away?'

Burun scowled at him. 'A tactical withdrawal. You can have the honour of leading it. Ride east for a day. I will catch up with you. Suragai, you come with me.'

'Where are you going?' Nogai's tone was petulant.

Burun sneered at him. 'To see T'ver, of course.' He pulled his st'lyan's head round and plunged off down-slope to the right.

Nogai's face was a study. He looked as if he was ready to shout after Burun, or even to follow him. Then he seemed to think better of the idea. He shouted to the troopers who were around him, and they moved off into the depths of the forest.

Rostov concentrated on catching up with Burun. The slope steepened and something charged through the brush to his left. He could not tell if it was a man or an animal. Suddenly the slope became more gentle and Rostov found that he could see the sky above the tree tops quite clearly. The forest was thinning.

Burun pulled up sharply, and Rostov almost ran into him. They were on a small plateau and there were no more trees ahead.

T'ver was huge. The walls and most of the buildings were constructed of stone, although many of the roofs were covered with wooden shingles. Beyond the inner wall there lay a vast harbour. Ships rode at anchor in it, their sails furled. There were no cultivated fields to be seen. Probably they were north and west of the city. Rostov had seen only a grain like wheat in the fields he had ridden past. He wondered if the Alan relied upon fish as a source of protein.

There were people outside the city wall. The ground had been cleared for almost half a verst and from their vantage point Rostov and Burun were able to see that there was a party close to the city gates. They seemed to be loading rocks into two carts. There was a single man wearing plate armour standing guard over them, and Rostov thought that probably the labourers were felons.

A small group of mounted men clattered out of the trees some distance to the left. The men who were working near the gate straightened up and called out to them as they passed. Then five or six woodcutters trotted down a track which led out of the forest and joined the main road. There were more mounted men behind them, shepherding them anxiously.

The city gate opened outwards. That was useful to know. There were people on the walls above the gate now, and they cheered as if the others who were riding in had won a victory. Probably they thought that they had driven the Yek away.

'When it is dark we will go down and have a closer look.' Burun slid out of the saddle.

'And then?'

'Oh.' Burun looked surprised. 'Then we will go home.'

Rostov looked at the sky. The sun was high, and he suspected that it was not yet midday. He dismounted and bent to inspect his st'lyan's hooves. The chestnut stood patiently while he raised each hoof in turn and cleaned out the wadded leaves and forest debris.

'There are other cities.' He looked sideways at Burun.

Burun was settling himself against the trunk of a large tree. 'I know it. But we have seen all the important ones.'

'Oh.'

Rostov hesitated. He had not yet found a suitable moment to tell Burun about the offer from Pereislav, although he had made certain that neither Mubarak nor Zukov was ever free from surveillance. When he looked up again he saw that Burun was watching him steadily.

'I have never seen reconnaissance carried out this way, Khan.' Rostov knew that his smile was strained. 'Now that the Alan know that we are coming, they will be prepared.'

Burun shrugged. 'No doubt. But now that we know how they fight, we can beat them. The more men you use to scout a place, Suragai, the more information you gather.'

'And of course you never consider the possibility of defeat.'

Burun laughed softly. 'Every plan suffers from setbacks,' he observed. 'But we cannot be beaten. We can only die.'

The concept was horrifying in its simplicity. Rostov shook his head and Burun laughed again.

Rostov tethered his st'lyan to the branch of a tree.

He searched his saddlebags until he found a lump of dried p'tar meat. The Yek delicacy had been smoked until it was rock hard. Rostov used the blade of his d'jaga to shave off a sliver. Then he placed it in his mouth, allowing his saliva to soften the morsel, and chewed slowly.

'Would your soldiers die, Khan, if they knew there was no hope of winning?'

Burun was watching the city. The gates had been closed, but there were still men working at the carts which were outside the walls.

He turned his head. 'Perhaps that is why the Yek have never been beaten. For how can any man win a battle if he has lost hope?'

The deep note of a horn was sounding inside T'ver. The gate swung open again, and a large body of mounted men rode out. They headed up a narrow road which seemed to skirt the forest and Rostov guessed that they had been sent out to try to establish the location and strength of the Yek. Most of the Alan wore plate armour and all of them were equipped with short muskets. The combination of firearms and armour seemed to represent a contradiction in terms, especially at the level of military development which appeared to have been reached. Then Rostov realised that the plate was probably being worn because at longer ranges it was sufficient to protect the wearer against low-powered shotfire. It suggested that the Alan were putting too much charcoal in their gunpowder.

Burun watched the riders out of sight. 'It is perhaps fortunate that the vessel which brought you to us landed first within the domain of the Kha-Khan.' His tone was thoughtful. 'For if you had come first to the Alan, then no doubt your knowledge would have strengthened them against us and next year's fighting would be harder.'

Rostov swallowed. For a moment he wondered if Burun already knew about Mubarak's betrayal.

'I doubt if we would have made much difference to the outcome, Khan.' He managed to respond calmly. Then he grinned. 'Everyone knows the Yek are invincible.'

Burun looked up sharply. Then he chuckled. 'That's the kind of answer I would expect from a foreigner. But you are Yek now.'

'Am I?'

Burun nodded cheerfully. 'Oh, yes. Or else you would have deserted to the Alan at the first opportunity.'

It occurred to Rostov that he had been tested once more, and had passed. He whittled another shaving from the p'tar meat, then sheathed his d'jaga.

'And if such an opportunity has been offered, Khan?' He did his best to speak casually.

'I would be surprised if it had not,' Burun said. 'I wondered if there had been something of the kind. You have not been yourself since Pereislav, Suragai.'

Rostov was perturbed to discover that his emotions were so transparent. He waited for Burun to demand to know what had occurred, but the Khan only resumed his study of T'ver and its surroundings.

'The wall is too high to be scaled by assault,' he observed. 'Do you think we could sap under one of the towers?'

Rostov searched his saddlebag again and pulled out a miniature version of the sighting telescope which had been designed for alignment of the heliographs. He scanned the ground along the wall.

'I don't think so, Khan. The foundations appear to be solid rock and in any case there is no cover. We would have to construct a mine. And that would take weeks.'

'Hunh.' Burun reached across, took the telescope and trained it on the wall. Then he nodded. 'You are right.'

'There are plenty of trees. We could build siege towers.'

'Yes.' Burun looked thoughtful. 'And maybe we could mount a diversion at one gate, then storm another or part of the wall. The gate timbers look old. If they are dry, they ought to burn.'

Rostov found it hard to concentrate on the problems of taking T'ver. He was still thinking about Burun's reaction to what had been said before. He waited until Burun handed back the telescope, then spoke.

'One day, Khan, I'll learn to understand the way your mind works.'

Burun grinned. 'Don't try. Even my wives say I am unpredictable. Tell me what Pereislav offered you if you like. But I trust you, Suragai, otherwise I would not have married you to my blood.'

Alan cavalry came into sight down the road round the edge of the forest. Rostov could not tell if they were the same as those who had ridden out earlier. When they arrived at the gate the men who were working outside the wall followed them inside. This time there were no cheers from the people who were on the walls.

Rostov settled back on his heels. He wondered if everyone had got away safely. It was only a short time since the woodcutters had been surprised, yet already the men of T'ver seemed to have lost interest in pursuit.

Burun led the way east without a pause for rest. There were bands of mounted Alan patrolling many of the narrow roads, but they seemed not to be organised, and they were easy to avoid. Plate armour made a noise every time the wearer moved, and several times Rostov and Burun waited with their st'lyan in the shadow of a stand of trees while armed cavalry clattered past.

They found Nogai on a plain which was situated in the centre of a range of low hills. Rostov saw the light of the fires when they were still half a verst from the camp, and he was surprised that it had not attracted an attack.

Nobody seemed to be particularly surprised when they rode in. Jotan and Nogai were sitting on opposite sides of one fire, and when Burun and Rostov dismounted neither of them even turned.

Teng stripped the chestnut's saddle and led her away. Rostov squatted and straightened in an attempt to ease some of the kinks out of his back. Then he strode stiff-legged over to the fire.

'So tell us about T'ver.' Nogai's eyes glittered in the firelight.

Burun tossed his reins to an orderly. He stamped his feet to restore the circulation. 'Tell him to go and look for himself,' he said.

Rostov shrugged. He met Nogai's stare. 'It's big,' he said. 'Probably it can be taken.'

Jotan laughed. 'What a report. A masterpiece.'

Burun snorted. 'It's as much as any of you need to know for the moment.' He sat down on his heels and held his hands out to the fire.

Nogai turned away. There were slaves beside a fire nearby.

'Someone bring the Khan his dinner!'

It was Teng who brought the food. Rostov felt too tired to eat, but he accepted the bowl which was placed in his hands. The meat was hot and when he tried to fork it into his mouth it burned him. He choked and swore.

'Did you talk to the prisoners?' Burun looked at Nogai.

'Yes.' Nogai nodded.

'Then probably you know as much about T'ver as we do.' Burun took a bowl from Teng's hands. He emptied it in a few mouthfuls and laid it aside.

Alexei walked into the light cast by the fire. When he saw Rostov he turned and walked away again. Rostov laid his bowl aside unfinished. There was a bitter taste in his mouth like bile and he was sure that everyone was watching his face for reaction.

'The hunting here is good.' Nogai addressed Burun. 'We could spend the whole season.'

'We would graze out the plain in no time.'

Jotan looked up. 'That's true. It would be different if we controlled the whole province.'

'We will control it.' Burun stood up. 'Next year.'

Mubarak disappeared during a patrol three days later. No trace of him was found by the men Yuan sent out to search, but the trooper who had been entrusted with the task of watching him was found dead in a ditch beside the Pereislav road.

Burun only shrugged when Rostov brought him the news.

'He is one man.' He showed his teeth. 'We will find him again next year.'

Rostov attempted to calculate the damage Mubarak could do by taking service with the Alan. There was little doubt that he would be able to upgrade Pereislav's defences. Probably he would improve the quality of the firearms, and would correct the errors the Alan were making in the manufacture of gunpowder. He was capable of designing the tooling necessary for the production of rifled gun barrels, and Rostov wondered if he would recognise the advantages of employing cannon against light cavalry.

There remained the question of the extent to which any advance in military science was capable of being communicated to other cities. Pereislav's duke was nominally a subject of the Alan king. However, in view of the offer which had been transmitted to Rostov, it was unlikely that he would willingly supply to others the technology which was the source of his military superiority. As soon as the Alan army possessed advanced weapons in any quantity the balance of power would be re-established. The duke's aspirations towards the throne would be overthrown. It seemed to follow therefore that he would attempt to retain control of new developments.

Rostov doubted if a year was enough time for Mubarak to initiate any kind of production line for military hardware. Even if Pereislav grew powerful, there seemed to be little chance that other cities would be brought under its control, either by force or by negotiation, before the campaign season arrived. He repeated his reasoning to Burun, who looked thoughtful.

'I had not thought that one man among you was capable of so much,' Burun said. 'I do not hold you responsible, Suragai, but it would be better if he had died.'

Zukov had made no attempt to leave. Rostov thought that even though he was removed from Navy discipline, desertion was not in his nature.

In the last light of the sun Rostov rode out on to a plateau which overlooked Pereislav. The gates of the city were tight shut and there were armoured men patrolling the walls.

Burun rode up behind. He wheeled his bay, goading her into a prancing curvet. She screamed, and at once someone on the city wall pointed and called out. The gong of an alarm began to sound.

'It is only another city,' Burun said. He sounded satisfied. 'See how they fear us.'

Every city had closed its gates. At M'skva the troopers of the vanguard rode beneath the walls. The people pelted them with rubbish, and threw stones, but there was no attempt to bring the passing Yek to battle.

Rostov felt tired and depressed. The sun was now oppressively hot in the sky, although at night it was cold and the ground was hard. The Yek forded the Moistr' a verst beyond the city. Yuan took a company of scouts to see if he could locate the Alan army which was rumoured to be riding to intercept them, but found no trace of military movement of any kind.

'They could have occupied the pass.' Burun sounded surprised. 'They could have made us fight.'

In the dead black of the night, just before the dawn, a courier rode in. Nogai's vanguard had encountered a group of peasants who were herding oxen away from the river. The herdsmen had fled.

'And the beasts?'

Burun was watching as Rostov made careful corrections to a map by the light of a lantern. He looked up.

The courier looked solemn. 'Khan, we slaughtered what we needed. Nogai Noyon sends you the gift of meat.' He indicated a laden pack animal.

'Oh.' Burun looked amused. 'Thank the Noyon for me.'

Rostov recollected that there was some kind of special significance attached to the custom of a meat gift. Jotan was riding with the command post and he laughed softly.

'Nogai should have sent honey. Or maybe the meat is sweet enough already.'

At first Rostov did not understand. Meat was only

sweet when it began to rot. Then he realised that Jotan was casting doubts on the quality of Nogai's sincerity. He remembered that the Yek used the meat bond as a pledge of everlasting friendship. He was used to the fact that Jotan and Nogai fought whenever they met, and the situation never seemed to trouble Burun. Jotan and Nogai were like two dogs of equal size and strength. They growled and snarled a lot, but the injuries they inflicted upon one another were never serious.

The dawn became a thin grey line which edged the mountain peaks. The Yek had been riding all night, and lack of sleep had given Rostov a headache. He made a last correction to the map, rolled it, and pushed it down into the sleeve lining of his mantle.

'How far is the pass?' Jotan asked. He had already mounted. Now he plucked the reins of Rostov's chestnut from Teng's fingers and led her over.

Rostov pulled himself into the saddle. 'A day's ride at this pace.'

'Why do you think the Alan left it unguarded?'

Rostov snorted. 'Who but a Yek or a madman would bring an army across the G'bai? Probably they think we came in by sea.'

The reconnaissance travelled through the gorge of the river without incident. The river was high and it tore at the clefts in the rock as it passed through them. The noise of rushing water drowned all conversation and Rostov was glad of the opportunity to withdraw into himself. He wrapped himself in his riding cloak, allowed his st'lyan to follow the trail and dozed in snatches.

Burun allowed the st'lyan a day's grazing on the lush grass of the plain which skirted the desert. Then he started them across.

Way stations had already been set up. The column moved by night and followed the light of flaming beacons from one vantage point to the next. Only a single brush with the *felahin*, the mutant sandpeople who inhabited the wadis, interfered with their progress.

Two full caravans of supplies had already been despatched across the G'bai, and the harassed captain of the principal depot reported that both had been attacked. Rostov remembered the horde which had rushed his scouts and wondered how so numerous a species had managed to survive in a place where there was clearly so little to eat.

In the clearing among the rocks which served the way station as a baggage park, a broken cart had been turned into a makeshift cage. Inside it, something prowled constantly.

'We captured two of them,' the captain said. He indicated the cage soberly. 'One was injured, but it would have lived, I think. We did not know when we caged them together that they were so hungry. They are cannibals you see, Khan.'

Jotan was peering between the bars. He stepped back, looking sick.

The *felahin* seemed to be annoyed by the presence of so many spectators. It crashed against the wooden slats making them shake, and uttered a snarl which was more animal than human. Rostov had a glimpse of the creature's face as it turned and saw nothing even vaguely manlike there. There was a wolf's muzzle instead of a nose and mouth, and its snarl displayed yellow fangs.

Both moons were visible in the night sky, but the way-station guards had lit fires in braziers set all along the perimeter and they patrolled nervously. Something moved in the sand and at once a st'lyan screamed.

Rostov shivered. The sandpeople were probably descended from human stock, but they were so mutated as to be unrecognisable as such. He could think only that they deserved nothing better than the extermination which they would doubtless suffer as soon as the Yek became tired of losing men to the protection of the desert caravan routes.

Imperial policy towards mutated species was brutally simple. The worlds they inhabited were quarantined. Rostov had never believed that isolation was the answer, but now he was no longer sure. Humanity was not a measurable quality, but it was possible after all that there was some kind of qualifying standard for measurement of the human species.

The sand of the desert was flat and hard packed. It stretched out seemingly endlessly in the heat so that riders in the distance seemed to float above the ground. Jotan's guidon hung limply and Rostov was able to identify it only because someone had attached a rod at right angles to the flagpole to hold the material out. He reined in and dismounted.

Jotan was sitting on a flat rock sipping his ration of water. He nodded when he saw Rostov, but made no attempt to rise.

'Do we camp? This march is madness.'

Rostov shook his head. It had been Burun's decision to continue riding into the heat of the day. The Altun had argued, of course, but the column was too close to the escarpment for their protests to carry much weight.

Alexei was crouched down against the base of a rock. He looked up when Rostov approached and at once assumed the stony expression which he now favoured whenever they met. Rostov bit down on his anger. He seized a handful of Alexei's mantle, pulled him to his feet and thrust him out into the sand until they were out of earshot of Jotan.

'We are going to talk.'

Alexei wrenched himself free. 'Are we?'

'Yes. I'm tired of your behaviour.'

'Oh.' Alexei sneered. 'Forgive me. The Amir is tired. The Amir is embarrassed, no doubt. The Amir's son is tiring him.' His voice was raw.

Rostov thought that most of his son's torment was self-inflicted. He back-handed Alexei as hard as he could. Alexei saw the blow coming, but he made no attempt to avoid it. He fell to his knees.

Rostov glanced quickly round. Jotan was sitting on the rock. His back was turned.

Alexei launched himself as he got up. Rostov caught his wrist. He bent and heaved, and his son tumbled into a shallow depression where the wind had scoured away the loose sand. Alexei was up almost at once. His feet kicked the sand into tiny cascades as he rushed up on to level ground. A rock a little smaller than his fist was lying at Rostov's feet. He picked it up. When Alexei charged, he stepped to one side and hit him below the left ear as he went past. Alexei sprawled on his face and lay still. Rostov bent down to make sure that he had not fractured his son's skull. Then he mounted his st'lyan and rode away.

With any luck Alexei would never know that he had not been knocked out fairly. Halfway back to the command post, Rostov let the rock fall. It had one sharp edge, and his fingers were torn. Carefully he wiped the blood off on the skirt of his mantle.

'We march as I command.' Burun was shaking his head.

'Damn you!' Nogai tossed his reins to Tulagai. He slid from the saddle. 'If you are in such a hurry, Khan, ride on. Why should everyone else suffer? This desert was never meant to be crossed in daylight. You are mad.'

'You think that when the campaign starts you will always be able to choose when to travel?' Burun hawked and spat. 'Push your men.'

'I am pushing them. If they were not Yek they would have revolted long since.'

Burun made a rude noise. Rostov grinned. He inspected the palm of his hand and picked away the shreds of dead skin which were still clinging to the inside surfaces of his fingers. It was several hours since the fight with Alexei and he had just received a message from Jotan to say that his son was unhurt.

'Well?' Burun stared at Nogai. 'What are you waiting for?'

Nogai looked as if he was trying to think of additional arguments to support his case. He threw up his arms, snatched his st'lyan's reins from Tulagai's hands and hauled himself back into the saddle. Then he rode away.

Burun watched. After a moment he dismounted slowly and carefully, as if every movement was painful.

'You think they are right.' He was watching Rostov's face as he spoke.

Rostov shrugged. He had passed the stage of extreme physical discomfort long since. The extreme heat made it next to impossible to breathe, he was dehydrated and every joint in his body ached.

'Khan, any fool can be uncomfortable. But the training should always be harder than the campaign.'

'Oh.' Burun grinned painfully. 'That's why I feel so terrible. Come on, get down. We'll walk for a while.'

Rostov dismounted. The hardpacked black sand stretched off to the horizon and the heat haze was so intense that he could no longer see the mountains behind. The dust which hung in the air turned the blue of the sky to violet. The red sun was a huge ball which hurt his eyes whenever he looked at it.

'We haven't lost a man or an animal to thirst,' Burun observed. 'I would worry if they didn't complain.'

A rider came pounding across the flat towards them. He was obscured by a cloud of dust, but suddenly Rostov knew that it was Alexei. His stomach muscles tensed with expectation.

'You will kill your animal if you ride her like that in this heat.' Burun waited until Alexei dismounted before he spoke.

'I was in a hurry.' Alexei's tone was harsh.

'Hunh. Your message must be urgent.' Burun looked amused. 'So speak.'

'Oh. It's urgent enough, Khan,' Alexei said. He hurled himself at Rostov.

Rostov jumped back. He jerked his reins and the chestnut reared and screamed. Alexei was forced to duck to avoid the mare's flying hooves and, before he could recover, Rostov let go of the reins and moved in. He hit Alexei three or four times in succession, driving him back, giving him no time to recover. Alexei dropped to his knees.

There was a d'jaga in his son's waist sash. Rostov jerked it free. He rested the point against Alexei's throat. Alexei froze.

'You have a message?' Rostov moved his hand so that the point just broke the skin. A tiny rivulet of blood started down Alexei's neck. 'So deliver it.'

'Father,' Alexei smiled artificially, 'I have forgotten what I wanted to say.' He got smoothly to his feet and backed off.

Rostov snorted. He looked at the d'jaga in his hand, then tossed it into the sand at Alexei's feet. At once Alexei bounded forward. He caught Rostov around the waist, and they rolled in the sand.

Two of Burun's aides were starting forward. Burun shouted at them and waved them back. Rostov was winded by the fall. He pushed Alexei away, but as he was climbing to his feet his son's arms pinioned him from behind. He took a deep breath. Alexei's grip shifted predictably to a chokehold. Immediately Rostov brought one arm up and back. He flexed, half rose and heaved, and Alexei flew over his head. Rostov followed, crowding in. He had to finish the fight quickly.

One of Alexei's boots caught Rostov below the knee and he stumbled. At once Alexei was diving forward. He wrapped his legs around Rostov's waist, forcing him over on his face. Rostov felt his son's weight pressing down, so that he was unable to move. He felt Alexei grab a handful of hair. His head was jerked back, and then a fist smashed him across the face. Rostov gasped. There was blood in his mouth and he spat it out. He heaved himself up off the ground on all fours, then lurched back so that when he fell Alexei was underneath.

Alexei was sobbing for breath, but he maintained his hold. Rostov jerked one arm free. He elbowed his son hard, and as soon as his grip loosened, rolled away.

Rostov shook his head. His sight blurred and it was hard to see. Alexei was already on all fours, rising to his feet. His face was like a stranger's. Rostov started to get up, but before he could stand something hit him in the face. He collapsed again. Off to one side Burun was standing watching. His eyes were remote, as if he was trying to make his mind up about something. Rostov was wondering why he was making no attempt to stop the fight when another blow hit him in the face and he fell into a pool of darkness.

*

'I never knew you were so strong.' Alexei moved the flap of the canopy so that it provided more shade.

'Is there any water?'

'Yes.' Alexei poured some into a bowl and held it while Rostov drank. 'I'm sorry,' he said. 'I didn't mean to hurt you.'

'Spare me the remorse. If I had the strength to get up I would break your neck.'

Rostov found that he was shivering as if he was suffering from a fever. Alexei soaked a cloth in some of the water and applied it to his father's face. Rostov flinched.

'There are cuts on your cheek.' Alexei dabbed carefully. 'I have to get the sand out of them.'

'You're a sorry nurse. Have I no other friends, that I must put up with you?'

Alexei snorted. 'Hah. It's because of your friends that I'm here. The way they were looking at me, I would have ended up with an arrow between my shoulder blades the first time I turned my back. They all gave up their water ration for you - Burun, Jotan, Orcadai, Nogai and all his brothers.'

Rostov closed his eyes.

'Are you all right?' Alexei sounded anxious.

'I'll survive. Alexei, I don't want to fight you.'

Alexei looked away. 'You'll feel better after you have rested,' he said at last.

'I mean it.' Rostov felt unbelievably tired. 'I won't fight with you any more.'

He watched Alexei's face.

'I didn't beat you, you know.' Alexei looked at his hands. His knuckles were red and skinned. 'I only knocked you out.'

'It doesn't matter. You would have beaten me eventually.' Rostov eyed the crop of bruises on his son's face. 'I'm not as young as I used to be.'

'No.'

Rostov closed his eyes, then opened them again.

'Stop agreeing with me. Where is everybody?'

'Burun made them move on,' Alexei said. 'Your guard is still here.'

'Wonderful. How long have I been asleep?' Rostov squinted through the flap at the sky and guessed that it was near nightfall.

'A few hours. You needed to rest.'

'Not here.' Rostov struggled to sit up. At once Alexei tried to make him lie down again.

'You're not well.'

'And whose fault is that? We ride on as soon as it gets dark. I don't care if you have to tie me onto the saddle.'

Alexei sat back on his heels, lips pursed. 'God. You're so stubborn.'

'You ought to be used to it by now.' The effort of sitting up made Rostov feel sick. He put a hand to his chest and winced at the pain. 'Name of God, I think you trampled me after you knocked me out.'

'Oh, well. Your new wife can soothe your hurts when you get to the escarpment,' Alexei said. Then he paused. 'I'm sorry. I didn't mean that the way it sounded.' He looked genuinely contrite.

Rostov took a deep breath. It hurt, and he wondered if he had cracked a rib. 'Alexei, we have to stop this.'

'I know.' Alexei looked solemn. 'It doesn't change anything, does it?'

Rostov moved until he was resting most of his weight on his right side. In that position he was more or less comfortable. A light wind hissed across the sand blowing the black grains into tiny flurries. The canopy of the shelter flapped a few times and then snapped taut as the wind grew stronger.

317

'Perhaps if we could start again, things would be different.' Rostov watched the ropes which anchored the shelter as they vibrated in the wind. 'But I cannot unmake the past.'

'Father, I -'

'No, wait. Hear me out. You are angry because I have married. Is it because you think I have forgotten your mother?'

'I - I just don't understand.' Alexei seemed suddenly very young. 'How can you marry someone who is -' He stopped.

'So much younger?'

'That, yes. But also she is -'

'An alien?'

'Yes.'

Rostov nodded, and said nothing. He waited until the silence seemed to be stretching into infinity. Alexei shifted nervously.

'Do you think we will ever leave this world?' Rostov met Alexei's eyes. 'Surely you can see that we are here until we die.'

Alexei hesitated. 'There is always a chance.'

'And are we to live our lives in anticipation of that chance? Is that what you want?'

There was an expression on Alexei's face which was somewhere between agony and distress. Suddenly it was as if an inner tension had been released. His shoulders slumped. 'No,' he said.

'Very well, then.' For the first time Rostov thought that everything was going to be all right between them. 'In that case you have to accept that we have a kind of duty to survive here the best way we can - to live as men and not to fall to the level of beasts. Whether or not you accept that the Yek are either human or civilised, we have to live out our lives among them.'

'I know that.' Alexei was looking at the ground between his feet. Suddenly he looked up. 'Father, do you love her?'

The question took Rostov by surprise. For a moment he could not find the words to answer sensibly.

'How can I explain to you?' he said at last. 'If you will tell me what you mean by love, then I will tell you if that is what I feel for Turakina. Or if you want to know if I love her as I loved your mother, then I would have to answer no. It is not the same. How could it be?'

'Loved.' Alexei caught at a single word. His mouth twisted.

'What?'

'You said loved. As if my mother was dead.'

Rostov clenched and unclenched his free hand. Irina was not dead, but he knew he had to forget her. Yet Alexei could not be told that, or not in those words.

'She might as well be,' he said at last. 'Do you think she believes that we are still alive?'

Alexei looked blindly away. Slowly he shook his head. 'I wish that there was some way to tell her that we are here,' he said.

Rostov flexed the arm upon which he was resting. There was blood under his finger nails and he could not understand how it had got there.

'Probably there is,' he observed. 'But what then? You seem to forget that someone went to a great deal of trouble to ensure that none of us survived. The fact that they failed makes little difference. Don't you think that advertising our presence - even if it is possible - could be rather risky?'

Apparently this was an aspect of the situation which Alexei had never considered. He frowned.

'You're saying that we are safer where we are.'

Rostov made a face. 'I'm saying that until exactly the right opportunity presents itself to alter our circumstances, we ought to do the best we can where we are. There's a difference.' Rostov lay back again. 'You know, these are good people, even if their ways are different from ours. Surely you are beginning to see how impossible it would be to try to impose our ideas and attitudes on them.'

Alexei stood up, uncertain. Rostov watched him.

'Tell me,' he said. 'Were you courting Turakina seriously? Would you have wished to marry her?'

Alexei looked confused. He avoided Rostov's eyes. 'I - I don't know. The question never arose.'

The evasion was sufficient answer. Rostov closed his eyes, and after a while Alexei went away.

Burun was standing in the middle of the yurt floor. His slaves were trying to dress him. Every box and chest in the chamber seemed to have been opened and emptied of its contents. There were silks lying everywhere. The hard riding of the reconnaissance had stripped every gram of fat from Burun's body and he had already spent several minutes complaining that none of his clothes fitted properly.

'You look terrible.' Burun eyed Rostov.

Rostov sat down on a stool. 'Thank you, Khan. I feel even worse.'

'Oh, well. You will have the summer to regain your strength. And if it is any compensation, your son's bruises are nearly as colourful.'

'I had noticed.'

Burun ducked his head so that a slave could place a chain made of flattened gold links around his neck. 'Of course you are reconciled now, you and he.'

Rostov was not deceived by the apparent lack of interest. He remembered Burun's face as he watched the fight. 'As much as we can be under the circumstances. We don't really like one another very much. It's best if we don't force matters.'

Burun did his best not to look disappointed. 'Hunh. You know best, of course.'

Rostov met his eyes squarely. He was fairly certain why Burun had not tried to stop the fight. So long as he and Alexei were preoccupied with one another, they were unlikely to combine to form a threat to the Yek.

'And have you visited your yurt?' Burun asked casually.

Rostov clenched his jaw. 'No, Khan. Not yet.'

'Oh, well. Probably you should. Someone will have told your wife that you were hurt. You should go to her.' Burun spoke prosaically.

A flush was rising to colour Rostov's features. He did not know what to say.

Burun was smiling tranquilly. 'It is not in the nature of any woman to remain indifferent forever, Suragai,' he said. He settled his feet into a pair of half boots. Then he looked up again. 'Go to her. You have my permission.'

The position of his yurt had been subtly altered and extensions had been constructed along each of the principal outer segments. An additional canopy had been erected over the whole structure and the ante-chamber was dim, cool and silent. Two slaves whom Rostov recognised from Burun's house in Pesth padded by, their heads bowed, eyes respectfully averted. They were wearing his livery and Rostov guessed that his household had been expanded in his absence. The main chamber was empty when he entered it, but as soon as he started to remove his mantle he was surrounded by servants. They took his clothes, removing the dust-stained garments as if they were offensive, and a pair of Y'frike women brought water and towels. Obviously he was expected to bathe, Yek style. Rostov stared frostily at the women until they departed, hiding their amusement politely behind raised hands. There was no nudity taboo on Tarvaras, at least so far as men were concerned, but Rostov was not prepared to shed the habits and customs of a lifetime to such an extent. He washed, standing naked in the wide shallow bronze basin while male slaves poured a constant sprinkle of water over his head. The Yek took a full bath in a similar fashion to the Manchu. It was a communal affair, conducted in water which was so hot that it almost stripped the skin from the bather's body. There was a bath-house attached to most Yek dwellings, and when a camp was constructed it was the first permanent structure to be erected.

The robes the slaves brought when he had finished were new, and their quality was finer than anything Rostov had ever encountered. The silks were so delicate that they bruised wherever they were touched. He had become so used to carrying a weapon that it was second nature to pick up first his long sword from the rest upon which it had been placed and then, as soon as it became clear that there was no way in which it could be worn in these clothes, to push the sheath of a *hiranu* into the sash at his waist. The silk was incapable of holding the weight of the short sword. It discoloured, and began to part. A slave knelt and replaced the sash with another, his eyes beseeching heaven for patience. Rostov grinned wearily and tossed the weapon aside.

The door hangings to the last chamber were midnight blue shot with gold. They parted like water. Rostov stood in the midst of silence. A single lamp was burning, an orb floating among fragrant petals in a golden bowl which was set upon a low lacquered table. He hesitated, his eyes adjusting to the light.

Turakina came out of the deep shadow on one side of the room.

'Lord of my life.' Her touch was light upon his shoulder. 'I have greatly desired your return.'

Her tone sounded sincere, but Rostov mistrusted Turakina's motives. There was no reason for her words to be the truth.

'Lady.' He spoke evenly. 'I am surprised.'

Turakina did not seem to take offence. 'Why then, I hope that it is to my advantage,' she said.

'Oh, completely.'

She was wearing a robe which looked as if it had been drawn from a single length of tissue of gold. Her hair had been combed out and it merged with the material so that he could not determine where the neckline lay.

'Lord, will you eat?'

Now that his eyes had become accustomed to the dimness, Rostov could see that there was a long low table on one side of the chamber. It was laden with covered dishes.

'Thank you, no.'

The message in her reception of him was unmistakable. Once more he had only to touch her and she would surrender. Only the knowledge that he would never know for certain if her willingness was genuine prevented him.

It was as if Turakina sensed his doubt.

'I would make a new beginning with you, Suragai.' She spoke low-voiced. 'Let us forget all that has gone before.'

Rostov took a breath. 'Lady, how can I refuse you?'

He was unconvinced, but he reasoned that there

would be time to discover if her attitude had truly altered. Suddenly the cumulative effects of lack of sleep, hard riding and his injury pushed themselves to the forefront of his consciousness. He knew that he needed to rest. There was a bed in the alcove, but to move towards it would be - he searched for the word - inappropriate.

'Perhaps I will eat after all.' Rostov eyed the couch which was parallel to the food table. His limbs ached and he wondered if the bruises on his face were visible in the poor light.

'Lord, you need rest.' Turakina's hand drew him towards the bedspace. 'And we should be reconciled.'

'Oh. We should?' Rostov was aware that he was no longer in control of the situation.

'Don't you think it is time?' Turakina stopped and looked up at him. The observation was tart. Then she smiled and took his hands and placed them on her waist. 'Or had you intended that I remain a virgin as a penance?' she enquired.

Vortai the Black was short, squat and swarthy. Except for a topknot which was bound with silver wire, he was completely bald. When Rostov entered the council chamber he looked up and scowled. Rostov bowed politely, then sat down.

Burun grinned. 'Good-father, this is Suragai Amir. Suragai is my vassal and Chief of Scouts.'

'Ho!' Burun's father-in-law looked down his nose. Then he sneered. 'I did not believe it when I was told that you were marrying my grand-daughter to a non-human. My brother the Kha-Khan must have been mad to give his permission. Such a match offends God. It is disgusting.'

Rostov's left hand clenched upon the hilt of his long sword. The temptation to draw and strike was overwhelming and he was dismayed by the strength of primitive emotion which Vortai's words aroused. It was easy to deduce that the insult was a deliberate attempt to provoke an attack so that Burun would be embarrassed. Rostov saw that Burun was readying himself to intercept any assault, and he forced himself to release hold of his sword. Coldly he bowed.

Burun sat back. 'Oh.' His response was mild. 'As to that, it was my feeling that drastic measures were necessary to counteract the inheritance to which my children have been exposed.' He showed his teeth. 'The legacy of Daijin's blood runs stronger in some of his kin than in others, don't you agree?'

Rostov did not understand the meaning of the remark, but it was clear that insult had been repaid with insult. Vortai went crimson.

'Now by God, Merkut, you go too far!'

Burun looked amused. 'Oh? I have a son who is the great-grandson of the most terrible man in history. He is married to a great-grand-daughter of the same line. Who has a better right to be concerned about the purity of blood?'

Vortai was restraining himself with difficulty. 'Were I Kha-Khan, I would order the marriage annulled.' He spat out the words. 'I would order all marriages between Altun and persons of lesser blood terminated.'

'No doubt you would.' Burun smiled unpleasantly. 'And then your kin would become even more inbred. But you will never be Kha-Khan, Vortai.'

It was apparent that Vortai did not trust himself to remain. He rose to his feet. 'If ever I am, then look to yourself, Merkut,' he grated. 'You and all your clan.' He stalked from the chamber.

Burun remained seated. Then he made a face.

'If actions were as easy to carry out as threats are to

make, the Merkuts would have been extinct long since. Suragai, you should not have been involved in this. I am sorry.'

Rostov shrugged. 'Khan, I am involved.'

'Hunh.' Burun nodded. 'You are right. The moment you married my daughter, you became part of the quarrel.'

Rostov had meant only that as Burun's vassal he was bound by the Yasa to serve him, but he said nothing.

'Did you understand the words I spoke about Daijin and his blood?' Burun watched Rostov's face.

'Not truly, Khan. Daijin was the Kha-Khan's father, was he not?'

'That he was - and Vortai's, and Siban's.' Burun nodded again. 'Men called him Daijin the Terrible, and rightly so, for he waded in blood.'

Rostov viewed the statement unemotionally. 'Kings often have blood on their hands, Khan.'

The history of the struggle for Imperial supremacy was a catalogue of murder and assassination. Rostov was not surprised to discover that similar events had occurred during the consolidation of the Khanate under a single ruler.

Burun looked up sharply. 'You would know such things, of course. But Daijin slaughtered whole clans - every man, woman and child. All who stood against him died.'

Rostov pretended awe. 'A terrible man indeed. And yet it seems to me that history is often harsh in its judgement of kings and princes. Was Daijin a bad ruler?'

'What?' Burun seemed to consider. 'No. For he made the Yek supreme in the land. He built the cities and palaces, and all who served him prospered.'

An orderly entered the tent. He laid a heap of requisitions for supplies on a table. Burun ignored the interruption.

Rostov was not sure where the conversation was leading. He waited for Burun to speak again.

'Have you observed Nogai?' Burun said at last.

Rostov was puzzled. 'Khan, I don't understand what you mean.'

Burun stood. He selected a pear from a dish and started to peel it. 'Nogai has Daijin's blood. Also he suffers from Daijin's weaknesses. Sometimes he has headaches which blind him. They last for a short time only, then he is well again. Sipotai, Vortai's son, has them, and Buratai, the father of Jotan's wife, was plagued by them all his life. Do you understand?'

Rostov nodded slowly. It was reasonable to expect that the in-breeding resulting from the marriage of closely related bloodlines would produce occasional genetic defects. If a blinding headache from time to time was the only manifestation, then probably the afflicted were getting off lightly.

'I think so, Khan. Such a thing may be caused by an element called a gene, which is transferred to a child at its conception. Sometimes it lies dormant for a generation, then reappears again.'

'Even so.' Burun looked mildly impressed by the exposition.

Rostov recalled the remark which had precipitated the explanation. 'Do you truly fear for the genetic inheritance of your children, Khan?'

Burun made a face. 'All things are possible. I spoke only to annoy Vortai. As to Turakina you need have no fear.'

Rostov shrugged. 'Why should I fear, Khan?'

'Oh.' Burun looked away, then back again. 'Well, for one thing Daijin was young by our standards when he died.' He used a gesture which the Yek sometimes employed when referring to the dead. 'The light that burns brightly also burns twice as fast, it is said.

Perhaps it is the truth. For although Daijin was a great Kha-Khan, he was also mad.'

'Your son is waiting for you in the antechamber,' Turakina said. She was bristling as if she had been insulted. Rostov grinned. Ever since she had found out who was responsible for the now-healing cuts and grazes on his arms and shoulders, Turakina had been behaving as if Alexei was a dog with mange.

Zurachina and Kiku both looked up. They were visiting with a gift of bed-linen, although in reality they were probably curious about Turakina's domestic arrangements. Zurachina waited until her daughter had gone into the other room, then she smiled.

'Your son does not live with you, Suragai?'

Rostov shook his head. In fact, Alexei divided his time between Jotan's yurt and Nogai's. The fact that Jotan and Nogai were still feuding did not appear to trouble him. Both accepted his presence without comment. Surprisingly they had made no attempt to involve him in their quarrel.

'No.' Rostov shook his head again. 'It would not be -' he searched briefly for a suitable word, '- fitting.'

'Aah.' Zurachina nodded thoughtfully. 'It is possible that you are right.'

Turakina came back. She had put on a cloak of light, reflective material. 'Take me riding.' She looked challengingly at Rostov.

At once Zurachina and Kiku stood up as if they had just remembered that they had business elsewhere.

Rostov hesitated. 'Very well.'

Turakina looked pleased. 'Good. I want to see the desert. I can't ride there alone.'

'Oh no.' Rostov shook his head at once. 'It's far too dangerous.'

She frowned. 'You go there.'

Rostov pursed his lips. Then he grinned crookedly. The way to win an argument with Turakina was to meet her with reason.

'I go because I have to. I can imagine what your father would say if I allowed you even a verst from the escarpment. Until the wadis are cleared of sandpeople no one is permitted to travel without heavy escort.'

Turakina seemed to realise that she was not going to get her way. 'In that case take me to the Khara Caves.'

Rostov cocked an eye at Zurachina, who nodded imperceptibly. 'As you wish.' He picked up his sword from its rest, then bowed to Zurachina and Kiku. 'Good-mothers, I beg you excuse us.'

'Peace, Suragai,' Zurachina said. 'We have others to visit, and your first duty is to one another.'

Turakina wrinkled her nose at the comment. Rostov laughed, and let her walk ahead of him out into the antechamber. Alexei was waiting, pacing impatiently from the door to the wall. He turned and his mouth opened as if he was about to speak. Then he saw Turakina. At once his eyes veiled, and he bowed stiffly.

'Step-mother, good morning.'

Rostov picked up his bow case from the stand beside the door. 'Turakina wants to go riding. Come with us.'

Alexei seemed to hesitate. Then he shook his head. 'I came merely to bid you good morning.'

Rostov smiled grimly at the lie. Alexei never did anything simply for the sake of courtesy. Clearly what he had to say was not for Turakina's ears. He shrugged. 'As you please. You are welcome, of course.'

The expression on Turakina's face belied the words. She was glaring rebelliously. Rostov busied himself with the fastenings of his bow case in order to conceal his amusement. Ever since the day he had returned to the escarpment Turakina had been a model of devotion and obedience. Only when she encountered Alexei was she incapable of maintaining the facade.

'Now that we are alone, tell me what you wanted to say to me this morning.'

Alexei was sitting with his legs dangling over the edge of the precipice which was the face of the escarpment at this point. When Rostov spoke he did not look up.

Rostov snorted. He walked a pace or two from the edge and sat down. At last Alexei turned round.

'The Yek are going to ask you to advise them on sieging the Alan cities,' he said. 'What will you say to them?'

Rostov did not meet his eyes at once. Burun had only spoken of the idea the previous evening. No one else was supposed to know.

'Your friend Nogai has long ears,' he said finally.

Burun would not have told Jotan and Nogai was the only other person who would have spoken if he knew.

Alexei ignored the observation. 'What are you going to say?' he asked again.

Rostov looked off along the escarpment. To the east it continued to form a rock wall against the desert until it was breached finally by the Serai Gorge, where the Y'ntze River flowed south from Keraistan. The land on the plateau was very dry but it was fertile, unlike the black sand of the G'bai. Where it was irrigated grass grew and st'lyan could be pastured.

'Windmills.'

'Eh?'

It was not until Alexei responded that Rostov realised that he had spoken aloud.

'Oh. It was just a thought I had. Water is too valuable and too scarce for the most part. The Yek don't use water power much because there are too few places where it can be applied the whole year round. Here on the escarpment, for instance. But there is always a wind off the desert.'

'I see.' Alexei swung his legs away from the overhang and stood up. 'Have you seen how they grind corn?'

Rostov nodded. 'You forget the Khan has given me a fief. They use animals - oxen or p'tar - to turn the stones. The stones run in a big basin; what they have ground the people sieve to take out the husks.'

'Have you ever seen a windmill? Could you design one?' Alexei's expression was unreadable.

'They had them on Antaeus, when I was there during the Federated Systems Wars. Probably I could put one together.'

Alexei sat down. 'What you are saying is that you can introduce primitive mechanical devices and the Yek will accept them. What are you thinking about for the Alan? Siege engines?'

'They already use those.'

'Yes. Have you seen them? The Yasa makes them wary of anything remotely mechanical, so everything they build is cumbersome, clumsy. It's as if their heart isn't in it.'

Rostov said nothing. In fact Alexei's assessment was probably accurate. The Yek were not mechanistic by nature. They refined the design of a machine only after long periods of trial and error.

*It is because their science was gifted to them. They did not discover anything for themselves. They are not inventors.*

Rostov wondered if the unknown benefactor of Tarvaras had ever considered the disservice he was doing the ancestors of the Yek by saving them from the effort of scientific discovery.

331

'There are other things you can suggest, besides siege engines,' Alexei observed.

'I know it.' Rostov stared out at the desert. To help the Yek to conquer the walled cities of the Alan without massive casualties he was going to have to make them a present of the horrors of medieval warfare: naptha and sulphur oil, Greek fire, mines and trenches. They would have to learn how to blockade a city; how to starve the besieged into submission until poisoned water brought plague and death.

'Of course,' Alexei said. 'There is a much simpler way.'

'Stone walls,' Tulagai said. 'How can we storm a wall we cannot burn?'

Burun threw a bone out through the open side of the tent and the dogs fell upon it, snapping and snarling.

'We can mine under a stone wall, or sap - dig away the earth below a corner or a tower so that it collapses.'

Taroutai made a face. 'That will take forever. How long is this campaign going to take? One year? Five?'

Burun shrugged. 'Well, there are other ways. Suragai is going to make some suggestions.'

Everyone looked at Rostov. They waited for him to speak and silently he counted to ten so that when at last he opened his mouth, they were straining upon his words. He saw Burun smile at the device.

'As Burun says, a stone wall can be sapped. It doesn't always take a long time. It depends on the soil.'

'God,' Targoutai said. 'Are we to be soldiers or miners?'

Some of the Altun laughed. Rostov waited until they were quiet before he spoke again. 'I think you have used siege towers.'

Nogai was sitting at one end of the long table. He looked up. 'Yes. But we always lost a lot of men getting them forward and, because they are made out of wood, they can be set on fire.'

'I see.' Rostov took the pile of sketches which were being carried by Hodai. He selected one. 'Well there is a way of moving a tower up to a wall without exposing the men who are working it. You need fairly level ground up to the wall. Under cover of darkness you should sink a pair of posts. Attach pulleys to them and run ropes joined to the tower through the pulleys. Then you can run the tower forward without exposing the men who are pulling on the ropes to fire. They can be some distance away from the wall.'

The drawing was passing down the table. Nogai looked at it. 'Clever. But that still leaves us with the problem that a siege tower will burn.'

Burun snorted. 'Have you never thought of placing bowmen to fire at the top of the wall to keep it clear of defenders?'

'Most of the cities we saw had a moat round the walls,' Tulagai objected.

'That's right,' Targoutai said.

Rostov sorted through the pile of drawings. 'What you say is true. However there is a siege counter-measure for every kind of defence. A ditch or a moat can be filled with fascines: bundles of trimmed branches which are tied together and rolled forward. It doesn't provide a particularly level or stable surface, but it does get you up to the wall. Walls can be weakened or even collapsed by use of a battering ram. You can cover a ram with a mobile roof, or you can mount it on a boat or a barge so that it can be used against a moated wall.'

He passed the sketches along the table as he spoke. All of them had been examined by the Sechem, who had confirmed that there was no breach of the Yasa.

'Every tuman will require a corps of engineers,' Nogai commented. 'None of us have ever fought this way before.'

'We never fought the Alan before,' Burun said.

Rostov let them digest the remark. 'There are many ways of attacking a city. I have observed that you use catapults. With only minor improvements in the design you can achieve much greater range and accuracy.'

Most of the Yek looked amused. 'Stones won't knock down a well-built wall, Amir,' one officer said.

'Hunh.' Arghatun nodded. 'I remember we used them at Pantai, in Daijin's time. They made the enemy uncomfortable, nothing more.'

Rostov waited for the objections to subside. 'Perhaps what you say is true, although I think that you will find that you can break down the gates of a city with a catapult if you aim it well enough. Besides, there are other things you can throw apart from rocks.'

'Flowers,' Tulagai said. 'We can charm the Alan out from behind their walls.'

'No, dung!' Nogai laughed. 'We'll stink them out.'

Rostov allowed the laughter to die. 'You could throw dung, certainly. If it lands in a city's water supply it will make life very unpleasant.'

Nogai was looking thoughtful. Tulagai said something to him in an undertone. Nogai shook his head.

'There are other substances which burn.' Rostov ignored the exchange. 'How do you make fire arrows?'

'Oh.' Targoutai thought for a moment. 'Usually we wrap soft fibre around an arrow head. Then we dip it in oil or pitch. Would a catapult fire large fire arrows?'

Rostov had not thought about designing a siege arbalest. In any case he was not sure about the operating principle of such a machine. He shrugged. 'I believe it can be done. But I was thinking that you could throw burning pitch, or a material similar. Fire is a useful weapon, even if it only takes defenders away from the city walls to act as fire-fighters.'

'Pitch would stick to the catapult,' Tulagai said. 'I wouldn't like to be in the vicinity when it was being fired.'

Rostov hesitated. Even though Burun had approved everything, he was aware that those who adhered strictly to the letter of the Yasa - the older men in particular - were about to have their sensibilities offended.

'Pitch can be distilled,' he said. 'In the same way that you distil the fermented milk of the st'lyan mare to make k'miss. When the distillate solidifies, a substance called naptha is produced. This also burns, but it can be handled much more readily.'

The Yek digested the idea. Rostov wondered if they could imagine the kind of wound which would be caused by burning naptha. Some of the faces around the table reflected disquiet.

'Suragai's words have my approval.' It was as if Burun anticipated the protests which were about to be made. 'And since I am in charge of the war under Siban, you may take it that Suragai also has the Kha-Khan's permission to try out both the ideas which he has outlined and a number of others. He will be assisted by Parin Sechem this summer, and both of them will report to me.'

Rostov was taken by surprise. It was the first time that he had heard that the Kha-Khan supported the ideas which had been put forward. Briefly he wondered if Burun had actually consulted Kinsai. If he had not, then he was courting disaster.

The Yek were muttering to one another. Clearly

some of them were unhappy, but Burun's words had prevented them from voicing their principal objection.

'Does anyone here dissent?' Burun looked around the table. 'No? Then I declare this kuriltai ended.'

Everyone seemed to be taken by surprise. Many of the officers got up to leave. Vortai was near the end of the table and for a moment it looked as if he was about to say something. Then suddenly he seemed to change his mind. He stared very hard at Rostov, then walked away out onto the canopied parade ground.

Burun looked surprised.

'He will make trouble, that one.' Nogai was resting one foot on the table.

Burun nodded. 'Yes. I expected Vortai to argue about everything. I don't think he opened his mouth. We will have to watch for mischief.'

Rostov was confused to find that Burun and Nogai were apparently on the same side. He wondered if their commitment to the prosecution of the war against the Alan was stronger than the personal differences which usually seemed to set them in opposition to one another. Possibly there were rules to the conduct of a feud which he did not yet understand.

He waited until Nogai had left the tent. 'I thought you were fighting with him?'

'No.' Burun shook his head. 'Nogai is feuding with Jotan, but that is a different matter. He thought he could bend me to his will, but he seems to have decided that since force isn't working, maybe he will do better if he is my friend.'

'Oh.' Rostov allowed himself to look perplexed. Burun grinned.

Yek attitudes towards personal relationships were quite unpredictable; their psychology in some cases was so strange that it was difficult to understand how

336

they had arrived at a specific point in the reasoning process. Clearly Burun accepted that under limited circumstances Nogai was a friend. At the same time he could be regarded as an enemy, his motivation suspect.

'You spoke as I desired.' Burun sounded satisfied. 'I did well to make you Amir.'

Rostov shrugged dismissively. 'I doubt if I said anything which could not have been said by the Sechem, had you asked them, Khan.'

'Maybe.' Burun's expression was unreadable, as it often was when events demonstrated the extent of Rostov's knowledge.

'There are other things I could have said.' Rostov paused. He was unsure of his ground. 'It is a pity the Yasa does not permit the use of gunpowder.'

He expected Burun's face to mirror disapproval, but he only looked surprised.

'Who says that it does not?' he demanded.

Rostov was bewildered.

'The Yasa.'

'The Yasa says that we may not use weapons which rely on anything other than the strength of our arms when we are in individual combat,' Burun said. 'And since a battle is essentially a large number of such combats, we interpret the law to mean that firearms are forbidden. But of course we employ gunpowder. Are we fools, to disregard such power and the uses to which it may be put?'

It took Rostov seconds to adjust. Clearly he was going to have to spend time receiving instruction in Yek law.

'I'm sorry, Khan. Pardon my misunderstanding. Tell me, if you will, how gunpowder is used.'

Burun gestured. 'A Sechem would tell you the uses better than I. It is employed to clear great obstacles and in the quarries to break up large masses of stone. Also it is used in fireworks.'

'Fireworks?' Rostov tried hard not to show excitement.

'Yes. I think the N'pani originated them. Certainly when we attacked T'sosei, they fired off rockets to scare us away.' Burun grinned. 'If I had been in command of the army, we would not have stopped running until we reached the sea.'

Rostov was only slightly disappointed. 'Are the rockets large?'

'Oh. I suppose so.' Burun appeared disinterested. 'But they are an amusement for children, Suragai. Nothing more.'

Rostov wondered if anyone on Tarvaras knew that chemical propulsion was the simplest method of powering spaceflight. He remembered that the *Simonova*'s landing boat had aroused minimal curiosity. A comment had been made to the effect that the principles of powered flight were known.

'It is said that rockets of the kind you describe were once used in war.' He watched Burun's face as he spoke.

'Those things?' Burun's disbelief was apparent. 'They cannot be controlled!'

'Oh. I think fins were fitted to the rear of the rocket, Khan. Fins work like the tail feathers of a bird.'

'Hunh.' Burun looked sceptical. 'Maybe so, but such a thing would certainly be forbidden by the Yasa. A rocket is not a weapon of the hand.'

'Then I am surprised that catapults are permitted, Khan.' Rostov made the observation innocently. 'Surely they are not weapons of the hand?'

'Eh?' Burun looked startled. He looked sharply at Rostov. Then he shook his head and grinned. 'Well, maybe they are, and maybe they are not. I don't think

338

anyone has ever thought to argue about the matter. You must have observed that few of us take such weapons seriously.'

'I suppose one could argue that storming a city is different from engaging an enemy in battle,' Rostov said. He watched Burun to see if the point had been made.

Burun laughed harshly. 'I will bear that thesis in mind. If you develop the catapult into a serious weapon, perhaps I will need to.'

It was difficult to know how to go on other than by speaking directly.

'If gunpowder is permissible for use in destroying an obstacle,' Rostov said, 'might it not also be permissible to use it against the wall of a city?'

Burun sat down on a bench. 'On the basis that a wall is an obstacle like any other, you mean? Yes, I suppose such a use might not be contrary to the Yasa. And interpretation of the law should be practical, should it not?'

The tone of Burun's voice was difficult to interpret. Rostov looked away.

'The force of gunpowder is difficult to direct, I have been told,' Burun commented. 'Is there a way to control its energy?'

Rostov hesitated warily. He had expected Burun to dismiss the idea out of hand. He wondered if he should attempt to describe the theory of shaped charges. Probably the Yek had never thought to consolidate their explosives and used gunpowder as a last resort, without much enthusiasm.

'There are means to direct explosive force, Khan. If, as I suspect, you use black powder in its loose form, then the power may be channelled to some extent by containing the explosive before it is ignited.'

'I see,' Burun said. He looked away towards the

parade ground; it was as if he had lost interest in the conversation. Rostov was afraid that he had said too much. He had intended to approach the subject gradually, in several stages.

'Khan, I do not wish to give offence.' Rostov chose his words carefully. 'There are suggestions which I may make out of lack of knowledge of your customs, which may not please you. If that is the case now, then I ask you to forgive my presumption.'

He waited. Finally Burun turned.

'You do not offend me, Suragai.' He shook his head. 'I do not believe that you are motivated by anything other then good intent. However, you should keep your own counsel on this matter, at least until I have had time to consult with the Sechem. Leave me now.'

It was cool under the canopy, but there was sweat trickling down Rostov's back. He stood up and bowed. Then he walked away.

Yuan and Alexei were outside. When Rostov tried to walk past, Alexei caught his arm. He looked hard into his father's face, then nodded as if he was satisfied by what he saw there.

'You told him.'

Rostov drew a breath. The hot dry air hurt his lungs and he realised that he had been breathing shallowly since the start of the conversation with Burun.

'Yes.'

'What did he say?'

'That he would consult the Sechem.' Rostov regretted that he had yielded to Alexei's pressure. Now it was too late to go back.

Yuan was contemplating the ground between his feet. When he looked up and spoke, his hand gesture was the mime for calm.

'*Yetekshi wa surimasen.*' - It is pointless to worry now. -

340

Rostov grimaced. Normally when he conversed in Manchu he omitted the gestures. Yuan understood facial expression, even though he made none of his own. Now the mime seemed to be fitting. Rostov's hand traced the cupping below his heart, followed by the offering which indicated acceptance of his fate.

'*Hai. Shirimasu.*' - Yes. I know. -

Rostov watched Yuan's eyes, as if he might find reflected there some expression of reassurance. The Manchu's irises were bright amber. Momentarily the black pupils set within them seemed to expand. Then Yuan folded his hands and bowed deeply.

# PART FOUR

# Campaign

Siban's riding clothes were encrusted. He stood in the centre of the main chamber of Burun's yurt and the slaves peeled each garment away until he was naked. The linens and silks were stiff with dust and every time they were handled they gave off tiny particles which hung in the air.

Burun noted the seams and creases in Siban's flesh. There were deep pouches under his eyes and, now that Burun had spent several months surrounded by young men, Siban seemed much older.

'Your reconnaissance is the talk of Kinsai.' Siban stepped into the wash tray. 'I am told that you rode all the way to T'ver, but that only you and Suragai saw the place. The Altun are in awe of you. Did you have any trouble with them?'

'Only what I expected.' Burun sat down on a pile of cushions. 'Nogai commands well enough once he sets his mind to it and his brothers usually do what he tells them. I gave him charge of the vanguard and he did not disgrace himself. He scouted Suslev and Shermetyev.'

'Amazing.' Siban turned so that the shower of water being poured by the slaves ran down his back. 'Are you and he now reconciled, that you will speak no ill of him?'

'Oh.' Burun made a face. 'He has stopped pestering me to support his claim to the Dragon Throne. Now he is wooing me instead.' He cocked an eye at Siban. 'Am I to take it that your return to command of the army means that you found nothing to keep you in the capital?'

Siban stepped out of the wash tray. The slaves swathed him in linen sheets. He took his time about answering. 'My brother knows how I feel about his offer to nominate me as his heir. Only a fool or a madman would desire the throne.'

Burun grinned. 'That eliminates only a few of the possible candidates.'

Siban made a rude noise. 'There is talk of nominating Artai.'

Burun was unable to hide his astonishment. 'Tulagai's son? Are they serious? He is a child. My youngest son C'zinsit is older.'

'Even so.' Siban freed one arm from the confines of the linen, and used the end of the sheet to scrub at the bald patch on his scalp. 'His mother is much about the Golden Yurt, and there is some support at court for the idea.'

'And if Arjun dies before Artai comes of age?'

'Oh, well.' Siban shrugged. 'Probably there would be a council of regents.'

'With Sunjara as Khatun.'

Burun made the observation expressionlessly, but Siban raised an eyebrow.

'Yes, I know she is a Ch'kassian. But her influence would be counter-balanced by the other women at court. The wife of your own eldest son is much in favour, for example.'

Jotan had received a private letter from Arkhina a day earlier. Now Burun wondered if he should take steps to find out what she had written.

'I take it that the Kha-Khan is no longer sick, or you would not be here.' He watched Siban's face.

Siban stopped drying himself. 'He gets sick. They take away the wine. He recovers.' His tone was a mixture of disapproval and sadness.

Burun thought about the Khanate and how it

346

consumed the men who ruled it. Probably Siban was right and no sane man would desire election.

'Sometimes I think that Nogai is the only candidate who is fit.' Siban stepped into a pair of loose silk trousers.

'I know what you mean.' Burun nodded. 'He has the way.'

'Would you support him?'

Burun stood up. It was a question he did not intend to answer until the day the throne fell vacant. 'Would my support make such a difference?'

'Well.' Siban's eyes were veiled. 'Let us say that it would be of considerable value.'

Burun looked away. He intended to gain the greatest possible advantage from his vote when the time came to cast it. No responsible Khan would do otherwise.

Siban pulled on a tunic and allowed a pair of slaves to wind a broad sash around his waist. 'I noted your camp industries as I rode in.'

The plant for distilling pitch and the workshops where Parin experimented under Suragai's direction with various designs of siege engine were some way from the main encampment. The production of naptha was only mildly dangerous, but the smell was not pleasant. The catapult trials had attracted a horde of spectators and Burun had been forced to decree that no one who was not authorised should be permitted in the area. He made a face.

'I don't know if Suragai is Chief of Scouts or Commander of Engineers.'

'Does he know that we are using him?' Siban asked.

'Oh.' Burun's mouth twisted in a wry smile. 'I think that there is a little using on both sides. Did I tell you that he had been experimenting with rockets?'

Siban's eyebrows rose. 'In the Name of God, what for?'

347

'Apparently flying vessels can be rocket-powered.' Burun grinned. 'Parin has been keeping me informed.'

'Is Suragai planning to leave us?'

'Oh. I think he is a long way from such a development. In any case there is something which he does not discuss which would prevent him from returning to his own people.'

'Really?' Siban looked relieved. 'Maybe we should find out what it is.'

'Eventually we will.' Burun poured wine from a flagon and gave it to Siban. 'Every day he is with us, we learn a little more.'

'Does he know that he is watched?'

'I expect so. He would be a fool if he thought that we trusted him completely.'

'Yes.' Siban nodded. 'You are right, of course. In that case he must realise that we will never allow him to leave.'

'There is no more pork, and the other meats are being rationed.' Zurachina seated herself on the large square cushion at Burun's side.

Burun pursed his lips. Kiku preferred roast pork over all other dishes. Sometimes she would eat nothing else. Five tumans had arrived during the previous week, and as yet the commissariat had not caught up with the demand for meat and grain. Vortai was now responsible for the management of the camp, and the fact that he was a poor administrator was beginning to cause problems.

'Are we going to starve?' He put an arm around Zurachina's waist.

She moved in against him. 'Not as long as Jotan and Orcadai keep us supplied with game.'

There was only limited wildlife in the rolling hills behind the escarpment. Burun made a face. 'I will speak to Siban. We should be receiving regular drives from both Pesth and Pantai.'

Privately he wondered if Vortai and the Gaijin were withholding stock. There was a fixed price for an animal requisitioned by the quartermasters, but if meat became scarce, then probably the amount of the payment would be increased to encourage the heads of clans to release more than the statutory minimum from their herds.

Kiku came out of the yurt. She eyed Burun and Zurachina for a moment, then went and sat down in the shade of the main canopy which had been erected to shield the yurts of Burun and his vassals. Two female slaves fussed around her, erecting a screen and placing a stand with paper and inks. Burun snorted, and Zurachina jabbed him in the side with her elbow.

'Don't laugh at her.' She turned her head and spoke into his shoulder. 'She is only pretending to dislike us.'

Burun laughed. He drew Zurachina closer and pressed his face against the warmth of her breasts. When he looked up, Kiku was watching, her mouth turned down.

Zurachina pushed him away. 'Sit and let me do something with your moustache.' She pulled him round so that he was facing her. 'You have been chewing the left side again.'

Burun grunted. He continued to watch Kiku out of the corner of his eye, but she pretended to be busy drawing. It was the yellow month, the hottest time of the year. The army was assembling from every part of the land, and every evening long columns of pack beasts vanished into the black sands of the G'bai, destined for the supply dumps which had been established along the line of march.

'How soon will you leave?' Zurachina spoke quietly. Her hands stilled as she waited for him to answer, and even Kiku stopped drawing.

'A month. Less, perhaps. Will you miss me?'

Zurachina trimmed the few hairs which were straggling down the side of his mouth. 'I will survive,' she responded tartly.

Burun grinned. Zurachina tried to look serious, but she could not keep her face straight, and ended up laughing. She shook her head. 'Oh, Khan. My days will be empty without you.'

Burun drew her close again, and closed his eyes.

Nogai and his brothers had been absent from the camp for over a month. It was rumoured that they had visited both Pesth and Kinsai, and there was a story going round that Nogai had been ejected from the Golden Yurt after a particularly unruly piece of behaviour. Now that he was returned, Siban had given him space to erect his tent in an area close to that which was occupied by Burun. Most of Nogai's slaves appeared to be female, so Burun sent some of his own and borrowed some from Suragai, so that the work of yurt erection could be completed.

'Khan, how pleasant it is to see you again.' Nogai settled himself on a stool. There was a new scar on his neck, part-hidden by his collar, and he had gained muscle. 'You had a good summer, I trust?'

'Oh, excellent, Noyon. It was peaceful in your absence.'

Nogai smiled and stretched like a cat. 'Now that I am returned I will make commotion enough. I have several new female slaves. One is a Suristani - quite untameable. You must visit my yurt.'

'I have all the women I need right now.' Burun moved so that he was out of talon reach. 'And if you cannot master your own women -' He broke off. Jotan was riding up. He dismounted.

350

'Nogai. I heard you had returned.' Jotan tossed his reins to an orderly.

'Did you. So?'

They were tensed like a pair of fighting cats. Burun waited to see who would attack first. Suddenly Jotan sat down.

'I'm not afraid of you.' He looked at Nogai.

Nogai stared back. 'Nor I of you.'

Burun held his breath. The silence seemed to draw out into infinity. Suddenly Nogai gestured. 'Very well then. Truce.'

'Agreed.' Jotan stood up. He seemed to notice Burun for the first time. 'Father, your pardon. I wanted to speak to Nogai –'

'So I see. Now go away.' Burun found that he was trembling. He glared at Jotan.

Jotan grinned. He leapt into the saddle and galloped away. Burun spat left and right to relieve his feelings. Nogai had not moved; his talons had remained sheathed the whole time. He stood up.

'Have you heard that my brother's son is being groomed for the throne?' His eyes were wide and innocent.

'I've heard it said.' Burun nodded.

'Good.' Nogai smiled. 'I just wanted you to know how desperate they have become.' He walked away.

Burun swallowed. Suddenly he knew how dangerous Nogai really was.

Everyone was dining in Jotan's yurt. Jotan kept only male slaves - silent N'pani who moved with unbelievable poise and grace. Their presence made Burun uncomfortable.

There was no discussion until the dishes for the first course were being cleared away. When the door hangings were pushed aside Burun heard the chatter

351

of the women who were dining apart in another chamber.

'Have you decided on the order of march yet?' Jotan caught Siban's eye.

Siban nodded. 'Burun leads the vanguard. I will take the main body. Nogai, you can ride with Burun or with me, as you choose. Kodai commands the rear.'

'I will ride with Burun, if he will have me.' Nogai looked across the table.

'My honour, Noyon.' Burun nodded.

'That's settled then.' Siban looked pleased. 'Burun, I was going to detach Jotan to follow the route he scouted south of the mountains along the coast. He can act as a diversion in case the Alan decide to defend the Moistr' Gorge. He can meet up with us at Ruysdal.'

'Yes.' Burun glanced at Jotan, who nodded. 'Although he ought to have enough men that he can fight himself out of trouble.'

'Agreed.' Siban gestured to the aide who was recording what was decided. 'He can take his own tuman and I will send Sidacai to march with him.'

Siban's son raised his eyes. He signified his acknow-ledgement, then concentrated once more on the chess board which was set up on a little table beside his place.

'Hulagai, Sodai and Haratai will ride with Kodai.' Siban looked around the table. 'But the major part of their tumans stay with me. The tumans of the Gaijin clan will form the rearguard, with Sipotai. I cannot imagine that Hodai will require more than twenty thousand men under any circumstances.'

Burun looked for Vortai but could not discern him. If Sipotai was under Kodai's command, he would be unable to create mischief.

'Once we are through the mountains we will split into three columns.' Siban gestured, and orderlies spread a map out on the wall so that it could be seen. 'I want to attack all the cities at the eastern end of the country simultaneously. That way they will have no time to think about aiding one another, and we will have a secure base in case the Alan army gets into the field sooner than we expect. We need to take Ruysdal, M'skva and the two cities Nogai scouted –' Siban searched for the names. He snapped his fingers.

'Shermetyev and Suslev,' Nogai supplied.

'Yes, those.' Siban nodded. 'We need to take them all during the first month of the campaign. Once the Alan know we are mounting an all-out attack, the fighting is bound to become harder. All the towns and cities will fortify.'

'They are fortified already,' Nogai observed. Everyone who had ridden on the reconnaissance nodded.

Burun remembered the man Barakai, the under-officer who was Suragai's vassal. Probably he was creating defensive measures in Pereislav, which was the first place they would attack after they had secured the eastern cities.

'If we take Ruysdal and M'skva, we will isolate the peninsula which runs south.' Jotan spoke. 'There is a city there. I think we ought to take it before we move west.'

Siban looked at Burun. He raised an eyebrow in enquiry.

'Miroselsk.' Burun pointed at the place on the map. 'The prisoners we took say that it's not very large, but it does control a stretch of coastline. I suppose if we bypass it the Alan will be able to land extra troops there from the sea. It could become a thorn in our side. On the other hand we can always use it to receive additional supplies from Y'frike if the need arises. I think Jotan's right. We ought to take it.'

'Very well.' Siban looked at Jotan. 'You brought it up. You take it. Strip the land bare, then catch up with us past M'skva.'

A movement at the far end of the table caught Burun's eye. Vortai was sitting down. He glared venomously at Burun. Burun stared back. He wondered why Vortai had been away from the table.

Jotan spoke again, his tone amused. 'Siban, if you are finished for the moment, I will tell the servants to bring in the next course.'

Siban sat back. 'Oh, by all means.'

Jotan turned towards the door and signalled. At once a line of servants entered. One of them carried a large covered dish to Burun's place. He bowed.

'What's this?' Burun raised the cover of the dish. The smell was mouth-watering.

'I came upon a deer when I was hunting yesterday, Khan.' Jotan turned back. 'My cook has prepared a venison stew for you.'

'It smells delicious.' Burun smiled. 'But Jotan, surely your cook knows by now that I don't like mushrooms. Suragai, let me help you to some of this.' He spooned a portion on to the offworlder's plate.

Jotan was frowning. He got up quickly and left the tent. Burun offered the dish to Nogai, but he shook his head.

'Thank you, Khan, but I don't like mushrooms either.'

Jotan came back into the chamber. He stopped at Burun's place and bent so that he was between Burun and Suragai.

'Suragai, don't eat the stew. My cook put no mushrooms in it.'

The spoon was at Suragai's lips. He went white, and then laid it down carefully. Burun gestured at the offworlder's body servant and the man lifted the dish and took it away.

Burun's face felt stiff, and Suragai looked as if he was carved from stone. Most of the people around the table had noticed nothing, but Nogai sat foward.

'Interesting,' he said softly. 'Who would want to poison you, Khan?'

'Poison?' Siban caught the word. His eyes questioned Burun.

'It is nothing. A misunderstanding.' Burun was furious. A slave laid a platter of meat in front of him and he stuffed some into his mouth. Suragai got up quietly and Burun guessed that he was going to talk to Jotan's cook. Suddenly he knew who had done the thing, and he looked down the table.

Vortai's head was down as if he was concentrating on his food, but he was not eating. An aide muttered something in his ear and at once he looked up. He stared at Burun expressionlessly, then his eyes moved on as if he was looking at no one person in particular.

Burun chewed slowly. The meat tasted like ashes in his mouth. Suragai returned and sat down.

'Khan, the stew was put to simmer this afternoon. There have been people through the cook tents constantly. Scores of them had opportunity.'

'Vortai?'

Suragai nodded. 'I thought of him. He was there only a short time ago and he conducted an inspection during the later part of the afternoon. He asked about the stew, but no one saw him do anything.'

'Hunh.' Burun felt the anger building inside. Poison was the most cowardly weapon imaginable. Its use was forbidden by the Yasa.

'I gave some of the stew to an old dog,' Suragai said. 'We will soon know if there is anything wrong with it.'

Burun accepted a cup of wine and drank deeply. The smell of the stew remained in his nostrils and the memory spoiled his appetite. Suragai accepted a platter of meat and began to eat as if nothing had happened. Burun thought that he envied the offworlder his ability to recover so quickly.

The meal lasted interminably. When it was over Burun got up quickly and went outside. If he had to talk to Vortai he would be incapable of controlling his actions.

Nogai came out of the door and walked over to join him. 'It is a pity you offered the stew to no one else.' He stood at Burun's shoulder, looking past him towards the edge of the escarpment. 'Then we might know who else was party to the deed.'

Burun considered. Certainly anyone who accepted the stew would have to be innocent. Nogai had refused a portion, but he did not like mushrooms.

'It would be a drastic method of identifying my friends.' Burun watched Vortai as he left the tent. He was surrounded by Gaijin as if he expected to be attacked.

'Oh, I don't know.' Nogai followed Burun's eyes.

Suragai appeared at Burun's shoulder. 'The dog is dead,' he said.

'What are you going to do about Vortai?' Nogai sounded interested.

'I'm not sure.' Burun stared after Vortai until he was out of sight. 'Something terminal.'


'The farmers in my province are all complaining.' Burun watched Suragai as he slid the tube packed with gunpowder into the hole in the rock.

Suragai smiled. 'I know. I've turned over every dung heap within a hundred verst to find saltpetre. The engineers can leech nitrates from the soil, but they have to find suitable soil first. It's easier to get it from manure piles, cellars and underground drains. Purification is the problem. I expect it's the reason the powder the Sechem were using wasn't very good.'

'Oh?' Burun was surprised. He had seen gunpowder used only a few times, but it always produced a satisfying bang and a great deal of flame and smoke.

'Well.' Suragai looked up. 'The proportions were nearly correct - saltpetre seventy-five per cent, charcoal fifteen, sulphur ten - but because the sulphur and the saltpetre were both impure, the end product didn't burn very well.'

There were lines of sulphur-evaporating pans down one side of the temporary engineer's encampment, laid out so that the fumes blew north. Two windmills had been built and these were connected to gristmills which ground the cakes of powder after they were formed.

'The changes you have made will make so much difference?' Burun asked.

'I can't say exactly how much difference yet, Khan. Maybe this demonstration will give you some idea. The powder you were using was what is called meal powder - a loose mixture of the three main constituents. What the engineers have been producing is called corned or grain powder.' Suragai did something with a length of what looked like cord. Then he stood up. 'Khan, you ought to move back now.'

'You're ready?'

'Yes, Khan.'

Burun was unimpressed. 'Very well, then lay your powder trail.'

Suragai was holding a big coil of the cord in one hand. He held it up. 'Khan, it isn't necessary for me to lay a powder trail. This is a fuse. It is very pure powder, sieved and mixed until it is like clay. It is sealed inside fine linen. I will run it out and light one end. A small explosion will run down its length and that will ignite the charge which I have placed here.'

'I see.'

'Unfortunately, the fuse is not very reliable yet. I'm still working on it. Sometimes it does not burn all the way to the charge, but other times it burns too fast. It's best not to be too close when it is lit. It doesn't give you very much time to take cover.'

'Oh.' Burun eyed the length held by Suragai. 'What are you going to do?'

'Well Khan, I have enough fuse to run back to that depression in the ground.' Suragai pointed. 'I'm going to light the charge from there.'

'Oh well.' Burun pretended poise. 'If it is far enough for you –' He met Suragai's stare.

Suragai shrugged. 'As you wish, Khan.' He began to pay out the cable.

'Why did you place your powder in this spot?' Burun walked alongside. The charge had been packed into a crevice in the rock about twenty lengths from the edge of the escarpment, at a point where the precipice overhung the desert below. The drop to the sand below was considerable.

'Oh, well.' Suragai smiled. 'I wanted to make an impression, Khan. If I can show what a small charge can do, then perhaps the idea will be taken seriously.'

'Hunh. I see.' Burun nodded. He looked up and shaded his eyes to find the assembled Altun. Most of them were sitting their st'lyan about a quarter of a verst from the escarpment's edge. 'Your audience is not very close.'

'Oh.' Suragai looked up. 'I think they're close enough.'

Burun was still not certain that he had been wise to give permission for the experiments in gunpowder manufacture to take place. The argument that the destruction of a city wall was the same as the removal of a large physical obstacle was difficult to refute, but it ignored the fact that enemy soldiers were liable to be standing behind the wall at the time. Briefly Burun wondered if Suragai had thought up the justification for himself, or if a Yek had advised him. Strictly speaking the idea was an evasion of the rule of the Yasa. On the other hand the Yasa was breached in little ways nearly every day.

When he reached the depression in the ground, Suragai sat down and dangled his legs into the hollow.

'Khan, you ought to lie down. We're still very close.'

Burun snorted. 'If I lie down, how will I see what happens?'

Suragai looked as if he was beseeching heaven for patience. 'Well, at least get into the depression,' he said. 'You can be sure that I will, as soon as I have lit this fuse.'

Burun stepped down into the hollow. The bank on the side which was towards the edge of the escarpment was at chest height. Suragai was carrying a leather satchel; now he opened it and took out what Burun thought at first was a firearm. He stiffened. Parin had said nothing about this. Then he saw that the implement was only the rear half of a gun. It had a butt, a trigger and striker mechanism, but no barrel. The flint in the striker was held down by a strip of sprung metal against a quarter-circular flashplate. Another spring mounted in opposition seemed to push the flint back after the trigger had been operated and, in the place where the spark was produced, there was a shallow pan which held a kind of wadding. When Suragai operated the trigger, sparks flew. The wadding ignited almost at once.

Suragai applied the flame to the end of the fuse. At once, he pushed himself off the side of the bank and dropped into the depression beside Burun. The fuse seemed to burn with a ripple of tiny explosions which ran along its length. The roar as the powder charge went off was simply a continuation. There was almost no flash and very little smoke. The blast made Burun duck. A chunk of rock sailed past his head.

Burun straightened again. There was a rumble and the ground appeared to shake. Then a section of the edge of the escarpment about thirty lengths wide disappeared with a crash into the void below.

'Name of God!' Burun spat to left and right.

Suragai climbed out of the hollow. He offered a hand to Burun and pulled him up on to the level. When Burun looked back at the Altun he could see that half of them had fallen off their rearing st'lyan. Gingerly he picked his way towards the new cliff edge. Most of the rock had split away cleanly, and there were only a few small fissures.

Burun was perturbed by the power of the new explosive, but also he was excited. Suragai had used only a small charge, and it had cut away a section of the escarpment big enough to hold a thousand men. A series of such explosions below the wall of a city would bring it down in neat sections. Even though Suragai's demonstration had been helped by the overhang of the rock and the drop below, Burun was impressed.

'Like this,' Turakina said. She kicked one leg, stepped crosswise and turned.

Burun smiled as Suragai followed awkwardly. It was the only time he had seen the offworlder out of his depth. 'If you can master that dance, Suragai,' he called, 'I will elevate you to S'zltan.'

Turakina demonstrated the step again. Suragai watched, attempted to copy her, then threw up his arms. 'Lady, in this at least, I think I prefer to be a spectator.' He came over and sat down beside Burun.

Jehan got up and joined Turakina on the wooden floor. He linked arms with her and they moved from side to side in perfect unison. Two slaves beat time on different sized tambours. 'Make me S'zltan, grandfather.' Jehan laughed, and he stepped, dipped, and stepped again.

Burun smiled. 'Ah, Noyon, if only I could.' He shook his head. He had not realised that Jehan had grown so tall.

The measure ended. Turakina came over and sat down against Suragai and Burun smiled approvingly. Jehan walked over to the slaves and said something. Then he walked back into the centre of the floor. The new beat was very fast. Jehan ran in a small circle and sprang into the air. He yelled, landed in a crouching position, then sprang into the air again.

'Name of God!' Suragai looked bewildered. 'Is that a dance?'

'A Merkut dance.' Burun watched Jehan. He had not thought that his grandson knew the steps.

'It is a dance for grown men.' Turakina made a disapproving face. 'He will injure himself.'

'What, girl.' Burun growled at her. 'Are you practising for motherhood already?'

Turakina blushed crimson, and Burun thought that Zurachina was probably right: she was pregnant. Suragai did not seem to have noticed and Burun wondered if he knew yet.

Jehan was dancing strenuously, his face red with exertion. The Merkut troopers who were standing guard turned to watch and they began to beat time with the butt ends of their lances. Two of the younger men laid down their arms. They walked to the edge of the floor and looked at Burun for approval. When he nodded they joined Jehan, linking arms with him. They circled so that they were back to back, then bounced, squatted and kicked. Jehan yipped happily.

Burun wondered if he should have warned Suragai about the dangers of having Turakina conceive out here on the edge of the G'bai. It was said that the desert was safe now; the discs which were used to detect radiation never discoloured. All the same, he could not help but remember the deformed monsters that had been born to families living as much as a hundred verst away. Jehan had an older sister called Jehana, but before her birth there had been another child. Burun shuddered at the memory, and thought that he was glad that it had not survived.

If God was concerned with the affairs of earth, as Suragai's son seemed to believe, then surely he would not have allowed such a thing to happen. Burun examined the thought. Then he nodded to himself. Certainly the absence of paradise from the earth was proof that God was interested only in his kingdom in Heaven.

The vanguard moved across the G'bai in excellent time. Now that the wadis had been cleared of sand-people there was little to hinder the movement of men and animals. Even small parties were able to ride without scouts.

On the third night Burun stood on top of the beacon platform at the largest way station and stared out into the distance at the signal lamps which advertised the presence of each thousand of each of fifteen tumans. There had been only one dust storm, but it had immobilised four tumans for half a day. Siban had marched them through the following night and well into the next day to make up for lost time.

'It's like a fleet of ships at sea.' Jotan perched on the platform at Burun's feet. 'How far away is the main body?'

'Twenty verst, maybe more.' Burun closed his eyes, then opened them again in an effort to improve his night vision. 'We can't see the rearguard from here.'

Even though it was dark, the air was warm. Small gusts of wind shook the platform and the oil flames from the brazier dipped and wavered.

'I hate the desert.' Jotan shivered. 'I never encountered anything so hostile before.'

Burun had slipped a small jug of k'miss into the sleeve end of his mantle. He got it out, uncorked it, and swallowed. The spirit was harsh. He wiped his mouth with the back of his hand, then tapped Jotan on the shoulder with the jug. 'Here.'

Jotan drank, coughing. 'God, this is raw. Are we no longer maturing our supplies?'

Burun grinned. Soldiers on campaign drank anything they could lay their hands on. There was no drunkenness, however, because there was never enough to go around.

He squeezed past Jotan and the platform swayed precariously. Jotan cried out in alarm. He edged to the far side of the platform so that he was counterbalancing Burun's weight. The trooper whose task it was to keep the beacon supplied with oil was clinging to the base of the tripod. His face was white.

Burun scrambled past him down the support. Pegs had been hammered into the timbers at intervals to provide hand- and foot-holds. He waited until Jotan joined him on the ground. Then they mounted and rode on towards the mountains.

The Alan had placed a solitary sentry post on the pass. The men who were manning it were not alert and the scouts captured them alive.

Siban shook his head in amazement when he was told. 'Our ambassadors told them we would come.

363

Why didn't they believe us?'

Burun shrugged. He was glad the Alan were so casual and thought that an enemy who took no precautions against invasion deserved to be conquered.

It took the army two days to traverse the gorge through which the Moistr' flowed. In many places the path was so narrow that only single-file riding was possible. In others, the constant passage of st'lyan broke down the rock shelving. The engineers had to be employed to clear obstacles so that carts could pass, and they were constantly filling the gulleys which resulted when portions of the hillside fell away into the river. When the vanguard and main body had emerged on to the river plain, Siban split the command. He sent six tumans under T'zin and Targoutai to attack Suslev and Shermetyev. The remainder carried on towards Ruysdal.

A screen of scouts and outriders moved in front as they marched. Burun did not believe that the Alan would allow the Yek to proceed unopposed and he had no intention of being caught in ambush.

There had been no word from Jotan. Every time a messenger rode up, Burun stood in his stirrups to look. Siban was unconcerned.

'Jotan will let us know if he runs into trouble,' he said. 'And we don't need his help to take Ruysdal.'

'Courier coming, Khan.' Hodai turned his head.

Ahead, a banner fluttered taut in the wind. Siban reined in and the spare st'lyan on his lead line halted in confusion. 'It's Orcadai,' he said.

Orcadai's piebald was flecked with sweat. He pulled up hard between Burun and Siban. 'We fell in with a company of Alan musketeers. They were marching south.'

Burun did not bother to ask how the encounter had ended. He looked at Siban. 'Ruysdal is south.'

'Yes.' Siban nodded. 'I wonder if they were expected. Maybe we can catch Ruysdal with its gate open.'

The column was starting to pass through a screen of trees. On the other side there was a meadow. A single rider was crossing it. When he saw the banners of the vanguard he stopped. Then he raised his arm in salute. He cantered across.

'Well?' Siban reined in.

The man was one of Nogai's personal retainers. 'Khan, Nogai Noyon sends to tell you that he is circling to the west of Ruysdal. He is a verst from the wall, and they have sounded no alarm yet.'

Siban looked pleased. 'This wind is covering the noise of our approach.'

'Yes.' Burun turned in the saddle. 'Suragai, do you think you can get some men up to the gate of the city?'

The offworlder nodded. 'I can try anyway, Khan. If we pretend to be Alan -'

'Yes. Take two hundred men. If you can stop them from closing the gate, do so. Hold until we get there. Orcadai, go with him.'

Suragai spun his mare and galloped away. Orcadai spurred after him.

Siban unfastened his bow case. 'Let's ride,' he said.

The wind shrieked in Burun's ears so that they ached. He pulled on the lead rope which attached his spare mounts, reeled in the chestnut, and jumped across on to her back. Then he threw the reins of the other animals to Osep. The orderly swerved away, leading the st'lyan towards the remuda which was already forming. Burun reached over the chestnut's back to fasten a strap, and attached his bowcase to it. The pace of the whole line increased as the army

365

sensed impending action. Burun yelled at the line on his right, and they reined in so that they were riding in formation once again.

'This is not how we planned matters.' Burun urged his mare up beside Siban's.

'I know. But if there's a chance to take the place without a lengthy siege -'

'Hunh. How many hours of daylight are left, do you think?'

Siban looked at the sky. 'I don't know. Four maybe.'

'In that case I hope Suragai can hold the gate. Otherwise we'll be trying to organise a blockade in the darkness.'

Burun remembered the distance of the exposed causeway which led to the gate. He wondered if Suragai would think to dismount his men and march them along it as if they were the musketeers who were probably expected.

'Nogai will need to throw a perimeter around the walls as soon as Suragai goes for the gate,' Siban observed. 'Does he have the experience to know what is expected of him?'

'Maybe. I think so.' Burun watched for signal banners. If Suragai timed his attempt badly, then both he and Orcadai would be isolated against the gate. Probably they would be killed.

'He has only half a tuman.' Siban pursed his lips.

There would be a moment when Nogai would have to choose between aiding Suragai and maintaining a secure cordon around the city. Burun thought about Ruysdal's low stone walls and the width of the moat. If the Yek could not get up the causeway and across the bridge, they would have to try to bridge the moat by breaking down the banks. The column passed through another screen of trees and emerged onto a plain. Signal flags waved.

366

'Khan, they are fighting at the head of the causeway!' Hodai stood in his stirrups and pointed.

'I see them. Double black at the zenith!'

Kuchuk was already attaching the pennants to his signal pole. The whole of the Yek line charged across the level ground and up the sides of the causeway. Troopers yipped and on the city wall, several muskets banged. An alarm bell was sounding somewhere.

Suragai and about forty troopers were fighting desperately in the small space in front of the gate. They were on foot, some of them using their bows to try to prevent the defenders from dropping missiles from the battlements above. The gate was wedged open about the width of a man. A length of tree trunk had been dropped into the gap so that the huge wooden doors could not be closed, and the Yek were shooting through the space into the narrow alleyway beyond. The enemy side of the gate was packed with men.

Burun leapt his st'lyan on to the bridge. He hammered across the timbers and his mare's hooves struck sparks off the cobbles below the gate arch.

'Get your shoulders to that gate!'

The troopers who had ridden up with him hurled themselves off their animals. A cascade of boiling oil fell from one of the gate towers. Men screamed and fell aside.

'Shoot at the towers! Keep that damned wall clear!' Burun pointed.

On the causeway there was a line of troopers kneeling to shoot. A single musket banged from the wall.

'Push!' Burun threw himself down from his chestnut. He shoved at the men in front of him. Everyone was heaving now, and suddenly one half of the gate tilted on its hinges. Then it fell inwards and the Alan howled in dismay. Burun was carried to one side of the arch by the packed mass of men struggling to get through the archway into the city. He backed up against the stone wall and stood in the shelter of the stone buttress until the press had eased.

Suragai was sitting with his back to the stones. His face was dirty and there was blood running down his neck from a wound in his scalp. He mopped at it with the sleeve of his mantle. Then he grinned wearily at Burun.

'Hot work, Khan. We lost more than half our number.'

Burun was shaken. 'So many?'

Suragai made a face. 'Those damned muskets. They are not much good at any distance, but a volley at close range -' He made a cutting motion across his throat.

'You did well. Where are your animals?' Burun hauled himself up the buttress using the crevices in the stone as toe- and hand-holds. He saw Orcadai on the other side of the archway.

'Back on the other side of the causeway.' Suragai took the material away from his wound and inspected the blood. 'We marched up the road. The gate was open. I think they thought we were their own men. By the time they realised they were wrong, we were halfway across the bridge.'

The Yek were in possession of both gate towers now. Troopers streamed on to the parapet which ran in both directions around the wall. An Alan musketeer was hurled screaming into the moat. Burun looked back at Suragai. He nodded. It had taken nerve to march steadily into the killing range of the Alan weapons.

Siban rode up. 'The damned fools are burning houses already, and we haven't even taken the wall.'

He gestured through the arch.

Burun swore. He searched the men riding past and saw Hodai, Kuchuk and Osep sitting their st'lyan calmly on the far side of the bridge. He waved, and they fought their way over.

Suragai caught up the reins of a loose animal as it went past. He pulled himself into the saddle, then reached down and offered Orcadai his arm. The two of them rode ahead of Burun into Ruysdal.

The narrow alleyway between the looming gate towers vented into a broad street. Several of the houses on one side of it were in flames. Two troopers ran out of one of the doorways. One of them was dragging a sack, the other had a woman slung over his shoulders. She was screaming and kicking, but the man who carried her did not even pause in his stride. Siban cursed and pulled his st'lyan across to bar their path. They stopped short.

'You can plunder when you have finished fighting! Leave your goods and the woman.' He turned to look at Burun. 'Khan, we should establish a collection point.'

Burun nodded. 'Several. Hodai, see to it. A leader of ten and a squad to act as custodians of all property and prisoners.'

Nogai rode through the arch. 'Are we winning? I saw smoke.'

Siban looked disgusted. 'We are inside the city, aren't we? Of course we are winning.'

Nogai looked amused. 'I would hate to run into you after a defeat. I left my men in a screen around the moat. There is a river gate which leads out into the bay and we are shooting fire arrows at any vessel that comes within range.'

'Good.' Siban pulled his st'lyan's head round. 'Now I think we'd better get organised. Burun, will you take

369

the eastern half of the city? Nogai, take the west. Start every man moving inwards. There must be a castle or a keep somewhere. It will have to be stormed, or maybe we can burn the defenders out.'

Burun nodded. He wheeled away and picked a sidestreet which seemed to run along the line of the wall. Every time he encountered a group of men, he directed them towards the harbour.

He rode into a dead end. Tall houses threw the narrow street into shade, their fronts tilting inward so that the crown of a roof on one side almost touched the gable end of one on the other. All the houses were deserted. He pulled his st'lyan's head round and rode back the way he had come. The sound of the hooves of the animals around him was unnaturally loud. Suragai rode on one side, Orcadai on the other. Several times Burun heard the noise of fighting but, by the time he found his way to the place where it had occurred, all that was left was the debris of combat, broken weapons and Alan bodies. The street widened, then narrowed again.

'We're swinging east again.' Orcadai edged in. The st'lyan he had found was black with white forehooves.

'I know that. But have you seen an alley running towards the harbour which doesn't come to a dead end?' Burun had expected the city to be laid out in a sensible pattern, perhaps like the spokes of a wheel, following the manner of Kinsai. But Ruysdal was a maze. Burun discovered that he could hear the sound of fighting ahead. Muskets banged irregularly and at least one large building was on fire. Cinders were floating down on the wind. Burun wrinkled his nose at the smell of the smoke and his chestnut reared nervously.

'That way.' He urged the mare down an alleyway which was barely wide enough for a mounted man.

370

The clash of weapons and the roar of men was getting louder. Suddenly, he emerged on to a packed square. The men with their backs to Burun were all Alan. Somehow he had ridden round in a circle, coming out in the rear of the retreating defenders. The far side of the square was a crush of Yek, all pushing forward, spilling out of alleys and sidestreets.

The men at the rear of the Alan line were armoured. One of them turned and when he saw Burun, he shouted in alarm. A tall blond pikeman lunged. Burun jerked at his st'lyan's reins. She reared, kicking out, and the man fell away with a cry.

Siban's voice bellowed from the other side of the square. 'Surrender, or we will kill you all!'

Burun took a breath, then bellowed the translation in Alan. The Alan cried out. Suddenly they seemed to realise that they were completely surrounded. Siban was urging his grey through the throng and Yek banners waved everywhere.

Burun forced his way forward. 'Did we take the castle?'

'There wasn't one. The city governor had a house. Can't you smell it burning?'

'I hope we looted it first.'

'Well, of course. Does a dog raise its leg to piss?'

Nogai rode into the square from one side. Officers started to organise the horde of captives, only a few of whom were women. Burun sat with one leg loose across the pommel of his saddle and watched as they were shepherded away into slavery. The troopers of the escort shouted harshly, their cries echoing from the rooftops.

'The problem is always the same. As soon as we enter a city, our force gets split up into small units. Unless the streets run to a pattern, it is difficult to organise an attack. The men see the richness of the places they are passing and they start to plunder. Who can blame them?'

Burun stopped. He hawked and spat into the fire. The embers hissed.

He had erected his camp on high level ground to the right of the causeway. Carts full of plunder went past in a steady stream, and much of Ruysdal was burning.

Siban stretched his hands out to the fire. 'Perhaps we should not have been in such a hurry. If we had attacked the way we planned, maybe the whole affair would have been better organised.'

'Oh well,' Burun grimaced. 'If you would rather be sitting out a siege –'

It had been Siban's decision to switch to a surprise attack. Now that he was able to view the chaos of the taking of the city in retrospect, he was unhappy that there had been such disorder.

'You know what I mean. We had everything planned.'

Burun shrugged. 'Suragai says that no plan of action ever survives contact with the enemy.'

'Oh well.' Siban looked at his hands. 'At least we took the place. But we lost half a tuman.'

Burun pursed his lips. Said like that, it did not sound so bad. But Siban was talking about the deaths of five thousand men. A courier galloped up the causeway. When he saw Siban's guidon he reined over.

'Lord, from T'zin Bahadur, we have taken the city of Suslev.'

'Good.' Siban nodded. 'Suslev is some distance. Have you ridden all the way?'

The messenger grinned. 'No, Lord. I came from the Moistr'. T'zin's messenger is on his way back by now.'

'Very well. Eat. Rest.'

The courier got down. He walked over to the fire, wrapped himself in his riding cloak, lay down like a puppy beside the warmth, and was asleep at once. Burun signed to an orderly to lead the st'lyan away.

Siban stood up. 'T'zin has done well.' He stamped his feet as if he had cramp.

'Yes, though we always thought that the early attacks would be easy. Now M'skva and Shermetyev will be prepared.' Burun looked up.

Siban sat down again. 'Cities. How can we rule such a land?'

There were more cities in the Alan country than there were in the whole of the rest of the Kha-Khan's domains.

'I know what you mean. They don't think the way we do.' Burun nodded.

The scouts who had come in from the west had reported that the fires in Ruysdal were visible in the sky from a distance of fifty verst. He wondered what the inhabitants of M'skva were thinking at this moment. Orcadai and Suragai rode up and dismounted. Orcadai was wearing a collar made from scores of fine gold chains which he had pillaged from the shop of a goldsmith in the city. He threw himself down beside the fire. 'God, I'm tired.'

Suragai said nothing. He lowered himself gingerly on to the log which had been set across two rocks to serve as a kind of bench. Burun wondered if he was concealing injuries received at the storming of the gate.

'Tired!' Burun made a rude noise. 'The campaign's scarcely begun yet.'

Orcadai stared up at the sky. Then he looked sideways at Suragai. The two of them grinned conspiratorially. 'I told you he would say that.' Orcadai sniggered. Suragai grinned.

Burun growled in his throat. 'If you don't show me proper respect, I'll have you disciplined.'

'Oh, Father - Mighty One -' Orcadai threw up his hands in mock terror, 'I fear your anger. Spare me, I beg you.'

Suragai stifled a laugh. Even Siban's mouth was twitching. Burun spat into the fire again. None of his sons were afraid of him any more, and he was not sure how he felt about the discovery.

The prisoners from M'skva were detained separately in a small stockade which had been built near the edge of the forest. The enclosure was uncovered and the men who were contained in it received the minimum of food and water each day.

The smell as he approached the place made Burun's nose wrinkle. Arghatun saw his expression.

'I know, Khan. But what can I do? They won't even keep themselves clean.'

'Hunh.' Burun nodded. 'Are these the ones we captured last year?' He wondered how the Alan must feel to have been dragged all the way across the G'bai to the escarpment, then back again.

'Two of them are, Khan.' Arghatun nodded. 'The rest we took three days ago. They were trying to scout us.'

The sentry on the gate saluted as Burun approached. 'Good morning, Khan.'

'Hah. It isn't a good morning. How can such a stink be good?'

'Oh, well.' The sentry grinned. 'We are relieved every hour, Khan.' He pulled the gate open to allow Burun and Arghatun to pass. The green wood squealed.

The captives were sitting in a line in the meagre shade provided by the raw posts of the stockade wall.

Arghatun pointed at the two on the end. 'Those are the two we took last year,' he said. 'Probably they have told us everything they know. They are fairly stupid.'

Burun thought that he too would be stupid if he were ever taken prisoner. The men Arghatun was indicating avoided his gaze.

'Have the others spoken yet?'

'Not so far, Khan. We have tried some persuasion, of course.'

Burun made a face. The Yasa was quite strict about the amount of ill-treatment to which a captive could be subjected. They were after all classed as slaves, and as such they had protection under the law. There were seven new captives. All of them were blond, bearded, with pale flat-faced features. They stared at Burun defiantly.

He pointed at one. 'Come here.'

'No.'

One of the men was older than the others. 'By the Name,' he murmured audibly, 'the barbarian speaks our tongue.'

Burun looked back at the gate. He waved, and at once the sentry and another trooper came into the enclosure. Burun pointed. 'Bring that one over here.'

The sentry passed his lance to the man who had accompanied him. He grabbed the captive by the neck, and hurled him on the ground at Burun's feet. The second trooper pricked the Alan's shoulder with the lance as he was starting to rise and the man lay still. The other captives growled in anger, but they did not move. Burun spat on the ground in their direction. 'What courage!' The prisoners dropped their eyes.

Burun walked back towards the gate. 'Bring him out.' The smell in the stockade made him feel ill and he did not want to show weakness in front of captives.

*

The captive was hobbled when they brought him to Burun's pavilion. The tent walls had been rolled up and secured, and beyond them the camp was bustling with activity. Burun sat at one end of a table. He stared at the Alan's face. The man met his eyes for only a moment, then he looked away.

'You are from M'skva.' Burun stood up.

The prisoner said nothing. He stared at the matting between his feet.

'Talk to me.' Burun spoke mildly. 'It will go much easier for you if you cooperate.'

The Alan's mouth tightened. He glared at Burun and shook his head. Burun shrugged. He turned his back, walked the length of the tent, then paced back again.

'Leave us.' He gestured at the sentry.

The trooper opened his mouth as if to protest. Then he nodded. 'The Khan wishes.' He went outside, but stood close to the door of the tent so that he would hear if Burun called out. Burun turned away to hide a grin.

The captive's eyes strayed to the side of the tent. Weapons were lying almost within reach, but there was nowhere to run if he tried to escape. He seemed to tense.

'Ordai!' Burun called out.

'Yes, Khan?' The other flap of the tent was pushed aside. A member of Burun's personal guard poked his head through.

'It's all right. I just wanted to make sure you were there.'

Ordai withdrew his head. The Alan captive relaxed again. He knew now that Burun was not being careless.

A flask of wine lay on the table. Burun lifted it. 'You would like a drink?' He picked up a cup.

The man said nothing, but his eyes watched the cup

as Burun poured wine. Burun set the cup down on the table. Then he stepped back. 'Go on. Drink.'

The Alan spilled some of the wine in his haste to get it down, as if he thought the cup was going to be snatched away from him. When he had finished he put the empty cup back on the table.

'Would you like more?' Burun picked up the flask.

The man started to nod. Then he shook his head. 'You are trying to get me drunk,' he said.

Burun smiled. 'Oh, well. Probably that would be easy. You haven't had much to eat, after all. Perhaps if you eat something, you can drink some more.' He walked over to the tent flap and pushed it aside. 'Ordai, the cook has some meat stewing for me. Bring two bowls.'

'Yes, Khan.'

When Ordai returned, Burun sat down on one side of the table. He indicated a stool. 'Sit. Eat.'

The prisoner looked puzzled. He had expected threats, maybe a beating. Steam was rising from the bowls of meat and Burun could discern the hunger in the man's eyes.

'Eat.' Burun gestured again.

The Alan took a step towards the table. 'I don't trust you. Maybe you are trying to poison me.'

'Poison?' Burun smiled. 'How would I benefit from such an act? But if that is what you fear, then I will eat with you, and you may choose the bowl from which you take meat.' He sat back.

The man sat down. He reached for a spoon, drew one of the bowls across and started to eat. At first he tried to eat slowly, but he was overtaken by his hunger. He gobbled down the stew, scraping every drop of the pungent gravy from the bowl.

Burun had eaten only a little, taking just enough so that the captive must see that the meat was pure. He pushed his bowl across. 'Here. You have seen me eat from this. You know that the meat is good. I can see that you are hungry.'

This time the man ate more slowly. When he laid down the spoon, his hunger seemed to be satisfied.

Burun smiled. 'I once saw a st'lyan as hungry as you. Our st'lyan graze, but this one was so hungry that it ate meat, just like you.'

The Alan looked as if he did not understand the connection. He shrugged.

'Do you know what the st'lyan ate?' Burun stood up and stepped away from the table. 'It ate the body of a man.'

The captive jerked in surprise. Then he laughed harshly. 'A story,' he said. 'You are making it up.'

'Oh, no.' Burun shook his head. 'I was there.' He went over to the tent flap and stood. 'I said that you would do well to cooperate with me. You should have listened.'

The Alan grinned defiantly. 'Do what you like. I will tell you nothing.'

'Well.' Burun shook his head and pretended to consider. 'In that case I think I will send you back to your friends in the stockade. Maybe I will tell them what you have just eaten. Do you understand why I told you that story?'

He saw doubt flare in the Alan's eyes.

'Hah. It was just meat.'

'What kind of meat?' Burun opened his eyes wide. 'Was it venison? Beef maybe? It didn't taste like beef.'

The Alan stood up quickly. 'No.' His face was pale. 'It was beef.'

Burun shook his head. 'My cook prepared the meat. Didn't you notice that the first bowl tasted different from the second? I saw it cooked. It was made from parts of a man - another Alan, I think.'

The captive leapt forward with a cry. Burun was ready. He knocked the man down. At once Ordai came into the tent. He forced the prisoner to his knees, and pinioned his arms.

'Yes.' Burun turned away. 'I will send you back to the stockade. What will the others do to you, when they know what you have done?'

'You ate it too!' The Alan flailed out with his legs.

'Ah.' Burun smiled. 'I ate from my bowl. I gave you the chance to choose which you would eat from, remember? But you were too hungry to care. You took the one you were given. Surely you noticed that the meat in the second bowl was different?'

The prisoner was trying to gag, to force himself to be sick, but with Ordai securing his arms it was impossible. Tears streamed down the man's face. He kicked and screamed, then subsided sobbing.

'I think you enjoyed it!' Burun pretended to be amazed. 'I didn't know anyone could be so greedy. Now I will have to send you back to the stockade. I can't do anything to harm you. Our law does not permit us to kill mad people and you must be mad to enjoy eating the flesh of your own kind.'

The Alan was shuddering with emotion. 'God.' He shook his head as if he did not believe what had happened. 'I didn't mean to.'

Burun signed to Ordai to let go of the captive's arms. 'Take him back,' he said.

'No! Wait, please. They'll kill me if they find out.'

Burun stopped. 'You refused to talk to me. Why should I care what happens to you?'

The Alan looked up sharply. Realisation dawned on his face. Burun let him start to feel angry at the way he had been tricked. Then he said, 'Help me, and maybe I will send you somewhere safe. No one need ever know what you have done.'

The captive's mouth set in a grim line. 'If I help you, I want more than safety.'

Burun shrugged. 'As to that, it would depend. I want M'skva, but I don't want to lose a lot of men taking it. Of course, I could catapult burning oil into the place. But that would burn up everything - the gold, the jewels, the furs, the people -'

'The people?'

'Why of course. Everyone would die. But it's easier to take a city with no people in it.' Burun counted to ten and then counted again. 'Have you family in M'skva?' he enquired casually.

The Alan's face worked.

'You - you -'

Burun gestured. 'Why should I be merciful?'

'But there are women and children in M'skva! You will kill them too?'

Burun shrugged. 'Oh, well. I have a certain fondness for children, I admit. But these are Alan children. They take the risks their fathers create for them by resisting us.'

The prisoner was crimson with self-righteous anger. 'You are barbarians! Animals!'

Burun waited. Then he spoke quietly. 'Tell me what I want to know. If there is a way into the city, I will use it. I would rather take the place intact, after all. Tell me and I will reward you. Fail to cooperate and I will send you back to your friends.'

The captive's eyes reflected the alternatives. Burun straightened.

'Ordai.'

'Yes, Khan.'

'Take him away and keep him somewhere. Don't put him back with the other prisoners and don't leave him alone. I don't want him to try suicide.'

'The Khan wishes.'

Burun caught the Alan's eyes. 'This man will take you away,' he said. 'Think about what I have said. I will speak to you again in a few hours.'

Ordai grabbed the prisoner's arm. He pulled him out through the open side of the tent. Burun walked outside. Siban was sitting on his saddle. He was sharpening arrows, and when he saw Burun he stood up.

'Well, you had him talking. Did he tell you anything?'

Burun showed his teeth. 'This afternoon he will tell me how to get into M'skva.'

'Really?' Siban looked disbelieving. 'How are you going to achieve that?'

Burun explained. Siban wrinkled his nose.

'I suppose the end justifies the means,' he said. 'But wasn't it a bit extreme?'

'At least we won't lose another five thousand men.' Burun waited for Siban to ask what kind of meat he had really given the prisoner.

'What did you use?' Siban said finally. 'Dog?'

Burun blinked. He wondered if Siban had spoken to his cook.

Siban was laughing quietly. 'And the fool really thought you were feeding him human flesh? I suppose the other bowl was p'tar meat.'

Burun made a face. It was incredible that the trick had worked. Only an Alan would believe that the Yek could be so barbarian, just as only an idiot would believe that a st'lyan would eat meat of any kind.

The tunnel which ran in under the city wall of M'skva was half full of water. Burun remembered that the river meandered across the plain, and he thought that probably there was a certain amount of seepage along the rock strata. There was a kind of tide mark on the walls which indicated how high the water was capable

381

of rising at certain times of the year. When the river was in flood, the water level would be greater than the height of the man. The tunnel would be impassable.

Wooden stakes had been set into the floor and walls. Their ends had been sharpened, but they were easy enough to pull out.

'Surely they will have a guard at the entrance.' Siban spoke at Burun's shoulder.

'Apparently not.' Burun peered ahead. 'Most of the time the water is high enough to stop anyone from coming this way. See how the roof dips in places. If the water was any deeper, we would not be able to pass.'

Burun could see only a little in the near darkness. Every tenth man was carrying a fire in a small clay pot, but the light was only sufficient to permit him to see the surface of the water an arm's length or so ahead. The water was filthy. Probably the inhabitants of the city fed their sewage into it. A trooper stumbled on something which lay unseen beneath his feet. He went under the surface and came up cursing and spluttering.

'Quiet!' Burun glared. He did not think that the tunnel was guarded. The Alan who had provided the information had too much to lose if he lied. All the same there was no point in advertising their presence until it became necessary.

Suragai waded through the waist-high water to Burun's side. The offworlder held the scabbard of his sword in one hand to keep it from getting wet.

'Khan, the diversion is ready.'

Burun nodded. He had awarded Nogai the privilege of leading half a tuman in a direct assault on the main gate. The attack was timed for the half-light just before dawn, so that as few men as possible would be lost to the Alan guns. In spite of that Burun did not envy Nogai the task.

Something scuttled along a ledge in the side of the wall. It entered the water with a splash, and swam away.

'Was that a rat?' Suragai asked.

'God.' Burun shivered. 'I hope so.'

Siban grinned. The comment was passed back along the line and some of the troopers chuckled. The tunnel was curving to the right and suddenly there was a patch of grey light illuminating the oily water from above. Burun stopped beneath the grating. 'Quickly.' He pushed troopers into position. 'Climb upon one another's backs until you can reach. Good. Now try to open it.'

The metal of the grating resisted for a moment. The troopers at the pinnacle of the human pyramid heaved and suddenly the hinges gave with a metallic shriek. Everyone froze. Then one trooper pulled himself swiftly through the narrow gap. It was only seconds before his head and shoulders reappeared again.

'Khan, we are in some kind of cellar. There is a storage barn above.'

Burun scrambled up the wall of bodies. He planted his feet on arms and shoulders, ignoring the muffled protests. When he reached the top he seized the trooper's outstretched arm and pulled himself through the gap.

The cobbles in the cellar were damp and mildewed. As Burun got to his knees, other men were already climbing through the hole. Someone found a torch and lit it. The oil-soaked bindings burned smokily and the temptation to cough was almost overpowering. Light was filtering into the cellar via a wide cobbled ramp at one end. It led to a much larger room above. One wall was piled high with sacks; Burun wrinkled his nose at the musty smell of old grain.

All the Yek were climbing up from the tunnel now. As soon as the men were in the upper part of the barn they knelt, weapons ready. There were double doors set in one of the shorter walls. They were the height of three men. Burun pressed his shoulder against the place where the doors met. They gave a little and he was able to see the stout bar which had been lodged across the outside. Siban came up. He placed one hand against the planks of the door and pushed.

'There is a bar across the outside.' Burun turned to look around the barn. Already the upper section was packed with men.

'We may as well stay here anyway.' Siban rested his back against one of the door pillars. 'Do you think we will hear when Nogai starts his attack?'

Burun shrugged. 'I expect so.' He sank down against the wood of the door and closed his eyes.

Everyone seemed to be breathing shallowly. There were only occasional whispers of conversation. Suddenly the steady beat of an alarm tocsin started in the distance. Burun could hear the sound of feet as they raced past the outside of the door. Hoarse Alan voices were raised. A musket boomed faintly.

'Nogai has started his attack.'

Burun stood up. 'Yes. All of you at the front, put your shoulders to that door. Now heave! Again!'

The door bar gave with a resounding crack. The men who were pushing fell out on to the cobbles beyond. The yard was like a small plateau. Steps and ramps descended from every side to a lower level which was like a great square. Off it ran streets of high-roofed houses.

The troopers were already splitting into thousands. Each was being directed to a different position. They fanned out, their bows ready, waiting patiently for the signal to begin their attack. More men emerged from the granary; there would be others still in the tunnel below.

There were lights in some of the houses, but no one appeared to be aware of the presence of the Yek.

'Which way is the gate?' Siban strode through the press of bodies.

'That way. Can't you hear the noise? Nogai must be keeping them occupied.'

'Well, I told him to make sure that he held their attention.' Siban grinned. 'He suggested that he might dance.'

'Hunh.' Burun grinned. 'I think we are ready.'

'Good. Maybe we can keep things organised this time.' Siban waved. At once files of troopers began to disappear along each of the streets which led off the square.

Burun jogged towards the sound of fighting at the gate. Suragai was at his shoulder. The offworlder had not uncased his bow, but his sword was unsheathed, the scabbard gripped in one hand, the hilt in the other. A group of men in half-armour appeared suddenly out of a doorway. As soon as they saw the Yek they shouted alarm. One of them knelt and Burun saw the flame of a musket. Something screamed off the wall of the house to his left, and the bang of the report echoed up the street. Troopers yipped and sprinted forward, and there was a brief bloody scuffle. Burun paused, then ran on. The noise of fighting ahead was much louder.

'Alan.' Suragai pointed. 'On the rooftops.'

Men were scrambling across the roofs of the houses above the junction of the streets ahead. Burun nocked an arrow and shot, and one Alan fell into the street. Several muskets banged, and then the space between the street and the roofs was suddenly black with arrows. The Alan who were not killed took cover. Yek troopers cheered triumphantly.

So far Burun had not seen an Alan armed with

385

anything other than either a musket or a sword. In adapting to the use of firearms, they appeared to have cast the bow aside.

Now that the Alan knew that their enemies were inside the city, a few troopers were beginning to loot the occasional house or shop as they ran past. More Alan appeared on the rooftops. They threw tiles, stones, sometimes even furniture down on the Yek in the street below.

Burun charged into the marketplace. The citadel at the far end threw a great dark shadow over everything. Stones and debris were landing all around. Suragai peeled away with about fifty men and raced off down a sidestreet. A woman screamed, very close, and a wounded trooper staggered out of an alleyway beside the gate towers and collapsed.

There were Alan up on the city wall; they occupied both gate towers as well as the space between. Some of them were piling sacks - soil or small stones, Burun judged, from the obvious weight of each - at the back of the double gate. Foot soldiers were being marshalled into a double line facing the gate. Burun saw the glint of musket barrels.

There were Yek coming out of nearly every street leading into the square. They gave a single roar and charged forward. Most of the Alan at the foot of the wall and in the space behind the gates were killed before they had a chance to turn. Those on the wall cried out. There was a battle for the steps leading into each of the gate towers. Then Yek troopers began to pour along the wall.

'Get the gate open.' Burun indicated the barricades which had been set up. A stray chunk of stone landed on the cobbles beside him. Splinters jumped away in every direction and he gasped as one sliced the skin of his cheek. The men who were opening the gate tore the wooden bar which secured the two sections off its mounts and cast it aside with a yell. Before they could stand to one side Nogai's men were forcing both sections of the gate inward. For a moment there was confusion.

'What kept you?' Nogai forced his st'lyan through the crowd. There was blood soaking the sleeve of his tunic.

'Oh, well. I wanted to give you time to distinguish yourself.' Burun waited while Nogai dismounted. 'Do you know you are bleeding?'

'It looks worse than it is. I think they were throwing old iron at us from the gate towers. Have we taken the citadel yet?'

'Not yet.'

Burun looked back at the great square tower. It was set on top of a rocky promontory. There were men on the walls and occasionally a musket boomed. The smoke from each shot was whipped away by the wind. It was almost light.

Suragai came up out of a narrow gap between two towers. 'Khan, there is only the one gate, just as we were told.'

'Good.' Burun nodded. 'Well, go on. You don't need me to command everything, surely.'

The offworlder grinned. He turned and waved. About fifty troopers rolled carts piled with wood and old hay out of the alleys in which they had been concealed. There was a slight downslope into the market place and, as soon as the carts were started on their way, they gained momentum, rumbling across the paving until they collided with the citadel gate.

'Fire arrows!'

A score of arrows streaked into one of the nearer carts. Its cargo had been soaked in oil and it burst into flames at once.

Suragai turned. 'Was that what you wanted, Khan?'

'Something like that. Now let's see if they have got the message.' Burun walked out into the centre of the square.

On the citadel wall a musket banged. The shot left a splash of lead on a stone at his feet. Burun raised his hands to his mouth.

'Shoot at me again and not a man of you will live to see nightfall!' He shouted the Alan words twice.

Several heads appeared cautiously above the level of the parapet. 'What do you want?'

The stupidity of the question made Burun grin. 'You can see that we have taken your city. Surrender, or we will burn your fortress about your ears.'

There was a long delay. Then the citadel door creaked open and three armoured men came out onto the short causeway. One of them was much older than the others.

'I am Duke Sergei, governor of this province. What terms do you offer for our submission?'

The name was the same as that which Suragai had once borne. Burun was startled. Then he recovered himself.

'One half of your goods now. One tenth of your young men to train for our army. A yearly tithe thereafter in the name of the Kha-Khan. Your people will be as slaves.'

The Alan duke looked shocked. 'Such terms are unacceptable!'

Burun turned. He looked at the Yek who waited. 'Oh, I think you'll find that they are acceptable enough once you have thought about them. Consider the alternative.'

'Barbarian!' It was one of the younger men who shouted. 'You will never leave our land alive!'

Burun smiled quietly. 'I will live longer than you,

388

boy, if your duke refuses my offer. For you will die today.'

The duke frowned. 'You offer us nothing more than slavery.'

'Oh, well. We are all slaves of the Kha-Khan. Submit to us now and we will throw the shield of our protection over you. Your people will live outside the walls of the city in peace. But as there is only one Lord in Heaven, so there must be only one on Earth. Defy us and you defy God.' Burun turned and walked back to the Yek line.

'Will they accept?' Siban asked.

'Do they have a choice? This one is a duke. His name is Sergei.'

Siban nodded. He walked past Burun into the square. 'I am Siban the White, brother to the Kha-Khan. What have you decided?'

The young man who had called Burun a barbarian was arguing fiercely with the others. Now the Alan duke said something to him sharply. He came forward. Then he drew a short sword from the scabbard which was at his belt. A hundred Yek bows were raised, but only the hilt was offered. 'I have no choice,' the Alan said. 'M'skva is yours.'

The troopers who had been detailed to clear the city were returning to the marketplace. Some of them guarded groups of disarmed Alan soldiers.

'What are we to do with all these people, Khan?' Arghatun gestured at the crowd which had begun to gather.

'Hold them outside the wall under guard for the moment. They may take half of their possessions - whatever they can carry. Let those who must, return to their homes so that they may take what is proper.' Burun watched the troopers as they herded the women, children and an occasional man out through the gates. The faces of the men were set and grim. The women had enormous shadows under their eyes.

'We will have to send men to watch when they remove their goods, Khan.' Arghatun looked as if he disagreed with the decision.

'Then do it and don't trouble me.'

Arghatun stepped back. His eyes were opaque. 'The Khan wishes.'

'I don't understand why we're not simply making them into slaves.' Nogai was sitting on a low stone wall.

Burun looked up. 'We cannot empty the whole country. If we release some of them, they will settle and build again. They will spread out and occupy the untenanted land which no one has farmed until now.'

'If you say it, it must be so.' Nogai did not smile.

Burun grinned. 'How delicately you avoid disagreement.'

Nogai made a face. 'What about the city?'

'Once we have taken what we want, we will burn it, of course.' Burun watched Nogai's face and thought that he detected a kind of distaste there. He turned away. If they did not burn M'skva after they had looted it, the people would simply re-occupy the place as soon as the army moved on.

'I hear that Jotan took Miroselsk without loss.' Siban handed his bowl to an orderly.

Burun grunted. The news had arrived a day earlier.

'Was it Daijin who said that cities are for burning?' Siban looked out across the valley. 'I forget. I don't know if we are doing the right thing here. These people are city dwellers. Most of them don't know how to live on the land.'

Burun was surprised at the words. 'You sound as if

you feel sympathy for them.'

'Maybe I do. How heavy were our casualties?'

'Light. Nogai lost more than I would have liked.'

'Yes. Well, he always fights in close.'

'And we lost a few score in the streets. On the whole we seem to have got it right this time.'

'Yes. I'm very pleased.' Siban turned back.

Burun sniffed. 'We won't always be able to take a city so easily.'

'No underground passages, you mean. No, but we will find other ways. The important thing is that we are learning how to deal with the way the Alan fight.'

There was no answer worth making. Burun waited for Siban to come to the point.

'You know the Kha-Khan has given the province to me?' Siban accepted a platter of meat.

'Yes.'

Siban ate a mouthful of the roast meat. He turned away to spit out a pad of gristle. A dog lying in the grass raised its head, examined the titbit, and wolfed it down.

'I don't intend to spend much time here, of course.' Siban studied Burun as he spoke. 'I will need to appoint a governor.'

Burun finished eating. He handed his platter to an orderly. 'It's a rich enough land. It will serve you well.'

'Yes.' Siban paused. 'I wondered if you thought that Jotan was ready for the responsibilities of overlordship.'

Burun concealed his surprise. He pretended to consider the idea. 'Jotan has never governed a fief, but he commands as well as any. Of course you would install stewards.'

'Oh, of course. One has to have an accounting. But the country is isolated from everything. The governor would be the true lord. He would rule in my name.'

Burun looked away. M'skva was dark and silent now that it had been emptied. There were still some people camped outside the walls, but they were dispersing gradually.

'Would that be in the name of Siban Khan, or Siban Kha-Khan?' he asked softly. None of the slaves and servants were standing within earshot.

Siban's hands were suddenly still. 'That would depend,' he responded at last. 'Would it make a difference?'

Burun considered. He had never believed that Siban had no interest in the succession. Finally he shrugged. 'Maybe not.'

Jotan stood beside the fire. A pair of slaves peeled off his mantle and tunic. Both garments were stiff with sweat and grime.

'I don't think Miroselsk was expecting us,' he said.

'You lost a few men.' Burun looked up. The reports that Jotan had taken the city without loss were clearly exaggerated.

Jotan made a face. 'More than I expected. A lot of them were C'zaki. They got split up when they got into the streets. When they ran into even small groups of Alan, some were always killed by the guns.'

Burun nodded. 'I know what you mean. And of course some got caught in burning houses, or were trampled by the men on their own side.'

'It sounds as if you experienced similar problems.' Jotan towelled himself with a linen sheet and put on a fresh tunic.

'In Ruysdal, yes. M'skva was different. And it was worth the taking. I have just sent a caravan-load of plunder off to Kinsai which was fifty carts long.'

'Was that everything, or just the Kha-Khan's tenth?'

'Only the tenth. I don't think I have ever seen a city

quite so rich outside of Kinsai. There were furs like none I have seen before, also gold, jewels and a great sapphire, to rival the one your wife wears. Most of the granaries were full. We could make our base here if we wished.'

'I see that you have not fired the place yet.' Jotan fastened his belt. 'Do we wish?'

Burun stood up and walked in a circle. 'I don't know. That could be a matter for you to decide.'

'Eh?'

'Well -' Burun watched Jotan's face for a sign that he had already been approached by Siban and saw none. 'You are going to be asked if you want to be provincial governor, once we have conquered the land.'

'I see.' Jotan adjusted the set of his mantle, his face expressionless. 'Would that be in Arjun's name, or Siban's?'

Burun shrugged. 'Would it matter?'

Jotan's face was thoughtful. 'Perhaps not. Whose idea was this?'

'Siban's initially. However his recommendation has already gone to Kinsai. It will have the Kha-Khan's approval.'

'I would have thought that the fact that I am your eldest son would bar me from elevation.' Jotan spoke musingly.

Burun looked at him sharply. Apart from the hereditary land of the Merkuts on the Khirgiz, the Kha-Khan had given him fiefs in Ch'nozia, N'pan and Suristan. Only the Altun had larger holdings, and if Jotan were to rule the Alan country Merkuts would control over a tenth of the known world.

'You know how my will is made.' Burun sat down. 'You are my heir. I expect you to award fiefs to your brothers. But everything I have done has been for you.'

'I know.' Jotan nodded. 'I'm just not sure that this particular fief would be worth the price we would have to pay.'

There were new fortifications surrounding Pereislav. A complicated series of earthworks enclosed the city walls and, where there had been gates before, there were massive towers.

'Clever.' Burun studied one of the new sections with the aid of Suragai's spyglass. 'But how do they get in and out?'

'There are platforms, Khan. They raise them on pulleys. I think there must be some kind of winch arrangement inside each tower.' The offworlder spoke. 'The main platform is big enough to hold a cart.'

'I see.' Burun closed the glass. 'They reason that if there are no gates, it will be next to impossible for us to gain entry.' He looked down at Nogai's camp which was setting up at one end of the principal earthwork. Patrols of Yek were riding innocently around the exterior. Apparently Pereislav was not wasting powder or shot, for the riders were within range of larger weapons like cannon or mortars.

Nogai rode up. 'Burun. I expected you yesterday. Is Siban with you?'

'He will be here in another day. Have you tried an assault yet?'

Nogai snorted. 'Do I look stupid? Wait until you have had a closer look. This one is going to be difficult.'

'Hunh.' Burun reined over. He kicked his st'lyan into a walk. Pereislav was the city to which Barakai had deserted, and he had expected its defences to be in good order. Yurts were going up all along the outer rim of the earth barricade. 'I see that you expect to be here for a while.' He looked for the pennant which marked Nogai's yurt and steered towards it.

Nogai smiled. 'Any fool can be uncomfortable.'

Burun dismounted. He looked at Suragai. 'What do you think?'

The offworlder shrugged. 'Khan, I need to have a closer look.'

'They must have started building this last year.' Nogai threw his reins to a slave.

'Probably.' Burun pulled his cloak off the back of his saddle. 'We will see. Maybe they have made some mistakes.' There was a wind coming off the hills. He wondered if it was going to rain.

Suragai was still mounted. He saluted Burun and rode off towards the first opening in the earthworks.

'You trust him for this?' Nogai got down.

Burun grinned. Suragai felt guilty because his man had deserted to Duke Yuri. He would expend every possible effort in the siege of Pereislav in order to convince the Yek that he was loyal.

'I trust him to tell me how to get through those defences.'

'Well.' Nogai looked thoughtful. 'Be careful. And if you ride in there, don't go alone.'

'Oh?'

'Wait and see.'


The earthworks had been constructed in a series of great concentric circles around the limits of the city wall. There were breaks at several points so that cart traffic could pass, but Burun guessed that the widest spaces had been filled as soon as the Alan heard that M'skva had fallen. Every earth wall was reinforced with stone and each barrier was about four times the height of a man and roughly as thick.

Suragai was walking his st'lyan just ahead. He reined

in and turned. 'We ought to dismount here, Khan.'

'Very well.' Burun uncased his bow. He threw his reins to Hodai.

'Khan, you should take more men.' Hodai looked unhappy.

'Not this time. I only want to look. Wait here.'

'Yes, Khan.'

Burun nocked an arrow to his bow. He followed Suragai into the first gap. In front there was only a blank wall. Anyone who drove into the maze would have to turn right or left, then drive until he came to another space. Eventually he would reach the foot of the wall, but there would be no direct road.

The next gap was filled with sharpened wooden stakes. There was an old blood sign on the hard-packed earth.

'We lost seven men here the first day,' Suragai said quietly. 'We were beaten.'

Something moved at the corner of Burun's eye and he turned swiftly. A man was moving almost out of sight around the curve of the earthwork. An arrow thunked into the wall beside Burun's head and he ducked. When he raised his head again the man was gone.

Suragai had not even raised his bow. 'That's what Nogai was talking about, Khan. Come and look, but watch out behind.'

The offworlder paced cautiously along the line of the earth wall. When he stooped, Burun saw that he was looking through a narrow tunnel.

'This is how they come and go.' Suragai stepped to one side so that Burun could see. 'The place is a maze of walls and tunnels. There are blind alleys. Probably they can see everything we do from the top of the city wall. Certainly they are always ready for us.'

Burun peered through the tunnel. He could see

through clear to the next barrier. 'Is the next circle the same?'

'I think so, Khan. No one has got that far yet.'

Burun wrinkled his nose. 'Let's look.' He went through the tunnel at a crouch. When he emerged from the end he saw four men crouching down against the curve of the far wall a short bowshot away. One of them turned. As soon as he saw Burun and Suragai he shouted. An arrow hissed past Burun's shoulder. He saw one man running and shot him. The others vanished.

'Well done, Khan.' Suragai rolled the dead man over on to his back. 'Usually we don't manage to kill them.'

'I can't think why.' Burun located the gap through which the Alan had escaped. It went part of the way through the next earth barrier, then turned at right angles. Burun frowned.

'We could cut a gap in each earth wall.' Suragai spoke at his shoulder. 'But you can see how thick they are. It would take time. The Alan know all the tunnels. They would pick us off at their leisure.'

'I understand.' Burun nodded. 'I want to see the rest of it.'

Suragai blenched. 'Khan, we wouldn't get past the next gap!'

'Oh, come. What are we? Yek or Ch'noze?'

'Well you may be Yek, Khan. But I'm just another alien. I'm not clever enough to go into a warren when I don't know all the tunnels.'

Burun grinned. He edged into the narrow passage through the earth wall. After a moment Suragai began to follow. At the place where the cutting turned sharply right Burun nocked another arrow. He went to the end of the trench and looked out. The gap between the two earthworks was empty.

'Come on.' Burun trotted across the space. He

rested his back against the hard-packed soil.

'There's a tunnel entrance to your right, Khan.'

'Good.' Burun sidled along the wall. 'Don't speak again. Just tap me on the shoulder. Use signs.'

They went on through to the next gap, seeing nothing. Burun began to wonder if the earthworks were as dangerous as Nogai and Suragai seemed to believe. He walked along the line of the next wall, counting his steps. Suragai tapped him on the shoulder and pointed. There was a tunnel entrance low in the barrier.

The tunnel was so low that Burun had to crawl on his hands and knees. When he got to the far end he took out four arrows and laid them on the ground. Then he nocked one and looked out. The outer wall of Pereislav was about thirty paces away. A score of lightly armoured Alan were clustered around the platform which had been lowered from one of the towers. The platform had side rails, at least one of which appeared to be capable of removal, and the whole affair was attached to heavy cables which led upwards into openings in the stonework above. As Burun watched, the men got on to the platform. It started to rise. Burun waited until it was about halfway to the top of the tower. Then he crawled out of the tunnel and shot a man who was standing at the end beside the rail. The Alan cried out, swayed, then pitched through the guard rail and landed on the ground. The other men on the platform shouted in alarm. The platform seemed to hesitate for a moment, then it rose more swiftly. Burun fired again, aware that Suragai had also emerged from the tunnel and was using his bow. A musket banged from the wall above, and the ball whined off the rock which had been used to reinforce the earthwork.

'Let's get out of here.' Burun crowded Suragai back

398

into the tunnel. 'I've seen all I wanted to see.'

Apparently the Alan had been withdrawing their men from the fortification. Burun and Suragai moved through the concentric circles without incident.

Burun took his reins from Hodai's hand. 'Do you think Barakai thought of this?' He looked at Suragai.

The offworlder hesitated. Then he nodded. 'I've seen something like it once before, Khan, on a world we both visited years ago.'

Burun cased his bow. 'In that case all you have to do is remember how it was defeated.' He mounted. 'In any case, when Siban arrives we will think of something.' He grinned at the offworlder's expression, and rode away.


'Suragai thinks we should use the explosives.'

The sentries on the outer ring of the earthworks had cut footholds up one side so that it could be climbed. Siban stood on the top and shaded his eyes to gaze at the looming towers of the city.

Burun nodded. 'Yes.'

Siban turned. 'You agree?' He looked interested.

'I think we ought to break through at least the outer rings that way. We can put enough men into them to prevent our engineers from being shot at all the time. And if the Alan are under the impression that we don't use gunpowder, maybe it will give them a surprise.'

'I hadn't thought of that.' Siban lowered his hands. 'Very well then.'

Burun started to climb down.

'I have despatches for you,' Siban said as he followed. 'They are from the escarpment camp.'

'Thank you.' Burun waved to one of the sentries. The man started to climb back on to the wall. 'I will send for them later.' He walked away towards his yurt. A light canopy had been set up beside it and Suragai was working there. He was sketching something for the Sechem, Parin, and when he saw Burun he stood respectfully.

'Good morning, Khan.'

Burun walked in under the canopy. 'Good morning.' He turned a sketch so that he could see the detail. 'What in the Name of God is that?'

'Oh.' Suragai had the grace to look embarrassed. 'It's a drawing of a glider. It's something like a large kite, only untethered. It flies well enough to carry a man. It can carry more if it's big enough. It depends upon the size of the wing area. I thought maybe we could build something like it. If we flew it over a city, we would be able to see what was happening behind the walls.'

'I see.' Burun studied the drawing. He shook his head. 'Well, you can forget about that for the moment. Siban has agreed to the use of explosives to breach the outer rings of the earthworks. I want you to survey the sections. The engineers will need to be told the best places to plant their charges.'

Burun had not thought that there was much science to the destruction of masses of rock with gunpowder. But a few demonstrations of the power of the refined explosive produced by the engineers had convinced him otherwise.

Suragai looked relieved. Burun guessed that he had been dreading an attempt to break into the rings by conventional means.

'That's good, Khan. I'm sure it's the best way to deal with the problem.'

Burun grunted. He stared at the sketch of the glider again. Then he walked away. A trooper of Siban's guard was waiting outside his yurt.

'Well?'

'Lord, Siban Khan bade me bring you these.' The man proffered a pair of scrolls. Both were bound with

400

the unmistakable crimson and blue of Zurachina's seal.

'Thank you.' Burun went inside, opening one of the letters as he entered the antechamber. The missive was from Zurachina, but Kiku had done the writing. As usual she had mixed N'pan characters with Yek script. The letter would take ages to decipher. Burun dropped it on the table and opened the other.

A second scroll dropped out. The outer parchment had been only a wrapping. The letter was in Yek and the seals were the Kha-Khan's. Burun bellowed wordlessly. At once Osep came quickly out of the back of the yurt. 'Khan?'

'Find my son quickly. And send to Siban Khan. I would be honoured if he would join me as soon as possible in my yurt.'

Burun started to scan the lines of script. Osep raced away.

Jotan must have been right outside. He came in almost at once. As soon as he saw the seals on the letter his eyebrows rose. 'What's this?'

'Wait until Siban gets here.' Burun forced himself to sit down. 'I'm not going to tell it twice.'

The manner of arrival of the scroll meant that normal communication from Kinsai was being obstructed. He wondered how long the letter had been delayed, and thus how out of date was the news it contained.

Siban came unhurriedly through the door hangings. 'What is it? Is one of your wives petitioning the Kha-Khan for a divorce?'

Burun held up the scroll so that Siban could see the seals. 'This is from Kinsai. It was inside a wrapping sent to me by my wife. I imagine she got it from our daughter-in-law, Jotan's wife, who is attending court.'

'Yes.' It was clear that Siban understood the implications. 'Who is it addressed to, you or me? Read it.'

'It's from Khotan, but the Kha-Khan has counter-signed the bottom of the page. It says - wait until I find the important part - yes, here. "From Arjun Kha-Khan by the hand of Khotan the Restless, to the Khan of the Merkuts, Burun. Know that you have my full and absolute authority to prosecute the war against the Alan, subject only to the will of Siban Khan."'

'I don't understand.' Jotan looked puzzled. 'The Kha-Khan is giving you authority you already possess.'

'Yes.' Siban nodded. 'But put that way, the authority cannot be revoked, even if the Kha-Khan dies. Arjun must be sick.'

'Possibly,' Burun agreed. 'In the next paragraph he says that Nogai is to be returned to Kinsai, under guard if necessary. He wants a report on Nogai's conduct under gold seal, copies by courier.'

'Artai has not come up to expectations.' Siban sounded unsurprised. 'Nogai is being considered as a possible successor again. And if he is not to be heir, then they want him confined at Kinsai.'

'That is my understanding.' Burun laid the letter aside.

Siban stood. 'It means that Vortai is obstructing the normal passage of despatches as they pass through the escarpment. I wonder how many copies of this were sent. I have had nothing from Kinsai for a month. I will go and speak to Nogai.' He left the yurt.

Jotan picked up the letter. He studied the text. 'The Kha-Khan is trusting you with a great deal.'

'They must have known that a letter sent through Zurachina would reach me. Also it was safe to assume that once I had received the order, I would tell Siban. Vortai can do nothing to prevent Nogai from returning to Kinsai. Too many people will know.'

'Name of God.' Jotan tossed the letter on the table. 'Use Nogai. Bargain with him. The Kha-Khan has put power in your hands. Why won't you use it?'

'Because it would be wrong.'

'Why?'

'Because until he dies, I serve Arjun.' Burun thought that the issue was clear enough.

Jotan swore softly but comprehensively.

Burun made a face. 'I have the Kha-Khan's favour because I have always been loyal. They could have had me killed a score of times. Instead Arjun has given me all I ever asked of him. And if I betray the trust of one Kha-Khan, why should his successor believe that I will be loyal?'

Jotan hunched his shoulders. 'We could be the foremost family in the Khanate.'

'We are great enough. You must not be so impatient.' Burun felt as if he was addressing a wilful child.

Jotan looked up. 'Can I say nothing to make you change your mind? How can you say that everything you do is for me?'

'It is. It is.'

Jotan walked out of the yurt. Burun sat and stared at the wall. Then he picked up Zurachina's letter and tried to read it. The important parts - where Kiku wanted something - came through quite clearly. The rest of the text was obscured by the fact that N'pani characters had no direct equivalent in the Yek tongue. Kiku said that she used them because they made the page look better. Burun wished that Zurachina was here with him. She would know how to handle Jotan, and would tell him what to do about Siban. She would know how far he should trust the offworlders. She would tell him that he was right to remain loyal to Arjun. Burun closed his eyes. Zurachina would sleep beside him at night, talk when he wanted her to talk, listen when he needed to think aloud. He thought about the wording of the Kha-Khan's order and opened his eyes again.

Jotan had not noticed and Siban had made no comment, but if Arjun died, Siban's direction of the war would be supreme. Burun picked up the letter again and tried to decide if the Kha-Khan was indicating a preference. If he was, then something would have to be done.

Burun moved back and forward on the edge of the tower and watched the gap in the first circle of earthworks. There had been a brief skirmish when the troopers escorted the engineers in, but no messenger had come. The outer earth wall prevented him from seeing a great deal of what was going on.

Every time he moved, the wood of the tower creaked alarmingly. Kuchuk was sitting on the stumps of the pyramid of poles where they were secured to make a place for the platform to be mounted. His signal flags were laid out ready and he seemed to be undisturbed by the commotion below.

Suddenly, men started to stream out of the two gaps nearest Burun's position. A green banner was being waved. Arghatun galloped his st'lyan out of the mob to the foot of the tower.

'We're ready, Khan.'

'Very well.' Burun looked for Suragai, but could not see him. 'Red banner.'

Kuchuk attached a square of crimson to his signal pole and waved it twice. When Burun looked down at the men who were waiting in ranks on the grass, he saw that the thousand commanders were telling them to hold their st'lyans' heads.

The explosives went off in continuous succession. First the earth circle seemed to vibrate, and then it was obscured by a rising cloud of dust. The noise came like a roll of thunder. The shock wave made the observation tower sway.

'Name of God!' Burun could see nothing. Suragai had said that the first charges might not altogether clear the outer barrier, that most likely they would simply redistribute the rock and soil so that an advance could pass over it. Most important of all, the concussion would destroy all the tunnels in the outer rings.

Suddenly Suragai came trotting up the slope towards the tower. He caught a projecting rung at head height and swung himself up on it. Then he swarmed up the outer surface of the support pole until he was on the platform.

'What's happening?' Burun pulled the offworlder to his feet. 'I can't see anything.'

Suragai was breathing hard. He waved a hand at Burun, telling him that he needed to catch his breath. Then he hawked and spat over the edge of the platform. 'Khan, we have reduced the walls of the two outer circles. There are still mounds of rock and soil, but there are spaces wide enough for you to move men forward in column. I don't think any of the tunnels in the third ring – what is now the outer defence – will have survived. I planted charges in most of them and the concussion should have done the rest.'

'Good. Kuchuk, white banner.'

A great roar went up from the men waiting below. They started to stream in through the gaps which had been blown. Most of them were on foot and they carried both bows and shields. Jotan and Nogai rode past. Jotan stopped long enough to deposit Jehan with an orderly at the foot of the tower. The boy climbed up to the platform, his mouth turned down with disappointment.

'Grandfather, can't I –'

Burun shook his head. 'No, Noyon. You have to stay

here. Your father is right. That earthwork is no place for you.'

Jehan sat down on the edge of the platform. His expression remained sulky.

The remains of the outer circles were now packed with men. Burun could tell which were Yek because they had their shields raised above their heads. He could see arrows sleeting down and guessed that the Alan were firing into the air from one of the inner circles. So far he had not heard a single gunshot, and wondered if it was Barakai who had persuaded the defenders of Pereislav to take up the bow again.

One of the disadvantages about the way Pereislav had sealed its gates was the fact that men could only be fed into the defensive rings slowly. Burun could see the platforms in the towers going up and down. Every time they descended they were crowded with armed men. Apparently the Alan had not thought to prepare ladders.

Siban rode up. He had been directing a similar invasion of the earthworks on the far side.

'It's slow, but we're gaining ground.'

'Yes.'

A tortoise of Yek shields now filled the whole of the first intact earth ring. More troopers were pouring into the gaps, and the sound of battle was a constant rumble. Suddenly the noise seemed to lessen, as if everyone had paused at the same instant to draw breath. Carts were being rolled into some of the new gaps, and Burun heard the sound of mallets striking timber.

'I hope you're right about this.' Burun rounded on Suragai. 'Otherwise we're wasting a lot of time and effort.'

The offworlder looked calm. 'Khan, they must have known we would get into the circles sooner or later.

406

They are bound to have a method of dealing with that.'

Inside the first ring a framework was being erected. As soon as a portion was complete, the troopers below climbed up and lashed their shields into place on top to form a roof.

'Burun, look.' Siban pointed.

'I see them.'

There were Alan soldiers running along the top of the earth wall. Several of them jumped on to the shield roof. Burun could see that they were bouncing on it to test its strength. Yek troopers were climbing the outer wall to shoot at the trespassers, but some of the Alan escaped back to their own side.

'I think they are going to try fire first, Khan.' Suragai sounded unruffled. 'We are ready for them.'

'Good.' Burun snatched the spyglass which was tucked into Suragai's sash. He focused it on the earthwork.

Already the Alan were running along the top of the outer barrier. Some of them were carrying buckets and several bore torches. Yek troopers were climbing up to shoot at them, but the Alan pressed forward with remarkable determination. They were being killed, but buckets were being emptied over the shield roof, and where the torches were thrown the oil-soaked surface burst into flames. Siban cursed and spat.

Suragai turned. He looked amused. 'Lord, we expected something like this.'

Signal flags waved. The carts pulled away from the gaps and the troopers raced out from under the roof. They took up positions just beyond the earthwork and knelt, waiting. Most of the shield roof was still intact. The flames had forced the Alan back, so that only a few arrows met the engineers placing ladders on the outer face of the earth wall in order to climb up and douse the fires.

Tulagai and Targoutai rode up from the gap. The standard bearer who rode behind Tulagai was waving a blue flag.

'They are asking for orders.' Siban pointed.

'I know. Kuchuk, tell them to wait.'

'Where is my father?' Jehan was standing up. He gazed at the smoke coming from the fires.

'He is inside. He is commanding the party which holds the first ring.'

'But he'll be killed!'

'No, Noyon.' Burun pointed. 'See, the flames have almost died. He is safe enough.'

Siban went to the edge of the platform. He looked over. 'The relief is ready.'

'Send them down, then. Put them in T'zin's charge.'

Siban nodded. He disappeared over the edge of the platform. Burun raised the spyglass again. When he trained it on the wall of the city, he saw that men were still being ferried down on to the ground. Every time the platform rose, it carried a full load of wounded.

Suragai was also surveying the city wall. 'Do you want to continue as planned, Khan?'

'I think so. Do you think they will believe we are giving up?'

'So long as we don't make any attempt to repair the shield roof. They must be able to see that we have drawn most of our men back.'

'Yes. The sun will set soon.' Burun looked at the sky.

The silence was so unnatural that it made Burun uneasy. The quiet nights on the steppe were different. Even on the G'bai a traveller would hear the whisper of the wind and the call of the wild things which dwelt among the sands. But in this stillness Burun's ears strained for sounds which never came. He adjusted his

408

short cloak, then walked through the lines of waiting men and into the roofed circle. The darkness under the shields was broken by the occasional chink of moonlight where it penetrated the places where they were joined. Nogai and Jotan were sitting under the largest of the intact sections. They were talking quietly, and when they saw Burun they stood up.

'Are we ready?'

Jotan nodded. 'We brought the timber in as soon as it got dark.'

Burun took a breath. Outside the circles the rest of the army was waiting, a vast number of men ready to surge forward to attack Pereislav.

'Very well. Make the signal.'

Nogai had a fire in a little clay pot. He covered the glow with the edge of his cloak, then uncovered it several times so that the light winked towards the greyness of the gap. An answering signal flashed along the curve of the earth wall. Everywhere, the Yek army rose out of the shadows.

Shields covered the mouths of the few tunnels not destroyed by the shock of demolition. Burun jerked the nearest one aside. He stooped and crawled through. Behind him others followed.

The next circle was full of the litter of the day's battle. Arrows lay everywhere, along with abandoned oil buckets and a few burnt-out torches. The smell of charred flesh made Burun stifle a sneeze. He realised that the shapeless lump at his feet was a man.

All along the wall the Yek were coming out into the moonlight. There was still no sign that the Alan in the city realised that anything was wrong.

'They aren't expecting us.' Nogai spoke softly.

'Maybe.' Burun looked upwards, but the top of the earth wall prevented him from seeing to the towers of Pereislav. 'Get some men up on top of the barrier.'

Troopers with axes hacked hand- and foot-holds. Other men armed with bows scrambled up on to the top of the wall and crouched to watch the city. The engineers were starting to bring timbers into the circle now. As soon as the noise of their mallets commenced, lights flashed in Pereislav.

'Is this the third circle out from the city wall, or the second?' Jotan moved out of the way of a pair of sweating engineers as they struggled to lodge a timber against one wall.

'The second.' Burun gestured. 'There were five. We destroyed two and took the third. There is one more ring beyond this, then we are beneath the city wall itself.'

It was something Jotan ought to have known. Burun opened his mouth to make a comment, then realised that Jotan had been making conversation to cover his nervousness. This was a kind of fighting the Yek had never tried before. Already the new shield roof was being lashed into place. Raw lengths of timber thumped down whenever someone was careless.

'Khan!' A sentry on top of the wall called down. 'They are doing something in the city!'

Burun looked for Suragai and saw him helping an engineer to shore up a sagging section of the roof. 'Everyone find cover!'

Nogai and Jotan repeated the command and it was yelled along the circle. The troopers who were in sections which were still unroofed dived back into the tunnels. Everyone else crowded in below the shields. They pressed against the wall which was nearest the city.

'Down!' A sentry howled warning. He flung himself off the top of the wall and dived for the shelter of the shields.

Burun pressed himself against the packed earth. A

hail of rocks swept down. Suragai had been right. The defenders of Pereislav had constructed catapults and had registered the range to each of the circles. The barrage seemed to go on forever. Rocks bounced and rolled in under the shield roof. Splinters pelted Burun and he gasped. Abruptly the hail of rocks ended and silence closed in.

None of the men who had remained on top of the wall had survived. They had been swept away as if they had never existed.

'Shake the timbers!' Burun shouted.

Troopers seized the supports and rocked them. Rocks and stones tumbled down, landing on stones already lying on the ground, splitting them. Burun saw that his hand was bleeding and bound it with a strip of material. The Alan must have tested their catapults for distance back when they first constructed the earthworks. They would have realised that if they could block an advance through the rings, a siege would be next to impossible.

'What now?' Nogai stood up.

'Send messengers out to Siban. Tell him to start sending the rest of the army through. I thought it would be enough to take this ring tonight, but I was wrong. We have to move right on through to the city wall.'

'Oh, well.' Nogai looked up at the sky. 'At least there is moonlight.'

'Yes.'

'More stones!' A trooper who had climbed up on to the earth wall scrambled back down again.

This time the rock shower was not so heavy. The stones were smaller, as if the Alan were loading their catapults with buckets of pebbles. A trooper who was caught in the open was brought down and when Burun turned him over he saw that the man had a

411

small stone lodged in his temple.

'Move into the next circle.' Burun wrenched a shield aside. He crawled into the tunnel entrance.

At once he knew that there was someone in the tunnel ahead of him. He lashed out with his talons and a man's voice cried out in Alan. Burun jerked out his d'jaga and stabbed the dimly seen figure in the chest. Blood flowed down over his hand and arm. The Alan sagged forward. There were others behind him but they could not get at Burun because he was holding the man he had killed upright in the tunnel. They shoved at the body, then tried to pull it out of Burun's grasp. He pushed hard, and Jotan and Nogai crowded behind him, adding their weight.

The dead Alan tumbled out of the tunnel mouth. Burun dived after him. An axe blade bit into the wall above his head, and he rolled desperately aside. A bearded face loomed above him and he stabbed at it with his d'jaga. Blood streamed from a gash across his assailant's cheek. The man yelled and staggered back. The space between the two earth walls was filled with Yek and suddenly the sounds of fighting died away.

Burun got to his feet and crossed the gap. Nogai was investigating a trench which seemed to pass through the final earthwork which separated them from the city wall. He sidled into it and Burun followed.

'Can we keep this up?' Nogai turned his head to see who was behind him. 'I thought we were going to take only the second circle tonight.'

'We were.' Burun squeezed past a projecting rock which was lodged in the earth wall. 'But we would have spent the day trying to stop the Alan from burning us out, and their catapults would have made movement impossible.'

The trench turned sharply to the left. Suddenly they

were in a space which was directly beside the Pereislav wall. It was about fifty paces wide and was packed with men fighting hand to hand. A platform had been part lowered from one of the towers and the men on it were shooting down at the throng below. Burun drew his short sword. A line of troopers was forming up between the earthwork and the city wall. They had shields up against a hail of arrows.

'We have to clear this space!' Nogai yelled.

An arrow thunked into a shield held by a trooper standing beside Burun. He flinched. 'I know. But so long as they can send men down off the wall, they can mount a counter-attack. We need to take one of the towers or a part of the wall. It doesn't matter if the Alan destroy the platforms.'

'I thought Suragai had something worked out to deal with that problem.'

'He has. But I haven't seen him since we left the second circle.'

A mass of Alan soldiers started to advance from the base of one of the towers. They wore plate armour and swung their swords like scythes. The Yek fell back. An arrow skipped off a breastplate, and Burun heard Jotan shouting at the bowmen to aim at their attackers' faces.

An Alan arrow thumped into Burun's cloak, but it did not penetrate the heavy fur. He yanked it out. Troopers were emerging constantly from the tunnels, but there was such a press that they were unable to use the advantage of their numbers to any effect. Burun glanced up at the city wall. He could see the heads of the defenders who were peering over. Missiles of all kinds were being thrown from above, but they were landing as often on Alan heads as on Yek. Nogai pushed men into line and they moved forward, battering at the Alan, their shields held high. Jotan was on top of the earth wall. He had archers

413

with him, and now they began to shoot down at the armoured men. The combination of the two assaults was too much for the Alan and they fell back. At first they retired in an orderly fashion. Then, as the storm of arrows became more intense, they broke and ran. They streamed away towards the base of the nearest tower.

The wooden platform which was suspended from the tower was about the height of two men off the ground. Before it had settled, Alan in plate armour were clambering on to it, fighting one another for a place. The platform started to rise almost at once and Jotan's archers switched their aim. As the platform came level with the top of the earth bank, they were firing into it at a distance of about half a bowshot. Most of the Alan on the platform were killed. The men who had been left on the ground below howled in dismay. They turned and tried to organise a new defensive line, but the Yek surged forward with a roar. For a moment the Alan armour reflected the moonlight, then it was submerged beneath a black tide. There was no colour anywhere, only blacks and greys. Even the blood was shiny black under the silver light of the twin moons in the sky.

The archers were using fire arrows now. A score or more thudded into the wooden platform as it continued to rise up into the tower. By the time it entered the embrasure it was burning fiercely. Suragai came through the narrow gap in the earthwork behind Burun. He was followed by a team of sweating engineers who staggered under the weight of pairs of cast-iron powder shells.

'Khan, if you can protect us, we can place these against the wall.'

'Yes.' Burun turned. 'Hodai, find twenty men with shields. Have them form a tortoise.'

414

The troopers who were detailed pushed lances through the arm straps of their shields so that they overlapped one upon another. At Hodai's command they raised the completed umbrella above their heads. More men moved in and held their shields so as to protect the sides of the formation. Suragai and his engineers filed into the narrow space between the shield holders, then everyone started to edge forward towards the buttress at the base of the nearest tower. A rock thrown from above caught one of the shield holders on the shoulder. He cried out and fell; at once two troopers ran forward and dragged him back out of range. The tortoise crept on until it arrived at the wall.

Engineers started to dig at the mortar which filled the crevices between several of the larger stones. They clamped the powder shells to the surface of the wall with pitons which they drove home with hammers. The powder shells were hemispheres of cast iron filled with corned black powder. The flat face was laid against the wall and the pitons were hammered through lugs on either side. A constant shower of rocks, timber and chunks of old iron showered down on the tortoise. Burun thought that he did not envy Suragai and the others who were labouring below its protection. Suddenly, the tortoise was moving away from the wall. As soon as they were out of direct missile range, the men carrying the shields cast them aside. Everyone ran back. Eight or ten powder shells were clustered on the surface of the wall like warts. A fuse sparked.

'Down!' Suragai shouted in Yek. 'Everyone get down!'

Burun threw himself flat just as the powder shells exploded in a ripple of enormous bangs. Pieces of rock whined away and something struck the ground beside him. When the dust had cleared he saw that there was a gaping hole at the foot of the tower. It was twice the height of a man and four times as wide. Burun was surprised that the first attempt had been so successful. He had expected the Alan to pile soil against the back of the wall so as to strengthen it against just such an assault. Apparently they had not had the time, or else they had relied upon the effectiveness of the outer earthworks to prevent the Yek from advancing so far.

Troopers charged into the gap. They yipped in triumph. There were Alan in the breach, but they were dazed, unprepared for the turn of events. Nogai ran up.

'We will take this tower, but it is a long wall. Can we do the same thing elsewhere?'

'Yes.' Burun looked at Suragai.

The offworlder gestured at the waiting engineers. 'Khan, I have ten shells here. After that I will have to send back to camp for more, but I can blow the wall in as many places as you want.'

'One will be enough,' Nogai said.

'Are you so sure?' Burun watched the Yek who were struggling to climb through the hole in the wall. There was no resistance now, but the space was fairly small and everyone wanted to get into the city at once.

'Does it matter?' Nogai waved his arms. 'Come on, let's get on with it! The light is getting bad!'

Burun stared at him. 'Don't talk to me like that. You are supposed to be wooing me for my favour, remember?'

Nogai snorted, then he grinned. 'Please, beloved, can we go and fight now?'

Burun raised an eyebrow. 'Give Suragai time to draw breath. Or maybe you would prefer to set the next series of charges yourself?'

Nogai laughed. 'Do I look stupid? Suragai, take your time.'

'I'm ready now, Noyon.'

'Good. Then let's do it.'

Suragai chose a place about two thousand paces along the wall to the east, at a place where there were two towers close together. Once again the Alan opposition was strong, but the offworlder blew a large hole in the wall between the towers. It was almost dawn. Already the fires in the western towers lit the sky and Yek war-cries rang out along the battlements. Burun watched as a horde of troopers poured into the new breach. They met almost no resistance.

Nogai looked pleased. 'Well, are you coming?'

'Do you need me?'

'God, no. The hard work's done now.'

Burun produced a twisted smile. 'In that case I place you in charge. Crush the Alan, sack the city. An old man like me needs his rest. I'm going back to camp. Suragai, come. You have done enough.'

Nogai turned away towards the breach in the wall. His officers crowded around him. Suddenly he turned. 'What am I to do with the city once it has been taken and looted?'

Burun snorted. 'Burn it, of course.' Pereislav had resisted to the last and its fate would serve as a warning to others.

'What about the Alan? Are we taking prisoners?'

Burun shrugged. The life of every man who had fought in the defence of Pereislav was forfeit, but he saw no sense in unnecessary killing. 'Use your discretion. If they will surrender, take them for slaves.'

'And Barakai, if we find him. Do you want me to hold him for your judgement?'

Burun considered. Then he looked sideways at the offworlder. 'Suragai? What is your pleasure? He was your man.'

The offworlder was wiping the grime from his face

417

with a scrap of wet linen. He looked up, then turned and stared at Nogai. His face was expressionless. 'If you find him, hang him,' he said shortly. Then he walked away.

Siban watched the line of carts as it headed west. 'Nogai has left for Kinsai,' he said.

'I know.' Burun did not look up. 'Did his brothers go with him?'

'Only T'zin. I expected that he would be the one to stay.'

Burun remembered what T'zin had once said about the Khanate. A man who would rather be a slave than be elected Kha-Khan was an ideal companion for someone who wanted so desperately to rule. Jehan was sitting nearby, just at the edge of the awning's shade. He was playing chess with Jotan, and he was winning. He looked up.

'Will Nogai be Kha-Khan when Arjun dies?'

Siban's face was a study. Burun grinned.

'There are better men,' Siban observed primly.

'None in the bloodline.' Jotan moved a piece. 'And Nogai has shown that he is capable.'

Jehan's eyes swivelled back to the board. He moved an elephant. 'Check.'

Nogai had said goodbye only to Burun and Jotan. Everyone else, Siban included, he had ignored.

'It depends upon what you mean by the bloodline.' Siban's expression was stiff.

Jotan looked up. 'The throne has always passed in direct line, hasn't it? No second son has ever been heir, nor any son of a second wife. Very well then, by rights Khotan should be named, and if he refuses election -'

'Khotan is a drunk -'

'Nevertheless,' Jotan continued as if Siban had not spoken, 'Khotan is in direct line of succession. Thus his eldest son is the most eligible candidate. Nogai.'

Siban walked round the tent. 'The Kha-Khan disinherited Nogai after the Manghutt plot.'

Jotan smiled grimly. 'Nogai was guilty of stupidity, not treachery. Even his grandfather knew that, or he would not have suffered him to live.'

Siban said nothing. His ulus was richer than any in the Khanate. He was the Kha-Khan's brother and his chief general. He stared hard at Burun, opened his mouth as if to say something, then closed it again. He shook his head and walked away.

Jotan turned back to the chessboard and studied his position. There was a fence of pawns around his overlord.

'I don't like him,' Jehan said.

Jotan looked up. 'Siban?'

'Yes.'

Burun was surprised. 'Why not?'

'We can't trust him. He isn't like us.'

Jehan was more Altun than Merkut, but Burun grinned. 'Maybe not.'

'Where the succession is concerned, we can trust no man's motives.' Jotan moved his overlord a space.

Burun made a face. He hated it when people told him things he knew already.


'Now for T'ver.' Siban sat on his st'lyan and surveyed the plain.

Only the cities in the far west of the Alan country were left. Three tumans were spread out across the lands which had been taken and the rest of the army was driving in two prongs towards an imaginary point situated between T'ver and Jaroselsk.

'Now for the Alan army.' Burun eased his feet from the stirrups and tried to stretch the kinks out of his spine.

'Well,' Siban gestured, 'that too. Their king is camped on the big plateau about forty verst east of T'ver. He isn't coming to meet us.'

'I know where he is.' Burun nodded. 'We camped there the day before we scouted the city. Maybe he is waiting for reinforcements.'

Siban looked doubtful. After T'ver, only the cities of Vaslav and Zēreislav would remain. Neither of them was likely to strip itself of its strength to aid a king who was in the process of losing his kingdom.

Jotan rode up from the command post. 'Are we waiting for a sign?' He glanced at Siban as he spoke. 'Or can we march?'

Siban's expression was frosty. Sidacai, his son, edged his st'lyan forward so that it crowded Jotan's. Jotan kicked his bay sharply in the barrel. The animal reared and screamed and, when Sidacai ducked to avoid the flailing hooves, Jotan hooked a foot under his stirrup and knocked him out of the saddle.

Burun glared. 'Behave, whelp.'

Jotan laughed. He rode back down the slope and Sidacai climbed into the saddle again.

'He is your son.' Siban had not moved. 'But I will not tell you to discipline him.'

Burun showed his teeth. Siban was being careful to avoid every situation which would lead to provocation. He had not said that he wanted Burun's support at election, but he would do nothing which would make Burun his enemy.

'Some men are not to be disciplined.' Hodai was sitting his st'lyan at Burun's shoulder. He spoke softly.

Sidacai adjusted his reins. Then he looked up. 'The Kha-Khan –'

'Those words were spoken by the Kha-Khan,' Hodai said. 'I was there when he said them.'

Sidacai glowered. 'He must have been talking about

someone special,' he said after a moment.

'Oh,' Hodai grinned, 'he was.'

Burun ignored the exchange. He remembered the siege of T'sosei during the N'pan campaign. He had found a virtually unattended gate, and had exploited the opportunity without waiting for orders, disobeying instructions to keep his men in reserve. Only the fact that the attack had been successful had saved him.

'So who was it?' Sidacai asked.

Hodai laughed. 'It was Burun, of course.'

Burun stared ahead. A flush climbed from his collar and in his mind's eye he saw the Kha-Khan's eyes as they surveyed him placidly.

*They tell me that men call you The Stubborn.* The Kha-Khan's tone had been mild. *They will call you Dead soon enough, if you do not learn to obey.*

Still Suragai did not appear to know that Turakina was carrying his child. Every time the offworlder received a letter bound with her seals, Burun waited for him to appear in camp wearing the silly smile which characterised an expectant father. But there was no change in Suragai's manner. It was as if he did not permit personal matters to interfere with military duty. Burun began to wonder if the offworlder knew how to unbend.

Burun was still not sure how important it was to understand the way the offworlder's mind worked. There was no doubt that he was useful. It was like having a Sechem who was more interested in the practical application of his knowledge than the theory, and, so far as Burun had been able to ascertain by means of a variety of tests, Suragai was loyal.

The problem was that Burun was not certain why. The motives of a human were easy enough to comprehend but, before he would trust an alien completely,

Burun wanted to be able to predict how he would react to every situation.

A steady wind blew from the west. During the day it was hot, but at night when the heat left the ground it was bitterly cold. The troopers who had not brought furs with them complained and raided small towns and settlements for warmer clothing. Suragai had acquired a sable riding cloak from somewhere. The furs had brilliant silver points; at night and in the grey before dawn he wore them constantly. It made him easy to spot. Burun watched to see who the offworlder's particular friends were and who visited him clandestinely in the darkness.

'Do you think he plots against us?' Jotan had been quick to notice what was going on.

Burun shrugged. If he had really mistrusted Suragai, he would have had him killed. 'He puzzles me, that's all.'

Suragai associated scarcely at all with the other offworlders. He dealt with the man Yuan on a more or less daily basis, because Yuan commanded the forward scouts who often rode deep into enemy territory, but he kept himself apart from everyone else, even from his son. Now that both Nogai and T'zin had departed, Alexai was usually to be found in Orcadai's company. Whatever the differences between father and son which had caused the fight the previous year, they had been resolved. In spite of this there was no closeness between Suragai and Alexai. Their relationship was similar in some ways to that which existed between Burun and Jotan, but it lacked the degree of contact; there was an ever-present wariness between the two whenever they met.

The Alan had waited in place while the Yek advanced on T'ver. Their positions were on level ground which was flanked on either side by forest. Unless the Yek wanted to detour around them and thus to expose a flank, they were blocking the road to the capital.

Burun sat his st'lyan on a low knoll. He surveyed the Alan emplacements through his spyglass and tried to count the men he saw moving there. His cloak was tied to the back of his saddle and his tunic was open to the waist in deference to the searing heat.

'Why have they put up those barricades?' Jotan pointed. 'See, there are more on that side.'

'I think they are providing a funnel for us to charge down.' Burun focused. The nearest barrier was made of carts which were chained together. 'I wonder what they are concealing in that central redoubt.'

A river flowed down the Alan left flank which bordered the trees. Burun suspected that the ground there was marshy.

'Will Siban be able to encircle them in time?' Jotan fussed with his reins.

'Of course. He only has to skirt the forest. It's thirty or forty verst, that's all.'

'And if there is a second army waiting for him?'

'There isn't.' Burun shook his head. The Alan did not seem to imagine that anyone would be able to coordinate the movements of two large forces which were some distance apart. They had posted no screens other than those which were designed to counter a direct move to outflank within a verst or so.

Burun pulled his grey's head round and urged her back towards the Yek front line. Loose st'lyan grazed in a pasture beyond, and troopers patrolled to ensure that the Alan did not try a raid.

'Obviously they intend for us to attack.' Jotan kicked his mare so that she moved up alongside his father's mount. 'They didn't even try to harass us when we brought up our vanguard.'

'That's the way they fight.' Burun turned his head.

'Two armies meet on a plain like this. They draw up facing one another. Then when they are ready, one side or the other mounts an attack. Occasionally opposing armies charge each other at the same moment. The victor is the side which holds the field at the end of the day.'

'Amazing.' Jotan shook his head in disbelief.

'Yes. It doesn't seem to have occurred to them that we might not be prepared to attack according to their design.'

A body of mounted Alan came out of a screen of trees close to the road which led down to the Yek camp. When they saw Burun and Jotan they increased their pace. Someone yelled a war-cry. Burun lashed the barrel of his st'lyan. She screamed and leapt forward. There was a stream with a bridge across it just in front of the Yek centre. Burun wondered who was going to reach it first. He spurred his mare and she stretched out, flying across the hard ground. The Alan shouted and waved swords and lances. Burun saw a puff of smoke and a musket boomed.

They were going to arrive at the bridge almost simultaneously. Burun uncased his bow and nocked an arrow. The Alan leader was ahead of his men, using his spurs in an effort to arrive first. Burun brought the head of the arrow down so that he was aiming about a handspan above the man's head and about five paces beyond. He loosed, the arrow took the Alan in the throat, and he pitched out of the saddle. Jotan yipped cheerfully.

The pace of the oncoming Alan faltered for a moment, then they charged on. Burun aimed his st'lyan at the centre of the bridge, and he and Jotan hurtled on to the timbers practically under the Alan noses. Jotan was facing to the rear, his reins loose on his animal's neck. He loosed an arrow. Another of the

Alan threw his hands up to his face and fell to the ground. Yek troopers who had walked out of the camp to watch cheered.

The Alan were turning back now. They seemed to slow their mounts with difficulty and Burun saw that they were riding beasts which looked like st'lyan without horns. He reined in calmly. His grey was barely panting.

The twin moons shone in the sky, but even so the visibility was poor. The ground on the left of the Alan position was a marsh and it was shrouded with mist. On the right the trees were close together. They cast shadows which made it hard to distinguish one man from another.

'Khan, Siban is in position.' A courier trotted up.

'Good.' Burun turned to look for Suragai. 'Amir, are you ready yet?'

'Nearly, Khan. The ground here is soft. We had problems bringing the catapults up as soon as we left the road.'

'Hunh.' Burun nodded.

The offworlder had spent most of the day supervising the construction of the four engines. The metal collars which replaced the usual lashings and bindings had been prefabricated and carried with the baggage train of the army. It had been necessary only to find and cut suitable timbers.

Burun peered through the screen of trees. The end of the barricade which protected the Alan right flank was about a hundred paces distant. Troopers were moving into position along the forest edge, their task to protect the artillery from attack if it became necessary.

'Ready now, Khan,' Suragai said.

'Very well.' Burun estimated ranges. 'If the Alan

425

retreat, can you still hit their centre?'

Suragai nodded. 'The range will never be more than three or four hundred paces, Khan. If we put blocks under the front of each catapult, we can strike up to a hundred beyond that.'

'After that it shouldn't matter.' Burun surveyed the line. A catapult frame was being hauled into place through a space which had been cut through the trees. 'If they retreat that far they'll run into Siban.'

Lights gleamed from the Alan line. They would have to be deaf not to have heard something.

'Kuchuk, red lantern.' Burun climbed into the branches of a tree so that he had a better view of the field.

The standard-bearer aimed a signal back towards the Yek centre. Suddenly, it was as if a whole segment of the countryside was moving forward. During the early part of the night three tumans had crept across the river. They had lain for over two hours in the long grass in front of the main Alan positions, but the Alan had never suspected that they were there.

Alarm tocsins began to sound in the Alan line. It was apparent that they were unused to night assaults; they seemed to be in some confusion at first about the location of the threat. Lines of Yek archers advanced to within a hundred paces of the central redoubt. They halted, and Burun heard the sharp commands of their officers as they loosed volley upon volley. Burun looked back over his shoulder. All the catapults were in position and the ammunition carts had been brought up. The gunners stood waiting, talking idly.

A rumble of noise rose from the Alan centre as they realised what was happening. Musketeers came tumbling out of the redoubt. They formed into a ragged line, the moonlight glinted on musket barrels, and when the first volley banged the sound was irregular, as if not every man had been ready.

As soon as the enemy opened fire the Yek dropped on their faces in the grass. Burun heard the whine of smallshot as it cut through the air. A few stray balls pattered into the trees. A full tuman of cavalry moved across the rear of the Yek line, its officers careful to follow a course which was out of gunshot range. In front of the Alan redoubt the Yek began to fall back. The archers retired in good order, volleying arrows every twenty paces until they were almost out of range. Every time the Alan musketeers presented their weapons to fire, the Yek threw themselves flat in the grass. Their casualties were minor, but the Alan appeared to think that they were winning. The sound of shouting increased in intensity. Mounted men rode out of the redoubt and formed into line. Apparently they intended to ride the Yek down.

Targoutai rode in under the trees. He stopped below Burun. 'They are forming up to charge. Are they mad?'

Burun straddled the branch. 'No. They think that they can chop us into pieces.' He peered across at the Alan right. A second body of cavalry was emerging. 'If your brother doesn't stir himself, he's going to get caught between those two attacks.'

'Hunh.' Targoutai nodded. 'Can't we do anything?'

Burun looked down and caught the offworlder's eye. 'Suragai?'

'Khan?'

'Can you find the range?'

'All I need is one solid hit, Khan. I can adjust from that.'

'Very well. Targoutai, as soon as the Alan start to fall back again, I want you to lead a charge up the flank. I don't want them to have time to think about attacking us here.'

427

'I can do that now, Khan. I have a tuman waiting behind that screen of trees.' Targoutai pointed.

'No, not yet. I'll signal you.'

'Yes, Khan.' Targoutai saluted. Then he rode away.

Burun jumped down out of the tree. Suragai was already striding towards the catapults and Burun had to trot to catch up with him.

'Do your loading numbers know the signals?'

Suragai looked offended. 'They ought to, Khan. They've practised often enough.' He waved at a signaller and the man ran two white lanterns up. At once the gunners moved into action. 'Yes.' Suragai's expression was satisfied. 'They do.'

'Good. Then try a shot at the musketeers who are advancing down the centre.'

Suragai nodded. He stopped beside the signaller and spoke once.

'Red flash.'

The lantern winked, the gunners pulled their levers and the catapults went off with a crash. Burun saw a stone smash into the armoured men who were advancing towards Tulagai.

'Number one was on target. Who saw the others?'

Suragai ignored the comment. 'Two and four, right ten degrees. Three, shorten your range by about fifty paces.' He nodded to the signaller and the catapults went off again.

'All solid hits.'

The Alan cavalry had finally started to move. They cantered down the right flank and, just as they rounded the end of the musketeer line, the catapults fired again. This time two were firing powder shells - pairs of the hemispheres which had been bolted together. One of the shells went off in the centre of the musketeers, throwing them into confusion. The other seemed to land directly in the path of the

428

oncoming cavalry. It exploded with a clap of noise and the whole leading section of riders seemed to fall. The few hundred who had ridden out of the barrier on the Alan right paused. They seemed to be unsure what to do.

'Kuchuk!' Burun turned. 'Flash Targoutai!'

'Yes, Khan.'

A full tuman came pouring out of the thin screen of trees beside the Alan, overwhelming them. The charge was over in an instant, but where it had passed there was nothing but a litter of dead, clad in half-armour. Riderless animals ran free down the front of the barricades.

'Red flash.'

Two more powder shells burst among the musketeers and tore their advance apart. The Alan in the right flank positions realised that the Yek were in the trees nearby. Muskets banged in an irregular volley and shot zipped through the trees.

'Number one, shorten range. Fire on that barricade.' Suragai spoke before Burun could open his mouth. 'All numbers flash.'

The loaders had set buckets of naptha this time. It bloomed in the night air and dripping fire fell on the Alan line. Where the stuff landed it stuck to armour and clothing. Men fled screaming and Burun was able to smell burnt flesh.

'Red flash.'

It no longer mattered what the catapults hit. The naptha was enough. Suragai altered the range of two of the engines so that they pelted the Alan who were still inside the main redoubt. The wagons and carts which formed the barricades were on fire, and all the firing had stopped. Tulagai's archers had reached the river now. They trotted across the bridge and forded the stream; mounted troopers took their place.

Burun waved at Kuchuk. 'Signal advance.'

The musketeer line was non-existent. Only the Alan in the positions on the far left were putting up a fight. As Burun watched, Suragai directed catapult fire onto them: naptha and powder shells landed along the enemy line.

The Yek roared. The mounted troopers in the centre moved in an orderly block up the field. They took sporadic fire from the Alan central redoubt, and armoured men came out and formed into a line.

'All numbers, increase range to maximum. Red flash.'

Powder shells exploded along the parapet which was at the rear of the Alan main position. The men in armour faltered, then broke.

'They've had enough.' Burun climbed into another tree.

'Yes.' Suragai nodded. 'Do you want me to hit them again?'

'Can you increase the range?'

'A little, Khan. We won't be very accurate.'

'It doesn't matter. I just want to start them running.'

The engineers hammered blocks under the front struts of two of the catapults and they fired again. Naptha streaked through the sky and fell on the Alan rear. A catapult caught fire and sweating slaves ran up with buckets of water to douse the flames. Yek cavalry thundered ponderously into the Alan who remained in front of the redoubt. The armoured men at the rear of the Alan line were already streaming away.

'Cease fire.'

Burun climbed out of the tree. He sat down on the end of the frame of one of the catapults, feeling suddenly tired. Another tuman was crossing the river, moving in pursuit of the fleeing Alan. Few of the enemy were likely to escape because, as soon as they

430

had passed through the rear of their own positions, they would encounter a line of ambushes commanded by Siban.

Suragai was sitting on the ground. He held an open flask of k'miss in his hand. He offered it to Burun.

'Shall we dismantle the catapults now, Khan?'

'Yes. Keep the timbers, though. Load them on to carts. We may need them again at T'ver.'

Targoutai rode up and dismounted. 'It's almost over. All the Alan are dead, or they are running.'

'Hunh.' Burun nodded. He drank from the flask. The k'miss was cool and sharp.

'Khan, you look tired.' Targoutai gave his reins to an orderly.

'I feel tired.' Burun saw that Suragai was watching his face. 'I don't think I like this kind of fighting much.'

Suragai seemed to hesitate. At last he nodded. 'I know what you mean, Khan. I don't suppose we killed more of the Alan than we would have in a conventional fight. It's just that this way seems more terrible somehow.'

Burun could think of nothing to say which would not have sounded trite. If they had not employed the catapults, the naptha and powder shells, the Yek would have been decimated assaulting the Alan positions. The Yasa was right, of course, to forbid certain kinds of weapons, but faced with a choice between death and progress, the sensible man chose progress every time.

Targoutai did not seem to notice the offworlder's expression. 'You have nothing to be ashamed of, Suragai,' he said. 'We could not have won such a victory without you.'

Suragai did not look impressed. Probably he recognised the exaggeration in Targoutai's statement. After a moment he shrugged and gestured dismissively. 'War

431

is always frightful,' he commented. 'A good soldier has no alternative but to be ashamed of his trade.'

The duke of T'ver was a youth no older than Orcadai. He stood surrounded by older men, all of them dressed in fine clothing, their garments trimmed with some kind of white fur. The duke was the only one who wore armour. The gold chasing on his breastplate glowed in the light of the afternoon sun.

'What terms do you offer for the surrender of the royal city of T'ver?' The duke's voice was unsteady with nervousness.

Burun hid a smile. He was seated on a dais which was constructed out of the floor of someone's yurt. He stretched his legs out in front of him and studied the toes of his boots. Then he looked up.

'One quarter of your goods, including our assessor's choice of furs, jewels and precious metals, and a yearly tithe thereafter in the name of the Kha-Khan. One tenth of your young men to train for our army and a levy as we require. Our governor will be your lord and you will be subject to his will.'

Most of the old men looked relieved. Burun thought that probably they had expected the city to be given over to sack.

The duke looked offended. 'We require assurances with regard to the continued status of our nobility. You leave us no honour, yet we are T'ver the Unconquered.'

Burun pursued his lips. 'Such a thing would be for the Kha-Khan to decide. I can make no guarantee.'

'Are you not his representative?'

'So far as you are concerned, yes I am.'

There was a tall man in dark robes at the duke's shoulder. He said something in a low voice and Burun caught the mention of Siban's name.

'We would speak with Siban Khan.' The duke stumbled over the unfamiliar name and pronounced it wrongly.

'Siban is not here.'

'His son, then.'

Apparently the Alan thought that Yek nobility was hereditary. Burun yawned. 'Siban's son has no authority here.' He saw Sidacai's head come up as his name was mentioned.

The Alan looked nonplussed. The tall man was whispering in the duke's ear again.

Burun stood up. 'Boy, I have been patient with you. The terms I offer are better than those I gave the king, your uncle. We looked for his body on the plain of J'slav, that we might return it to you for burial according to your custom. I regret that we could not identify it. Too much of the high command was burned and the bodies were not recognisable.'

The Alan all went white. Several of the old men were trying to offer the duke advice. He ignored them, his eyes fixed on Burun's face.

'If we choose to resist you, we will fight you for every inch of ground. We will burn T'ver house by house, street by street, before we will allow you to take one koban of profit from its capture.'

Burun shrugged. 'If that is what you wish, we will fight you to the death. We are sworn to conquer the world for our sovereign lord, the Kha-Khan, and to do so we will fight until the sun falls.'

The Alan heard his words in silence. Burun judged that few of them had any stomach for a battle. They would commit their young men quite cheerfully to the most hopeless fight, but most of the army of T'ver had perished on the plain of J'slav. The duke turned to his councillors and said something in Alan. His face was set and determined.

433

Jotan was standing at Burun's shoulder. 'What's he saying?'

'He's going to offer himself in single combat with any one of us who desires to advance his honour.' Burun had not caught all the words, but he guessed the general meaning. Single combat was not a Yek custom, but he had learned enough from the Alan prisoners to know what to expect.

The duke took several paces forward. It was as if he no longer wanted to be associated with the old men. When he began to issue the challenge he spoke in Yek, faltering over unfamiliar words and vowel sounds.

Burun was mildly impressed. The rest of the conversation had been conducted in Alan. He had not expected an enemy to take the trouble to learn the conqueror's language until he had been conquered. He waited patiently for the duke to finish.

'You are a brave young man. What is your name?'

The duke met his stare without flinching. 'I am called D'mitri. Which one of you takes up my challenge?'

Burun grinned. 'I am sorry, but we don't fight that way. You can see that we don't use armour and our weapons are much lighter than yours. Would there be honour for you in such a contest?'

The duke seemed to consider the point. 'I will remove my armour,' he said after only a moment. 'And I will fight on foot with only a sword and shield.'

Jotan muttered. 'I'll fight him.'

'Don't be a fool.' Burun shook his head. 'Look at the size of him. With a bow it would be impossible for you to lose. Hand to hand he would simply beat down your guard and smash you. He's got a longer reach, and he outweighs you by about a hundred diram. You wouldn't stand a chance.'

Jotan scowled. 'He'll think we are afraid.'

434

'Let him. I'll tell him that he has gained enough honour by offering to fight when everyone else was ready to surrender.'

'Are they going to give in?'

'They will if the council of T'ver has anything to do with it. But if they decide to fight, then I want that duke alive. He's the only man I've come across in this country who might be worth something.'

Siban gestured the slaves away. 'Is it over?'

'As good as.' Burun nodded. 'We haven't taken Vaslav yet, but the way things are going we will meet their ambassadors on their way to surrender to us long before we are ready to mount a siege.'

Siban sat back. 'I hear you have taken a valuable hostage.'

Burun snorted. 'D'mitri, the duke of T'ver, or he was. He isn't a hostage. I just told that to his family to keep them quiet.'

Siban looked amused. 'You have a gift for attracting unlikely additions to the army. Since we're recruiting a full tuman of Alan, I don't see why you shouldn't have one on your staff. Is he any good?'

'Oh well, he thinks with his sword arm, if that's any indication.' Burun chuckled. 'But I believe that he is young enough to change. I've put him with Suragai. If that doesn't make him question his knightly training, nothing will.'

'You know best.' Siban accepted wine. 'I gather you have been busy while I have been at Jaroselsk. Tell what you have been doing.'

Burun considered his reply. 'Well, we hold the whole country with the exception of Vaslav and the country about. As I said, I expect it to be ours within the month. I'm sending Targoutai and Tulagai down there. I don't think they will have to fight, but if they

435

do then an independent command will give them some practice.'

'Very well. Go on.'

Burun took a cup and filled it to the brim with k'miss. 'M'skva and T'ver we have not burned, as you know. The people from the rest of the towns and cities are dispersed across the countryside. Much of the disputed territory on the borders of the city states was never cultivated, so there is land for everyone. Next year we will be able to hold the whole province with two tumans or less. We will need to patrol on a regular basis so as to ensure that no settlement tries to establish control of the land around. Under the system which was in operation before we came, every city demanded tribute from the farmers and landowners within their area of influence. That was why they fought each other over the boundaries of their provinces.'

'You are going to allow them to govern themselves?' Siban looked astonished.

'To a large extent, yes. Unless we install a ruling council in every town, village and hamlet, they will go ahead and elect their own. They have to have someone to defer to. That is the way they behave. As long as each council is accountable to our officers, the end result will be the same as if we were ruling directly. Most of them aren't trained soldiers. They won't revolt so long as they can see that they are getting benefit from obeying us.'

Siban drained his cup. 'It isn't quite what I anticipated.'

Burun shrugged. 'Well, you gave me a free hand. The Alan will behave and they will accept our taxes. Surely that's all that matters?'

Siban's expression remained unconvinced. 'Slaves would be easier to control.'

'The Ch'noze aren't. They fight us at every turn. How many tumans is Berke commanding?'

'Four at present.'

'To keep control of an area one quarter the size of this land. I rest my case.' Burun set his cup aside. 'What is a slave anyway? He's someone who does your bidding, having no choice in the matter. The Alan are slaves, but their peculiar concept of honour demands that they are not required to acknowledge the fact, except perhaps to themselves.'

'I can see that you have thought the matter out most carefully.'

Burun guessed he was being patronised. He opened his mouth to retort, then glanced quickly at Siban. It was obvious that he realised that he had said the wrong thing. Burun sat back. 'You want my son to rule this land. If one method does not work, he can easily try another.'

'That's true.' Siban nodded. 'Forgive me. I did not mean to criticise.'

The slaves brought platters of meat to the table. The meat was dark and ran with juice. It was not spiced, but had been cooked in a gravy made from marrow. Burun's mouth watered and he helped himself to a large portion.

'You have turned city dwellers into farmers.' Siban forked meat on to his plate. 'Will they be able to feed themselves?'

'We will have to give them food this winter.' Burun looked up from his plate. 'I am going to make the ruling council in each area responsible for the needs of those who are breaking new ground to the plough. Our officers will have orders to see that the distribution is fair. But the land is fertile; next year they will be feeding us.'

Siban had eaten only a little. Burun wondered if it

was a sign of his age, that he had such a small appetite.

'And so there will be order.' Siban took another cup of wine. 'Have you ever wondered what we are doing here?'

Burun was not sure how to answer. At last he looked up and met Siban's eyes. 'Yes. Sometimes.'

'And?'

'And nothing. The Ancestor said that we should conquer the world. So here we are.'

'But we hold everything now. From the Sea of Tears to the Gulf of Mists. Is it enough?'

'You mean, what do we do next? Well, the old maps show another continent on the far side of the Great Sea.'

Siban pushed his platter aside. 'It does not say much for us that we carry on simply because we have started. Surely we have to stop somewhere.'

In theory the earth was enough. The earth under one lord, the Kha-Khan. But now the Yek knew that the Sechem were right. There were other worlds.

'Could we stop if we had to?' Siban was watching Burun's face for a reaction as he spoke.

'If we had to, why not?' Burun frowned. 'Can't we simply say "This is enough" and then stop?' He knew that his answer was simplistic. It was easy to talk about it. It would be harder to do.

'I will never be Kha-Khan.' Siban spoke quietly.

Burun said nothing.

'Everyone looks to you.' Siban's tone was thoughtful. 'And yet I think that you are the cleverest and the most cunning of us all. Why should that be?'

'I am a Merkut,' Burun said simply. 'You could kill me tomorrow.'

'You mean we trust you because you are not a threat to our aspirations?' Siban grinned crookedly.

'Yes. Maybe. I don't know.' Burun threw up his hands. He felt confused. 'Why do you ask such questions of me? Talk to your own kind.'

'I can't.' Siban looked solemn. 'They all want the same things I do.' He stood up. 'That's why we don't kill you, I think. Who would we have to talk to?'

Vaslav capitulated without a fight and suddenly there was peace in the land. Burun rode from T'ver to M'skva where Jotan was already in residence as provincial governor. At every stop Alan grooms ran to hold the reins of his st'lyan, and Alan serving women brought wine and smiled. The places where they had fought - the plain of J'slav and cities like Pereislav and Shermetyev - were already becoming overgrown. The bones of the dead had been stripped clean by the birds and in another hundred years no one would remember the carnage or recollect that such places had ever existed.

Where the plains had been deserted, now they were alive with activity. There were low Alan farmhouses on every hillside and new walls were everywhere.

'I don't know why they ever lived in the cities.' Jotan was riding out with Burun to show him a farm which had been established for the breeding of st'lyan. 'They are natural farmers.'

'Tell me why one man grows up learning to tend a plough and another to follow the banner.' Burun was amused. Jotan was suddenly civilised now that he was responsible for the government of so many people.

Jotan had the grace to smile. 'I know I sound impatient with them. But they lived under the yoke of the cities for so long and never thought to change.'

'There is safety in familiar things.'

'Is habit ever a good reason to shun progress? At least we are different.'

'Are we?' Burun thought about his conversation with Siban. Once a pattern was set, it was hard to

439

break. It was as well that the Yasa provided rules for living in time of peace as well as for making war.

'I am bringing Arkhina out from Kinsai,' Jotan said suddenly.

Burun tried not to appear surprised. 'There will be other campaigns.'

'The land across the Great Sea?' Jotan sounded amused. 'No. Let someone else go. It is time one of us learned how to rule.'

The fiefs which the Kha-Khan had granted to Burun were all governed in his absence by stewards or by officers of his household. Most of the Khanate was managed the same way. Burun tried to think of a comment, but only doubt surfaced. There had always been another campaign, another new land to conquer. It was not possible that a time would come when things would be different.

'What will you do now?' Burun watched Suragai's face.

The offworlder smiled. 'You gave me an Amirate, Khan. I have never seen it.' Then he shrugged. 'I am a soldier. What else is there to do?'

Burun nodded, satisfied. 'In that case I will find work for you. A soldier's employment.'

The military administration of the Alan had thrown up enough logistical tasks to keep the whole staff of the army busy for a year. Never had the Yek tried to rule so many people in one province.

Burun looked past Suragai at the Alan duke who was serving as one of the offworlder's aides. 'And you, D'mitri, shall I send you to the Kha-Khan's court as befits your station?'

The young man frowned. 'Lord, I think I would rather stay here. A soldier's occupation is considered honourable enough among my people, and I desire to learn your ways.'

It was the kind of response Burun had expected. He nodded. 'So be it.'

Burun had set up camp on a grassy promontory which overlooked the meeting place of two tributaries of the Moistr' River. Although Jotan ruled from M'skva and had occupied a house there, the place made Burun feel uncomfortable. The streets were narrow and cobbled, the rooms in the houses were too small, and their slated roofs were so high that the gables of buildings on opposite sides of the street seemed to touch, patching the space below with deep shadow. Yurts and tents were dotted around the level top of the plateau in no particular order, and there were more servants and orderlies in the camp than there were troopers. A guard patrol from the city passed regularly, but since the province was free from bandits - even the disaffected elements of the Alan army had now been dispersed - Burun had seen no reason to maintain more than the minimum strength.

'Have you heard from Turakina?'

Suragai was standing at the open door of the yurt. He turned. 'Not since the last letter, Khan.'

'Hunh.' Burun nodded as if it was of no conse-quence. They had both received letters shortly after the surrender of T'ver. Zurachina's had been marvel-lous for its complete absence of news about anything other than her own household. As usual half of the missive had been indecipherable thanks to Kiku's inclusion of N'pani ideograms. There had been no mention of Turakina's pregnancy.

Three troopers galloped past leading loose strings of st'lyan remounts. They were stripped to the waist, and were bronzed and fit after the rigours of campaign life. They yipped cheerfully when they saw Suragai, and he waved.

'Is there some reason for your enquiry, Khan?'

441

Suragai was watching Burun's face as he spoke.

'What? No.' Burun wondered if the offworlder felt about separation from Turakina in some way which was incomprehensible to the human mind. Burun did not ache for Zurachina, or for Kiku, when he was engaged in a campaign. Both of them were like pleasant memories in the back of his mind, yet when he was with them it was hard to believe that such longing had never existed.

Burun got up and walked over to the door. Suragai moved quickly and he flinched. The offworlder's size still made him nervous at times. He was like one of the big male breeding st'lyan, full of scarcely concealed power and energy and it was hard not to jump when he moved.

'Someone is coming.' Suragai pointed.

Burun followed the direction of the offworlder's arm. Three riders charged downslope towards the camp. When they came closer Burun saw that Jotan was in the lead, followed by Orcadai and Jehan.

Jotan reined in hard. 'Is my father in here?'

Suragai stood to one side. Burun stepped past him into the sunlight.

'Name of God, you're in a hurry. What has brought you out in the heat of the day?'

'Our wives are almost here.'

'Eh?' Burun gaped. 'I thought Arkhina was in Kinsai. You said she was in Kinsai. How did they get so close without anyone telling us?'

'She was in Kinsai the last I heard.' Jotan shook his head. 'They must have decided together. They came by pack train across the G'bai. They are coming through the pass. With carts they will be at least another day getting here.'

'Name of God.' Burun ran a hand across his scalp. 'You'll have to loan me another yurt.'

Jotan grinned. 'I expect I can find one. Not as fine as this though. Which woman will you put in which yurt?'

'Who knows?' Burun threw up his hands in agitation. 'Do you think there is space behind this one for another?'

Jotan and Orcadai both laughed. 'You could reorganise your camp,' Jotan said.

'Name of God.' Burun sat down on a rock.

Jotan dismounted. 'You old goat, you'll have to start living like a civilised man again.'

Burun ignored him. He wondered why Zurachina had decided to travel without warning. If Vortai had been inhibiting her freedom or had interfered with the transmission of private letters, he would answer for it before the Kha-Khan.

'At least you will have enough servants.' Orcadai slid out of the saddle. 'I've never seen so many in one place.'

Burun stood up. 'Osep! Bring my cloak and send someone to saddle my grey.'

'Yes, Khan.'

Jotan nudged Orcadai. 'Where are you going?'

'To meet them, of course. Are you coming?'

'I might as well.' Jotan grinned. Then he looked at Suragai. 'You too, Amir. Your wife is with them, and she has your new son.'

'What?' Suragai's jaw dropped.

Orcadai elbowed Jotan gleefully. 'I told you he didn't know!'

Burun took his cloak of coated linen from Osep's hands and walked down the slope towards the lines where the st'lyan were tethered. If Turakina had brought the child across the G'bai, he was healthy and not deformed. A glow of happiness engulfed him. Suragai was hurling questions at Jotan. Jotan spoke only a few words, then his reply was drowned out by the offworlder's whoop of exultation.

PART FIVE

# The Dragon
# Throne

Rostov adjusted his grip on the centrebar, extended his arms to alter the distribution of his weight in the harness, and the kite soared. The foothills to the east of M'skva were ideal for gliding. The wind was always from the west and there was a constant warm updraught which made flying possible during all but the hottest hours of the day when the currents rising up off the ground made landing difficult. Early in the morning the conditions were usually excellent.

He leaned very slightly to the left, pulled forward, and the kite began to spiral slowly towards the ground. The meadow where Turakina and the others were riding was to the south. Rostov pulled himself towards the centrebar again, and when the glide steepened, moved his weight back once more. Air rushed past the fabric on the surface of the wing and hummed in the wire stays. Rostov swooped deliberately on the st'lyan as they trotted on the grass and whooped with exhilaration as he passed overhead.

The act of removing his feet from the stirrups which formed the base of each leg of the harness required a mild feat of physical dexterity. The kite rocked for a moment and then he was free, settling like a stooping hawk in the grass. Orderlies ran forward to support the kite frame as Rostov unclipped the harness from around his waist.

The kite was shaped like a joined pair of bat wings. The fabric which covered the framework was like silk, but much stronger. It had been coated with the same resinous mixture which the Yek used to make reflective tent canopies. One of the engineers had mixed pigment with the coating substance and it had dried unevenly so that the final effect was slightly psychedelic. Underneath the wing a pair of triangular supports were joined by a central bar and the main clip for the body harness was situated so that the body weight could be shifted in any direction for the purpose of steering.

St'lyan came towards him across the meadow. Rostov accepted a loose mantle from an orderly, took his sword from another and inserted the scabbard into his waist sash. Jotan reined in beside him, followed by his wife and son. Behind them came Turakina, guiding her bay mare slowly and sedately. Rostov watched her, ignoring everything else.

Jotan dismounted. He tested the tension of the coated fabric of the kite with his hand, then shook his head. 'If men were intended to fly -'

'God would have given them wings,' Rostov quoted. 'It is not the man who flies. It is the kite.'

'Hah.' Jotan smiled. 'An equivocation. How high were you that time?'

'Two hundred drem perhaps.' Rostov used the Yek measurement quite naturally. A verst contained a thousand drem, two hundred was therefore the equivalent of about four hundred metres. 'I have been much higher.'

He had demonstrated the flying capabilities of this primitive version of a hang-glider to the Sechem and to a number of the Altun. So far the thing was little more than a toy. The Yek flew kites for sport and did not take the idea of one which was capable of supporting a man particularly seriously.

Jehan slid out of his saddle. Jotan's son was tall and lanky like his father, but he had his mother's Altun colouring. 'I wish I could fly.' His tone was wistful.

Rostov caught the look which passed between Jotan

and Arkhina. Jotan laughed. 'Oh no, Noyon. Not until you are much older.'

'You would have to be much taller, Noyon, in any case.' Rostov made the observation mildly.

Jehan's expression was typical of adolescents who think that adults exist to spoil their fun. Arkhina smiled and nodded acknowledgement to Rostov. Turakina brought her mare into the space between Jotan and Rostov at the walk. She was managing her reins with one hand, cradling her son with the other as he lay in the folds of the shawl which bound him to her breast. Her st'lyan was a palfrey, light chestnut with a blond mane and tail.

'Lord husband, your son advises me that he is hungry. Will you ride with us?' Turakina's face was placid; there was only a hint of the wifely amusement which she sometimes displayed at what Rostov guessed she considered were his more eccentric pastimes.

An engineer was driving a light cart across the meadow. The orderlies began to dismantle the struts which held the kite rigid while it was in flight. Rostov's body servant brought up his mare, leading her on a long head-rope. He mounted. Then he reached across and gently pulled aside the material which protected his son from the sun.

Kadan Noyon was six months old. He had his mother's red-gold hair and wise grey eyes. Rostov tickled him under the chin and the baby laughed and drooled.

*An Imperial geneticist would say that this is impossible.* Rostov looked at the perfection of his son in Turakina's arms. *How can the genes of a human and an alien mutation combine to produce a normal child?*

He dismissed the thought. Kadan's birth was like so

much which had occurred since he had come to Tarvaras. It did not bear reasoned explanation. It was better simply to accept that it was so.

'Lady, our son must speak a language I do not yet comprehend.'

Jotan's wife laughed. She could have been Turakina's twin, except that there was a livid birthmark high on her left cheek. 'All babies have a private language which only their mothers understand, Suragai.'

Rostov looked at Jotan; simultaneously they made the face that husbands make when they feel that their wives are talking over their heads. Kadan squirmed in Turakina's arms. He tried to burrow into her robe and his mouth made sucking motions.

'You see?' Arkhina said, and both women laughed.

'Why did you name him Kadan?' Burun poured wine. 'That's a Ch'noze name.'

Rostov accepted the cup which Burun held out. He had been displaced from his yurt because Turakina was turning one room into a nursery and his house was full of cooing women.

'It was your daughter's choice, Khan. I have found it politic to let her have her way in small matters.'

Burun snorted. 'And in larger ones too, I daresay. You are too easy with her.'

Rostov shrugged. He could imagine nothing touching upon his relationship with Turakina which would be of so great a concern that he would wish to maintain his point of view above hers. 'Khan, all men are easy with those they love.'

Burun smiled crookedly. 'Hah. Maybe you are right. I am not the man to lecture you, that is true.'

Rostov drank. His mouth puckered as he tasted the sharpness of the k'miss. Burun saw the expression.

'You have become too used to wine,' he said.

Alan wine was light and pleasant. It had been worth conquering the country for the taste of it alone.

Burun drained his cup and poured another. 'I had a letter from Nogai. He asked to be remembered to you.'

Rostov choked on a mouthful of k'miss. Burun chuckled at the reaction.

'Yes.' He nodded. 'He sent his regards to Jotan and Orcadai also.'

'He is still wooing you then, Khan. Is he at Kinsai?' Rostov's eyes were streaming. He shook his head to clear them. The k'miss burned his throat and nasal passages where he had swallowed the wrong way.

'It would seem so. He mentioned a banquet which took place to mark the end of the campaign, so probably he is being permitted access to the Golden Yurt again.'

'And the posts are travelling without interference, or his letter would not have reached you.'

'Oh, well.' Burun sat back. 'My father-in-law has been relieved of his command. That was in Nogai's letter. Siban arrived in Kinsai one day and the order dismissing Vortai was issued the next. He is summering in Losan.'

Rostov looked up sharply. Losan was a western coastal city. It was only a few verst north of the escarpment, perhaps eight days' ride from the Moistr' Gorge. Burun's expression was innocent, but Rostov was not deceived. 'You mean to pursue your feud.'

'Wouldn't you?' Burun tossed the gold chalice from which he had been drinking high in the air. It rose almost to the hangings of the roof, then fell back into his outstretched hand. 'For that matter it was you, not I, that he almost poisoned.'

Rostov nodded. A fine point of honour was involved, a matter of face. The Yasa did not permit any

451

overlord to involve a vassal in the pursuit of a personal quarrel; however, Vortai's act had been completely reckless. He had employed poison, a weapon which was forbidden by the law because it did not discriminate between one man and another. He had not cared who he killed in his attempt upon Burun and, as an injured party, Rostov had the right of kanly.

It was like accepting an insult. Nothing in the Yasa required a man to respond. But to do nothing was to lose face before anyone who had witnessed the act.

'Khan, your issue is with both father and son.' Rostov met Burun's eyes squarely. 'I have no quarrel with Sipotai.'

'I know.' Burun laid the chalice aside. 'But if I go to Losan, you will come along.'

Rostov thought about refusal. It was certain that Turakina would oppose his involvement. She would not understand the issue which was at stake. Finally he nodded. 'Yes, Khan. If you go to Losan, I will come.'


Slaves had spread carpets from the yurt on a level place beside the bend of the river. Turakina was nursing Kadan in the bright sunlight of the early morning. Kiku and Zurachina were sitting with her.

Rostov lay stretched out on a long Ch'kassian rug. He was on his stomach so that he would not have to stare into the oppressive red glare. His elbows and forearms propped his head and he was watching Kadan who lay naked on his back in the centre of the soft pile of the carpet upon which Turakina sat.

'When will you return from Losan?' Turakina was not looking in his direction as she spoke.

Kadan kicked and chuckled. One of his feet found its way somehow into his mouth and he sucked noisily.

'When I am finished,' Rostov said patiently.

She did not turn. 'You don't have to go.'

'I know that.' Rostov wondered if Turakina was concerned for his safety, or if her reaction was the result of a woman's natural distaste for affairs of violence.

Zurachina reached out and scratched the sole of Kadan's other foot. He kicked reflexively.

'He is a sweet baby.' Zurachina looked in Rostov's direction. 'Mine were all brats. Only Kiku's were happy and peaceful.'

Kiku turned. 'My babies were good because they knew that if they cried or were troublesome, I wouldn't go near them.' Her tone was remote.

Zurachina smiled. 'That's an exaggeration.' She gathered Kadan up in her arms. 'Jotan had croup all the time when he was this one's age.'

Turakina rose. She was wearing a long gown of ivory silk. There were fine gold threads through the material and it rippled and glittered when she moved. She looked down at Rostov, then held out her hand. 'Walk with me.'

Rostov got to his feet at once. Ever since he had told her that he intended to accompany Burun on his *venda* against Vortai, her mood had been unpredictable. Beneath the trees along the river it was cooler. A light wind stirred the branches of the trees so that the sun changed the shades of the grass and the fallen leaves until they looked like the patterns of a carpet. The river ran past with almost no sound at all.

Turakina walked ahead as the path narrowed. Rostov was tempted to close with her, to draw her to him. He knew that she would submit, but in the midst of a disagreement it would mean nothing. She stopped by the side of the bank and bent down. There were small smooth pebbles everywhere. She picked one up and tossed it into the rippling water. It disappeared with hardly a splash.

Rostov squatted on the bank. He was carrying the scabbard of his sword loose in his hand and now he laid it aside. There was no danger, but it felt unnatural to go unarmed.

Turakina chose a larger stone. This time the splash threw drops of water in an arc. Almost at once she turned and threw a rock the size of a fist into the water beside the place on the bank where he was waiting. The resultant splash drenched him. Turakina laughed and ran off along the bank.

'Ah, would you?' Rostov shook water from his collar. He stalked after her.

Turakina took to her heels. He began to trot to keep up with her. She looked behind to see if he was coming, and stumbled on a soft piece of overhang. The bank crumbled and she fell into the river. When she stood up her gown was clinging to her breasts. Rostov stood on the edge of the bank and laughed.

'Come.' He held out a hand to pull her up.

Turakina drove the heel of her hand into the water. 'Come and get me.' She splashed him again.

Rostov squatted on his heels. He thought that he was just out of range. 'We could do this all day. Come out of the water.'

Turakina looked up. It was as if she was calculating how far she could go. He held out his hand again and she grabbed it and jerked. Rostov yelled as he landed in the river with a splash which sent waves up the bank. Turakina backed away. She lost her footing for a moment and went under the surface of the water. Then she pushed herself up, watching him.

Rostov stood. The water was just above the level of his waist. 'This is ridiculous.'

She laughed. 'You are, certainly. You look like an angry bear.' She arched her hand through the water and splashed him. Water streamed down his face. His clothes were sticking to him.

'Now I am angry.' He dived forward.

Turakina yelped. She backed away, splashing water at him as fast as she could. Rostov ploughed after her and she scrambled up the bank.

Rostov made his way to the place where he had fallen in, intending to climb out. Turakina grabbed a branch and fended him off with it. Her eyes were alive with mischief.

'I will let you up when you beg my pardon for upsetting me.' She poked at him.

'I will break my hand over your backside.'

'And I want a new gown, and a dog, white with long hair like the ones which are bred for the Kha-Khan.'

'No!' Rostov glared at her. 'I'm your husband. Let me up. You're making a fool of me.'

Turakina nodded happily. He charged the bank and when she poked at him again with the branch he seized the end and pulled it out of her grasp. She gave a small scream and turned to run. Rostov tackled her and she fell.

His weight was on top of her so that she could not move. 'Got you!' He spoke in her ear.

She twitched experimentally. Rostov grinned and moved so that he was kneeling astride her.

'Now –' He started to speak when she arched suddenly. Rostov was so surprised that he was unable to maintain his balance. He fell to one side and Tura-kina leapt up to run. Rostov caught her ankle. He pulled her down again and dropped her flat on her back. She looked up at him and it was as if they had both stopped breathing. Rostov reached out and began to loosen the laces of her gown.

'Let me up.' She made no effort to intercept his hands.

'Oh, no.' He shook his head. 'You don't escape as easily as that.'

'You're mad, the pair of you.' Jotan paced the length of the chamber and then turned.

Burun was in the middle of a chess game with Jehan. 'We have a just cause. Would you have us lose face? What else can we do?'

'Name of God.' Jotan threw up his arms. 'For a start you could go to the Kha-Khan. Vortai used poison. That's against the Yasa.'

Burun moved a warrior. Jehan grinned and moved his overlord a square to the right. 'Check, grand-father.'

Rostov craned to see the board. Burun studied the position of the pieces for a moment, then looked up. 'I have no evidence, you know that. Besides, I want satis-faction.'

'You expect either Vortai or Sipotai to fight according to the rules? They'll have you ambushed and killed.'

'Oh, well.' Burun smiled crookedly. 'I hadn't exactly intended to announce that I was coming for them. What do you take me for?' He turned back to the board. After a moment he moved one of his archers.

Rostov whistled softly between his teeth. Burun was not paying attention to the game. Jehan moved an elephant and almost at once Burun moved his over-lord.

Rostov closed his eyes. 'Khan.' He spoke in a pained whisper.

Jehan looked up and saw the expression on Rostov's face. He laughed. Then he moved the other archer into place so that it threatened Burun's overlord. 'Check and Mate.'

Burun was turning to speak to Jotan. Now he

looked back. 'Aaah!' He shook his head ruefully. 'Someone else play this demon. He's practically unbeatable.' He stood up.

The Yek version of chess was similar enough to that which was played in the Imperium for Rostov to have achieved a degree of mastery. 'Your mind wasn't on your game, Khan.' He took Burun's place at the table. Jehan began to lay out the pieces again.

'Hunh.' Burun snorted. 'That's true enough.'

Rostov wondered if Burun was beginning to have second thoughts about going to Losan. Every member of his family was against the idea and had made some kind of adverse comment.

Jotan sat down. 'Your feud against Sipotai has waited nearly two years. You shamed him at Pesth. Isn't that enough?'

Burun did not answer. He glared at Jotan and after a moment Jotan looked away. 'Well.' He seemed to draw a deep shuddering breath. 'If you must, you must.'

Burun took a cup of wine from a slave. He was brooding, watching almost absently as Rostov tried to create a defence against Jehan's warriors as they marched across the board.

'I wish you would remember that I have a province to govern.' Jotan's tone was long-suffering.

'So?' Burun turned.

Jotan looked down his nose. 'You don't think I'm going to let you ride off to Losan without proper escort. And anyway, if it comes to kanly, you will need seconds.'

Burun made a rude noise. 'You don't have anything to say about the way I conduct this affair. As it happens I will be well attended. I'm taking my personal guard and so is Suragai. Arghatun is coming and he commands two hundred of the first tenth of my own tuman. I'm not stupid.'

'Only reckless.'

Burun looked as if he was struggling to keep his temper. 'The war is over.' He drank from the cup then set it aside. 'There are minor feuds and quarrels being settled all over the Khanate. I have done what is required of me by the law. I have sent to the Kha-Khan to advise him that I intend kanly against the head of another clan.'

Jotan tipped his stool back. He placed his booted feet upon the table. 'You don't intend to fight any fairer than Vortai.'

Burun shrugged. 'If Vortai is prepared to meet me according to the code, well and good. If not, well there is more than one way of breaking a st'lyan to harness.'

Jotan looked disapproving. 'If you place yourself in the wrong, you'll forfeit everything. We both know Vortai will never accept a challenge.'

Burun gestured. 'Jotan, your grandfather and your uncle have been trying to kill me, or failing that to dispossess me, since before I married your mother. Vortai only gave his consent to my marriage to his daughter because it was the Kha-Khan's command and he thought he could gain an advantage over me through her. I have been patient long enough. I mean to rid myself of these thorns that prick me.'

Rostov was not sure how to interpret the look which passed between Jotan and Burun. Burun had a clear grievance against the Gaijin, but there was much more to his hatred of Vortai and Sipotai than that. There was an inner compulsion which drove him, and Rostov wondered if he had done the right thing by allying himself to such a cause. Every so often an incident occurred which made him realise how little he understood about the way the Yek mind worked. He looked up and saw that Jotan was staring at him.

'You are misled, Suragai, to follow my father in this venture.' Jotan's tone was harsh and accusing.

Rostov met the stare with as much composure as he could muster. 'Noyon, I owe your father a debt of loyalty, and, if that is not enough, according to the law Vortai has wronged me also.'

Jotan seemed to consider the answer. It was clear that he thought that it was insufficient. His mouth closed in disapproval and he turned away.

In the middle of the night Turakina woke. She lay bathed in perspiration, crying. Rostov woke slowly. He felt as if he had been drugged and wondered if the tiredness which he felt was a sign that the effects of the Longivex were departing from his system. A cat was sleeping in the hollow between them in the bed, and he lifted it out of the way. It howled and lashed out at him.

'What is it? Are you sick?' Rostov drew Turakina into his arms.

She nestled against him. She was trembling, but as he held her, gradually the shuddering of her body ceased. She turned her face into his chest. 'It was a bad dream. I don't remember.'

The walls of the yurt deadened all sound. Rostov knew that there must be some movement in the camp outside, but he could hear nothing. It was about the third hour of the night watch. Soon it would be dawn.

The cat leapt back on to the bed. It was a Suristani, given to Turakina by Kiku. Turakina reached out and stroked the animal and it arched its back and purred.

'Are you angry with me?' She glanced up at him.

'Oh, furious.' He hugged her.

She smiled and moved against him. 'I am afraid for your safety. You should be pleased.'

Rostov grunted and made a face. Lying on his back

459

the dome of the ceiling was almost invisible. It was like sleeping beneath a moonless sky. There were tiny metallic threads in the material of the hangings and the lamplight reflected off them so that they twinkled like stars.

Turakina raised herself on one elbow. She moved so that her weight was resting on his chest and started to stroke the inside of his calf with one of her feet. 'Have I tried to dissuade you?' She raised her head and looked at him.

'No.' He shook his head.

'Then heed me.' She put her head on his shoulder. 'A feud is a private matter. It is ridiculous for you to become involved. The Yasa will not permit you to engage in kanly. You have no talons, so how can you fight?'

The law was a code designed for the True People. It did not provide for humans, and kanly, the only permitted form of duel to the death, was fought without weapons of any kind. Only the races who had talons - the Yek, the N'pani and the Ch'noze - were capable of engaging in it.

Rostov drew a breath. 'I don't suppose I will come to harm. Vortai is your grandfather. How can Burun kill him?'

Turakina did not move. 'My father is an evil man,' she said. 'He cares for nothing but his own ambition. You think it is a feud which concerns him? Vortai is a candidate for the Dragon Throne. That is why he intends to deal with him.'

Rostov considered her words. He thought that the idea was improbable. No one took Vortai's claim seriously.

Turakina looked up again. 'Burun means to humiliate Vortai so that he can never be considered. Vortai knows this and he will kill my father if he can. Sipotai covets my step-mother and, if my father is killed, her hand will be in Vortai's gift. Their quarrel matters not. You cannot afford to trust any of them.'

'You mean that I am in the middle.'

'Exactly.'


'There has been no word from Kinsai.' Burun tossed the report aside.

Ten days had passed since Burun had sent to the Kha-Khan to say that he intended to pursue his feud against Vortai. It was ample time for a prohibition to have been received.

Burun was frowning. 'You think I am wrong in this,' he said.

Rostov was making notes in the margin of a list of grain requisitions. He laid his pen aside and looked up. 'Khan, where you lead I will follow. I confess that I do not altogether understand this business.'

'What does my daughter say?' Burun's stare was challenging.

Rostov hesitated. 'She says that you mean to see Vortai humiliated.'

'Oh?' Burun showed his teeth. 'What else?'

There was something in Burun's eyes which warned Rostov to be completely honest. 'She says that I should not trust your motives.'

'Hunh.' Burun nodded. He got up and went to the open flap of the tent. Then he turned. 'You should be careful of such openness. With another man it would get you into trouble.'

'You would have known if I lied.'

'Maybe.' Burun sat down on a stool which was placed just inside the entrance. 'Turakina is right. Look to yourself.'

Rostov was not sure how to react. 'Khan?'

Burun's eyes were watching intently. 'If I gave you a

461

choice in this matter, would you still follow me?'

'Khan, you already gave me a choice. But the answer is yes.' Rostov was careful to display no hesitation.

'And if I tell you that my quarrel with Vortai is not a true reason?'

Rostov shrugged. 'Khan, I did not suppose that you had told me everything. But it seems to me that I have little choice. I will always be a stranger here, so I must trust you because I cannot do anything else. I need your favour. I will follow you.'

Burun's face was expressionless. Rostov wondered if he accepted the statement at its face value or if he understood that the words had been spoken for effect. Only a fool would talk himself into a situation where he forfeited the trust of his lord.

'You speak well,' Burun said at last. 'And it does not matter that I do not entirely believe you. A man is not wise who trusts another without good reason. It took me most of my first year's ruling to learn to ignore what men said, and to watch what they did instead. You know the story of the hunter?'

Rostov grinned. 'Yes, Khan.'

There was a Yek fable which illustrated the quality of trust. The story went that one day a hunter took his bow into the fields to shoot quail. The wind was cold and soon his eyes began to water. 'It is well,' one bird said to another. 'The man has pity, for see, he weeps.' But another bird said, 'Never mind his tears. Watch his hands.'

'The story describes us well.' Burun stood up. 'I will try not to betray you, Suragai, for in this as in many other things you are an innocent and it would be wrong. Serve me and I will reward you. But you should always be wary.'

Huge tented inns had been constructed at the principal desert way stations, for the caravans which crossed the G'bai were full of traders who preferred the landward route to the Alan country to the journey by sea. On the second night of their journey towards Losan, Burun stopped at a place which was crowded with N'pani; small powerful men, none of whom seemed to bear arms. The traders wore dull grey silks and every time they finished a sentence they hissed and bowed. Their language was similar in many respects to Manchu. When they displayed their merchandise, Rostov saw that they were carrying the substances like dried st'lyan blood which were employed in the remedies administered to ordinary men. The races of the True People had no use for such things, because they did not get sick.

The N'pani were fascinated by Rostov's size.

'I had forgotten I looked so different.' Rostov rested his head on his arms. It was late and he was tired. The inn did not appear to possess separated sleeping quarters and he guessed that he was going to have to lie down on one of the benches in the public room if he wanted to rest.

'Not different.' Burun smiled. 'Just a lot bigger. You would make two of most of us.'

The caravan leader was similar in appearance to the N'pani, but his skin was darker and he was more heavily built. Arghatun said that the man was a native of N'czuan, which was the general name given to a group of islands situated to the east of the continent of Y'frike. When he was introduced, the N'czuani bowed and touched his finger tips to his forehead.

'This man is called Joden.' Arghatun spoke Yek. 'His caravan came through Losan six days ago.'

'I am Buratai.' Burun nodded acknowledgement of the salutation.

Rostov hid a smile. Burun had used the name of

463

Jotan's deceased father-in-law, the half-brother of Khotan. The N'czuani bowed again.

'Lord, your officer says that you intend to travel through Losan.'

'Yes.' Burun nodded. 'Did you have good trading there?'

'No, Lord.'

'Oh? Why not?'

The caravan master scowled. 'Lord, Vortai Khan summers there this year. The city is under martial law and the sentries do not like strangers. The market is permitted to open only one day in three and there is a tax upon all goods which prevents an honest man from taking a profit.'

'Then perhaps I will travel by another route.' Burun sat back and smiled easily. 'I am no trader, but in time of peace, men should be free to come and go as they please.'

When Arghatun had drawn the N'czuani away, Jotan leaned forward and spoke. 'Vortai has been warned you are coming. Why else is he taking such precautions?'

Burun shook his head. 'No. Vortai imposes that kind of control wherever he goes. It is said that he sleeps in his mail, he is so afraid of treachery.'

'Hunh.' Jotan gestured. 'Yet you hope to issue your cartel. No wonder you are using a different name.'

Rostov watched Burun's face. The Khan's eyes were hooded and it was impossible to tell what he was thinking. Rostov knew he would not be bothering to travel to Losan unless he had a plan.

'If Vortai knows I am coming, it does not matter,' Burun said after a moment.

Jotan made a rude noise in reply. Then he got up and went outside.

*

They came up out of the G'bai at a place where the natural barrier of the escarpment had been eroded away by the wind and by the changes in temperature between night and day. Huge blocks of stone lay split away from the main mass of the cliffs. The black desert sand had been blown into the space and there was a steep but manageable gradient.

'How far is it to Losan?' Rostov allowed his st'lyan to find her own way up the slope.

'Three or four days at this pace.' Jotan urged his mare around the side of a shelf of rock which protruded out across the path.

Burun was riding in front. He turned his head when Jotan spoke, but he said nothing. The ground under the hooves of the st'lyan was changing from the black crystalline sand which characterised the G'bai to a peaty red-brown. Rostov thought that the desert had once been basalt flats, eroded to sand over thousands of years. Up on the escarpment trees grew. They were stunted and the trunks were twisted in weird shapes. Where the grass showed it was harsh and spiky, the colour of old iron. At the edge of the plateau a family of *mirkat* raised their heads inquisitively. The animals were like squirrels, but they were much larger and their tails were short. They lived in burrows in the soil and moved in groups of a score or more. This particular breed was distinguished by a streak of darker fur which ran down the spine. The adults stood on their hind legs like sentries while Burun's party rode past.

'The wildlife is different up here.' Rostov loosened the *burnoos* with which he had shielded his face from the wind-borne desert sand.

Burun looked amused. 'Well, of course. Would you live in the G'bai if you had a choice? The creatures here are all native to the steppe. They don't venture down into the desert.'

465

'And the things which live down there?'

Burun shrugged. 'Who knows?'

Rostov thought that anything which had evolved so that it could live in the black sands probably required the minerals which were found there in abundance. An Imperial ecologist would take a lifetime to study the fauna of Tarvaras. Apart from a few large canine and feline species, there were no predators north of the line of the escarpment. There was, in nature, a kind of balance which had been disturbed only a little by the way of life of the people. The G'bai however was populated almost entirely by predators of one sort or another. Mostly they were reptilian, and without exception they preyed not only upon other species but also upon the young of their own kind.

The sun was at its zenith, but it was clear that Burun had no intention of calling a halt. At this time of day the solar intensity was so great that sweat evaporated to vapour as soon as it came into contact with any kind of surface. Every member of the party was wearing a riding cloak of reflective material, but even so some of the troopers were voicing complaint.

'How do the st'lyan survive in these conditions?' Rostov kicked his mare into a sidestep so that he was riding stirrup to stirrup with Jotan. 'They don't sweat much.'

A corner of Jotan's mouth twisted for a moment. It was as if he was amused by such curiosity. 'St'lyan are like the True People, Suragai. Extremes of heat and cold mean little. When it is very hot the lungs expand. The blood circulates faster and changes. Ask a Sechem for a better explanation.'

If the st'lyan were genetically engineered, then of course they would be built to withstand climatic extremes. If the Yek physiology was similar, then perhaps they too had been adapted. Rostov wondered how long men had survived on Tarvaras, and if he would ever know more. The True People themselves were supremely incurious about their early prehistory.

Shadows which moved on the ground made him look up. Birds wheeled overhead.

'V'ltar.' Jotan glanced up briefly. 'Eaters of carrion. They are found everywhere in the hot lands. They follow the caravans and every band of riders.'

A few of the creatures were hopping around on the ground beside a fallen tree. Something had died there, or perhaps had been killed, and they were scavenging noisily for titbits. The v'ltar were huge, almost as big as a man, and they had untidy black plumage. Their beaks were wicked hooked affairs. The advance guard gave them a wide berth. Burun spat left and right as he rode past them, and everyone seemed to be glad when they had been left behind.

The further west the party rode, the more the land changed. It was still hot, but now it was apparent that there was a water table below the surface of the soil which provided life and nourishment. The road wound through groves of tall trees; the grass of the plain was lush and green. The st'lyan dipped their heads whenever there was a halt and grazed contentedly.

Jotan stopped and gazed around. 'Whose land was this before we came? I don't remember.'

Burun was releasing his feet from the stirrups. He turned his head as he spoke. 'Most of the country belonged to the Southern Khitai. We killed them all years ago.'

Arghatun had dismounted to clean out his st'lyan's hooves. He straightened slowly. 'We fought the final battle against them on this plain, Khan.'

'Yes.' Burun nodded. 'You're right. Their standards

were up on that hill. We attacked towards them, into the sun. That was a day.'

'It was Daijin's first great campaign.' Arghatun lifted one of his mare's fore-hooves. 'Before that he occasionally made mistakes.'

Rostov dismounted. He went behind a thicket to make water and, when he looked down at the ground, he saw that the bushes were growing up through a matrix of dry bones.

'It's good land. Fertile.' Jotan pulled up beside a flat-topped rock. He stepped out of the saddle on to it, and stretched.

Arghatun spat to one side. 'It's Gaijin land. The Kha-Khan gave it to Vortai for all time, just as he gave the Khirgiz to your father.'

Jotan sat down on the rock. He swung his legs. 'And if Vortai dies?'

Burun said nothing. It was as if he had not heard.

Arghatun made a face. 'The Gaijin are as many as fleas on a mangy dog. Sipotai has half-brothers.'

'None of them acknowledged,' Jotan said at once.

Rostov watched Burun's face for a sign of what he was thinking. Burun folded one free leg across the pommel of his saddle. Then he turned. His smile was grim. 'This isn't about land. The Gaijin are welcome to the Khitai.'


Losan had started life as a fishing port. It was only partially fortified. Houses followed the line of the low white cliffs around the curve of the bay. Most of the buildings were white or light grey and the roof covering appeared to be grey slate. The water in the bay was a deep uniform blue; there was no sign of a beach.

'Deep water everywhere.' Burun surveyed the town

with Rostov's spyglass. 'It's the best anchorage in the Khanate.'

Rostov guessed that the cliffs were either chalk or soft limestone. Two roads were visible from the rise above the city. One was the route which Burun's party had been following from the south for most of the day. It was deserted. The other road wound north out of Losan into a range of low hills. Carts moved on it and there were occasional groups of mounted men. On a low plateau at the northern end of the bay there was a keep built out of grey stone.

'For a place which is under martial law,' Burun closed the glass, 'there is a remarkable amount of activity. There are boats moving in the harbour and carts on the road north. Vortai must be allowing some commerce. The traders would complain to the Kha-Khan if he did not.'

'I don't see that it matters.' Jotan dismounted. 'You are here and Vortai is there.' He indicated the citadel. 'If you go in and issue a challenge, you're a fool. And if you imagine for one moment that he will accept a cartel and come out to fight you according to the code, then I should be Khan of the Merkuts, and you should go back to the Khirgiz and sit by the fire, telling tall stories the way old men do.'

'Be quiet, whelp.' Burun growled. 'I'm not in my dotage yet.'

'Oh, well. That's a matter of opinion. We aren't really going to ride in, are we?'

Burun slid out of the saddle. 'You can do what you like. I'm going to watch for a while. Send the guard back about a verst. Keep them away from the road and make sure they don't light any fires.'

Arghatun nodded. He rode away and the troopers followed him.

'Even if you could get to the keep,' Jotan nagged,

'Vortai would not meet you in a fair fight. Give it up.'

Burun ignored him. He led his st'lyan into a grove of trees near the roadside and tethered her. Rostov followed suit, and after a moment Jotan muttered something which sounded like a curse. He slapped his st'lyan angrily on the rump. She screamed and then trotted docilely in under the trees.

An hour passed. A mounted patrol came out of Losan and rode past the place where they lay hidden. Some time later the same patrol returned, riding with no haste so that it was clear that they had not observed Burun's escort.

'Careless.' Burun shaded his eyes to watch the progress of the patrol back down the road to Losan. 'They are only patrolling the roads, and that not very efficiently.'

'Do they have to maintain better security?' Jotan was sitting with his back propped up against the base of a tall tree. He looked up. 'If Vortai has less than half a tuman I will be surprised. Against that you have three hundred.'

Rostov listened but did not raise his head. Burun kicked the sole of his boot lightly to attract his attention. 'Suragai, tell me what I ought to do.'

Rostov was taken by surprise. He did not believe that Burun had made the journey to find Vortai without a definite plan in mind. 'Khan, I'm not sure what you wish to achieve.'

Burun stared. 'I want to make Vortai break the Yasa so that I will have an excuse to kill him.'

Jotan snorted softly. 'If Vortai tries to kill you other than by kanly, you will have reason enough.'

'I need to be able to show just cause.' Burun looked down his nose. 'Anyway murder is not usually witnessed.'

'No.' Jotan sounded amused.

'And besides, I'm reasonably fond of life.'

Rostov managed a smile. 'We all are, Khan.'

'So tell me what I ought to do.' Burun's gaze was steady.

A small rodent like a field mouse ran along the ground almost at Rostov's feet. Its track through the grass was like the wake left by a ship moving through the water, then suddenly it was gone.

'If you attack Vortai,' Rostov met Burun's eyes, 'how will he respond?'

Burun grinned. 'Like a p'tar with a burr in its hide.'

'The trick will be to avoid getting killed,' Jotan commented mildly. 'And of course if you attack Vortai, then you too will have broken the Yasa.'

'I don't intend to get caught.' Burun wrinkled his nose.

Rostov hid a smile. Now that he was better acquainted with the Yasa, he was aware that there were as many loopholes in it as there were in Imperial law. No man could live a normal life without breaking the minor provisions.

'Khan, if you enter Losan without an escort you will be running a considerable risk.' Rostov spoke musingly. 'On the other hand if Vortai tries to kill you and you escape him, then maybe he will use a fairly small number of men to chase you. As you have said, murder is best carried out without witnesses. Your escort can set up an ambush along the road, and you can lead Vortai into it. There are some good places.'

'Yes.' Burun looked interested. 'And as to the risk, I care not if I can deal finally with Vortai.'

Jotan looked unhappy. 'Can you be sure that Vortai will come after you?'

'When he knows who is attacking him?' Burun snorted. 'Of course he will. Vortai has wanted a chance to kill me for years.'

The city gate was guarded by Losani militia. They gave the small party of riders consisting of Burun, Rostov, Hodai and Kuchuk only a cursory glance, and did not attempt to hinder their passage.

Burun urged his st'lyan past a line of carts which were waiting to be unloaded. 'Suragai, I should have left you behind with Jotan. Sit low in the saddle and cover your face. With any luck everyone will think you are Ch'noze or C'zak.'

'Look to your own appearance, Khan.' Hodai's tone suggested that he was on the verge of mild hysteria. 'Your face isn't exactly unknown. If just one Gaijin identifies you, we are all dead men.'

Burun scowled, but he said nothing. He had removed his gold arm rings at Hodai's insistence, and had wiped dark stain on to his eyelids to conceal the Merkut clan tattoo. All of them had stripped their harness of the gold and silver decorations which would have marked them at once as something more than ordinary soldiers.

The Losani houses were narrow structures with roofs which leaned all to one side. The chimney pots were ornately decorated, some of them capped with tiny towers or pagodas. Rostov guessed that the light colouring which surfaced most of the buildings was a kind of lime wash. There were smooth flints in place of cobbles in the streets and quartz glittered in the stonework of the few big buildings which were uncoated.

'There are Gaijin watching us from the yard over there, Khan.' Kuchuk did not turn as he spoke. His eyes moved on down the street as if the men he had noticed were of no consequence.

'I see them.' Burun sounded calm. 'It's an inn.' He

kicked his mare into a sidestep, and turned without apparent hesitation into the enclosure which had been constructed.

'Hold! Identify yourselves.'

A thin man who wore the gorget which signified that he was an officer barred their path. His hand caught at Burun's bridle. Burun's dun mare reared and screamed.

'Take your dung-sodden hand off my harness!' Burun snarled. Hodai and Kuchuk crowded their animals in on either side of him, and the officer backed off a pace. A few of the troopers who were lounging on the terrace outside the inn looked up. One or two reached for their weapons.

'Identify yourself!' The Gaijin was insistent.

'Name of God!' Burun kicked his feet free from the stirrups. 'Yours is the fifth challenge I've answered since I entered this misbegotten excuse for a city. I'm from Kinsai, damn you. The Kha-Khan's business. I've just delivered a despatch to your Khan. He offered me no lodging, curse him, so now I'm seeking a night's shelter.' As Burun spoke he wrenched an empty courier's wallet from the binding behind his saddle. He flourished it.

Rostov held his breath. The Gaijin's attention had switched and he was inspecting Hodai and Kuchuk. The suspicion was plain upon his face.

'And these?'

'My escort,' Burun said shortly.

A pair of Gaijin troopers had strolled out into the yard. 'Name of God!' One of them laughed and jostled the other. 'How many men does it take to deliver one letter?'

Burun was unfastening his saddle girth. He turned and his voice took on a querulous tone. 'How many indeed? If your Khan would clear the damned bandits out of the hills, a man could ride alone and in safety. Fifty verst I was forced to travel out of my way because the coast road is unsafe.'

'Oh peace, in the Name of God.' The officer let go of Burun's bridle. He gestured rudely. 'Let me be spared the noise of your whining. Enough.' He turned away.

The troopers on the terrace and in the yard chuckled. The men who had picked up weapons laid them down again, and Rostov released the breath he had been holding. Burun spat so that he just missed the departing Gaijin's heels. He tugged his saddle off his st'lyan's back and threw it down under the cover of a lean-to which seemed to lead to the stables attached to the inn. A servant came out of the back and led the mare away. Hodai dismounted. He was joined a moment later by Kuchuk. Their faces were strained, and they busied themselves with the task of unsaddling to hide the fact. Rostov gigged his mare in under the shelter of the lean-to and slid quietly out of the saddle. It was nearly dusk now and his height was less noticeable in the lengthening shadows.

'Am I mad?' Hodai's voice was low. 'Or did the Khan just deceive that fool?'

Burun looked up. 'Would you look for the Khan of the Merkuts here?'

Hodai shook his head and laughed wildly.

The public room of the inn ran the whole length of the lower floor. There were only a few traders; they sat in tight little groups and scowled occasionally at the soldiers who occupied the other tables.

'Vortai's restrictions on trade are unpopular.' Burun chose a table which was partially screened by one of the pillars which supported the balcony constructed across part of the upper floor. He sat down.

'It is peacetime, Khan.' Hodai looked around the room. 'Some people are saying that there will be no more wars. Now that the Alan have been conquered, the Kha-Khan rules the whole land from sea to sea.'

Burun snorted. 'Some people are fools. Are the Ch'noze at peace? What about the lands across the Great Sea? There will always be wars.'

It occurred to Rostov to wonder what a race which bred every male child to the sword would do when finally every part of the world had been conquered. It seemed to him that peace-keeping was a poor excuse for maintaining a whole nation under arms, but he said nothing. The Yek were passing through a phase which was similar in many respects to the medieval period of pre-atomic Terra. The actual possession of large tracts of land was a measure of power and influence. In order to maintain control over new territory the greater proportion of the male population were employed as soldiers. At the same time it was clear that there was never going to be the transition which would have been brought about under other circumstances by the discovery of science and technology. The Yek did not need to be shown how to use land and resources more efficiently. The core of knowledge which would carry them - if they wished - towards industrialisation was already in existence. Their approach to life had been delineated from the beginning by the Yasa, although if there was a basic principle to their philosophy, it bore no relationship to anything which would be either recognised or understood by human civilisation.

Hodai was looking doubtful; it was as if he disagreed with Burun's summary. Rostov remembered that, like many of the Merkut officers, he was also Burun's vassal, and held a fief in the fertile north of Keraistan. Even though he followed the banner as Burun's aide, Hodai was concerned with the stewardship of his land. Possibly he took his feudal responsibilities more seriously than most.

'Khan, I don't quite understand what we are going to do now that we are here.' It was Kuchuk who spoke, his expression perplexed. 'It makes sense for you to conceal your identity. To do otherwise would amount to suicide. But if as you say you want Vortai to attack you, then you will have to reveal yourself. How can you achieve your purpose and hope at the same time to remain alive?'

'Oh, well.' Burun's features betrayed no hint of concern. 'There is some element of risk. Suragai, those were your words I think.'

'Risk!' Kuchuk laughed harshly. Suddenly he sat back and shrugged. 'Well. Whatever you intend, Khan, I am your liegeman. I will follow you.'

Burun produced a crooked smile. 'If I thought you followed me out of loyalty alone, I would release you. Anyway you know perfectly well that the Yasa does not require your duty in this matter.'

Kuchuk looked exasperated. 'Name of God, Khan, it must be wonderful to be right all the time. Saving our duty to you, it is true that we know what has to be done. Now tell us what you intend and let us make a start.'

There were three troopers on the quay below the citadel wall. Probably they were supposed to be walking sentry, but in fact they were gathered around a brazier which had been placed in the lee of a low stone wall. The glow of the coals lit their faces.

Kuchuk came stealthily through the piles of panniers and baskets. He knelt at Burun's side. 'There are no other guards, Khan.'

'Good.' Burun nodded. 'Pick your targets.'

Rostov selected the man who was sitting on the wall. He brought the head of the arrow down until it

476

was centred at chest level, then loosed. The man tumbled backwards over the wall and there was a faint splash as he went into the water below the wharf. Both of the other sentries collapsed without a sound. Hodai and Kuchuk lowered their bows. Burun was glancing up at the parapet of the keep, but there was no indication of alarm.

Rostov cased his bow again. Kuchuk and Hodai were already arranging the bodies of the dead men on the wall so that it looked as if they were huddled over the heat of the fire. When they had finished, they moved silently along the base of the wall.

The postern gate of the citadel was at the end of the wharf. It was set into the wall of the keep at the head of a short flight of stairs. Hodai and Kuchuk began to carry timbers and bales over from the piles which were lying along the quay. Gradually they built up a heap of inflammable merchandise against the timbers of the gate. Rostov followed Burun to investigate the contents of a small warehouse.

Burun levered the bung out of one of a line of small barrels which were stacked just inside the entrance. 'Fish oil. I thought we would find some.' He pulled a second barrel over on to its side. 'Help me.'

Rostov wrinkled his nose at the smell. 'Khan, I hope this works.'

'Of course it will work. Vortai is not a clever man and his son is no better.'

'A fire and an attempted assassination.' Rostov strained to lift his end of the barrel. He was surprised that it was so heavy. 'You would have to be mad to think that such a plan would succeed.'

Burun grinned. 'My father-in-law has never thought very highly of my intelligence. Vortai will reason that I feared to send him my cartel in case of treachery on his part. A fire here is calculated to bring someone out to see and a botched attempt to kill him will only re-assure him. He will think that I am desperate and that I have been forced into this because I have no support from my vassals.'

Rostov shuffled out of the warehouse, his hands losing their grip slowly on the barrel staves. It was out of the question to roll the oil along the wharf. The sound would alert the citadel before Burun was ready. 'Khan, let me try and get this onto my shoulder. We can't carry it this way.'

'There should be a barrow somewhere.'

'No, I can do it.' Rostov heaved the barrel up, then straightened. The weight was just manageable and he staggered towards the postern.

Kuchuk splashed oil cheerfully over the timbers and bales. 'I haven't played with fire since I was a child at my father's knee,' he commented. Hodai laughed softly and Rostov raised an eyebrow at Burun. Hodai and Kuchuk were barely restraining their hilarity. It was as if they could not believe their situation.

Burun's tone was only mildly annoyed. 'Be quiet, you two. Are you done yet?'

Hodai nodded. 'It needs but a spark, Khan.'

'Very well. Give me that lamp.'

The lantern was suspended from a bracket set in the wall leading down into one of the alleyways which disappeared off into the northern end of Losan. Kuchuk stood on Hodai's shoulders to lift it down.

Burun adjusted the wick until the flame was high. Then he threw the unshuttered lamp so that it landed at the base of the timbers which were angled against the postern. Flames sprang up at once. They ran along the wood and licked at a pile of baskets. The face of the gate began to burn.

'Khan, we should move back.' Hodai uncased his bow nervously.

'Yes.' Burun nodded. 'That archway there.'

The place he indicated was the entrance to a short covered street. Rostov uncased his bow and laid arrows on a ledge at his side.

'What if no one comes?' Hodai stared at the blaze which now enveloped the postern.

'Someone will come.' Hodai sounded amused. 'We just can't be sure it will be Vortai or Sipotai.'

'Sipotai at least will come.' Burun's voice was calm.

An alarm tocsin began to boom in the citadel. It was joined by a second, then several smaller bells started to ring in the city. Rostov heard shouting and the sound of running feet.

'Here they come.' Kuchuk's tone was matter-of-fact.

Most of the firefighters were on foot. Men streamed down a street which came from the direction of the citadel causeway. They were followed by a few mounted troopers, and townspeople ran beside them.

'Watch your targets.' Burun spoke. 'Don't waste arrows.'

Kuchuk loosed and a man who was wearing officer's medallions fell off his st'lyan. The animal shied, but the people ran on over the body without stopping.

'Maybe we should wait.' Hodai seemed to hesitate.

Burun snorted. 'Either my in-laws will come, or they will not.' He nocked an arrow and fired into the crowd running along the street. Another man fell.

The troopers at the front of the crowd reached the wharf. A figure in half-mail climbed up onto the low wall which ran along the quay. Commands were screamed, and a bucket chain formed between the postern and the steps which descended from the quayside to the water. Several troopers were trying to drag burning bales out of the blaze, using their lances as grapples.

'Sipotai.' Burun watched the man on the wall. 'I

knew he would come.' He sounded pleased.

Rostov aimed at a Gaijin trooper who was standing in the stirrups to direct the movement of buckets towards the flames. 'Khan, if we get out of this, remind me to show you how a simple pump works. They could put the fire out in no time if they had the equipment.' He shot, and the trooper fell off his st'lyan into the bay.

'Are they blind?' Hodai had started firing at last. 'They must know they are being attacked.'

'Someone will tell them.' Burun sounded amused. 'Stop shooting.'

'Are we going?' Hodai looked relieved.

'Soon.' Burun was surveying the chaos along the quay. The timbers which had been dragged out of the fire at the postern had started a second blaze among a heap of cordage on the wharf. He nocked an arrow, then stepped out into the open. 'Sipotai!'

On the wall Sipotai's head turned. His features were clearly illuminated by the bonfire which was all that was left of the postern. He seemed to search for the source of the voice.

'Over here!' Burun loosed. His arrow screamed over Sipotai's head.

A cloud of smoke billowed down, obscuring everything. Then a gust of wind whipped the smoke away again and it was as if everyone on the quayside saw Burun at once. Sipotai pointed and screamed wordlessly and Gaijin troopers charged towards the archway with a roar.

'Now we can go.' Burun turned as he spoke and ran easily along the street in the direction of the yard where the st'lyan had been left tethered. Rostov pounded along at his shoulder.

Hodai and Kuchuk were already several paces in front. Kuchuk turned his head and laughed breathlessly. 'Go?' He gasped, his face creased with amused incredulity. 'Go where?'

Rostov rode with his head down. He still found it hard to believe that he was at liberty; a sense of unreality pressed down upon him. By any rational principle - by the principles which governed normal human existence - the acts in which he had been involved since arriving in Losan were meaningless. They lacked discernible motive.

*Is this how it ends? Like a driverless cart running down a hill?*

Rostov was oppressed by a sense of the futility of attempting to control the course of the events in which he was involved. Only a Yek steeped in the arcane traditions of the Yasa would understand and appreciate Burun's method of attacking the Gaijin. Only a native Tarvarian would react in such an illogical and yet apparently predictable fashion.

There were lights in the windows of many of the houses now. Alarm signals - drums, horns and a few small gongs - sounded a counterpoint to the steady boom of the tocsin which tolled from the citadel, and the whole northern end of Losan appeared to be in an uproar. Burun was riding confidently, as if he knew exactly where he was going. A company of armed troopers on foot ran across the junction ahead, but he did not pause or falter. To the casual observer they were four more mounted men whose harness and equipment resembled that which was worn by members of the citadel garrison. Their presence excited no interest. Yet to Rostov it was beyond belief that they were not being hotly pursued.

They turned the corner, and Burun stopped abruptly. The street was lined on both sides by buildings which were clearly warehouses and storage

481

barns. There were occasional narrow alleyways with high walls. One entrance seemed to provide access to a half-enclosed yard.

'Khan?'

Burun ignored Hodai's unspoken question. He guided his mare up a narrow opening between two buildings. At the end there was a high wooden gate set in a stone wall. 'Kuchuk, see if you can get this open.'

The standard-bearer stood on his st'lyan's hind quarters. He hauled himself up onto the top of the gate frame, then dropped into the darkness beyond.

'Can't we simply ride away out of the city?' Hodai had turned so that he was watching the opening out into the street. A small party of men clattered past without stopping. 'There have been no checkpoints so far. Why should anyone suspect us?'

'No.' Burun shook his head. 'Even if the guard commanders have not received word, they will allow no one to leave while an alarm is being sounded.'

The gate in the wall creaked suddenly and everyone jumped. Kuchuk appeared in the gap. He showed his teeth in a smile. 'It was only barred, Khan. There must be another entrance somewhere.'

'Good. Everyone inside.'

There was an open lean-to shed along one wall. The roof was low and Rostov was forced to bend almost double in the saddle as he rode in below it. Burun dismounted at once. Hooves rattled loudly out in the street and they all tensed. A voice shouted something which was either a question or a challenge. At once a number of voices answered so that the words of the response were garbled and unintelligible. The light of the street beacons threw huge shadows against the wall and Rostov estimated that a full company of mounted men was riding past the end of the alleyway. Minutes passed, then it was quiet once more. Occasional footsteps hurried along the paving in the street, but no one paused beside the entrance to their refuge.

Hodai and Kuchuk were watching Burun like mice watching a cat. Rostov guessed that they were wondering if there was a plan by which they would get away safely. Somehow Burun had to let Vortai know that he had escaped from Losan, and the direction of his flight, otherwise the whole exercise was a waste of time.

There was a smell of smoke on the night air. Hodai sniffed and made a face. 'Khan, I think the fire must be spreading. Maybe it will cause a diversion. What are we to do now?'

For a moment Burun's face remained hidden in the shadows under the lean-to. He did not answer and suddenly Rostov was sure that he had come to Losan to sacrifice himself. The reason was not to be guessed at.

Burun glanced up at last. His face was expressionless. 'Now we separate.'

'What?' Hodai protested. 'Khan, you're mad.'

'Oh? The Gaijin will be looking for four men. Correction, the Gaijin will be looking for me. Don't you think we will all have a better chance if we split up?'

'They will start examining eye tattoos.' Kuchuk slid out of the saddle. 'And Sipotai will have anyone who can recognise you watching the roads out of the city.'

Burun's expression was calm. 'My point exactly.'

Hodai seemed to consider. He gestured. 'We can't stay here, that's for certain. Khan, what are you going to do? You'll be discovered in no time.'

'I'm not suggesting that anyone should stay here.' Burun looked down his nose. 'It's a good place to leave the st'lyan, that's all. Personally I intend to head back in the direction of the harbour.'

'Eh?' Kuchuk's expression was comical. Hodai laughed uncertainly.

'Why not?' Burun started to unsaddle his mare. 'It's the last place Sipotai will look for me, and in case you hadn't noticed, there are scores of small boats in the bay.'

Rostov thought about Burun's words, and did not believe them. The bay was a possible escape route certainly, but a flight from Losan which was undetected would not bring either Sipotai or Vortai in close pursuit. A change in the wind blew smoke down into the yard in a swirl and Kuchuk's st'lyan backed up nervously. Her horn scored the timber of the lean-to and she screamed.

Kuchuk grabbed at the piebald's head-rope and quietened her. 'Khan, I hate to leave my animal here. I've only just trained her to my hand.'

Burun shrugged. 'If we survive, we can come back. You will see her again.'

Survival equated with success over Vortai and Sipotai. Rostov realised that if Burun killed his in-laws, or disgraced them so that they were dispossessed by the Kha-Khan, the Gaijin would no longer control Losan. Merkuts would be able to come and go as they pleased. He got down out of the saddle. 'If we don't survive, the loss of a few st'lyan will be the least of our troubles.'

Burun turned. He stared innocently. 'That's right.'

'Khan, I can't imagine you in a boat.' Hodai loosened his saddle girth. 'You're no sailor.'

Burun snorted. 'It doesn't take much skill to work a pair of paddles. I don't intend to try to walk on the water. What else do you suggest?'

Rostov felt hollow inside. It was as if every moment of his existence had led up to this point. The inevitability of it shocked him so that he was unable at first to speak. He swallowed and hesitated.

'What do you suggest for us, Khan?' Kuchuk's stare was intent.

Burun did not turn. He was watching Rostov's face as he spoke. 'There are parts of Losan where there is no real city wall, only the walls around the houses. I thought you could find a quiet spot and lower yourselves over into the ditch. Is stealing a rope too much trouble?'

'God!' Hodai threw up his hands. 'It's no use to talk to you. We'll draw lots and one of us will come with you. A boat needs two men.'

Burun opened his mouth to argue. Rostov cleared his throat. He was not sure why he felt he had to speak. It was as if some compulsion was driving him. Burun's eyes were still on him.

'There is no need to draw lots.' Rostov thought that his voice sounded like the croak of a bird. 'I am more of a sailor than any of you. At least I have handled a boat before.'

Burun's stare was appraising. It was as if he was seeing Rostov properly for the first time. After a moment he shrugged. 'As you wish,' he said. His tone was disinterested. He turned away.

There were fires in two of the warehouses adjoining the quay and the roofs of several of the houses were burning. Some of the structures built around the bay had shingles in place of slates, and Rostov guessed that sparks rising from the fire at the postern had set them alight.

'Damn the fools.' Burun sounded annoyed. 'I did not mean to burn the town.'

One of the warehouses exploded with a roar. Heat washed over them and Rostov gasped. The timber of most Yek buildings was seldom anything other than bone dry and fires were a serious risk at any time. Unless the Losani did something to create a firebreak, the blaze which Burun had started would soon be leaping from street to street. A squad of men raced past even as he arrived at the conclusion. They formed themselves into a bucket chain and began to damp down the walls and roof of a building which was in the path of the fire.

Scores of small boats bobbed in the water of the bay. They were secured in groups to buoys. The light from the fires cast a glow across the wavelets which lapped against the quay wall, and it was difficult to tell what hour it was or if dawn was near.

Another group of men ran past and Burun paused beside a pile of nets. 'I forgot to ask if you can swim.'

Rostov managed a smile. 'Better than you, I expect, Khan.'

The larger vessels which had been berthed along-side the principal wharf were putting out to sea. A single carrack rode at anchor perhaps fifty drem from the quay and it was surrounded by fishing dorys.

'We will need oars if we are going to steal a dory.' Burun followed the direction of Rostov's glance. 'We can float them out and swim behind them. But we have to get them into the water.'

Rostov gazed along the line of the wharf. 'Khan, there are boathouses over there, but a bucket chain is working beside them. Any flat piece of timber will serve as a paddle. We only want to get clear of the harbour after all.'

Burun made a face, then nodded. 'You are right. There are too many people along the quayside. Someone is going to see us going into the water.'

'It's the same all the way along the front, Khan.'

'Yes. I did not think they would allow the fire to spread so. The people will hate us.'

Rostov raised his eyebrows. Burun's approach to the pretence of an attack on Sipotai had been so reckless as to demonstrate a complete disregard for the consequences for the city. It did not make sense for him to be worrying about the feelings of the people now. He followed Burun towards a flight of steps which led down to the water. There was a floating pier secured against the quay wall below. Suddenly armed men ran out of a sidestreet opposite. The officer at their head paused in mid-stride when he saw Burun.

'You there! What are you doing? Identify yourselves!'

'Don't stop.' Burun did not turn his head. 'Keep walking.'

They were nearly at the head of the stairs. Rostov tensed himself to run. If they could make it into the water ...

A boat the size of a ship's cutter appeared out of the smoke which was blowing down across the water. It came towards the floating pier and Rostov saw that it was packed with armed men.

'Those two! Stop them!' Behind him the officer's voice rose shrilly. Men ran to intercept.

Hands caught at Rostov. He tore himself free. His blood hammered in his ears and he lashed out at the two men who were trying to hold him. The two or three who were in his way backed off.

'Hold him!' A new voice yelled the command.

There were men surrounding Burun. Rostov saw the flash of silver talons and someone fell back with his face streaming blood. The boat was in against the pier now. Troopers came surging up the stairs. They crowded Rostov back against the stone wall of the quay. He drove fists and knees into them. A man gasped and Rostov felt bone break beneath his knuckles as he struck out. His assailants clutched at him and brought him down. His face was pressed against the rough wood of the edge of the wharf and his arms were pinioned from behind.

For a moment there was confused shouting. Someone was ordering the men who were holding Rostov to drag him away from the stairs. He got both feet under him and with an effort stood up. There were men hanging on to his arms and shoulders. He swung them off their feet, but they did not let go. The Gaijin officer was watching. He seemed to think that the struggle was over. Rostov took a pace towards him, dragging the men who were trying to restrain his movements. The officer looked alarmed and backed away. A boot caught Rostov behind one knee and he fell on his face again. His wrists were forced up between his shoulder blades. He tried to roll over, but someone was pressing down on his back so that he could not move. He subsided, panting, and after a moment he was dragged onto his knees. Burun was thrown down beside him.

'Tie them.' The voice was Sipotai's. He came through the crowd of troopers and stood looking down at Burun. His eyes glittered.

A kick took Rostov in the ribs and he gasped. Sipotai seized Burun's queue and pulled his head back. 'Merkut, I have dreamed about this moment.'

Burun's smile was ghastly. He spat in Sipotai's face. Sipotai jerked back, then he lashed out viciously, talons unsheathed. Burun cried out.

'Hold them!' Sipotai's voice was as high as a girl's. 'The rest of you stand back!'

Men were wrapping cords around Burun's wrists. They pulled on the ends so that Burun's arms were pulled out from his body. He could not break free. Others dealt with Rostov the same way. He saw that Sipotai was shaking out a whip - the kind which was used to drive oxen. It was bound with hide and when Sipotai flicked it out to its full length, it lay across the timbers of the wharf like a long snake.

Sipotai's arm came up, then he sent the lash forward. The end came over with a crack; it caught Burun across the shoulders. By the tenth stroke Burun's tunic was hanging in tatters and long deep cuts had been opened down his back. He made no sound. Sipotai's breathing was laboured, and there was spittle flecking his lips. He swung the lash again and this time the tail curled around the side of Burun's head and tore the side of his face. At last he cried out. Sipotai stopped. He laughed like a pleased child, then threw the lash to the officer who was standing among his men.

'More. Let me see his spine.'

The officer looked uncertain. He licked his lips. 'Lord, I –'

'I said more!' Sipotai's voice rose up the scale so that the last word was a scream.

The officer seemed to shrink back. He nodded quickly. 'Yes, Lord.'

The whipping recommenced. Burun slipped to his knees and hung between the ropes which were fastened to his wrists. Blood soaked into the timbers of the wharf and Rostov thought that he was unconscious. When the men who were holding the ends of the ropes let go, he slumped in a heap.

'Now the other one. The same.'

Rostov had expected the command. The first cut of the lash was like a knife across his back. It cut through the material of his tunic and laid the flesh open. He cried out. Clenching his teeth he hauled on the ropes which bound his wrists. There were three or four men hanging on to the end of each. They surged back against the strength of his pull and Rostov's arms were jerked so that the sinews of his shoulders cracked. The lash came down on his back without a pause.

There were men in the crowd whose faces were grim, as if they did not like what they were watching. Rostov found that he was on his knees. He stared at Sipotai, willing his tormentor to meet his eyes. There was no curse strong enough to express what was in Rostov's heart, but Sipotai would remember the look on his victim's face and he would know.

Someone shouted a hoarse command and the whipping stopped abruptly. Rostov struggled to keep Sipotai inside his field of vision. There was a red haze which blurred every detail, but he saw that Vortai had arrived on the scene. He was shouting angrily at Sipotai.

Rostov pulled on the ropes which bound his arms and to his surprise the men who were holding them let go. He fell forward onto his face, and unconsciousness when it came was a blessed relief.

'Is he still alive?'

'I think so. Name of God, look at the blood.'

At first Rostov thought that the voices were far away, but then after a moment he realised that he was listening to whispers. He was lying on a wooden surface. It rocked as someone pushed against it and he guessed that it was a cage of some kind. A chill breeze was blowing across his back and he felt weaker than he had ever felt before.

'Hold this. I can't unfasten the bar.'

That was Kuchuk's voice. Rostov tried to turn his head. Pain lanced through his neck and across his shoulders.

Metal shrieked and the cage rocked again. Rostov felt an arm sliding beneath his chest. Someone lifted him gently.

'Suragai. Suragai, can you hear me?' This time it was Jotan who spoke.

Rostov tried to lift his head. A hand restrained the movement. 'Yes. I can't see.'

'There is blood sticking your eyelids together. Hodai, give me some water.'

Hands were easing the rags of tunic away from his back. Some of the material was stuck to the wounds. Rostov gasped as it was pulled aside and he heard Jotan swearing softly.

'The Khan.' Suddenly Rostov remembered Burun.

'Peace.' Jotan spoke. 'He was in another cage. We have freed him already. He is in a better state than you.'

Hodai came back with water. Jotan started to wash the crusted blood out of Rostov's eyes. Grey detail swam into focus through the red and Rostov blinked in an effort to clear the particles of dried blood which still obscured his sight.

It was just past dawn. Pale light filtered between the iron bars of the cage in which Rostov lay. He could make out the expanse of the main square of Losan. The buildings which faced onto it were shuttered and there was none of the movement which was to be expected from any city which relied for its livelihood upon trade. The door of the cage was open. Hodai was framed in the gap and behind him Kuchuk was supporting Burun. A Gaijin officer and a solitary trooper stood a little way off.

Jotan and the others were armed, so they were not prisoners. Rostov grasped the bars of the cage and pulled himself up on to his knees. 'What's happening?'

'We're getting out of here.' Burun freed himself from the support of Kuchuk's arm. He staggered, and Hodai and Kuchuk watched him as if they expected him to fall flat on his face at any moment.

491

'Old goat.' Jotan pulled Rostov's right arm across his shoulders and stood up. The cage rocked alarmingly.

Burun gestured rudely. 'Whelp. You disobeyed my orders. I told you not to come after me.'

Hodai positioned himself in the doorway of the cage and caught Rostov's weight as Jotan released his hold. The movement opened the cuts on Rostov's back and he felt the blood running down into the waistband of his trousers. Jotan climbed down out of the cage. 'I saw the fires,' he said. 'And anyway, you knew it was an order I would not obey.'

'Fires?' Rostov raised his head.

'Your little fire spread.' Jotan took a pot of salve from Kuchuk. He started to smooth some of it onto Rostov's back. 'Losan has had no rain for four months. The people stopped the blaze before it destroyed everything, but they lost the section around the old port.'

'Which meant that Vortai had to let the people evacuate,' Burun said.

Jotan nodded. 'The gates were opened before first light. Hodai and Kuchuk simply put their weapons inside bales of cloth and carried them out past the guards. I met them on the way. I knew you would need help.'

Burun sniffed. He glanced at Hodai and Kuchuk. 'You should have kept going,' he observed sourly.

Hodai looked offended, but Kuchuk only laughed.

'Name of God.' Jotan spat to one side. 'Even when we save your miserable life, we are wrong. You ungrateful old pig.'

The ointment which Jotan had smeared on to Rostov's back burned at first, but gradually the sting went out of the wounds. Rostov breathed in the smell of the stuff and realised that he had seen the same salve used on a st'lyan with swollen hocks. He moved his shoulders experimentally. His legs felt stronger now, and so long as he held onto the side of the cage, he did not need Hodai for support.

The Gaijin officer had been shifting nervously from foot to foot. Now he inclined his head to Jotan. 'Lord, you should leave now. Sipotai will come soon.'

'Yes.' Jotan nodded. He slid a shoulder in under Rostov's arm again. 'Do you think you can ride?'

'Try and stop me.' Rostov looked at Burun. 'You're going to deal with Sipotai, aren't you?

'Oh, yes.' Burun nodded. 'And of course now you also have a quarrel with him.'

'That's right.' It occurred to Rostov to wonder if he had been manoeuvred. 'I do.'

'Very well.' Jotan nodded to the officer. 'Totai, we are going now.'

The material of the tunic which Hodai spread across Rostov's back clung to the wounds left by the lash. He hoped that no one was able to see the fresh blood which was already seeping from his shoulders. Burun's face was a mess and his back was marked, but already his cuts had closed. The Khan's skin would be raw for a few days, the weals of the lash would be visible as fleshy ridges for a while. It was hard to believe that only an hour or two earlier he had been huddled in a pool of his own blood on the quayside.

'Vortai ordered you kept for the Kha-Khan's judgement.' Jotan supported Rostov away from the square. Burun walked unassisted a few paces in front. He was flanked on either side by Hodai and Kuchuk.

'Let me guess.' Rostov could feel the blood running down his back. The waistband of his trousers was soaking again. 'Sipotai intends to kill us without his father's knowledge. Why does he fear a trial?'

Burun turned his head. 'Sipotai should not have used the lash. It is forbidden by the law.'

'Is that why the Gaijin are letting us go?' Rostov struggled to follow the line of reasoning.

Jotan snorted softly. 'The officer is Vortai's man. He let me release you because he knows that Sipotai will come in pursuit. If we are killed there will be no trial. Whatever happens, Vortai will not be embarrassed.'

'And Sipotai?'

'Vortai has other sons,' Burun said. 'And Sipotai is out of control.'

There were small fires in several places, but they were being put out by busy teams of Losani. Streams of people were moving along the streets. A few were pushing carts and others carried bundles.

'When this is over, we must come back and help them rebuild,' Burun said.

'Losan is Sipotai's fief.' Jotan gigged his st'lyan to one side to avoid a cart which was being pulled by a pair of oxen. 'When you have killed him, you can do anything you like.'

Rostov rode at Burun's shoulder. He concentrated on staying in the saddle and ignored most of the activity going on around him.

'Are you all right?' Burun reached across and caught at the reins of Rostov's st'lyan. He looked concerned.

Rostov tried to produce a smile in reply, but the effort hurt his face. He wondered how Burun was managing to keep going. Even though the Khan's wounds had closed, there were bruises all over his upper body, and from the way he was managing his own reins one of his arms had been either broken or dislocated.

'I can manage, Khan.'

Jotan leaned down out of the saddle. He took Rostov's reins out of Burun's hand. 'I'll lead him.'

Burun turned stiffly in the saddle and looked back

over his shoulder. 'Are the Gaijin still trailing us?'

Hodai stood in the stirrups to look. 'Yes, Khan.'

'Hunh.' Jotan did not look surprised. 'I wonder if they are concerned to make sure that we get safely out of the city, or if they intend to kill us as soon as we ride out onto the road. That Totai is a clever man.'

'Why do you say that?' Hodai's head came round.

'Well.' Jotan made a face. 'You don't think he consulted Vortai before he let us free the Khan, do you? He pretended to be outraged by Sipotai's breach of the Yasa. But what about your breach of the law? To keep the Khan and Suragai from Sipotai, he only had to move them to a place where they could not be found. Instead he sent a herald to find me with an offer of safe conduct. Now whatever happens, the interests of the Gaijin will be protected.'

Hodai looked thoughtful. 'I hadn't thought of that.'

Burun was behaving as if he had not overheard the exchange, but Rostov was not deceived. Whatever Burun's real motive for coming to Losan, every permutation of reaction by Vortai and Sipotai had been anticipated and provision had been made.

Kuchuk reined in. 'I have lost my sense of direction. Are we far from the gate?'

Rostov looked up at the buildings, but they were not familiar. Jotan pulled on the leading rein by which he was guiding the chestnut. 'Another two streets,' he said.

Hodai looked worried. 'What do we do if there are guards?'

Burun snorted. 'What do you think?' He urged his mare forward.

Embers cascaded down from the burning roof of a house which was on one side of the street. Rostov's mare reared and he clung to her mane. Jotan was hanging on to the leading rein, cursing in anger. A burning piece of timber fell between them. One end of it caught Rostov across the shoulders and he gasped at the pain.

'Hold on.' Jotan hauled on the rein and Burun side-stepped his st'lyan so that he could kick the chestnut in the barrel. She screamed and kicked out, then began to move forward again.

Rostov nodded. He was sure he was going to faint. Every movement was agony and he felt Hodai moving in on one side while Burun edged closer on the other. Clearly they expected him to fall.

They were riding in the middle of a constant stream of people now. The gate was visible at the end of the street ahead.

'The fires are luck for us.' Hodai reached out and slid his hand in under Rostov's arm. 'They are a diversion which works in our favour.'

Burun snorted softly. Rostov remembered the care with which the blaze at the postern had been set. Given the Losani's minimal fire-fighting capability, the extent to which individual conflagrations had spread was hardly chance.

An alarm bell began to toll steadily. The sound came from the direction of the city square behind them. Burun sat up in the saddle.

Jotan looked back. 'Do you think that is for us?'

'Probably.' Burun was staring over the heads of the people crowding along the street behind. 'I don't see the Gaijin.'

'Well.' Jotan's eyes were opaque. 'You wanted to be pursued.'

The movement of people through the gate out of the city had not slackened. Rostov searched the crowd for sentries and he saw that there were armed men perched in the embrasures above the main portal.

'Khan. Above the gate.'

'I see them.' Burun nodded. 'So much for our safe conduct.'

'Yip! Yip! Yip! Yip!'

The shrill cry cut through the confusion of noise in the street. Armed troopers appeared in one of the narrow archways to the side of the gate. They started to shoot at the men who were on the parapet above.

'That's Arghatun.' Hodai pointed. He sounded relieved.

'Well of course.' Jotan turned as he spoke. 'You didn't think I was fool enough to trust a Gaijin promise? I told him to take the gate if he heard an alarm.'

There were Gaijin running along the city wall from the north. Some were pausing to shoot, but it was apparent that they were having difficulty identifying the Merkuts in the crowd, whereas the men around the archway were able to see their targets clearly. Arrows flew, and a man pitched out of an embrasure into the space between the pillars of the gate. The Merkuts who were in the archway cheered.

'Gallop!' Jotan lashed his st'lyan.

Rostov grabbed for his reins. He spurred the chestnut and she thundered along the street. The Losani who were moving towards the gate dived out of the way. Some were jammed in the archway and had nowhere to go. Rostov had a momentary impression of pale faces reacting in panic to the men and animals which were crashing into the accessway. A Losani who was directly in Burun's path threw up his arms as he realised his danger. Then the onrushing hooves were upon him and he cried out. Rostov heard a thump and the chestnut ran over something solid. Suddenly he was out in the open, riding flat out along the road.

Arrows whipped past his head from the wall. Jotan reined in briefly. He threw up his shield to cover

497

Rostov's exposed back and the flying shafts thumped into the toughened oxhide. Suddenly they were out of range.

Burun pulled up and looked back. Merkuts were racing out of the archway below the gate. Arghatun was at the rear, riding low in the saddle. When he reached Jotan he reined in hard. His black st'lyan reared and screamed.

'Khan, I'm happy to see you.' Arghatun clapped his mare on the shoulder. He grinned at Burun.

'And I you. How many men did you lose?'

'Only two.'

Burun looked satisfied. 'Good. They will send men after us to see which way we ride. Cover us. Kill a few if you wish and don't let them get close enough to us to do any damage.'

'The Khan wishes.' Arghatun saluted. He shouted at the troopers who had ridden away from the gate and they formed up in a screen across the road, reins loose across the necks of their st'lyan, bows ready.

'We ought to ride on.' Jotan gathered his reins.

'We have some time.' Burun shook his head. 'Sipotai has never liked level odds. If he thinks we have twenty, he will wait until he has assembled at least a hundred. All we have to worry about at the moment are his scouts.'

'You want them to follow you, don't you?' Jotan looked back.

'Yes, of course. But if it is too easy, Sipotai will suspect. We have to kill some of them every time they get too close. That way they will think we are trying to discourage pursuit.'

Jotan made a face. 'How complicated.' He rode off along the road.

A small group of mounted Gaijin rode out of the city gate. They rode through the evacuees who were crowded on the open ground outside the wall and advanced at a walk. Arghatun's men loosed a single volley towards them and at once they stopped. They fired in reply, but they were shooting into the wind. Their arrows fell short and the Merkuts stood in the stirrups and jeered.

'Your back has stopped bleeding.' Hodai offered Rostov the damp cloth which he had been using to sponge away the crusted blood. 'How long will your wounds take to heal?'

Rostov dropped the sodden mess of his tunic on the grass. Hodai had been forced to soak the material with water in order to work it free from the stripes on his back. 'I don't know. A few weeks.'

Hodai picked up the tunic. He stuffed it into the hollow bowl of a nearby tree. 'I didn't know anyone could bleed so much and go on living. How do you feel?'

Rostov snorted. 'How do you think?'

Burun was sitting on the grass. He was drinking from a leather bottle filled with k'miss. He gave a short bark of laughter and shook his head. 'You hurt.' He drank and then met Rostov's eyes again. 'I would be dead, I think, if I had to suffer from wounds as you do.'

The place where they had stopped was among the low hills which overlooked the steppe. Behind them lay Losan and the coast. It was late in the afternoon, and the sun was sitting on the western horizon like an enormous red ball. A heat haze distorted the ground in the distance so that any movement in the long grass made ripples like waves stirring in a great golden sea. The rider who was coming across the plain seemed to float above the ground.

'Here's Arghatun.' Jotan was cleaning his st'lyan's hooves. He straightened.

Arghatun rode without hesitation up the slope. He dismounted and saluted Burun. 'They are still following us, Khan.'

'Their scouts?'

Arghatun nodded. 'Yes.'

'And where is Sipotai?'

'About five verst behind, Lord. Two to three hundred men, riding fast.'

'More than you expected,' Jotan said.

Burun ignored him. 'Only Sipotai?' he asked Arghatun. 'Or is Vortai with them as well?'

Arghatun's face was expressionless. 'I cannot tell, Lord. The standard-bearers carry the Gaijin totems, but that is to be expected.'

A totem implied the presence of either a Khan or his eldest son. Rostov was amazed how calmly everyone was taking the situation. They were in open country, riding away from a force of at least equal strength. If they were caught before they were able to reach a suitable spot to establish an ambush, there would be a slaughter.

'Do you want to keep riding east?' Jotan took the k'miss bottle out of Burun's hands. He drank.

Rostov climbed to his feet. He was still stiff and sore, but remarkably he felt that he was beginning to recover from the beating he had taken. It was hard to believe that his body still retained a residue of Longivex. The last treatment had been two years earlier, but it was the only possible explanation.

Burun shook his head. 'No. We must turn south.'

Jotan had the bottle raised to his mouth. He stopped as if paralysed. 'The G'bai? You're mad.'

'Oh? Why?'

Jotan gestured. 'Well, for a start, the Gaijin animals are fresher than ours. They will catch up with us in no time.'

Burun's mouth twisted wryly. 'They will catch us anyway. That is the idea. Better it should be on ground of our choosing.'

Jotan squatted on his heels. He looked troubled.

'We have never fought in desert,' Hodai said softly.

'Neither has Sipotai.' Burun took the k'miss bottle out of Jotan's unresisting hands. He tilted it and drank.

Arghatun let the reins of his st'lyan trail on the grass. He bent down and pulled a seed stem from a tuft of grass. 'Whatever happens, it won't be like fighting the Alan.'

'Obviously.' Burun looked up impatiently. 'It will be like fighting ourselves.' He tossed the bottle to Rostov.

Rostov drank slowly. The k'miss was sharp. He watched Burun's eyes. 'We need an advantage.'

'Exactly.' Burun nodded. 'What have you in mind?'

Rostov collected his thoughts. There was a method of ensuring Sipotai's defeat, but it was contrary to the law. His mouth twisted in amusement. The prohibitions of the Yasa were meaningless here.

'Riders, Khan.' Kuchuk called out before Rostov could speak. The standard-bearer was perched on the bough of a tree. He pointed west.

One of the men who spurred up the slope was Y'zan, the commander of Rostov's guard. He swung down from the saddle and saluted Burun. 'Khan, Sipotai is only a verst or so behind his scouts now. Once he is up with them, we won't be able to keep them at a distance.'

'Very well.' Burun sat back against the base of the tree. 'How much time do we have?'

Y'zan shrugged. 'Two hours at the most, Khan.'

'That settles it.' Burun put one hand on the tree trunk to support himself and stood up. 'We ride south.'

Jotan untethered his st'lyan and swung himself into

501

the saddle. 'I still say you're mad.' He kicked his mare into a sidestep and looked down at Burun. 'The Gaijin match us man for man. We should run for the escarpment. Give yourself up to Siban's custody and you need have no fear of Sipotai. In the desert anything could happen.'

'Well that is true enough.' Burun's tone was amused. 'But I want the satisfaction of killing Sipotai myself. I won't get that if I surrender to Siban.'

Jotan's lips compressed. 'If you let the Gaijin chase you out into the G'bai, it is as likely that it will be you who will be killed.'

'Such confidence.' Burun made a sound in his throat and Jotan's st'lyan snorted and backed up. Jotan had to fight to control her. Burun spat to one side. He did not look at Rostov as he mounted and rode away.

'Tell me how to beat Sipotai.' Burun edged his mare in until he was riding stirrup to stirrup at Rostov's side.

Rostov snorted softly. He had known what Burun was going to ask. 'Do you care if you break the law, Khan?' He pushed up in the stirrups and slid back in the saddle. The ache in his lower back did not subside.

Burun laughed harshly. 'What do you think?'

Rostov settled himself in the saddle again. 'Khan, I think you will do anything you have to.'

'Hunh.' Burun nodded. 'You are right. So tell me.'

Rostov did not answer at once. They were riding across the narrow plateau which led to the edge of the escarpment. It was almost sunset, and the dust which was kicked up by the hooves of the st'lyan in the column hung in the air like a red haze. The Merkuts were riding fast, but there was little noise. Every sound was deadened, as if the harness had been wrapped in cloth.

'Will Sipotai suspect that our strength is as great as

his?' Rostov pushed the hood of his cloak of reflective material back so that it lay across his shoulders.

'No.' Burun shook his head. 'His scouts cannot get close enough to see how many we are. Y'zan's rear-guard is killing them every time they ride into range.'

'Won't that make them suspect?'

Burun made a face. 'It is possible. But probably they think that we are trying to deter them from coming on so fast.'

The troopers ahead of Rostov were riding in twos so that only a narrow trail was being left on the hard ground. Outriders rode behind, dragging brush across the tracks to disguise the numbers.

'Khan, in the first place, I think we should imitate the *felahin*.'

'Aah.' Burun produced a grim smile. He nodded. 'You mean we should conceal ourselves beneath the sand. Yes, but that will put us on foot.'

Rostov unfastened his cloak. He let it fall back so that it lay across the chestnut's hindquarters. 'I wasn't suggesting that we should fight the Gaijin hand to hand, Khan. All I want to borrow from the sandpeople is the element of surprise. We can hide men in Sipotai's path, leaving a trail for him to follow. If they volley when he is in bowshot range, then retire, they will sting him into a charge.'

'Which we can intercept.' Burun looked thoughtful. 'If we kill Sipotai's scouts as they ride down off the escarpment, he will assume that we are trying to get further ahead. He will imagine that we are hoping for a windstorm to cover our tracks so that we can escape him. Maybe he will forget to be cautious. Is that all of your plan?'

'Not all, Khan, no. One of the pack animals being led by my guard carries a thousand diram of corned black powder.'

Burun's expression did not alter. 'And so?' He spoke after a moment and raised an eyebrow. 'There is no wood for catapults in the desert.'

'Not catapults.' Rostov gestured. 'Mines. The powder is packed in twenty containers. We can lay them in shallow pits filled with small stones. The mines will have to be set off just as the Gaijin ride over them, but the effect will be the same as using powder shells.'

Burun seemed to digest the idea. He looked away towards the setting sun. 'You serve me well,' he said after a pause. 'It is easy to forget that you are not one of us.'

Mines were a military solution which the Yek mind would find shocking. Rostov wondered about the conflict of emotions which Burun must be experiencing, and suddenly he knew why Vortai and Sipotai had to be killed. There was only one motivation which explained Burun's actions.

Burun turned back. 'If we do this wrong, we will all die.' He spoke softly. It was as if he was reading Rostov's mind.

Rostov shrugged. 'Khan, you once said that if men let the thought of death deter them, the Khanate would still be a short day's ride from Kinsai.'

'So I did.' Burun grinned. 'I am impressed that you remember.'

Rostov nested the container of powder in the pit, then stood back so that the troopers could pile stones on top of it. There were jagged shards of basalt all through the sand and teams of men had been organised to gather them.

'Is this the last?' Burun watched the troopers as they sprinkled sand lightly over the mine.

'Yes.' Rostov paid out the fuse. There was just

enough to reach the fold in the dune. Rostov tied a strand of material to the end of the fuse so that he could identify it, then wiped his hands on what remained of the skirt of his mantle. His robe stank of gunpowder and he thought that if he stood too near a fire he would probably explode. One of the containers of powder had been leaking and the material of his garments was saturated with the stuff.

The depression which Rostov had chosen as a firing point for the mines was situated on a slight rise to one side of a narrow wadi. The dunes on both sides were steep; a recent windstorm had blown irregular ridges down them and spilled a covering of sand across the valley between so that it was ideal for concealment. About forty troopers trotted their st'lyan slowly down the length of the wadi so that they left a clear trail. Every other impression in the sand was being obliterated by troopers who trailed cloaks and robes behind them. A light wind blew constantly and the drag marks soon merged with the surrounding irregularity of the surface of the dunes.

Rostov had personally supervised the laying of every one of the twenty mines. An officer of Burun's guard had been given a crash course in their use and he was stationed on the other side of the wadi. It only remained for Rostov to hope that he would not be too eager to ignite the fuses when the Gaijin rode into range. Splitting the fuses had been necessary, both as a precaution in case Rostov's position was attacked and because twenty mines were too many for one person to control.

'This wind is good for us.' Burun squatted on his heels. 'A windstorm would cover every trace.'

'We wouldn't be able to see Sipotai, Khan.' Rostov laid the flintlock igniter on a rock. He settled himself on his knees.

'Blue lantern, Khan.' Kuchuk was occupying the centre of the depression. His lanterns were laid out in readiness and he was pointing north. A light flashed twice on the crown of a dune near the wadi entrance.

'I see it.' Burun uncased his bow and laid arrows in front of him on the sand parapet. 'Their vanguard is passing our outposts.'

'They will be cautious,' Hodai said. He looked worried.

Burun showed his teeth. 'They ought to be very nervous indeed. We have killed over a score of Sipotai's scouts and I imagine he is running short of willing men to ride ahead.'

A second lantern flashed from the crest of a dune which was on the opposite side of the wadi. Both of the moons of Tarvarus were visible in the night sky and their light threw everything into sharp relief.

'That's Jotan.' Hodai shifted from a crouching position to a kneeling one. 'Sipotai will see our signals.'

'If he does, the hundred commanders know what to do.' Burun did not turn his head. 'Everyone knows what to do.'

Rostov stared along the wadi. At its mouth a group of four men were walking their st'lyan slowly between the first ridges of sand. They seemed to pause for a moment, then they came on again. Rostov whistled softly through his teeth. 'Khan, we ought to signal Arghatun.'

'Yes.' Burun nodded. 'Kuchuk, two greens to the south.'

'Yes, Khan.' The standard-bearer jerked the lantern cord twice. A single white light blinked in response from the folds of dunes which were almost out of sight beyond the exit from the wadi. 'He is acknowledging, Khan.'

Burun grunted. The Gaijin scouts were riding

steadily down the centre of the depression between the highest dunes now. They moved in line abreast and studied the steep slopes with no more than casual interest. Everyone burrowed into the soft sand as they passed. Harness jingled and Rostov heard one scout murmur an indistinguishable something to his companions. After a minute the intruders disappeared into the folds of sand which marked the start of another deeper wadi to the south. Burun raised his head.

'Arghatun will take care of them. Here comes the main body.'

Rostov got up onto his knees again. About three hundred men were nearing the wadi. They rode in extended order, their pace an easy canter. There was a bottleneck where ridges of sand formed a partial barrier across the level floor which filled the space between the highest dunes. The oncoming riders squeezed through it and then fanned out again. Burun grunted satisfaction.

'Hah. See the totem? If that's not Sipotai in that group beneath the banners, I'll piss naked on the Dragon Throne.'

The Gaijin had ridden perhaps a third of the way along the wadi floor when the dune slopes on either side of them seemed to stir. One moment the sand was apparently smooth and featureless. The next the cloaks and saddle blankets with which Burun's men had covered their foxholes were thrown aside and arrows were sleeting down.

The Gaijin roared. Rostov saw men in one rank reaching for their bow cases. Most of them fell before they had a chance to nock an arrow. The Merkut hundred commanders' voices rang out as they ordered each volley. Then, as the Gaijin were organising themselves to reply, their ambushers hurled themselves

507

downslope onto the hard sand of the wadi floor and started to run. Sipotai's men seemed to gather themselves and they charged with a yell.

Rostov worked the trigger of the igniter and lit a cluster of four fuses which were draped across a rock. He watched the pace of the Gaijin charge and lit four more.

Men who had been hidden along the crests of the dunes on both sides were shooting down into the depression now, but they were making little difference to the impetus of the horde of Gaijin which was flying along the wadi floor.

'If they get this far, we're done for.' Burun made the observation calmly. He nocked an arrow.

A string of mines went off with a crash and the front half of the Gaijin charge seemed to disappear suddenly in a curtain of sand. Two of the mines had been planted in the floor of the depression, but two more had been placed so that they were on the dune slopes. The explosions sprayed the first five or six ranks with razor-sharp shards of basalt. The riders toppled and the men who were behind rode headlong into a chaos of fallen. St'lyan screamed and men cried out. The second set of four mines went off directly beneath the main part of the charge and a further set lit by the guard officer on the far side of the wadi exploded a second or so later among the Gaijin who were in the rear. Forward movement ceased and the charge dissolved.

'Name of God!' Burun sounded shocked.

Individual bangs signalled the fact that single mines which were situated under the groups of milling riders were being set off by the officer of Burun's guard. Rostov ignited the remaining fuses in a group. He was sickened by the slaughter and by his part in it. It did not matter any longer which mines exploded.

Their effect was enough to prevent the Gaijin from organising a second charge.

The troopers who had been running away along the hard sand of the depression were now halted in a line which stretched from one dune slope to the other. They began to volley arrows into the confusion.

'White flash.' Burun's expression was grim. 'Let's finish this.'

Kuchuk raised a white lantern on a pole. He worked the shutter cord energetically and the Merkuts who had been concealed around the entrance to the wadi formed up in ranks and advanced on the Gaijin rear. They were shooting constantly, their targets thrown into silhouette by the bright moonlight which shone down. Bunches of st'lyan were being brought up by the troopers who had been detailed to guard the remuda. A force of about a hundred Merkuts mounted and they encircled the Gaijin and picked off the survivors in the ranks around the fringes of the milling formation. Troopers on the dune crests poured arrows into its centre.

'It's a massacre.' Hodai turned. He sounded amazed.

'Not yet.' Burun nocked an arrow. He drew his bow to full stretch and loosed. The arrow skipped off a shield which was thrown up by a Gaijin who was attempting to organise an outer defence and it took a man behind in the chest.

It was clear that at least a few of the Gaijin command had survived. A tortoise of raised shields broke away from the mass, and the men formed up inside its shelter moved slowly back towards the wadi entrance. The commander of the Merkuts who were lined up on foot there seemed to realise the danger. The dismounted formation moved back out of range, firing steadily. Its place was taken by troopers mounted on st'lyan. They circled the tortoise, killing the shield-holders. A few Gaijin fled back towards the chaos of the wadi. They ducked as they ran, but they were quickly cut down.

Some of the Gaijin in the depression were raising their helmets on lances or swords in token of surrender.

'Khan?' Hodai pointed at the truce signal which was being raised beside the Gaijin banner.

'Green lantern.' Burun's tone betrayed no hint of emotion. 'They all die.'

Hodai looked sick. He opened his mouth to protest, then closed it again. Kuchuk attached the lantern to his signal pole and raised it. He pulled the cord and lashed the end around the wood so that the shutter stayed open. Green lights bloomed on both dune crests and in the wadi entrance, and the slaughter continued unabated.

It was only moments later that an avalanche of sand flowed down the steep slope into the hollow. Jotan came sliding the last few drem into the dip, the loose sand cascading behind him.

'Khan, they are beaten. We have them at our mercy.' Jotan got to his feet. He caught Burun's arm. 'Spare the common men,' he said urgently. 'How have they offended you?'

Burun shook Jotan's hand away. 'Let go of me, damn you!'

'But this is murder!'

Burun turned away from the carnage. His face was grim. 'You know the Yasa. What choice have I?'

Every trooper in the wadi was a witness to Burun's breach of the law. The testimony of even one man before the Kha-Khan would mean his execution.

Jotan stepped back as if Burun had struck him a blow. He stared intently into Burun's face, then he spat to one side. He brushed past Rostov wordlessly, and started to climb back towards the crest of the

510

dune. Burun watched him thoughtfully and Rostov felt a chill of premonition. The perversity of Yek law quite often set a son against his father.

In the wadi a new tortoise was breaking away from the killing ground around the Gaijin banners. This time it moved south towards the exit between the dunes. Because it was much smaller and the troopers along the dune crests were concentrating on targets clustered beneath the totem, it went almost unnoticed in the dust and confusion.

Suddenly Burun pointed. 'Name of God, that's Sipotai!'

Rostov had already observed the face which appeared for a moment in a gap between two shields. The features were imprinted upon his memory like the scars which would always be visible on his back and across his shoulders. He did not wait for Burun's reaction, but snatched up his bow case and hurled himself over the rim of the hollow.

Loose sand moved under Rostov's feet so that he was carried downslope as if by a river. Dust hung in the air above the level floor of the wadi like a misty curtain. In places the visibility was only a few drem. Rostov was up and running as soon as his feet touched the hard-packed sand at the foot of the slope. The line of the dune crest above and to the right was the only visible landmark and it was easy to understand why Sipotai's attempt at escape was proceeding unde- tected. Merkuts knelt in a line to the left. They were shooting at the indistinct movement of men around the Gaijin totem as if they were taking part in a macabre kind of target practice. Two men were resting their bows, talking quietly, while a third was adjusting the flights of an arrow.

'You, follow me!' Rostov did not break stride as he shouted the command.

A Merkut officer looked up. 'Yes, Amir.' He responded without hesitation, and his shouted command brought troopers to their feet. Rostov raced on, tearing the cover from his bow case.

Sipotai's tortoise came out of the sand haze twenty or thirty drem to the left. The shield-holders were jogging now; the men who were sheltered inside were only visible as grotesque shadows in the gloom.

Rostov snatched an arrow from his belt and loosed. 'There.' He pointed. 'Aim for the gaps. Stop them.'

The troopers who were following him began to shoot, but it was already too late. The tortoise was engulfing a trio of mounted archers. Rostov heard one of the Merkuts shout in alarm, then the Gaijin under the shields surged forward. They pulled the troopers from their st'lyan and butchered them. Men knelt to volley arrows at the threat posed by the presence of Rostov and the four or five troopers who had followed him, while others lunged to secure the reins of the rearing st'lyan.

'Merkuts! Behind you!'

Burun's voice rang out. He was up to his waist in the soft sand of the slope down from the hollow. He pointed at the Gaijin and every man within bowshot turned at the sound of his cry. When they saw Sipotai they roared in anger. Arrows began to fly.

Sipotai was already mounting in an effort to escape. He had one foot in the stirrups of a skewbald mare, but the st'lyan was a clear target against the black sand. The animal screamed as it fell and Sipotai rolled out of the saddle. One of the two surviving st'lyan had broken loose and on the back of the other was a young Gaijin ensign. He reined in, shouted, and offered Sipotai his arm. Sipotai wrenched his would-be saviour out of the saddle, mounted swiftly, and galloped away. The young officer got to his feet shouting. An arrow took him between the shoulders, and he pitched forward on to his face.

Burun bounded down the slope. He skidded to a halt at Rostov's side. 'Damn Sipotai! That boy gave his life to save him!'

Rostov did not respond, but watched as Sipotai fled out of range. None of the arrows which were fired after the racing st'lyan found their target. Sipotai was crouched low in the saddle and it was only moments before he was hidden by the curves of the dunes to the south.

Burun was shouting to Kuchuk for a signal to be made to Arghatun, but Rostov did not wait. There were loose st'lyan trotting on the wadi floor and he caught at the reins of one as it ran past. Hurling himself into the saddle he galloped in pursuit. South of the wadi there was only the trackless expanse of the G'bai. There was no refuge anywhere for a fugitive and Rostov already knew that for Sipotai there must be no escape.

It was perhaps the third hour of the night watch. The two moons were high in the sky, and the rolling dunes looked like frozen silver waves in an enormous sea. The tracks of the st'lyan ahead led directly south-west, and Rostov guessed that Sipotai was heading for the coast. If he had intended to circle towards Losan, he would already have started to turn north. There were no towns on the coastline below the escarpment, but it was possible that Sipotai knew of a place where Losani fishing boats beached for the night.

It was wrong that everyone else should die and that Sipotai should escape. Rostov wondered if Vortai was lying among the dead in the wadi basin. If he was, Sipotai was now Khan of the Gaijin. A wind whipped across the desert so that grains of sand were blown

513

into the hoofprints left by Sipotai's st'lyan. Rostov spurred on. He did not know if Burun and Jotan were following, but if they were, they would ride hard to catch up. Sipotai was silhouetted briefly as he rode up the side of a low dune about half a verst in front. He was riding flat out.

Rostov reined in for a moment, then urged his st'lyan on at a gentler pace. The need to catch Sipotai was an urgent one, but it was matched by the knowledge that no animal was capable of continuing indefinitely at such a gallop.

To the west the G'bai ceased to be true desert. Great segments of basalt reared up out of the ground, showing how the original volcanic basin must have broken up prior to erosion. There was still sand, but it was a thin coating which blew constantly over the rocks and there were patches of dark soil in which a few plants grew. Rostov remembered that volcanic soil was supposed to be fertile. He wondered if eventually the character of the G'bai would change, and crops would grow where there had been desolation.

Sipotai came into sight again. He had increased his lead and was nearly a verst ahead now. Rostov allowed his mare to find her own pace through a patch of broken ground, then he stopped, amazed. There was a field on the level plain between two great outcrops of black rock. Blue seed pods streaked with purple waved on tall blue-green stalks across its expanse. It was a sight which Rostov knew was to be seen only on two other worlds of the Imperium. It was a sick joke that he was seeing it here.

It was by chance that he glanced down at his harness. Like every other Yek saddle there were radiation-sensitive discs attached to the pommel by means of a leather thong. At first Rostov thought it was the effect of the moonlight, but then he looked closer.

Both of the discs were discoloured.

'Name of God.'

Sweat broke out on Rostov's forehead. He wondered how accurately the constituents of the discs had been measured, but if he had already received a lethal dose it was too late to do anything about it. There were no anti-contaminants on Tarvaras.

St'lyan came through the broken ground and up the slope. Burun reined in, while Jotan pulled up on a low rise.

'What, haven't you caught him yet?' Burun sounded amused. The st'lyan he was riding was flecked with foam and he was carrying his bow loose in one hand.

'He is there.' Rostov pointed. Sipotai was crossing a patch of open ground. Probably he was riding on sand, for there was a cloud of dust which marked his position.

'Hah.' Burun gathered his reins. 'We will have him within the hour.'

Rostov snatched at Burun's bridle. 'Khan, look at the discs on your saddle.'

Burun's face went white. Jotan trotted his mare back down the slope. He saw that Burun was examining his discs, looked at his own and started to swear quietly.

'We are dead men.' Burun's tone was prosaic.

'Not necessarily, Khan.' Rostov did his best to display confidence. 'If a disc turns black, the dose is lethal. If we turn back now there may be no ill effects at all.'

'And Sipotai?' Burun stood in the stirrups. The st'lyan in the distance was a mere speck which was entering another patch of broken ground.

'He is dead as if you had killed him with your own hand.'

Rostov was sure of his judgement. The radioactives

were trapped beneath the basalt. As the sheets broke into segments they were released. In other areas of the G'bai the rocks had been eroded to fine sand, and the irregular rains had washed the contaminated elements into basins. The concentrations were the reason why the G'bai had only recently become passable. Previously the Yek had not known what areas of the desert to avoid.

'Khan, we have to ride east, away from the broken ground.' Rostov indicated the tilted basalt fragments which projected out of the slope.

Burun seemed to accept that Rostov knew what he was talking about. He nodded and pulled his st'lyan's head round. For a moment he turned back and stared south. 'I would have killed Sipotai.' Burun met Rostov's eyes as he spoke. 'But I would not wish such a death on any man.' He urged his mare downslope and was followed by Jotan.

Rostov gazed once more at the field which stretched out between the black rocks. The seed pods waved in the wind. *Papaver longiverus*, the Imperial poppy, the source of human immortality. Cut the pods and gather the sap; dissolve the resin in hot water and precipitate it by adding lime; filter the precipitate and allow it to dry. Taken regularly as a thirty per cent solution it was capable of prolonging life indefinitely.

'The Tree of Life.' Rostov shook his head and laughed softly. He took one last long look, then turned his st'lyan's head towards the east and rode away.

They stopped when they reached the escarpment. At Rostov's insistence everyone showered naked in the water of one of the streams which trickled off the rocky overhang and meandered out into the desert. A fire built out of brushwood summoned Arghatun and a squadron of Burun's guard. Arghatun paled when he learned why Burun had returned and the troopers gave the place where Burun sat with Rostov and Jotan a wide berth.

Rostov could not summon up the energy to produce a smile. He had already slaughtered all three st'lyan, and had thrown every stitch of clothing and harness into a deep crevice in the rock. An orderly brought fresh clothing. He bowed to Burun, his face grey with fear, and hastened away.

'How long before we know if we are sick?' Burun laced the silk trousers. He stepped into the boots and stamped his feet.

Rostov shrugged. 'A day. A week. Khan, I do not know.'

'Name of God, Suragai.' Jotan spoke drily. 'My father thinks you know everything. Don't disillusion him now.'

Burun snorted. 'If we die, we die,' he said.

Jotan made a rude noise. Rostov pulled a clean tunic over his head. He stood up. 'Khan, the first sign of sickness is nausea, followed by sweating and chills like a fever. Sometimes the nausea passes and there are no other symptoms. If none of us falls ill within the week, then probably we have not been affected.'

There was no point in mentioning the long-term effects which could arise. One of the benefits of Longivex was the prevention of cancer. Rostov wondered if enough of the drug remained in his system to provide protection.

'Riders, Khan.' Arghatun suddenly pointed east.

'It's Siban,' Jotan said. He did not sound surprised.

Siban's escort was a full tenth of a tuman. The outriders swung out to encircle Burun's guard. Their weapons were drawn. Burun sat down on a rock. His face was expressionless.

'Khan?' Arghatun looked as if he expected to be

ordered to fight. His hand was resting on the bowcase which was secured by bindings to his saddle.

'Wait.' Burun lifted a hand. He did not turn.

Siban reined in a length from the fire. 'Khan, surrender,' he called. 'Submit to justice.'

Burun stretched out his legs. Then he looked up. 'Is there a complaint against me?'

'You know there is.'

'Speak it then.' Burun got to his feet.

Siban's expression was frosty. 'Very well. Burun, Khan of the Merkuts, I charge you with a breach of the law. You have made war on another Khan, laying waste the city of Losan. Where is the Khan of the Gaijin. Show me that he lives, or yield.'

'Vortai?' Burun looked surprised. 'Vortai is in Losan.'

Siban spat left and right. 'Vortai is dead. Sipotai is Khan of the Gaijin now.'

'Oh, well.' Burun traced a pattern in the dry soil with the toe of his boot. 'If Vortai is dead, Sipotai killed him. Saving the fact that he has saved me the trouble, I never thought he had the wit for such an act. Have you no complaint against him?'

'Does he live?' Siban kicked one foot free of the stirrups. He drew his leg up across the pommel of his saddle.

'Oh, probably.' Burun gestured carelessly towards the desert to the south. 'We followed Sipotai into the dead land to the west of the G'bai. The earth there is still poisoned.'

'Then he is a dead man.' Siban made the observation smoothly with no apparent change in expression. 'And since Sipotai was attempting to escape you, his death is on your head.'

'That is for the Kha-Khan to decide, surely.' Burun spoke mildly. 'By what authority do you take the Gaijin's part?'

518

Siban did not answer at first. He was looking out at the G'bai. Then his head came round. 'Vortai was my brother,' he said. 'Sipotai was his son. I have blood right.'

Burun's eyes were raised. He showed his teeth. 'Blood right? Yes, I see.'

Rostov picked up a k'miss bottle from a heap of harness and other items which had been left beside the rock. The movement made Burun's head turn. He saw the bottle in Rostov's hand and gestured. Rostov tossed it to him. There was a plop as Burun pulled the cork. He drank. Siban shifted impatiently. His face displayed irritation.

Hooves rumbled in the distance. Rostov heard the shout of a challenge, then Tulagai and Targoutai rode together into the space beside the fire. More men charged between the ranks of Siban's escort. Arghatun's hand moved towards his bowcase again, and Burun held up one hand to prevent others from copying the motion.

'Hold, in the name of the Kha-Khan!' Tulagai stood in the stirrups. His men were forming a screen between the troopers of Burun's guard and the tenth of a tuman which rode with Siban.

'Burun Khan, come forward. Siban, come forward.' Tulagai did not have to shout. His voice rang out crisp and clear and everyone heard him.

Burun walked past the fire. Siban seemed to hesitate. Then he put his foot back in the stirrups and rode a few paces towards Tulagai.

'By what right do you use the name of the Kha-Khan?'

Tulagai let his reins fall loose on his st'lyan's neck. 'Siban. The Yasa gives me the right. You came here to take Burun prisoner and yet it is you who makes the complaint. By what right do you justify your actions?'

'Blood right.' Siban looked annoyed.

Tulagai looked as if he was considering the claim. 'Blood right gives you grounds for complaint. You intended to judge Burun. Blood right gives you no authority.'

'Burun has killed another Khan –'

'Be quiet,' Tulagai said. 'This is a serious matter, and if we were at Kinsai I would take you to the Kha-Khan for judgement. I claim the right of the Yasa to deal with you both.'

'You are the son of the son of the Kha-Khan.' Siban kicked his st'lyan into a sidestep. 'You are Burun's friend.'

Burun made a noise which sounded like a laugh. Tulagai ignored him.

'I am the Kha-Khan's voice in this.' Tulagai looked squarely at Siban as he spoke. 'My personal preferences are of no moment. Each of you give me an arrow.'

Siban muttered something. He took an arrow from his quiver and handed it to Tulagai. Burun already had an arrow in his hand and he gave it to Tulagai head first.

Tulagai gave the arrows to Targoutai, who pushed them into his belt. 'Your arrows are your pledges of good conduct. Ride to the escarpment camp, both of you. I will send to each of you when I am ready to judge. Go.'

Burun turned and walked back past the fire. He picked up the k'miss bottle from the place where he had left it on the rock and drank. Siban was gigging his animal round and his men were pulling back. Tulagai trotted his animal around the fire.

'Whelp.' Burun corked the k'miss bottle. He looked up. 'Who asked you to interfere?'

Tulagai laughed. 'You should thank me. Do you

know Vortai is dead?'

Burun made a face. 'Siban told me. Why are you getting involved in this?'

'I had no choice. A messenger arrived from Losan last night. Siban rode out at once. Did you kill Sipotai?'

'No. The G'bai is doing that.'

'Ugh.' Tulagai produced an expression of distaste. He dismounted.

'Suragai should not be judged,' Burun said. He looked past Tulagai as he spoke and met Rostov's stare steadily.

'Oh?' Tulagai's tone was severe. 'He is your vassal, it is true, but he also holds the rank of Amir. If he has privileges under the Yasa, then also he has responsibilities.'

Burun's expression suggested that he thought that Tulagai was being unnecessarily exact in his interpretation of the law. 'As you observe, Suragai is my vassal. I required him to follow me. He should not be judged.'

The last of Siban's men were riding away now. Targoutai was in command of the screen which encircled Burun's camp. He seemed to be relieved that he had not been called upon to fight. Rostov estimated that Siban's men had outnumbered the combined strength of the escorts commanded by Burun and Tulagai by about three to one and he wondered why a battle had not taken place. There was no reason why Siban should have baulked at using force to achieve his objective of capturing Burun.

'I will consider your argument on Suragai's behalf.' Tulagai's tone indicated that he intended to do nothing of the kind. 'In the meantime you are responsible for his conduct.'

Rostov laughed harshly, and at once both Burun and Tulagai turned. They stared at him.

'I am responsible for my own actions,' Rostov said.

He was careful to look at neither Burun nor Tulagai as he spoke. Burun smiled grimly, but Tulagai flushed. He mounted again and rode away.

'I am trying to protect you.' Burun sat down on the rock again. He picked up the k'miss bottle, looked at it, then laid it aside.

Rostov shrugged. He could think of nothing to say. Jotan had not moved the whole time since Siban's arrival. Now he got up quietly, mounted, and rode after Tulagai.

'How did Siban know what had happened?' Rostov watched Jotan as he rode away.

Burun laughed softly. 'You noticed that. I thought that I was the only one who caught Tulagai's slip of the tongue. If warning reached the escarpment camp last night, it must have been sent before we attacked Sipotai. Jotan will be cursing Tulagai now.'

Rostov was taken by surprise. He had not been suggesting that Jotan was the traitor.

Burun saw Rostov's expression, and he showed his teeth in a smile. 'What, are you surprised, Suragai? Jotan owes Siban a duty. He is his governor in the south. He was protecting his interests, that is all.'

'And Siban?' Rostov was struggling to adjust to the idea. The way Burun described it, Jotan's treachery was the only sensible conclusion.

'Siban wants to be Kha-Khan.' Burun shrugged. 'I have always known that. He would have released me in exchange for a promise to support him at the election.'

Rostov knew how much effort Burun had expended in the past to avoid committing himself to any single candidate. 'Then Tulagai's interference was your good fortune, Khan.'

'Hah.' Burun snorted. 'Fortune had nothing to do with it. Jotan sent to Tulagai at the same time as he sent to Siban.' Burun's tone betrayed grudging admiration. 'If the charges against me are proved, it will be Tulagai's duty to take my head,' he said. 'Jotan cannot be condemned because he sent warning. He will become Khan of the Merkuts and our line will continue. In his place I would have done the same.'

Tulagai laid his wine cup aside. 'Don't expect me to be easy with you,' he said. 'Whatever his reasons for it, Siban was right to raise a complaint against you. You burned half of Losan and, one way or another, your actions caused the deaths of both Vortai and Sipotai, not to mention several hundred of their men and a number of civilians who had no part in the matter. I intend to judge this thing properly, without consideration for any friendship which may exist between us.'

Burun produced a twisted smile. Rostov said nothing. He signalled towards the door of the tent and Teng moved silently around the table removing the remains of the meal.

'You cannot condemn us.' Burun turned his cup between his palms. 'Or if you do, I will appeal to the Kha-Khan. I acknowledge your right to act as judge; but don't imagine that I will allow either you or Siban to gain face at my expense.'

Tulagai seemed to hesitate. At last he shrugged. 'Probably Siban could have acted sooner. His case is that he did not attempt to intervene while you were fighting Sipotai because he could not properly judge the matter of provocation. At the same time Vortai was Siban's brother, so Siban had a right to act once he heard that Vortai had been killed.'

'Are you saying that I had no right to deal with Sipotai?' Burun's hands stilled. He looked up.

Tulagai made a face. 'There is no doubt that Sipotai broke the Yasa by his use of the lash on you and on

Suragai. If you could not capture him, then you were within your rights to order him killed. How he died - by your hand or by another means - should not concern anyone.'

'Oh.' Burun produced a snort of amusement. 'I'm glad you don't dispute my right to vengeance, otherwise we would argue this until sunfall.'

Tulagai looked offended. 'You are mocking me,' he said.

Burun gestured. 'Not at all.'

The point at issue is not your right to kill Sipotai.' Tulagai's tone was prosaic. 'What you did cannot be excused by the laws relating to kanly. There was no intention on your part to engage in single combat. Instead you set out to make war.'

It was dim and cool inside the tent. Even though the side walls had been rolled up, there was only limited light because of the huge over-canopy which was suspended above. It covered the yurts occupied by Burun and his guard. The paths between the structures were always damp because slaves watered the stone paving daily.

Rostov rose. He went past Tulagai and stood in the shadow cast by the reefed-back hangings at the door. He was wearied by the interminable discussion about points of law which appeared to be a preliminary to trial.

'Have you sent for your wife?'

Rostov sensed that Burun had risen and was standing at his shoulder, but he did not turn. 'Not yet, Khan. Is there time?'

'Probably.' Burun sounded amused. 'Tulagai will send to Kinsai before he decides anything finally. There has been little word from the court for over a month.'

The words were spoken softly, but Rostov turned to

see if Tulagai had heard. 'I thought Siban was at Kinsai before he came here.'

'He was.' Burun sniffed. 'But he doesn't have any better contact with the Golden Yurt than anyone else.'

Rostov examined the statement. Burun's tone as he mentioned Siban was positively malicious. 'I thought you and Siban were friends, Khan.'

Burun wrinkled his nose. 'Siban and I were junior officers together under Daijin. Siban was his son, but he never showed him any favour. We are friends when it suits us.'

The explanation was simple enough to be the truth. Rostov turned to look out of the door again. It was late afternoon, and only slaves and orderlies moved on the pathways which had been laid from one end of the escarpment camp to the other.

'Send for Turakina,' Burun said. 'It will be some time before we travel south again.'

Rostov tried to interpret the expression in Burun's tone. If the Khan was concerned about Tulagai's verdict, he did not show it.

'Khan, I will write to her.'

'Good.' Burun sounded relieved.

It would take an arrow messenger four days to reach Turakina. Even if she set out at once, it would be two weeks before she arrived. Rostov stared past the tents at the escarpment edge. It was eight days since the battle among the dunes. The bodies of the slain had been cremated in a funeral pyre which had been visible for ten verst or more, but no trace of Sipotai had been found.

'If Sipotai was alive, we would have had word.' It was as if Burun read Rostov's mind.

'Yes.' Rostov nodded. The Losani who fished the Inner Sea were telling a story about a ragged figure seen haunting the shore close to the Forbidden Land.

525

No one had landed to investigate because the radiation levels at that spot were known to be deadly.

'Are you well?' Burun made the enquiry casually.

Rostov smiled grimly. Perhaps it was due to the precautions taken after they came out of the desert, or perhaps the radiation to which they had been exposed was minimal, but none of them had experienced anything more than slight nausea, and that had passed after a day.

'Khan, I am well.'

Burun turned away for a moment. He poured wine from a jug which had been placed on a table near the door and offered Rostov a cup. Rostov drank.

*This has become a habit.* Rostov estimated that he drank wine and k'miss in quantities equal to the amount of tea and cachac which he had consumed while he was a servant of the Empire. *The Yek only get drunk when they want to. Am I less human than I was?* Rostov held his cup up to the light. Although there was still daylight, one of the moons was visible in the sky. Its face was pitted with craters and Rostov thought that if they were capable of being seen at such a distance, each of them must be the size of a province.

'Have you worked out why I did it yet?' Burun asked softly.

Rostov turned. He saw that Tulagai was engaged in conversation with Jotan. 'Not to help Siban, anyway. That's what most people think, in spite of the trial.'

Burun made a face. 'I know,' he said. 'They are saying that Tulagai's judgement will be a sham.'

Rostov managed a smile. Burun was not worried about Siban's complaint. Probably he knew that he could obtain the Kha-Khan's pardon. Burun raised his own cup and drank. Then he wiped his mouth with the back of his hand. His talons flashed.

'Jotan will never be Kha-Khan.' Rostov pitched his voice low.

Burun stood motionless. Then he lowered his hand. 'I knew you would reason it correctly.'

'You did it for your line.'

'Yes.' Burun nodded. 'I told Jotan that, but he did not believe me. You're right. He will never be Kha-Khan. But Jehan could be.'

Rostov understood. 'It is said that Nogai will never marry.'

Burun grimaced. 'I don't know where you heard that tale. Probably it's true.'

Rostov visualised the line of succession. 'After Nogai, the Khans will elect Tulagai's son.' Suddenly he saw why Tulagai had chosen to interfere in the dispute between Burun and Siban.

'If he is old enough.' Burun made the observation calmly. 'Artai is still a child.'

'Jehan Kha-Khan.' Rostov tested the phrase. 'People might have trouble saying it.'

Burun made a rude noise. 'People can get used to anything.' He drained his cup, then placed it on the table.

News of the trial had brought people in from every nearby province. The solar intensity was at its height and dust hung in the air above the plain where the st'lyan had been put out to graze.

'If Tulagai does not give you justice, you can over-throw him.' Jotan reined in at Rostov's side. 'He can't have heard from Kinsai yet.'

'If he does judge it properly, we will have to go to Kinsai anyway.' Burun spat to one side. 'I'm not ready to die.'

Jotan shoved him. Burun reeled in the saddle, recovered, then shoved back. Jehan rode in between them singing and they were forced to separate. Rostov looked at Burun and saw that he was grinning.

The people who were crowded into the centre of the camp were all dressed in their best clothes. The air was heavy with the smells of cooking. When a woman led a p'tar past them with panniers laden with ch'leve, the yeasty bread which was made from rice flour, Jehan snatched a loaf and rode on with it. 'This is like a festival,' he said cheerfully. He broke the bread in half and offered some to Rostov.

The big kuriltai tent was draped with the decorated banners of the Khans.

'Where is the flag of the Merkuts?' Jotan stood in the stirrups.

'It's in a chest somewhere.' Burun reined in. Rostov studied the insignia which were displayed. Nearly all the clans were represented.

'You should have brought it.' Jotan turned.

'It's in the chest back home on the Khirgiz.'

'Oh.' Jotan frowned. 'We look like beggars in the middle of all this finery.'

'Nonsense.' Burun snorted. 'We look like honest Merkuts.'

The space in front of the central canopy was packed with people. When they saw Burun they cheered. The men rattled swords and daggers. Hodai came out of the kuriltai tent. He was smiling.

'Khan, Siban is already here. The people are cheering you. Him they only saluted.'

'Hunh.' Burun dismounted. He looked unimpressed. 'Let's go in and get this over.'

The heralds who were lined up on either side of the tent entrance blew a fanfare. At once there was silence; Rostov followed Burun into the tent. Jotan and Jehan walked behind.

Tulagai was standing on a raised dais. An expanse of

528

polished floor had been laid within the tent, and Siban was standing to one side of it with his officers. Burun strode into the centre of the floor and stopped. Merkuts crowded into the space behind him. Siban scowled and he shifted from foot to foot. His personal standard-bearer was standing among the men who were at his back. The guidon which he held had the emblem of the Darjin clan embroidered on it in gold thread.

When it was clear that no more spectators could crowd into the tent, Tulagai held up his hands. 'In the name of the Kha-Khan, I call those here present to attend my judgement. If there is any man here who disputes my right to hear this case, let him speak now.'

There was silence. Burun was standing in a relaxed posture. He glanced once at Siban and seemed to smile.

'Very well.' Tulagai looked satisfied. 'We are here to listen to the complaint of Siban the White against Burun Khan. First, it is said that Burun attacked Vortai Khan, having no right or authority.'

'Vortai is dead.' Burun spoke.

Tulagai ignored the interruption. 'Second, Burun Khan is accused of causing the death of Sipotai Noyon.'

'Sipotai killed Vortai,' Burun said. 'Also he attacked me. He deserved to die.'

Tulagai frowned. 'Burun, you will have a chance to speak. I have to list the charges which have been laid against you.'

'The charges are nonsense and Siban knows it.' Burun looked amused.

'Nevertheless.' Tulagai sounded as if he was having difficulty restraining his temper. 'Thirdly, Burun is charged that he set fire to the city of Losan and caused its partial destruction.'

A hum of comment ran round the tent. Tulagai

529

raised his hands, and after a moment there was silence again. Tulagai looked around. 'Who stands surety for Burun?'

'I do.' It was Targoutai who spoke. 'Who stands surety for Siban?'

Siban looked offended. 'A surety is not necessary. I am the complainer.'

'Oh?' Targoutai smiled his disbelief. 'What if your accusations are proved false. Is Burun to have no recourse?'

'Then I will stand my own surety.' Siban spoke angrily.

Targoutai looked at Burun. 'Khan?'

Burun seemed to be studying the polished planks under his feet. He looked up after a moment and shrugged. 'Siban is the complainer. How can he provide surety for himself?'

Tulagai looked as if he thought that the discussion was getting out of hand. 'If no one else will come forward, I will guarantee the surety for Siban,' he said.

Burun laughed. 'You are the judge, Tulagai.'

'Are you suggesting that I am biased?' Tulagai's face was crimson.

Burun was smiling. 'Not at all. I withdraw my objection.'

Jehan nudged Rostov with his elbow. 'If Tulagai demonstrates a preference, my grandfather can use it to overturn the judgement when he appeals to Kinsai.'

Rostov nodded. There was something unreal about the whole proceedings and he suspected that it would never be necessary for Burun to go to Kinsai.

Tulagai gestured. 'Very well. All men know the background to this affair. It seems to me that the situation is thus: Burun was involved in a feud with Vortai and with Sipotai his son. The cause does not concern us here, but it has been said that Vortai attempted to interfere between Burun and his wife, Vortai's daughter. Also it has been suggested that Sipotai offended Burun by looking with desire upon Burun's second wife. In any event Burun was within his rights to declare kanly. We do not know if Burun in fact sent his cartel. Certainly he signified his intention to do so in the required manner, but it is apparent that Vortai would have refused to see Burun, so Burun went to Losan, where Vortai was, and attacked him.'

'Who says I attacked Vortai?' Burun stuck his thumbs in his belt. 'I never saw him.'

The Merkuts in the tent laughed. Rostov realised that the accusation was nonsense. By the time Vortai had appeared on the quayside at Losan, Burun was unconscious.

'You attacked Sipotai,' Siban shouted. 'It is the same thing.'

'I had the right.' Burun was looking at Tulagai. 'The Gaijin tried to kill me.'

'No Khan has the right to make war on another without the permission of the Kha-Khan.' Tulagai returned Burun's stare. 'Are you claiming that you had authority?'

'I am,' Burun said.

There was a stunned silence. Siban looked as if he had swallowed bad meat.

Tulagai seemed to search for a response. When he spoke his tone was wary. 'If that is true, then you have no case to answer,' he said. 'Have you proof?'

'I have sent to Kinsai.' Burun showed his teeth. 'As you have, Tulagai. Have you received a reply to your letter yet?'

Tulagai shook his head.

'If Burun cannot provide proof, the matter should be judged.' Siban took a pace forward.

Burun smiled grimly. Rostov studied Siban's face,

and guessed that he sensed that his advantage was slipping away.

Tulagai's expression was a frown. 'Without confirmation one way or the other, judgement would be pointless,' he said.

Burun let his hands fall to his side. 'Good. Then I take it this trial is adjourned?' He looked first at Siban and then at Tulagai.

Tulagai nodded. Burun turned, pushed his way through the crowd and went outside. At once the people started to cheer.

There are still places where we do not rule.' Burun pointed at the map.

Rostov followed the pointing finger and made a face. 'The land south of the G'bai and east of the Y'ntze. Isn't it desert?'

'Ask Jotan.' Burun had raised his head and he was gazing north as he spoke. 'He found a city at the place where the Y'ntze reaches the sea. It was empty, but maybe there are people around somewhere.'

Rostov stood up. A rider had appeared, floating on the heat haze above the plain. As he rode nearer, Rostov caught the glint of gold on a cross-strap - a courier's pouch. The st'lyan had been ridden hard. It stumbled every few paces. Siban was sitting under an awning a few drem away. When he saw the messenger he got to his feet.

Even a letter from the Kha-Khan would not come with such haste. Rostov's stomach felt hollow inside. If Burun had really obtained permission to attack the Gaijin, he would have told someone long before the matter was brought to judgement. The courier was at the outer picket line now. He called out something, and at once a sentry turned and pointed towards the awning where Siban stood.

'An arrow messenger.' Burun spoke quietly.

Rostov nodded. The courier pulled up beside Siban. His st'lyan staggered, and when the man dismounted, it stood exhausted. Siban took the packet which was held out to him. He ripped off the seal and unrolled the scroll which was contained inside the outer binding. Rostov saw that Burun's face was filled with expectation.

Burun was walking towards Siban. Rostov followed. Siban looked up. 'Call everyone to a kuriltai,' he said. He looked suddenly old and very tired. He handed the scroll to Burun and walked blindly away. Burun barely glanced at the script which was inscribed upon the parchment.

'What is it?' Rostov knew of only one message which could have caused Siban to react so.

'The Kha-Khan is dead.' Burun turned. He threw the scroll carelessly on to a table under the awning.

Jotan came running between the maze of stays and cables which supported the huge over-canopy which floated above them. 'Is it true?'

'Yes.' Burun nodded. 'Find the commander of my guard. Make sure that they have remounts. Go on.'

'What?'

'Just do it!'

Jotan nodded quickly. He turned away.

*This was the message Burun was expecting all the time.* The realisation sprang unbidden into the forefront of Rostov's brain. He stared at Burun.

Burun met the stare without expression. 'Arjun died over a month ago. They kept it a secret. He must have died about the time Siban left Kinsai, and Siban never knew.'

'They thought to put Artai on the throne.' Rostov made the deduction without effort.

'Yes. At least they hoped to get support.' Burun

533

shook his head as if the idea amused him. 'Of course they could get none. Now it has to be Nogai. I'll send Jotan ahead to tell him that we will vote for him.'

The news was spreading swiftly through the camp. Old men stood with tears streaming down their cheeks. The women were attaching red scarves to the doorposts of the yurts; troopers were hitching strings of st'lyan and leading them off to strategic points around the central canopy. Rostov tried to recall the Kha-Khan's face, but it was only a blur in his memory. All Arjun's death meant was that Burun would have no case to answer.

'I want you to travel south.' Burun laid a hand on Rostov's arm. 'Bring our wives to Kinsai. It will be a month before an election can be held. You will have enough time. I entrust you with their safety.'

'Yes.' Rostov met Burun's eyes and examined the expression within, but he could see no hint of triumph. 'Khan, you knew this was going to happen.'

Burun was suddenly still. Then he showed his teeth. 'Did I?'

Rostov nodded. 'I think so.'

It was as if a shadow passed across Burun's face. Suddenly he seemed wary. 'You are a clever man, Suragai.' He nodded as if he had made up his mind about something. 'I am glad that you serve me.' He released Rostov's arm. Then he turned and walked away.

Men were already filling the kuriltai tent. It was clear that most of them had heard the news. Outside the tent the escorts of individual Khans stood waiting, pennants streaming from their lances, while advance parties were galloping away to the north. The moment the kuriltai was ended everyone would ride off to Kinsai. None of them would dare not be there while Nogai was deciding every petty claim and the allocation of every fief in the Khanate.

Rostov guessed that Burun had stolen a march on all of them. Probably he had already sent to Nogai to indicate his support. He was sending Jotan because that way everyone would believe that the news had come as a surprise.

Jehan ran past. 'Suragai, are you coming?' he shouted.

Rostov shook his head. He walked down past the orderly lines of the yurts below the outer canopy and did not stop until he had reached the edge of the escarpment. A pulse was beating in his forehead, and he wondered if everything that had happened was a dream.

'Amir?'

'What is it?' Rostov turned. He saw that the commander of his guard was waiting with his men. Rostov waved his hand. Then he turned and looked out across the G'bai. It seemed to stretch into infinity. Even the mountains sat on a layer of haze which it was impossible to define.

Rostov sat down on a rock and crossed his legs. He closed his eyes, then opened them again. Nothing had changed. He tested the surface of the rock with his fingertips. The perspiration which dripped from them sizzled when it came into contact with the hot limestone. Rostov grimaced, then searched the pouch at his waist for the horn container of eye shading which he knew was there. It was still some hours to midday, and it was a long time until sunfall.